Corpora Delicti

Manna Francis

CASPERIAN
BOOKS

I'd like to thank my publisher and editor for their hard work and patience, and also my husband, who read this story when it was a quarter of the length it is now and told me that it wasn't finished. Well, I finished it.

Chapter One

❖

I had a call from Medical Citidigital first thing this morning," Toreth said. "Apparently it was all a false alarm—the data breach and threats were internal. They're very sorry that they wasted our time."

The reaction from his assembled investigative team covered sighs, shaken heads, and grumbles under their breath. No one looked surprised.

"Lone disgruntled employee?" Nagra asked.

"No, this one was different—emotionally unstable. They want us to drop the investigation and allow them to handle everything. The word 'counseling' came up a couple of times."

"Counseling, right," Nagra said cynically. "Sounds like their security had a break and found the sabs themselves. Maybe we'll get the case back when the bodies turn up in the marshes."

Toreth grinned. "We can hope. Anyway, I told Tillotson and he said shut it down. No point chasing uncooperative corporates for crimes they say don't exist. So the Investigation in Progress isn't anymore. B-C?"

Barret-Connor had been rubbing his injured leg above the edge of the brace. He looked up when Toreth said his name.

"Para?"

"Where are you with the music corporation sabbing? Was the suicide okay?"

B-C grimaced slightly. "It was definitely suicide, yes. The submission went off yesterday, so we're waiting for the Justice systems to process it. I don't expect any problems."

"Good work," Toreth said. "Well, then it looks like until we get another case—and we have some suspects to talk to—Nagra, you're back down in Interrogation."

Toreth had expected a protest, or at least a complaint, but the junior para merely shrugged and nodded. "Right you are, Para." She looked at Barret-Connor and grinned slyly. "Or should I wait to see if someone gets killed after you close the case this time, B-C?"

5

Barret-Connor looked pained but didn't reply. Well, if he wanted to let the junior para take the piss, that was his lookout.

"So that's our exciting Tuesday morning," Toreth said. "Maybe all the criminals have decided to start their New Year holiday early."

The team smiled politely, but Toreth knew what was at the back of everyone's mind. Were there no cases, or were they just not showing up in General Criminal? Were other teams in General Criminal getting assignments? At coffee time everyone would be asking casual questions of people from other teams, or maybe having coffee in another section to check out the situation there. As the year drew to a close, the ripples from the revolt were still running back and forth across I&I and the rest of Int-Sec, and a section in favor one month might be struggling for budget the next. After a slow start, General Criminal had appeared to rise steadily in the new hierarchy, but that didn't stop people from getting nervous whenever the caseload lightened. Days wasted on a case closed with no results didn't help matters.

"Cheer up," Toreth said. "If no corporates have killed each other by lunchtime we can use some time from the training budget."

Jasleen Mistry and Andrew Morehen exchanged unenthusiastic glances. Alex-Ann Jameson wrinkled her nose like someone had farted right next to her. Toreth had picked her out of the pool rather hastily before the approval to bring his team back up to four permanent investigators vanished again; her case record suggested she was an active and aggressive junior investigator, but she hadn't entirely impressed him so far. Still, if hating training courses was a sign of a bad investigator, then no one at I&I would ever get a bonus.

Except, apparently, Barret-Connor, who looked honestly enthused by the prospect. Maybe it was the painkillers.

"Really?" B-C said. "Because a useful-looking systems security course just came onto the list. I was planning to have a word with you about it, anyway, Para. Since, well." He glanced around. "Since Wrenn was the one who specialized in that area, and she..."

Spinelessly crawled away after the revolt. While they had access to specialist investigators from Systems when needed, it never hurt to have some expertise on the team. "Fine, I'll approve it. Everyone else find something that's actually useful, not just taking the piss and eating biscuits for a couple of days, and let Sara know. I wouldn't want anyone getting bored."

"Para?" Nagra said.

"Sorry, you'll just have to be bored doing your job. Interrogation is screaming for staff."

To his surprise, she didn't object this time, either. "Well, then, Para, you know where *I'll* be if you need me."

"Sara," Toreth said as the others filed out, and she stopped and came back to his desk.

"Yes?"

He waited until Jameson closed the door, then said, "What's up with Nagra? That's the first time I've sent her down to help out in Interrogation that she didn't at least roll her eyes about it. And not just once—twice."

"Huh." Sara frowned. "I don't know. She hasn't said anything to me. But then if she had something new lined up she probably wouldn't, would she?"

Another senior poaching, maybe, or even a job outside I&I. "Could be she's just in a good mood. See if you can sniff anything out, though. It's hard enough finding useful investigators, and there's supposed to be a surplus of those. God only knows when we'd get another decent junior if Nagra fucks off."

Sara nodded. "Oh, by the way, Systems is looking for people to try out some new transcripter. They think this one can really cut down the amount of time we—which is me—have to spend processing interrogation transcripts. If no case comes through today, can I tell them I'll help?"

"Sure," Toreth said. "Just make sure they know you'll have to drop it if there's some real work to do."

Sara bristled slightly. "This *is* real work! Lorraine May in Systems is running the trials, and she says on some of the test data they had a hundred percent accuracy."

"Sounds amazing." Just like every other attempt in the past to completely automate transcription, which had performed perfectly in the trials with data carefully filtered by the corporation selling the system, and proved a miserable failure when faced with the messy world of real interrogation. Still, he couldn't blame Sara for her eternal optimism that she'd be able to ditch one of the more boring parts of her job. "Want to bet on it working?"

Sara gave him the eye roll that he'd missed from Nagra earlier, but she didn't take him up on the bet. All she said was, "Do you want a coffee in here later?"

"No. I think I'll get it myself. Stretch my legs."

Fulfilling his own prediction, Toreth went over to Corporate Fraud at coffee time, hoping to find someone he could pump for information. The first person he met in the coffee room was another stranger to CF—Christofi. The senior para's own section, Political Crimes, had initially done all right after the revolt, but Sara had relayed recent gossip about falling caseload and budgetary snubs. Toreth's former junior, Chris Doyle, always a man with an eye for the prevailing winds, had won himself a promotion from PC back to General Criminal only a couple of months earlier.

"I wasn't expecting to find you here," Toreth said to Christofi as they filled their mugs at the coffee machine.

"I live here. Or I will, come January. I'm scouting out an office and making sure HCT has remembered to tell the section head and everyone else I'm coming."

Human Capital and Training were the only people in the building who seemed to have thoroughly enjoyed the aftermath of the revolt. Months later, they were still enthusiastically embracing the excuse of systems disruption for losing information and making mistakes, even though systems failures had rarely hampered Toreth's investigations for months.

Anyway, it sounded as though things weren't improving at Political. "Bringing the team?" Toreth asked.

"Most of them. I'm dropping a grade and I'm losing my second junior, but at least there'll be something for the rest of us to do." Christofi shrugged. "De Alba is a waste of a desk, anyway, so leaving him behind is almost a bonus."

Whatever he said, the loss of the junior had to sting. Toreth still hadn't had permission to replace his own second junior. "So who gets him?"

"No one. They're making him a senior." Christofi snorted. "Which tells you all you need to know about what PC's turning into. You know, one day a bunch of resisters will pop up and assassinate half the Council, and they won't be able to find one senior in Political able to do jack shit about it."

"Don't worry," Toreth said. "We can always take the case in General Criminal. It's our new motto: we do everyone's jobs, only better."

"Ha. Hilarious. Come on, let's sit down."

As Toreth followed him over to a couple of vacant chairs in the corner, he found himself thinking that Christofi looked older than he remembered—there were a few more silver hairs sneaking in among the black, a few deeper lines on his face. It hadn't been so long ago that Toreth had last seen him, so either Toreth had simply had other things on his mind back then, or Christofi had suffered some sleepless nights lately.

"I thought PC was getting a permanent section head at last?" Toreth asked.

Christofi grimaced, like he'd bitten something sour. "And that's why I'm leaving. You know, I never realized Ravi actually did anything useful until some bastard resister shot him in the head. He might've been able to tickle a corporate appendix with his tongue when it came to arse-licking, but at least he could fight for a budget. I hung on while Djaout was temporary section head, because he did a decent job, considering. But now he's pissing off, and—"

"He's leaving?" Toreth said in surprise. Sara hadn't passed that on.

"Not *leaving* leaving, no. We're all supposed to keep it quiet until they find a new PC deputy section head to replace him, but I don't give a shit anymore. He's been offered the ADCF section head job, and he was so sick of being dicked about that he said yes, and so we're getting this Whittaker bloke from outside instead."

8

Another sign of changing times. Toreth knew Djaout only by reputation, but that reputation was for management ambition. In the old world, section head of Administrative Department Corruption and Fraud would probably have been considered less prestigious than even deputy section head of Political Crimes.

"Not waiting to give Whittaker a chance, then?" Toreth asked.

"He was Political deputy section head at I&I Dublin. I know someone over there, and she's over the fucking moon that he's leaving. She swears the resisters didn't kill him in the revolt because he does more damage to the Administration alive."

Toreth laughed, but Christofi didn't.

"Now I bet you're glad you didn't come back to PC when Ravi took over," Christofi said. "Although, you know, that's probably the last thing Shaughnessy said to him when he retired. 'Welcome to Political, good luck, don't let that smooth bastard Toreth back in unless you want to come home and walk in on him fucking your wife.'"

Toreth shook his head. "It wasn't at home. He did a c&p on her and found the hotel, so it was his own fault."

"She should've paid cash. Serves him right for marrying her, anyway," Christofi said. "She was what? Thirty years younger than him?"

"At least." Toreth didn't remember her very clearly, but he did remember she'd been a lot more attractive than the Political Crimes section head. "So, you like the idea of Corporate Fraud?"

"Oh, absolutely," Christofi said with bitter sarcasm. "I can't wait to spend all day wanking over databases and listening to cocky finance specialists who think they're real investigators droning on about indicative stats. You should see the training material list—Administration finance regulations, corporate accords, corporate *protocol*. The whole team is moaning about it, the ungrateful shits."

The coffee room was sparsely populated, but behind Christofi one or two heads had lifted. Still, Toreth wasn't the one insulting his future colleagues. He made a vaguely sympathetic noise and sipped his coffee.

"I told them they could stay with fucking de Alba or shut up and stop giving me grief. But PC's finished, unless the resisters get off their lazy arses and give us a hand. The rumor is someone high up—way above I&I—doesn't like the name. Political. Not trendy these days." Christofi slumped gloomily lower in his seat, coffee held in both hands. "You know, I even thought about getting out completely, but where? Ex-paras in your security team used to be something for corporates to show off. Now we're the 'wrong image' and they won't touch us. Not unless it's such a shithole corporation that you're better off here."

"It'll change," Toreth said.

"Will it? I know you don't give a crap either way—you aren't leaving."

"Now you sound like Chevril."

That made Christofi smile. "Yeah, you're right. But everyone except him knows he's never leaving, either. I suppose at least in CF I'll be getting some corporate exposure. Maybe I'll run into someone who still knows the value of I&I."

"A new IIP arrived while you were gone," Sara said as Toreth passed her desk on the way back from Corporate Fraud.

"Looks like B-C doesn't get his training course, then."

"I wouldn't cancel it yet if I were him. Justice picked up something unusual in a stolen property surveillance, and they thought it might be more in our line. Restricted tech or something. The file's a bit vague," Sara added disapprovingly. "Not very well organized, either. It's hard to tell if there's anything to it."

One penalty of having no active Investigation in Progress was the inability to turn down whatever crappy noncase might roll in next. "Tillotson is trying to fuck my career. When did he last hand over something decent?"

"The music case turned out all right," Sara said. "Blackmail and murder, and we closed it."

"Only because B-C let someone take a potshot at those—" Toreth frowned. With the case closed, the details had already moved to *who cares*. "The singers. 343. When it arrived it was a threats-to-kill, and who the hell wants those?"

Sara just shrugged.

"Fine, I'll take a look. Maybe there'll be something worthwhile in it. Anything about Nagra yet?"

"Oh, yes." Sara glanced casually around, then lowered her voice. "I had a word with one of the senior admins in the assignment section in HCT—she was one of the first ones who came back after the trouble, so I got to know her quite well when we were trying to get HCT up and running again. Anyway, Nagra put her name up for a senior para post. They're about to start filling a fresh round of replacement teams. We're getting at least two or three, probably more."

"What about the other sections?" Toreth asked, temporarily distracted from his own problems. "Corporate Fraud?"

Sara nodded. "They're getting the same. So is Information and Communications Crimes. One team at Administrative Department Corruption and Fraud—basically, everywhere except Political gets something."

Looked like Christofi's assessment of PC's future was spot on, if even the historically underresourced ADCF section was beating them to replacement staff. "So is Nagra going to get a team?"

"Well, I actually managed to get hold of the cleared candidates list, and her name's definitely on it."

"Nice." HCT usually kept the names of juniors ready to move up to senior tightly locked down, because of the trouble caused when approved juniors didn't find a promotion. "What are her chances?"

"The assignments won't be finalized until the new budgets next year, so I couldn't find out for sure. There are people above her with better experience, though, including a couple of seniors, so probably not this time." Sara shrugged. "Apparently she put her name in for the last round, too, but Chris Doyle beat her and all the other juniors here on time and case points."

Doyle, equally as good a para as Nagra, had only a few years' more experience than her. "When she finally goes, where the hell am I going to find a new junior?" Did no one in his team have any fucking loyalty at all?

Sara didn't seem to have an answer, because she said, "It might not happen for ages. There are always paras transferring in to take senior places. And they're still talking about rolling out the investigator team lead scheme next year."

A sign of desperation, as far as Toreth was concerned, done purely because more investigators than paras had survived the revolt. "Investigators trying to do paras' jobs?" he scoffed. "They might as well merge us with Justice; then I can just fucking resign."

"Corporate Fraud has had senior specialists leading teams for years, and they manage all right. And besides, a few paras are still coming back from medical leave," Sara added soothingly.

Toreth doubted many people who'd been so badly injured—or were that talented at spinning out medical leave—would return as seniors. Not enough to stop Nagra from eventually getting her promotion, anyway. "You know, Christofi told me one of the PC interrogators is still on the sick. Psych reasons. He developed claustrophobia in the cells, so now he can't go down to the underground levels." Toreth snorted. "Sometimes I think it's a pity they finally shut down Psychoprogramming."

"Reorganized," Sara said. "What was left of them."

"The 'Division of Neuropsychology'? At the Department of *Medicine*? Or whatever they're calling it these days."

"Department of Health Care and Research, I think. Unless they've changed it back again."

"Well, whatever the name is, that isn't a reorganization, it's a burial. Mindfuck is finished," Toreth said with satisfaction.

And with them the mindfuckers' perennial threat to interrogation as a way of extracting information. That was something to be optimistic about, Toreth thought as he went into his office. Politically significant crimes might be out of favor at the moment, but at least, unlike Psychoprogramming, I&I was still alive and functioning inside Int-Sec.

11

Sara had been, as usual, right about the IIP. It was uninspiringly sparse. An anonymous tip-off had led Justice to a storage unit where a brief search had revealed cases of high-grade fabrics, purportedly of Indian origin. The cases had the required ID chips containing import and movement information, but a more detailed check showed them to be fake, so Justice had assumed the fabrics to be stolen or counterfeit. With unusual enterprise, they'd then decided to plant trackers to trace the distribution routes. Opening the eighth case, they'd found not supposedly natural silks, but far more illegal electronic surveillance equipment.

And there the Justice investigation had stalled. The unit had been reserved remotely, using stolen information. The storage facility had no surveillance of its own, as might be expected when someone had chosen it to hide specified equipment. Forensic examination had been uninformative, suspiciously so—tests on a stained piece of silk suggested the place had been sprayed down at least once with an enzyme mix designed to wipe out organic evidence. Then someone at Justice had had the bright idea of declaring that surveillance equipment possibly sent from a foreign country plus high-tech forensic cleanup must equal political, which thus equaled I&I. So the case had flown, like a mercaptan grenade at an anti-Administration demonstration, into Toreth's lap.

To Toreth's eye, the list of items looked more like a cache belonging to a sab team. But an investigation still needed to be made. He tagged the IIP for Jameson and Morehen, then decided to give the instructions in person.

B-C was still hanging on to the spare senior para's office he'd claimed during the revolt, which meant that until Jameson's arrival Toreth's three investigators had had the luxury of an office each. During the fight for Wrenn's replacement, Tillotson had tried to pacify Toreth with a promotion to Senior Investigator for Mistry, which left Morehen sharing with the new junior investigator.

The pair were drinking tea and chatting when Toreth opened the office door. He leaned on the door frame and regarded them silently.

"Mandatory study break, Para," Morehen said, and gestured at his screen with his mug.

Toreth had always wondered if the optimized learning algorithms did help information retention, or if Human Capital and Training had worked out that only by dangling the lure of officially sanctioned slacking could they ever get anyone onto a training course in the first place.

"Of course," Toreth said. "Well, maybe you could squeeze a new IIP into your schedules."

The mugs went down on the desks in unison, and Toreth smiled.

He explained the unpromising origins of the case, then laid out his plan. "For now, maintain surveillance. Justice already installed some cameras, so just check that they aren't stuck over the door with a flashing red light on top. Cover the ap-

12

proaches and the door itself, and we'll see if we can get a clear ID on anyone who visits. Got that?"

"Yes, Para," Jameson said. "Discreet watch, clear facial images. I'll get on it right away."

She always sounded so bloody enthusiastic. Sometimes Toreth wondered if she was taking the piss.

"Now, this place is on the other side of New London. If there's anything to it, then whoever shows up will probably be a pro. Our best chance is a physical tail. I want one of you two or someone trustworthy from the pool nearby at all times when there's access to the facility. Luckily for you, it isn't twenty-four hour. Don't arse around right opposite the entrance, mind. And no uniforms."

"Of course not, Para," Morehen said.

He only wished everyone found it obvious. "Make sure if you get a pool sub in, you tell them the same. Work out the rota between yourselves. The unit is only paid for until the end of next week, so if no one shows up by then it's a wash. I'm sure you can finish your courses while you're on surveillance."

The investigators exchanged glances, then Morehen said, "Yes, Para."

Chapter Two

❖

De Nijs had been anticipating one of the less comfortable professional sessions of his career, and Warrick's first words did nothing to alter his opinion.

"This is ridiculous, and an outrageous intrusion into my private life," Warrick said as he sat down in the SimTech psychologist's office.

He'd taken one of the four more casual, low chairs by the window, instead of the chair opposite De Nijs across his desk. Making De Nijs come over to him—such a blatant display of bad manners from Warrick left no doubt how angry he was.

"I'm sorry," De Nijs said as he went to join Warrick. "If it's any consolation, I helped Linton look for an alternative key personnel insurance policy without the partner assessment clause. None of them covered SimTech's needs."

Apparently it wasn't consoling. "Considering they've managed to insure me without this information for the last five years, I fail to see why they need it now."

"Well, you're now cohabiting with a registered partner. And there've been some changes in the policy terms. Para-investigators have been given an increased risk level." De Nijs hesitated, but avoiding the truth was rarely productive in the long term, especially with Warrick. "Not without some justification. If anything, *as a group* they were underassessed before."

Warrick grimaced. "But you've met Toreth."

"The policy mandates a formal, recorded, interview. I can hardly give them an assessment based on a couple of social evenings and hearsay."

"Office gossip," Warwick said with distaste.

"People tell me things, and I listen to them—that's my job. Although I wouldn't call it gossip. More like natural concerns leading to a flow of information. People notice when one of the directors comes to work with unusual bruises. Other people reassure them. Have you heard of Fitcherson's dependency-interest model for corporate dynamics?"

"Corporate social theory, isn't it?" Warrick looked upwards for a moment, then gave a small nod. "It uses individuals' perceptions of their colleagues' importance to them personally to construct a map of key social nexi in a corporation. Is that right?"

"That's it," De Nijs said with some surprise. Warrick wasn't known for his interest in formal psychology, even corporate psychology. "Well, for a lot of SimTech employees, you'd be strong in both financial and professional scores."

"If not so important on the emotional axis," Warrick said dryly.

"You might be surprised—maybe I should run a scoring project and find out." Which was something he'd meant to do for a while, but SimTech generated more genuine clinical work for a corporate psychologist than most corporations. "You know, some people would say Fitcherson's is an outdated model. But for me, a lot of the criticism comes because people can't resist the temptation to add new criteria they think will make it better meet their specific needs. Sticking with Fitcherson's original scheme, I find a lot of value in it ... and we're getting sidetracked. Now—"

Warrick held up his hand. "Before we start, can I ask a question about the flexibility of the scoring?"

"What specific aspect?"

"In the context of ..." Warrick paused for a moment, rubbing his wrist. "Suppose there's a question along the lines of 'has Toreth ever hit you?' In that case, is there room for 'only in a consensual sexual scenario,' or are we limited to yes and no? If it's the latter, then we're going to run into problems."

"Ah! I did take the opportunity to discuss that with their risk assessment department in advance." Which had gone rather more smoothly than De Nijs had expected. "They're willing to let me exercise discretion, and take my opinion as to future risk."

"Really?" Warrick sounded surprised.

"It's possible they'd try to use my lack of impartiality as a way to avoid paying up, but they have as good a reputation as any corporate insurers."

"Still, I suppose I'd better try not to die, just in case." The joke and small smile didn't entirely hide Warrick's underlying irritation. "What happens to the recording of this session?"

"We keep it. They only see my report. If they dispute my conclusions, then excerpts might help negotiation, but only with your permission. Otherwise the interview is completely confidential."

Warrick nodded. "Inside SimTech, too?"

"Yes. Inside and outside—unless you're planning to tell me anything that threatens the safety or stability of the European Administration. That I'd have to report, of course."

Warrick didn't comment on the standard qualifier. "Then we'd better get on with it."

De Nijs marked the official start of the recording on his hand screen. "Dr. Hendrik De Nijs, interview with Dr. Keir Warrick. Now, your relationship with Valantin Toreth has lasted...?"

Warrick was already frowning, but he answered readily enough. "Five or six years, give or take. I'm afraid it doesn't lend itself to an exact start date."

"That's fine. And he's a senior para-investigator at the Investigation and Interrogation Division, correct?"

"Yes. Which is why this nonsense is apparently necessary."

De Nijs ignored the comment. "Does he have any convictions for violent offenses?"

Warrick hesitated. "Not as an adult, so far as I know. I think he had an incident as a juvenile, but he only mentioned it once, and I don't know the details. A stabbing, if I recall correctly."

The carefully casual tone made De Nijs raise one eyebrow slightly, but he confined himself to making a note.

"Has he ever been violent towards you?"

"Not outside the context of entirely consensual sexual situations," Warrick said clearly, glancing at the recording camera.

"And have you suffered any injuries in those situations?"

"Nothing beyond some superficial tissue damage, just scrapes and bruises. Oh—a broken wrist. That was an accident, though. A chair overbalanced while I was handcuffed to it, so you could say it was partly self-inflicted."

"So, how often do accidents happen?"

"Very rarely. He knows what he's doing." There was a certain brittleness underlying Warrick's voice. "I hope the risk factors for para-investigators at least acknowledge that they have expertise in the area."

"Mm." De Nijs checked the list of indicators provided by the insurers, using the pause to signal a change of topic. "Has Toreth ever forced you to have sex, or to take part in sexual activities that made you feel uncomfortable?"

"No. Or—" Warrick hesitated. "Define uncomfortable."

While there was a potential—although somewhat technical—ambiguity under the circumstances, De Nijs wondered if that was all. "On balance you would've preferred to refuse, but felt you were unable to, for any reason."

"Mm. Then no. On either count."

"Are you ever afraid of him?"

Warrick stroked his palms together, his expression meditative. "On rare occasions, yes, I have been. He can be somewhat...intense, under certain circumstances."

He'd expected to have to push harder for the admission. Still, infuriating as he could sometimes be in a professional context, Warrick had a strong basic honesty, refreshing in a successful corporate. "What kind of circumstances?"

Warrick gave him a careful inspection, letting De Nijs see him make the assessment whether or not to trust him with the knowledge. "He can be jealous, for

16

one thing. It's caused some problems in the past." He stressed the final three words.

"And how do other people find Toreth, do you think?"

"Are they afraid of him, too, do you mean? I expect so, in the sense that his job has a certain reputation. His personal assistant is wary about upsetting him, but of course he's her boss. You've probably noticed Lew Marcus avoiding Toreth at SimTech functions—I wouldn't like to say whether that's fear or just dislike, though." Warrick sighed. "My sister doesn't like Toreth either, but I'd say she's more afraid *for* me than *of* him."

"In what way?"

"She's never...accepted, I suppose, that the bruises don't mean anything more sinister than if I'd got them playing rugby. But yes, I think she's found him a little intimidating in the past."

"I see. You mentioned jealousy?"

Warrick shrugged. "We all have our weak spots."

"True, but we also all choose how they affect others. For example, does Toreth ever try to stop you from spending time with people?"

"No. Well, not anyone I have the slightest desire to see, anyway."

"Oh?"

"A man named Jean-Baptiste. But Toreth's dislike of him is amply justified, and shared by me."

Warrick's cold tone gave De Nijs no reason to doubt his sincerity. "And how about your sister?"

"There have been disagreements on both sides in the past. But honestly, I don't think for most of the time he gives her a moment's thought."

"So he doesn't affect your relationship with Dillian at all?"

"I—" Warrick hesitated. "I admit, I hadn't thought about it quite like that. Immediately before I moved, she'd been working on Mars for a few months, so obviously we'd only spoken on the comm. But now...." He frowned thoughtfully. "Yes. Perhaps she does visit the flat less often. But of course she's busy with her own life. It might simply be a coincidence. I'll talk to her about it—I'll see her at New Year."

"And what about SimTech?" De Nijs glanced down at Warrick's file. "You're on the full trials list. How does Toreth feel about that?"

"Yes, it used to bother him. But I explained that sex in the sim is just work— he understands emotional detachment from work situations very well. Also, that the sim is not negotiable."

"And that satisfied him?"

"I'm sure it wasn't his perfect outcome for the situation. But he hasn't mentioned it for years, now. I assume he prefers not to think about it." He smiled rather tightly. "Which is something we're both quite good at by now, really, regarding one another's jobs. It makes for a more harmonious home life."

17

De Nijs had considered asking Warrick his views on Toreth's job. But it wasn't required by the insurers; even these days, in a commercially and medically confidential interview, some opinions were best not examined. "So in general, how's the cohabitation working out?"

"Surprisingly well. At least, it's still ongoing, which is more than I honestly expected. The whole project was rather unexpected. It wouldn't have happened at all if Toreth hadn't lost his flat during the trouble earlier in the year, at the same time as SimTech asked me to move somewhere more secure."

Trouble. It was the word that seemed to have slipped into general use for the revolt. Nonspecific, and de-emphasizing the political ramifications of a Europe-wide uprising. It caught De Nijs's attention every time he heard it, but it wasn't relevant to the interview.

"So you're happy with the situation?"

"Yes. Well. It's required some adjustment, but I'd lived on my own since Melissa and I separated, and one gets used to having everything just so." Warrick smiled slightly. "In my case more than some other people, I'm sure."

"Any particular areas of conflict?"

"Mm." Warrick's look of careful consideration suggested he'd got past some of his annoyance with why they were there. "Nothing really new, I suppose. But... one doesn't care about towels left on floors that one can't see. However, when one is sharing a flat, they're rather more obvious."

"Are those actual or metaphorical towels? Because if they're the former, then I'd suggest adding 'put the towels in the hamper' into the flat management system's daily routine. They won't be folded, but they'll be in one place."

"I never thought of that." Warrick shook his head. "I suppose it's because the vac only comes out when I'm not there."

"Probably. And even though most vacs have a pickup function, I'm always surprised how many people turn it off because they can't be bothered to train them what to move and what to leave. So, now that we've solved that, how about the more metaphorical towels?"

"Those are my problems, not Toreth's, and not relevant to the question of risk."

"I'm afraid that's my professional assessment to make."

"Very well." Warrick's voice had tightened again. "He sleeps with other people. Frequently. He picks someone up at the gym, or he goes out in the evening to find someone. And while it wasn't an issue when I didn't have to be aware of it, now it... has become harder to ignore, even though he rarely mentions anything specific. But I knew that going into the situation—or I should have done."

"So you didn't hope his behavior might change once you were cohabiting?"

"No," Warrick said, then held up his hand. "Or... I'd like to think that I didn't. Knowing Toreth as well as I do, it would be a frankly stupid thing to expect. Looking at the situation more positively, I suspect his overall level of, ah, extracurricular activity has gone down, simply because I'm more conveniently to hand now."

To De Nijs it sounded like a miserable situation. But it wasn't his life. "Overall, though, are you happier than before?"

"Overall . . . yes? No less happy, certainly. Adjustments have to be made, that's all. They always do."

"Have you told Toreth about the change in how you feel about his other partners?"

This time Warrick actually laughed.

"I take it that's a no?"

"Ah, yes. Exactly." Warrick shook his head. "It wouldn't be a productive use of my time. Before he moved into the flat I told him that he couldn't bring people back there, and he agreed to the condition. As far as I know, he's kept to that. Asking him to stop, though, or even implying he should—no." Warrick shrugged, apparently relaxed, but De Nijs thought he could hear a faint undertone of resentment, again, at being forced to expose so much. "I honestly don't think that he could, even if he were willing to try, which he wouldn't be. He'd see it as an unreasonable attempt to control him."

If the insurers were looking for a sticking point, this seemed a good place to find it. "And that would make him angry?"

This time the hesitation was pure reluctance, not uncertainty, until Warrick said, "Yes, it would."

"And what—"

"I imagine he'd slam a few doors and disappear for a week. Maybe two. Luckily, his admin can always reach him, so it isn't too much of a problem." If De Nijs hadn't been so confident in Warrick's ultimate understanding that De Nijs was only doing what SimTech required, the dark flash of resentment in Warrick's eyes might've made him wonder if he should be looking for a new job. "The question is theoretical, in any case. I have no intention of asking anything of the kind. The situation is something I've accepted. Or thought I had. As I said, it's my problem."

And just that quickly, Warrick had regained control. He steepled his fingers as he waited for the next question.

"Has it caused conflict before?" When Warrick nodded, De Nijs added, "And how did you deal with it?"

"The last time? Extraordinarily badly." Warrick shook his head, his expression pained. "The insurance company certainly wouldn't have approved. If you want occasions I was afraid, that's one of them, although as you can see, I'm still here to tell the tale some years later."

"So, would you like to tell me more about it?"

After a long silence, Warrick said, "Not particularly."

"Because it shows Toreth in a bad light?"

"God, no. Quite the opposite. Me, on the other hand . . ." Warrick sighed. "In brief, I allowed myself to become overly concerned by the idea that he was seeing other people—having sex with other people, rather. Rationally, I knew they meant nothing to him, in a very literal sense. No more than masturbation would. Nevertheless."

He paused, and De Nijs nodded. "If we could all be rational all the time, I'd be out of a job."

Warrick smiled reluctantly. "True. Anyway, selfishly, I had an affair. Not even that. Just a few days at a conference, with someone who certainly didn't deserve to suffer for my stupidity."

"You felt you were putting them in danger?"

Warrick hesitated, then said, "I suppose I must have been aware there was a possibility. At the next conference, I invited Toreth along. I rubbed his face in what I'd done, he walked out, and yes, for a while I was afraid he'd come back and I might be in danger, too. But he didn't. In fact, he handled it far better than I did."

"You say you felt afraid. Did you take any practical steps as a result?"

"Such as?"

Such as something the insurers would definitely take note of. Had Warrick realized that? "Did you call the hotel security? SimTech security? Leave the hotel? Find a place with other people?"

"No." Warrick looked honestly surprised. "I didn't even think about any of that. I just lay on the bed in the dark and felt like an idiot. I suppose you could call it instructive, but please tell the insurers I'm not planning to repeat the lesson."

"So what happened between you afterwards?"

"He came back a day or so later, and we talked about it over breakfast. All ridiculously civilized, really. Although—" Warrick hesitated minutely, but carried on before De Nijs could speak. "It took a couple of days more to finally settle out, but we had a very pleasant holiday in the end. Good skiing, or at least Toreth enjoyed it. I find skiing outside the sim to be a little too unpredictable." He smiled. "I hardly go looking for gratuitous physical danger."

"I see." Phrased appropriately, that could probably make a reassuring part of the assessment report. "Now, there's one more thing that I'm afraid I'd like to go over. I have a report from Emma Queen about a security incident last spring, where—"

Warrick actually groaned. "Is that really necessary? Unfortunate as it was, that had nothing to do with my personal safety."

De Nijs ignored the deflection. "Why did Toreth hire a detective to watch you?"

"He didn't. Well...I suppose it depends on how you look at it. You recall I mentioned Jean-Baptiste?"

"The man Toreth doesn't want you to see?"

"Yes. Technically, it was Jean-Baptiste being watched."

20

De Nijs frowned—he knew it wasn't his memory at fault, and it was unlike Warrick to lie, at least so obviously. "That isn't the name in the file Queen gave me."

"No—that would be Alex Welham, if I recall?" He waited for De Nijs to nod. "He was here under a different name, for commercial and confidentiality reasons that had nothing to do with Toreth." Warrick smiled wryly. "Although I'm sure you can imagine the fake name didn't help when Toreth unfortunately found out. Hence the surveillance. But since Jean-Baptiste had been assigned to SimTech to perform a safety and security assessment for an Administration department, it had the obvious side effect of scaring the hell out of Queen."

Curiosity made him itch to pursue the idea of "safety and security" issues, but that wasn't the purpose of the interview. "Obvious to you."

Warrick nodded. "Toreth's interest in SimTech is situational at best. He enjoys the sim. Apparently he didn't think through the logical consequences of personnel surveillance."

"Rather surprising. He must interact professionally with corporate security, surely?"

"Yes." Warrick sighed. "But as you pointed out, if we all acted rationally all the time..."

"Yes, of course. Queen's report said that you confronted him about the surveillance. How did he react?"

"He was angry and embarrassed that he'd been caught. He apologized; I told him I didn't care, and that if anything similar happened again, then our relationship was over." Warrick's cool, factual calm had returned in full force. "He took that part of it very well, actually, but then I suppose he would. I'm sure the embarrassment alone would've made him reluctant to do it again, whatever I said."

"And you don't think he's carried out any surveillance since then?"

Warrick looked down at his hands, turning them over, curling his fingers to inspect his nails. "Not professionally, or at SimTech," he said finally.

"Meaning?"

"Since we began cohabiting, he sometimes checks up on me via the security cameras in the flat." Warrick looked up. "It doesn't bother me—I have nothing to hide."

For all Warrick's control, it was impossible not to empathize with the humiliation of having to lay out such personal details involuntarily. "Does he know that you know about it?"

"Honestly, I don't know." Warrick frowned. "He ought to be able to guess. I've never mentioned it, though. Toreth is—" He paused, then said, "I know this is confidential, but I just want to emphasize this must stay between us."

"Of course," De Nijs said. What could Warrick possibly have more interest in keeping quiet?

"Toreth works for I&I, I'm corporate. He's living in a flat owned by SimTech, in a complex he could never afford, if they even take noncorporate primary residents. He's as used to having his own living space as I am. So I think that using the security feed lets him feel some sense of control over the flat—and over me in the flat. I can understand that."

Because Warrick of all people could certainly empathize with a need for control. "And if he found out that you knew about it? What would he do?"

"Nothing dramatic, I'm sure." Warrick sighed. "At the old flat he used to check the drawers and so on when he was alone there. It happened to come up in conversation that I'd noticed, and he was mildly embarrassed, that's all. I imagine his reaction now would be much the same."

"Then I think that's enough to let me answer the insurer's questions, thank you."

"So, what's your professional opinion?" Now Warrick sounded genuinely curious. Having looked at some old files before the session, De Nijs wondered if his assessment would be compared with that of his predecessor.

"It isn't a risk-free situation. You could even call it playing with fire. But then some people play with fire for years and never burn themselves. Not badly, at least. Of course, some do. You certainly have a good grasp of how to handle Toreth's personality type, though. Firm consequences, clearly laid out and enforced."

Warrick smiled.

"What's funny?"

"Jean-Baptiste told me something very similar at the end of his visit to SimTech. Interspersed with warnings about the risks of making pets of dangerous wild animals. I sincerely hope the insurance assessors never solicit *his* opinion." After a moment's contemplation, he apparently dismissed the memory with a shake of his head. "Your report?" he asked briskly.

"Still needs to be written. But I don't think it'll cause any problems with the renewal, or even put your premiums up too much."

"Excellent." This time Warrick's smile was warm, and he put his hands on the arms of the chair as though about to stand. Then he stopped and sat back. "Actually, since I'm here, there are a couple of unrelated things I'd like to discuss."

Stamping his authority on the relationship again. "Of course."

"Is everything going smoothly regarding your sim safety programs? I was looking at the allocation of resources for next year—"

"And I'm taking too many?"

"Not at all. There are a few minor projects wrapping up soon, though, and if you need more people involved now would be a good time to ask before they're all reallocated."

Ever since Warrick's abrupt about-face on the subject of sim safety, every conversation they'd had about it had been infused—on Warrick's side—with a level of dutiful determination De Nijs had never seen from him in any other context.

"I think I have what I need, but if you'll give me a day or two, I'll mull it over and let you know."

"Please do. Further to that, I'm hoping to make another claim on your time. Next year we're setting up a new strategic planning group, largely made up of lawyers, and Asher will be the director with oversight." Warrick smiled. "I thought it best if I took a hands-off approach in this case."

"A group looking at what?"

"Oh yes, of course. Re-evaluating potential corporate risks." Warrick brushed his palms together as he talked. "We benefit from all the standard corporate protections against product liability, but the sim isn't a standard product. There are areas where future liabilities could exist outside the legislative framework, and probably other areas we haven't even considered yet. As the old saying goes, there are known unknowns and unknown unknowns. The directors have decided it's time to make a concerted effort to review all previous assessments and pin down as many of those unknowns as we can. No matter how painful that process might be in terms of circumscribing future development."

De Nijs could already imagine the expressions on the faces of the lawyers if he raised some of his predecessor Marian Tanit's old concerns. "I'm pleased you think my input would be valuable."

Warrick frowned slightly. "It's a genuine investigation, not a box-ticking exercise for regulatory compliance. In fact, some of the legal team are of the opinion that we'd be in a better position if we didn't plan to look quite so hard. But others think it's a sound strategy, provided we deal appropriately with any concerns we find. Which we will," he finished crisply.

"It sounds like a valuable process. I'll be delighted to participate in any way I can."

"Good. As I said, Asher will be dealing with it by and large—I'll make sure you're included in the planning. And finally, a new behavioral psychologist will be joining us this week—Dr. Marley Thomas."

"Oh? I didn't hear about an interview." De Nijs thought he might have sounded even more surprised than he felt, because Warrick hurried on in a reassuring tone.

"There wasn't one, as such. She led the fan management team at a subsidiary of UnLTD Ent, dealing with their virtual performer portfolio. We happened to hear she was considering other options, and we were able to make an attractive offer. She's coming in on the practical development side, not as a staff psychologist. But I'd still like you to brief her on all the concerns about the sim, past and present, especially as regards the Yeses."

"That's what she'll be working on?"

Warrick nodded. "The main area, anyway. The regulatory discussion with the Communications Systems Assessment Division stalled after the trouble, but there's movement again. Finally. The EES program has real potential for solid licensing revenue." He looked intently at De Nijs. "What do you think about the Yeses?"

"I think they're one of the largest cans of worms out of all the many cans that make up the sim."

Warrick smiled broadly. "Then I'm sure you and she will have a lot to talk about."

Chapter Three

❖

To Toreth's surprise, the surveillance produced a result after only three days. He would've put money on the whole thing being a waste of time—not least because he couldn't believe anyone trading in highly restricted tech wouldn't have the inside of the storage unit monitored, or fail to notice Justice blundering around the area.

It seemed somehow fitting, though, that the result was as vague and confusing as the original file.

"So he didn't actually go inside?" Toreth said.

"No, Para," Jameson said over the comm. "I was watching the whole time. He walked up, checking the unit numbers, and he stopped right in front of our door. He got his hand about halfway to the screen, and then he turned around and walked directly out of there."

"Huh. He didn't visit any other units?"

"No. The cameras had him covered the whole way in and out. We got a clear ID, and there are no units reserved there under his own name or his business's name."

Toreth contemplated the security file on his screen. The pictures showed a tall, well-built man with a light, even tan that suggested a certain level of vanity, and dark hair worn longer than was fashionable. Good-looking, in a square-jawed, sharp-cheekboned way that would make him stand out from a crowd, often not an advantage in crime. Kelvin Richardson, aged 33, with an ex-wife and a son, and the owner of a small but modestly profitable company working in the field of systems security. Urban Fox Security had full registered corporate status via a franchising system—not illegal, but interesting. There were many reasons a small company might want to buy that level of respectability.

"Anything else?" Toreth asked. "Don't suppose he dropped any litter on the way out?"

"Not quite, Para. There is one other thing, though. The car he arrived in looked like the corporate car—there's one registered—but on the off chance I checked the Department of Transport tracking, and that wasn't the ID showing up according to the traffic monitoring and control. I followed him when he left. Someone's definitely been mucking around with the chip; according to the DoT system the car never left the parking space behind Richardson's office, which is funny because I saw him pull back into it."

"Good work," Toreth said. "All right. We'll start looking at Richardson as a sab. Get back to the storage unit and hope someone else turns up who knows the unit code this time."

"Are you still coming back to my flat this evening?" Sara asked as she delivered a late afternoon coffee.

Toreth looked at her blankly. "I don't know. Am I?"

"To talk about the thing. You know—the not-work thing. The thing you wanted me to look at with you?" Obviously his face was accurately reflecting his complete memory failure because she added, "Wood?"

"Oh! Right, of course. Yeah, then I suppose I am. Tell Morehen I'm sorry, but he'll have to stay at home tonight and wank. Send him a nice naked picture or two."

Morehen's unreturned interest in Sara had morphed into a long-running team joke. Or, at least, it amused Toreth. Sara, as usual, just shook her head.

These days, when Toreth wanted to plot anything related to Warrick, he had to do it at Sara's place. True, he'd done much the same before, starting with the collar and manacles, fucking years ago now. That had been at her old flat, though, from before the revolt. Now they both lived in different flats, and the original manacles were gone, too. Sometimes he wondered how the hell his life had become so fucking domestic, and what else might be waiting around the corner to blackjack him.

He shook his head. Depressing ideas for what was supposed to be a fun evening.

Sara was sitting beside him on her sofa, beer bottle in her hand. She was paging slowly through the designs on the screen, flipping back and forth to compare them.

"What do you think?" he asked her. "Picked one yet?"

"I think you should get the sun ray design, with the three colors of wood. That goes best with the rest of the flat, doesn't it? Although I don't really remember what the bedroom looks like—I only saw it the once with the furniture in, at the flat warming. Which one do you like?"

"I don't really care." They all looked good enough for the game, and that was the extent of Toreth's interest in furniture. "I sent her some pictures, along with the measurements, so everything she suggested ought to match."

"What did you tell her?" she asked.

"That I wanted something to fit in with the rest of it, and that it had to be the right shape and solid enough to tie someone to and fuck him as hard—hey!" he exclaimed, as Sara spluttered beer over the screen.

"Sorry," she gasped, still coughing. "You didn't?"

"Why not?" Toreth looked around and spotted a disposable napkin that had probably arrived with some takeaway, lying on the floor. He picked it up and wiped the screen. "It's what it's for. I'm paying enough, so she might as well get it right."

"Yes, but the woman is . . . I mean, she makes bespoke furniture. For really posh people. She doesn't even advertise anywhere—all word of mouth. It took me ages to find her, *and* I called her for you."

"So? You're not planning to order anything, are you?"

"No . . . no, I suppose not. Definitely not now that she knows I work for a pervert. What did she *say*?"

Toreth grinned. "That they'd better use all-wooden pegged joints because they squeak less. And that those were more expensive."

Sara stared at him, then started giggling. "My God. You are so *bad*." She finished her beer and waved the bottle. "D'you want another one?"

"I'll get it."

Sara had piled the remains of the Thai takeaway on the kitchen table. Sara's cat, Bastard, stood in the middle, lapping up the tom yum soup Sara had been forced to leave because it was too hot. Toreth lifted his hand and raised an eyebrow, causing Bastard to crouch down and flatten his ears. As Toreth started the swing, Bastard hissed malevolently and shot off the table and out of the room.

No doubt gone to pretend to Sara that he'd been cruelly abused. Toreth grinned and opened the fridge. Inside he found mostly beer, along with an assortment of revolting-looking metabolically optimized liquid nutritionals; it was only the second week in December, so Sara's traditional pre-New Year-blowout health regime looked to be underway in good time this year. At least some things didn't change.

When he carried the beers through, Bastard was curled up on Sara's lap, looking as woebegone as any cat could that weighed seven kilos and had teeth like a nightmare. Toreth handed Sara's beer over at arm's length, then made a tactical retreat to the chair opposite.

"Does Warrick know you're getting it?" Sara asked, tickling Bastard under the chin.

"The bed? Wouldn't be much of a surprise present if he did, would it?"

27

"Oh." Sara frowned, opened her mouth, then pressed her lips together.

"For fuck's—don't make such a production out of it. What?"

"Well, he's very...particular, isn't he? About his belongings."

"He's an obsessive fucking freak, yes. But he mentioned a new bed months ago. He wanted something to match the rest of the flat, just like you said. It's perfect. And anyway, it'll be his New Year present."

Sara grinned. "So you think he's far too polite to say if he hates it?"

"That's right. And I'm going to test it out beforehand, so at least I'll know it's comfy."

"You'll never get someone to deliver it on New Year's Day, though," Sara said. "Not without paying a fortune."

"New Year's Day doesn't matter. I expect he'll be at Kate's place. Jen's place, now, I suppose, not that it makes much difference. Same old fucking family drama, anyway, I'm sure."

"With—oh, you mean Tarin?"

Toreth nodded shortly.

"Right, yes, of course. How is he?"

"How the hell should I know? Not dead, yet, as far as I heard. I expect Warrick would've mentioned that."

"So Warrick's going to be there with Jen and—what's her name?"

"Tarin's wife? Philadelphia. Philly." Toreth shifted in the chair, then downed half of his beer. Why the hell Sara was interested in Warrick's family crap he could never fathom. "And the kid, I assume, and Dillian and Asher and Cele, and God knows who else. Warrick's usually there for a few days. I suppose I should find out exactly when, so he doesn't walk in while they're carrying the bed up the stairs."

"What are you doing for New Year, then?" Sara asked, looking inexplicably anxious about the answer.

"I don't know. A nice juicy case might pop up—if one does, the holiday rota's always thin, and this year it's bound to be worse than usual so I should be able to pick and choose. We could do with a strong result. The Bureau might like what I did in Washington, but Tillotson doesn't care. There isn't a metrics box to tick for America. Otherwise...find a party or two. Heard anything from Daedra about a bash yet?"

"You mean you aren't going with Warrick?" The anxiety hadn't gone away.

"Any reason why I should?"

"No, none at all. I just thought—I mean, you don't. Um. Yes. So, you ought to get the bed delivered before New Year, then," Sara said briskly. "I mean, presents after are no good. It always looks like you forgot, or you organized it too late, even when you didn't."

Toreth kept his gaze pinned on her for a few moments more until she started to squirm a little, then he shrugged.

"It shows up when it shows up. It'll be sometime around New Year, anyway. I'll just make sure he knows it is a present when he does see it, that's all. Tie a bow on it or something."

Not that it would matter, because Warrick would love the bed. Still, he wished Sara hadn't brought up the chance that he might not. Buying presents for someone significantly richer than you was fundamentally tricky, and Toreth hated to fail at anything.

"What are you doing for New Year?" Toreth asked, as a diversion. Not that there was much point asking, as Sara always did the same thing—get drunk at an astonishing number of parties, then have a happy, hungover day or so recovering with her family.

To his surprise, she said, "Oh, I haven't decided yet."

Toreth sat up a little. "No? More party invites than you can choose between?"

"I was thinking I might go away somewhere for a few days. Do something different. You know."

Was that why she'd been worried at the thought of him sticking around on his own? "Something different like what?"

"Well, Andy—"

Bastard growled suddenly, and Sara yelped—he must've jabbed his scythelike claws through her thin skirt. She jumped, and beer splashed over Bastard and the sofa.

"Ow! No, sweetie pie, please don't do that to mummy's legs!"

Bastard leapt down, probably more in response to the beer than the very mild reprimand, and stalked off in an offended huff towards the kitchen, no doubt to register his displeasure by stealing more food and throwing it up. Sara mopped at her skirt and the cushions with the napkin Toreth had left behind on the arm of the sofa.

"Oh, bother," she said.

Toreth was more interested in the sentence the cat had interrupted. "Andy—Andy Morehen?" If this development was common knowledge in the team not a whisper had reached Toreth. "Finally reeling you in, is he?"

Sara was concentrating very hard on the cleanup. "If you want to put it like that. He's found a hotel somewhere nice and quiet—he wouldn't tell me where—so we could have a couple of days to ourselves. We both booked the holiday off," she added.

Not, as she well knew, that Toreth ever checked the bookings. While he had a reputation as a tolerant boss, if he needed his team in for an important case, then they came in, holidays or not.

"So when did this start?" he asked. New Year away didn't sound like an opening move. "Why the big mystery? Why didn't you tell me?"

"No reason. And...a few months ago, I suppose. Maybe a bit more." She scrunched up the tissue, dropped it on the table, and finally met his gaze. "I don't really know. After he came back with his new leg, anyway. It started with drinks after work, and then we went to a few other places. Just as friends. It was fun, and then he asked me and I thought, well, why not? He's—well, he's a lot nicer than he seems."

"He'd have to be." The investigator was rather hard-edged, but maybe that was camouflage he'd developed at Political Crimes. "So—" Toreth raised his eyebrows. "What's 'nice'?"

Sara actually blushed. "Just little things. Like…we were walking to the bar after work yesterday, and he mentioned he was going to cut his hair short again. And I asked if he'd keep it longer, because I liked it. And so he said he would."

Not what Toreth would classify as nice. "No ring yet?"

"No! It's far too soon."

Not by the standards of some of Sara's conquests. "Slowing down in your old age?"

She frowned. "We're taking things easy. He's asked me a couple of times to make it more…more of an official thing. At least tell people, meet each others' parents, that sort of stuff. But I don't want to rush into it. Not this time." Sara trapped the bottle between her knees for safekeeping and rubbed her fingers together. Her collection of engagement rings and other mementos was another loss to the revolt. "I rushed into lots of things in the past, and it never worked out very well, did it?"

"Hm." It sounded plausible, but years of training and experience made Toreth question anything out of character. Of course, Sara made a terribly unreliable witness when it came to anything about her boyfriends—no distance at all from the suspects. "Well, ring or not, when you break up with him, do it *nicely*. He's a good investigator, and I don't want him pissing off back to Political Crimes." Unlikely as that might be, if Christofi's assessment of its future was correct.

"Sometimes I don't know why *I* don't put in for a transfer," Sara said.

"Because your next boss wouldn't do his best to get himself taken off the New Year rota so you can have a dirty weekend fucking one of his investigators?"

Sara smiled. "That's probably it, yes."

"There you are, then." Why hadn't she just asked straight away? The old Sara, before the revolt, would've done it without hesitation. It was a change he couldn't seem to get used to. He didn't really want to. "I'll put Nagra's name down on the interrogation rota to keep Tillotson happy. I'm sure she won't mind."

30

Chapter Four

Toreth wasn't claustrophobic, never had been, but the curve of the scanner top hung only centimeters from his nose, and the air inside the scanner was beginning to taste stale. He was naked, but the carefully warmed air didn't stir a hair on his body. He hated lying motionless.

"How much longer?" Toreth said.

"You—ah. I told you not to say anything." Warrick sounded annoyed. "When you can talk, I'll tell you. And how long it takes depends entirely on how many rescans it needs."

Fine, Toreth thought irritably. I'll just lie here and . . . and nothing. Which was the problem. For this he'd cut short a Saturday morning at the gym. When was he going to learn not to listen to the lively, glowing enthusiasm in Warrick's voice which sounded so much like fun and fucking, and take better note of the actual content?

The scanner had internal lights, but Toreth had asked Warrick to turn them off after contemplating his own distorted face had got to be too much. The only light was what leaked in from the ends of the machine. The steel, dull and dark, felt closer than ever.

Toreth shut his eyes.

"If you could not do that, I'd be grateful," Warrick said after a few seconds. "I did ask at the beginning whether you preferred open or closed."

It must be showing up in the neural scanning. Toreth wondered if there was any way Warrick could actually tell what he was thinking at this point. He tested the idea by spending a few minutes with as vivid and detailed a picture of Warrick in the cabinet as he could summon up. It drew no reaction whatsoever from Warrick, but it passed the time. And gave him a hard-on, but Warrick didn't complain, so he probably wasn't scanning that.

The machine beeped—a noise which sounded very much like all the other beeps it had made. This time, though, Warrick gave a satisfied exclamation.

"Perfect head scan. You can talk now," Warrick added after a few seconds. "Just subvocalize into the microphone, though, please. I don't want the muscles moving more than they have to."

"Thank fuck," Toreth said, voice coming back to him from the scanner's speaker, disconcertingly disembodied. "I feel like I've been in here for hours."

"Hm. One hour and forty minutes, that's all."

"*All?*" Toreth fought off an intense urge to push the scanner away and swing his legs off the edge of the couch. Moving would feel so fucking good. "Seems like forever. What're you doing?"

"Not very much, actually." Warrick's voice moved. It was hard to tell from inside the thick shell, but he sounded to be going towards the foot of the machine. "As I said, the scan's going very well, so I'm just monitoring progress, watching the results come through. Of course, it's only the most superficial analysis, but part of the charm of the new system is the wider variety of real-time output."

Charm? Surely no one else in the world would describe a neural scanner as charming. "I can't believe this shit doesn't bore you to death."

Warrick chuckled. "I'm enjoying it a great deal. I spend far too much time in meetings and not enough on the technical side. Besides, it's a new way to look at your body. Not exactly a hardship."

Warrick's hand landed on his thigh and stroked up, briefly unprofessional. Toreth twitched, unable to prevent the reaction to the surprise.

"Sorry," Warrick said. "That one was my fault. But you're as engaging in detail as you are in total."

"I can get compliments somewhere I'm not bored out of my fucking mind."

"Mm. Not quite the same ones, I imagine. Your tongue has fascinating microphysiology, has anyone ever told you that?"

"Um." Actually, he had to say no. Many people had mentioned how well he used it, but admiration of its physiology, not that he could remember.

"That's one of the things I was scanning before." The hand lifted away, and Warrick's voice moved closer again. "The new system produces a relatively crude three-D visual representation as it takes the scan. You see, we can do a genetic profile to establish your individual flavor receptor gene alleles, and we can use a fast scan and some modeling to roughly map them out. However, to replicate your exact personal cell-to-cell variation we need the molecular expression scan. In a sense it's trivial, certainly compared to the olfactory receptor scanning, but it's another level of detail. In combination with the refined topological scanning of the mucosal layers in the nasal and oral cavities—which are more important in flavor perception than you might think—it's a step forward."

"But what's so great about mine?"

"Unusual might be a better word. You have a notably biased spread of receptors, in expression and position. It could be an aberration from your normal pattern—one problem with this level of detail is that changing expression patterns over time require rescanning, and it's a relatively poorly studied field. On the other hand, you don't like overly sweet things, so perhaps these are consistent values."

His voice had turned speculative. "It would be extremely interesting to do a longitudinal study, if you'd be willing to have a few more local scans. They wouldn't take anywhere near so long."

Toreth almost shrugged, stopping himself just in time. "Sure. If you make it worth my while."

"Mm?" Warrick's voice lowered in pitch and volume. "I expect I can think of an inducement."

And, yeah, he probably could. "How much longer is this going to take?"

"Not long at all—well, considering the level of detail. One incidental advantage of the new system is that because some initial processing is done in parallel instead of waiting until scanning is complete, missing or errant data can be rescanned instantly, which cuts down match-in errors from the passage of time. So in theory, the new sim bodies generated from it should be almost flawless point-in-time replicas."

"I've got a sim body that works fine. And the old scan didn't take this fucking long either."

"That's because this will ultimately allow us to create much better bodies." Warrick chuckled softly. "Although probably still not doing justice to the original."

Flattery, of course. But, Toreth felt, well deserved. "Is this better as in I'll actually be able to tell the difference, or better like the last time?"

"The last time you *did* get a better body. Technically speaking, the resampling produced a much faster neural simulation as the end result, so the rest of the sim world ran at a higher resolution on multiple scales."

"Looked about the same to me."

Warrick made a noncommittal noise which Toreth assumed equaled conceding the point. "This time, though, we're taking a fundamentally more detailed peripheral neural scan. Not merely more precision in the old metrics, but qualitatively improved. Now, admittedly, we've been pushing hard to get this idea into the main development stream because of the commercial benefits from making the user input more generic. It should cut a significant proportion of the sense-memory simulation patches required, possibly to the point where they're a rare exception. But, discounting the financial aspect, the whole sensory simulation mechanism will be made fundamentally better in concept and design—more organic. The virtual becomes more real, if you like."

Toreth was surprised to find he actually understood most of that. Understood it and reached a rather irritating conclusion. "So I won't be able to tell the difference?"

"Mm...perhaps not always in the sim as such, no. But if, for example, you were on a deep sea base and there was a chemical spill, any smell novel in the real world would be far better matched to sim training experiences."

"And, out of curiosity, exactly how fucking likely is that to happen to me?"

"It's merely an example. There are others. To select one that might be of more interest to *you*, should you kiss a stranger in the sim, they'll now taste the same if you later kiss them outside."

"Oh." The concept sounded familiar, although it took Toreth a moment to— "Yeah, I remember that."

"You actually noticed a flavor mismatch in kissing someone?" Warrick asked, his voice suddenly lively with curiosity. "That's unusual. Not many people have that level of discrimination, or sense memory."

"Not kissing—it was sucking you off. Tasted totally different in the real world, the first time."

"Ah, interesting. And then afterwards in the sim, once you had the outside experience?"

Toreth thought back. At the time he hadn't noticed. "Not sure. You taste the same now."

"Yes. The sim is pulling up the matched sense memory, or rather your brain is, with a little prompting. Which in itself is actually part of the problem we're hoping to correct here. It's an old, old flaw in the system, which is that the sim is affected far too much by expectations. This is something we might test later— under the old model system, if you tasted someone else but thought it was me, then you would taste me. One difference you'd hopefully notice with the new system is that even if you thought it was me, you'd get the taste of someone else. Of course, you might still end up confused, since the brain's vulnerable to distortions caused by expectation outside the sim, too. But at least the sim won't be worse than reality anymore."

"Amazing," Toreth said. "Fascinating."

Warrick laughed dryly. "Perhaps not for the average user. But that's the way it should work, at a conceptual level. One day the sim will be an absolutely seamless experience."

"Not if people have to lie totally fucking immobile for a week first. I think most people would notice the seam there."

"Well, faster scanning will come with time, and validation of the underlying concept. This is very much a proof-of-concept trial; sadly the hardware we were able to hire is rather less than state-of-the-art, and not really intended for this depth of scanning. Budgets, as usual. So I do apologize for the time required. I'll make it up to you later, I promise."

Toreth sighed, trying not to take too deep a breath and disturb the scan. Normally by now he'd be able to feel every single point along his body where his bones pressed into the scanner bed. Not this time, though. The pressure was smoothed away by the dynamically reactive cushioning. He hadn't listened to the details when Warrick explained it, but the stuff molded itself to him so supportively it was like floating in dense salt water. Extremely comfortable, but his body had begun to feel unreal, weirdly disconnected and diffuse. The physical memory of Warrick's hand on his thigh had long faded, and the growing urge to move, to feel the reassuring pull of tendon and muscle, only added to his unease.

"Lying in here is like the sense-memory stacking," he said.

"Yes—one of the other volunteers mentioned SMS. Unfortunately, this doesn't have the same user payoff."

"So I'm not the first gullible fucker you've tricked into this thing."

The silence stretched out long enough that Toreth felt a flutter of unease in his gut. "Warrick?"

"Hmm? Sorry, I was looking at the results. No, you're the sixth. I'm hoping if we can generate a sufficient amount of data, the final analysis can be completed by the end of the year—or the beginning of January, at the latest—and if the results look good, we'll expand the program."

New Year. A perfect chance to find out what Warrick was doing for New Year, and when Toreth could have the bed safely delivered.

"You're going to be working over New Year, then?" Toreth asked with what he hoped was convincing nonchalance. Warrick might be distracted by the scan results, but he could be annoyingly sharp at times.

"No. Once we have all the samples I'll leave the analysis running and hope it's done when I get back. Even with the systems here, the processing time required to generate and test the new sim models will be horrific. At least in these initial phases—the neurocognitive modelers assure me it can be streamlined and made workable in the end."

"So, what are your plans?"

"Plans? For the modeling?"

"No, for New Year. Where you're going, what you're doing. I need to make sure I can book the time off work, that's all, if you want me to be around."

"Ah, right, of course." Warrick still sounded a little bemused, which was understandable since Toreth had never asked before. Hopefully he'd put it down to them being at the new flat. "Well, at the moment, it looks as though I'll be at Jen's place, as usual. That might change."

"Oh?"

"Depending on Tarin's condition." Warrick sighed. "We were all hoping he'd be able to come to the house for New Year, at least for a few days, if we make sure there's adequate care provided. But apparently the risk of infections is still very high, so the doctors at the rehabilitation center aren't willing to commit to a definite yes or no until the day."

Damn. That was no help at all. "So it's all up in the air?"

"And likely to remain so until the last moment. We—Dillian, Philly and Val, and myself—might well be spending New Year's Day at the center, while Jen stays at the house to cook dinner, and then traveling all the way back."

"Why not stay somewhere nearby?"

"Valeria's insistent we have dinner at Granny's house, as usual, even though Granny's not there. I think she still hopes Kate will come back."

Toreth imagined Warrick shared his own view of how likely that would be. There was a silence, then Warrick sighed again so quietly that Toreth barely caught it. "What?" Toreth said.

"Nothing important. I was thinking about New Year at the house without Tarin there. For all the arguments we've had over the years, it would be very strange."

"Quieter, at least," Toreth said.

"Yes. I should just be grateful he's alive, of course. After New Year I'm going to help Philly look at rehabilitation centers nearer to her and Jen, with day units. A few months ago we would've given anything for a guarantee we'd need to do that one day."

The idea of Tarin away from the intensively monitored, secluded medical environment and interacting with family and friends again was an unwelcome one. Since the accident, Toreth had generally been content to push worries about Tarin to one side; there was precious little point in expending energy on the man when there was a decent chance his death would solve all their problems. Now, though, it would have to be faced.

"I guess I could come with you, then," Toreth said. "For New Year."

"Do you want to?" Warrick said, with unsurprising astonishment.

"I might as well. Sara has a new boyfriend, so she was begging for time off to go fuck him in some hotel he's probably fiddling on expenses. So it's either go with you or hang around here on my own, get drunk at Daedra's party, and fuck someone who's bound to be worse at it than you are."

The last part of the sentence might not have been there, for all the reaction it got from Warrick. "I'd love to have you there, of course, but I can't promise much in the way of entertainment. It's a long drive to the rehabilitation facility and back, for one thing."

And Warrick didn't like the idea of keeping his friends and relations cooped up in a car for hours with Toreth? Toreth had to admit there was a pretty good chance of him managing to offend someone. Boredom was a powerful provocation to liven up the atmosphere.

"From what you were saying, you might not even be going to the center," Toreth said. "Anyway, I can always stay behind and help Jen with dinner. She's not bad company. And she's easy on the eye, considering how old she is."

He half expected a "don't you dare!", but Warrick knew him far too well to engage his interest like that. "I'm sure she'll be glad of the help," he said blandly.

"I'm not—but then, I've eaten shit I've cooked. Anyway, I can't guarantee I can make it," Toreth added. "There could be a development in the current case at the last minute, or even something completely new, and I'd have to stay. I hope not, though. Sara would kill me."

"And that would be very unfortunate for everyone."

Silence again, and Toreth wondered how much time the conversation had eaten up. He counted his breaths for a while—in, out—until he had to ask.

"How much longer?"

"A while. You're doing very well."

"Can't you give me a countdown or something?"

"I could, but trials suggest constant indications of time passing actually increase user discomfort." Warrick paused, then said reluctantly, "There's something in the region of an hour left."

"Shit. An *hour*?" Toreth stared up at the dark metal, then said, "That's it, I'm giving up."

"Oh, come on. You've already done the difficult part."

"I can't feel my legs anymore. Or my arms." He didn't want to admit how much that was beginning to unsettle him, but he suspected Warrick would know anyway. "I'm not joking."

"One moment," Warrick said.

One? Way too many moments, that was the problem. But now that Toreth had something immediate to anticipate, he could keep waiting.

"I'm going to touch you again," Warrick said after an indeterminate amount of time had passed. "On your hip."

This time he was prepared, but he barely managed to resist jerking away, his skin oversensitized by the lack of stimulation.

Warrick's hand didn't linger long on his hipbone before it moved to stroke his cock, and Toreth was almost surprised to find he was still partly hard. The touch felt strange, though, too smooth and dragging slightly against his skin. Not necessarily unpleasant in itself, he decided after a moment, but he needed to know—

"What the hell is that?"

"I'm wearing a glove to delimit my hand and let the scanner know exactly who is who."

"Isn't this going to fuck up the scan? I don't want it to end up taking twice as long."

"Oh, no, that won't happen. Plus, arousal is physiologically complex. A scan of the authentic organic process will come in very useful when we're running the data analysis. You have to keep still, though," Warrick said a moment later.

"Okay."

"Are you sure you can?"

"Of course!"

"And—no—your eyes open."

"Fuck. Okay."

That was trickier, because closing his eyes was a pretty automatic reaction to a hand on his cock, at least when there was nothing to look at. Like Warrick's face.

He tried to conjure the picture onto the steel above him: Warrick's smile, his intent dark gaze, the slight frown of concentration as he watched his hand moving. Or was he working by touch, hand under the scanner edge? Maybe looking on the monitor to see the detailed neural response?

Toreth pressed his fingertips slightly down into the bed, feeling the resistance as the reactive surface pushed back, keeping him in place.

"Don't move," Warrick murmured. "I mean it. If you move, I'll have to stop."

Fuck. "No wonder this gets you off. I might as well be tied up."

There was a pause, then Warrick said, "I hadn't thought of that."

Toreth took a moment to firmly suppress a grin. "Now both of us are having fun."

Although, Toreth decided soon, a decidedly skewed fun. Warrick kept his cock remarkable still, pressed against Toreth's belly while he stroked up and down. The stimulation had a maddening edge, delicious, especially compared to the rest of his body's motionless boredom, but intensely frustrating. Five or ten—or who the hell knew how many—minutes in, Toreth could tell he wasn't going to come like this.

"Get on with it," Toreth said.

"No, sorry," Warrick said. "If you came, then you'd move. And that *will* mess up the scan."

"Fuck. No way. How much longer is there left?"

"I told you," Warrick said, mock serious, "that information is reliably shown to distress the subject."

And Toreth was going to demand a closer look at *that* study when he came out. Right now, though, it was obvious that Warrick had no intention of telling him for a quite different reason.

Time crawled by in maddening heartbeats. Every tiny thing he tried to relieve the tension—clenching his jaw, curling his toes, tightening his buttocks—was met with a murmured, "Mm-mmh" from Warrick. After a while Toreth realized he was sweating, a stickiness to his skin which every now and then concentrated into a cool drop and ran ticklishly downwards to vanish into the disposable surface layer of the reactive couch. At least it gave some sensation which wasn't Warrick's sudden scientific interest in inducing a heart attack through wanking.

"Warrick," Toreth said, mildly impressed he remembered the subvocalization. "I can't fucking—how long?"

"Soon."

"*How* fucking soon?"

"Soon."

He tried to count seconds, but he couldn't keep any time in his head except Warrick's relentless, steady stroking. Every muscle in his body seemed to quiver with tension, although he couldn't risk clenching them or Warrick would bitch about it again. He'd better see some fucking outstanding virtual results from this real torture next time he went into the sim. Although Warrick could go fuck himself if he thought he'd get a longitudinal study out of *this*. Fuck, fuck, fuck—

Warrick's hand tightened suddenly on the downstroke, and Toreth bucked up, pure reflex with no chance to stop it. He expected another reprimand, or even for Warrick to let go, but instead Warrick curled his fingers snugly around Toreth's cock and stroked him again.

"*Fuck*." Toreth couldn't stop the shout, reflected immediately back from the metal curve above.

Warrick laughed. "Scan's over."

"Thank fucking *God*," Toreth said, and closed his eyes and came.

Chapter Five

❖

Even after so many years of introducing people to the sim, Warrick still liked to use the water meadow. Of course, saying "still" ignored the enormous improvements and developmental effort that had gone into it over that time. For Dr. Marley Thomas, though, he'd picked something different. The room appeared around them, an odd combination of a very formal office at the front and an opening in the wall behind leading to a low-lit bedroom almost filled by a thick-mattressed bed.

Thomas looked around with the confusion of someone finding something familiar radically out of place. Then she snapped her fingers. "This is the set of the last production I worked on. But—" She turned to Warrick. "It isn't even for sale yet."

"There was a short promotional clip available as part of a monthly montage of upcoming releases."

"Oh, yes, of course. But..." She looked around, then bent down and pressed a button under the desk. A section of wall slid into place, hiding the bedroom. She pressed the button again, and the wall opened. "You got all this from a few seconds? That's unbelievable. It even smells the same. At least—" Thomas sniffed the air. "I think it does. Now I'm not sure."

"It's part of the next iteration of the fast creation system we're trialing, trying to push down the amount of preparatory detail we need to generate a room. Because you're flagged as someone who knows the original scene, the sim is actually infilling details from your sense memories as we stand here. If there were three or four people here now who'd visited the set, it would combine, weight, and adjust their recollections."

"That's memory scanning," she said after a moment.

"Not exactly—or rather, not illegally. Prompted recall and translating thoughts into sim experiences is absolutely fundamental to the function of the sim. Otherwise users couldn't even decide to pick up a rock. This is an expanded application, that's all. It's all been cleared by the relevant regulatory authorities."

"Well." She sat down cautiously on the edge of the desk, as though unsure it would support her, and picked up a ruler. She smacked it into her palm twice, then shook her head. "It's still... unsettling."

"Are you feeling okay? Sim sickness is extremely rare these days, so we do rush the briefing a little. Don't forget, if you feel you need to get out—"

"There's a safe word, yes. No, I feel fine. It's just..."

She scanned the room slowly, and Warrick gave her time to think while he studied her. He'd only met her once before, at the director's interview, when he'd been concentrating on her qualifications and experience rather than her appearance. He thought perhaps she'd had her hair up, then, because he didn't remember shoulder-length blonde waves, only the vivid blue eyes and square jaw. Maybe she wore her hair up at work and down at the weekends? Sunday had been the only day he'd been able to schedule a sim introduction before the New Year break, but she hadn't seemed to mind.

Finally she looked back to him. "It's overwhelmingly real. I know a lot about fantasy and imagination, and created locations and people, and I had an idea that somehow I'd be able to tell. But I can't. It's as real as anywhere else I've ever been, and that's what unsettled me."

"That's how we like it," Warrick said.

She raised her eyebrows. "Unsettling?"

"Real. That's what the sim is built to be. Although I must confess that some people do still find it generally emotionally unsatisfying—too unreal. For others the unreality's only an issue at certain times, under certain circumstances."

"Maybe the sim just isn't for everyone?"

Warrick smiled. "Probably true, but not helpful for sales. If there are ways to develop the sim to give it even broader appeal, then we should be looking for them and assessing their viability. SimTech can always use new perspectives, new approaches. Even though we're in production now, R&D is still core to the corporation."

"Glad to hear it. To be honest, that's one of the reasons I left Big Damn Sexy Movies. I joined not long after it was founded, when having fun was as important as making money, so long as we could pay the content provider license. And then—" She shrugged. "The usual story. We had too many successes, and finally there was an offer the founders found too tempting. You can't blame them, of course. And I can't honestly complain about the way UnLTD Ent treated us as employees. But every project had to turn a guaranteed profit, which meant sticking closer to tested formulae and less room to experiment. Every fan interaction modality had to be cost-justified—and the fact I just said 'fan interaction modality' like it was English is depressing enough."

Warrick nodded, thinking about some of the arguments in the past at SimTech about giving the developers leeway to have fun. "I know exactly what you mean."

"Do you?" She looked at him for a moment, then smiled. "Maybe you do. I have to say, not many corporate directors would. So—" She slid off the desk and brushed her hands together. "Tell me what's wrong with the sim that you want me to try to fix."

"All right." He snapped his fingers and the familiar control panel appeared on the surface of the desk. "Shall we go somewhere else?"

"Where—"

Before she could ask, he shifted the room to the water meadow. Thomas laughed, shading her eyes.

"That's just fucking—excuse me!"

Warrick laughed in turn. "No need to apologize."

"No, I'm sure not." She was still smiling. "You must love that kind of reaction."

"Yes," he admitted. "And I don't get to see it as often as I used to do. These days there's usually something else I have to do, unless an important enough sponsor arrives or someone sufficiently senior joins SimTech that I can justify a personal introduction. And our turnover of senior staff is so low."

They walked down to the river and along the sandy path. From the corner of his eye, Warrick caught sight of the panther slipping out of the edge of the trees. He must not have removed it from the room last time he used it. As always it made him think of Toreth, and of the real world danger and unpredictability that the sim could reproduce in appearance only.

He erased the panther with a thought, then said, "There's something I forgot."

Thomas looked around. "Do we need to finish?" She sounded pleasingly disappointed.

"No, but I meant to do it in the last room. Never mind."

Warrick adjusted the cuing and then clapped his hands. A tray appeared in the air beside them, keeping pace. In the spirit of the summer meadow, he'd changed the usual gin and tonic into a rum punch.

Thomas laughed. "Very neat." She took a glass, pausing to rub at the condensation before she took a sip. "It tastes perfect." She drank again and then said, "Should I be doing this in the middle of the introduction?"

"It's nonalcoholic, in the real world—although it can get you drunk in here, depending on the settings. Recreational pharmaceutical dosing was part of the original design, but eventually we managed to model most of the effects within the sim. That allowed us to avoid a raft of regulatory compliance." Warrick picked up the other drink and took a refreshing mouthful. "There can be an issue with functional intoxication on leaving the sim—a placebo effect on the nervous system. A lot of alcohol-induced behavior is actually learned."

"Interesting." She set the glass back on the tray. "Does expectation flow back into the sim, too, then?"

"Very much so. There's a lot of processing that goes into separating useful intent from preconceptions that can spoil the user experience. It's still imperfect, unfortunately." Warrick let go of the glass, and it vanished, along with the tray. "Would you like a specific example of one of the user issues we were talking about?"

"I'm always better working outwards from specifics."

"There's a particular sexual experience I've never been able to replicate inside the sim. It's in your field of expertise, too—bondage, some pain."

She looked him over, then said, "Dom or sub?"

"Sub."

"Okay. So, what's missing?"

"It's difficult to explain. The essence is . . ." He thought of Toreth, who might look to an outsider to be as tamed as the sim panther, caged in Warrick's corporate flat, but still as feral as ever at heart, and then of his interview with De Nijs. "Controlled fear. Danger that's real, although not excessive. But it's not the danger itself, exactly. More . . . knowing that, ultimately, I am vulnerable. My helplessness is real and absolute, and entirely outside my control."

"Mm." Her pace hadn't varied as he spoke. "And that's why the sim doesn't work for you?"

"Oh, it's perfect for everything else. But for that one thing, yes, it's incomplete, and the missing element is part of the fundamental nature of the sim—the sim *cannot* be dangerous, and I can't forget that. Of course, I don't know how generalizable that example is to the root cause of anyone else's dissatisfaction, although 'awareness of artificiality' is a measured category. We have a lot of subjective user experience data to which you'll have free access."

"That sounds fascinating," Thomas said. "Will you have time to work on your specific issue, if I need a test case?"

"I can't guarantee to be free on demand, but I'm on the full trials list," Warrick said.

"I'll think about it and examine that data you mentioned, and I'll let you know if I have any ideas."

They stopped on the bank of the river and looked around. After a few seconds a fly dipped down over the river, and a brown spotted fish jumped clear of the surface in a shower of water drops, sunlight sparkling on its flanks, and snapped the fly out of the air. The fish splashed back down, and the rings spread and vanished as the river flowed on.

Thomas pointed. "It's still down there."

"Oh, yes. It's a real object, as was the fly, autonomous within the sim. Actually, the fly still is—if you caught the trout and cut it up, the fly would be inside, until it's digested."

"So you didn't make that happen, just as we stopped?"

"Not at all. Although it's possible the sim triggered it. User attention and experience tracking means the sim will sometimes initiate object interactions previous users have enjoyed, depending on the room."

"Amazing." She knelt down and dipped her fingers in the water. "Absolutely amazing."

Warrick crouched beside her and trailed his own fingers through the water. He remembered the first water trials, trying to marry nerve induction and fluid modeling

"We're fast reaching the point where improvements in the naturalistic user experience are so incremental they're difficult to justify unless they bring other benefits, like processing gains," he said. "Most of our research now is on other aspects, like the recall-driven room construction you saw. And we've recently started to focus on time compression, using the brain's natural flexibility in subjective time perception to compress user experiences into a shorter session."

"And the Yeses are part of the new research focus?"

"Exactly, although they're much less experimental. We have firm hopes they'll turn into a major revenue stream. Creating legislation-compliant virtual people is a hard problem, tightly bound up in red tape, and if we can crack it we can supply tailored solutions more cost-effectively than other corporations can develop their own." Warrick shook the water from his fingers and was about to dry them on his trousers when he paused, turning his hand over as the breeze touched the wet skin. "Evaporative cooling," he said when Thomas made an interrogative noise. "Something I remember working on with Lew."

On the far side of the river, a kingfisher perched in the reeds, scanning the water below. Warrick called it over with a thought, and settled it on the back of Thomas's hand. She lifted it up, scrutinizing the bird minutely. It cocked its head, beady eyes looking back at her, its iridescent feathers fluffing. Finally she stretched out her hand; Warrick released control, and the bird flew away.

"Now, you definitely did that," she said. "But I didn't see any panel this time."

Warrick held his hand over the river and pulled the surface up in a column shaped like his handprint, then let it fall down.

"With enough practice it's possible to control everything in the sim, animate or inanimate. Even other user representations. It's just a question of developing the mental tools to perform the manipulation."

She looked at him seriously. "See, if *I* were a sub—which I'm not, quite the opposite—but if I were, I imagine I'd find that interesting. Or even intimidating, depending on who was doing the controlling."

Warrick shook his head and stood up. "There's always the disconnect available. And anyway, not to sound immodest, not many people can do it as well as I. It takes years, and it certainly isn't commercially reasonable to ask most users for that depth of commitment. We need to appeal to the casual majority."

Thomas stood up slowly and brushed flecks of grass and soil from her knees. Suddenly she smiled broadly. "Talking about how to model sex, in a virtual field full of flowers. I think I'm going to enjoy working here."

"I hope so." They started walking again, and after a moment Warrick said, "Asher Linton and I are going to an entertainment industry convention in Valencia in January, then on for some private meetings with potential clients, and finally to the Brighton virtual reality expo. I'd like you to come along."

"I'm not sure how much I'll be able to contribute, even by then," Thomas said doubtfully. "I'm still working through the introduction to the Evolved Expert Systems material."

"But you do have more industry-specific experience of content delivery than Asher or I, and you know what people look for in virtual interactions. I think it might be helpful for you to see the kinds of markets we're considering, and perhaps spot where we've missed others we should be looking at."

Thomas shrugged. "In that case, I'd love to."

Chapter Six

Toreth picked up one of the unfamiliar, irregular biscuits from the plate Sara had delivered and gave it a cautious bite. Shortbread, he thought, although it was rather solid, but at least not too sweet.

"Where did you get these?" Toreth asked, gesturing with the half-eaten biscuit.

"I made them," Sara said. "Happy Wednesday."

"*You* made them?"

Sara managed to look impressively indignant. "Yes! And why not?"

"I don't know. Maybe because you've been working for me for twelve years, and you never baked anything before?"

She smiled, a little sheepishly. "Well, okay. Fair enough. I thought it might be nice, that's all, for a change. I thought they came out okay, but I'm sure I'll get better."

Toreth finished the rest of the piece and rinsed his mouth with his coffee, trying to dislodge the lumps welded to his teeth. How many of the things had she brought? "Don't forget to share them. I don't want the team in a huff because you gave biscuits to me and Andy bloody Morehen and not to anyone else."

Sara sniffed in mock offense, then opened her hand screen and examined it. "The other thing is that Tillotson wants to see all the seniors who're free. I guess it's the New Year's rota meeting." She looked down at him with unspoken appeal.

"So, tell me something else that's happening. Anything."

"Well..." Sara scanned her screen, moving between schedules. "Andy called in a location change in the Richardson surveillance. He says the subject is taking the hacked car out again, so he thought he might as well pin another DoT on Richardson while he has the chance."

"Sounds good. Give me half an hour, then tell Tillotson there's been an urgent development, and I can't get back. No comms."

Sara smiled. "Will do. Thanks."

46

The end of movement notification formed an ongoing inconvenience at I&I, but that had only ever been a part of the mechanisms allowing the Administration to keep track of persons of interest. Even though citizens were no longer required to register their travels, credit and purchase checks still functioned as well as ever, as did those monitoring systems which had a benign alternative purpose.

All vehicles in the Administration contained chips allowing the Department of Transport traffic systems to control them safely. Even after the revolt, no one had wanted that system dismantled. Toreth had heard of some resisters demanding that vehicle location data be deleted after its immediate usefulness was past, or at least anonymized. The DoT had stalled with feasibility studies and technical complications, until the proposal was lost with another change of Council.

So DoT data still allowed I&I to track easily the kind of citizens who probably didn't care anyway. Those people who didn't want their movements monitored found ways to deceive the system. An arms race, as in so many areas, between the criminals and resisters on one side, and the various departments that tried to eradicate them on the other.

Charges of tampering with traffic control systems was a lever which had been left in I&I hands because of safety laws, depressing as it might be to be reduced to threatening suspects with DoT violations. And that was why Toreth and Morehen were sitting out of uniform and in an unmarked I&I car outside a building in a Peterborough industrial area, waiting for the suspect they'd followed there to re-emerge and hopefully allow them to follow him back to New London, all so that if he later denied being there, they could prove otherwise.

And, in Toreth's case, because Sara wanted a dirty weekend away. Maybe there'd be enough paras looking for New Year overtime that Tillotson could make up the numbers at his meeting. If not, though, tradition decreed the meeting would be followed by a tour of the section, during which Tillotson would happily pin the New Year rota on the next paras he saw. So, Peterborough was the safer option.

"How's the new optical microphone coping?" Toreth asked.

Morehen consulted his hand screen, scrolling up and down through the automatic transcript. "Not too bad, Para. Much better than the old model would've managed, anyway. We're losing parts to the wind vibrations in the glass; otherwise it's coming through fairly clear, even when there are three or four conversations going on at the same time. What the transcript can't pick out live, I think we'll be able to get from the recording."

The new microphones were one of the unexpected benefits of the revolt. With much of I&I's equipment destroyed, replacements had often turned into upgrades. Toreth remembered sending lists to Carnac, detailing losses. The bastard had authorized replacement purchases, of course—at the time he'd been planning to kill Toreth along with all the other paras, interrogators, and investigators at I&I, so the financial details of refurbishing I&I hadn't been a consideration. And even a disgraced socioanalyst's name was enough to scare later budget reviewers into leaving his orders alone.

So now they had a surveillance device that could deal with the wind hammering relentlessly in with nothing between them and the North Sea except the ugly concrete wall of the East Anglian flood defenses. The heavy drizzle it brought with it was trying its best to be as wetting as any thunderstorm.

"Pity they aren't saying anything interesting, really," Morehen added.

"Nothing useful at all?" Toreth asked.

"All perfectly legitimate business, so far. Corporate protection planning, mostly...although it's nothing you couldn't deal with over a comm, which is suspicious in itself."

"Hm. Security reasons, I'm sure, or so they'd say. What's Richardson talking about?"

"Not much. Again, strange when he's come all this way." Morehen peered forward as though he could see inside the building. "I wonder if he's subvocalizing on a short-range link?"

Toreth, who'd been wondering exactly the same thing, leaned over to look at the screen. "We have names for everyone in there, right? Start the system crosschecking and find who's not speaking at the same time Richardson's not speaking."

Any correlation would have piss-poor evidential value, but was still the best option they had right then.

"How long are we going to watch Richardson?" Morehen asked.

"Until he does something else interesting. Or, more likely, until Tillotson says we've spent too much money. Why? Don't like the overtime?"

"The overtime is great. It's the time itself which isn't so much fun."

Toreth smiled. "I remember a case when I was a junior—at Political Crimes, in fact. Christofi and I were watching a Parliament of the Regions rep, and for some bullshit reason the senior in charge, Harry Hinde—before your time, he must've retired before you joined—couldn't get permission to monitor his comms. So for nearly two weeks we had to stick as close as we could, on a twenty-four-hour tail. Christ, I've never known anyone who spent so much time in brothels. Almost every night. You should've seen the expenses claims the team put in. Fucking hilarious. And we got paid, too, in the end."

Morehen looked around at the rain-soaked collection of drab buildings. "Richardson doesn't seem to like brothels."

"No. More's the pity." Toreth glanced at the screen, where yet more uninteresting conversation was transcribing itself, and sighed. "At least we'd have something to look at."

The most interesting place Richardson had ever been, in fact, was the storage unit where he'd first come to their attention. The rent on the unit was almost due to expire, with no other visitors so far, leaving Richardson as their only suspect—

a suspect who, as Tillotson would no doubt soon be pointing out, they couldn't even solidly connect to the unit's contents. Why had Richardson walked away? Had Toreth's team done something to tip him off? Had he received a last-minute warning they'd missed? Had it been a bizarre coincidence, and Richardson had somehow gone to the wrong place? Whatever the truth, the illegal equipment was still there, still being monitored, waiting for Toreth to kill the case and send the retrieval technicians to collect and destroy it.

Toreth tucked his hands under his arms. The car was heated, of course, but just looking at the water smearing across the windows made it feel damp and chilly. "Did I see a place back down the road selling coffee?"

"Yes, Para, I think so." Morehen closed the screen. "Do you want me to get us something to eat as well?"

"I'll have something hot. Bacon sandwiches, or whatever they've got that's close enough." No doubt nothing as nice as the bacon he'd got used to eating at Warrick's flat. Their flat.

"Will do." Morehen put his hand on the door, then hesitated.

"Run," Toreth suggested. "It'll keep you warm."

Morehen didn't look very warm by the time he opened the door again. Of course, he'd had to be reasonably careful on the way back not to spill the insulated cups.

He didn't grumble, though, just handed Toreth his cup and a slightly damp paper bag and settled into his seat with his own lunch. Now he was no doubt regretting letting Sara talk him out of a haircut, as the rain had soaked his hair completely and was probably trickling down the back of his neck.

As Toreth ate his roll—not too bad, any defects in the ersatz bacon slices concealed with plenty of brown sauce—he covertly studied Morehen. The man wasn't unattractive, but Toreth still couldn't imagine what the hell Sara seemed so enthusiastic about. How long would it last, Toreth wondered, and what would happen when Sara finally met someone richer and more fun? Assuming that was what did happen, and Morehen didn't end things first, one way or another.

Since that little prick Jonny Kemp had proved Sara's inability to spot a certifiable psycho on her own, Toreth liked to give her boyfriends the once-over himself, as soon as possible, and impress on them that Sara had someone in an I&I para's uniform looking after her interests. At least that wouldn't be necessary with Morehen. The man had been on Toreth's team for three and a half years and, excellent investigator that he was, he ought to be able to deduce what would happen to anyone who treated Sara badly. And while he'd been a successful and commended investigator at Political Crimes, that didn't automatically make him an arsehole.

Still. A hint or two never hurt.

"Have any plans for New Year yet?" Toreth asked.

"Para?" Morehen said with wary surprise.

"Just wondering if you have anything fun lined up. Going anywhere?"

"Oh. Did, er, someone mention something to you?"

"Sara said she had something different planned this year. Holiday—she didn't seem to know where."

"Ah. I wanted to keep it a secret, because—"

"I don't give a shit what you're doing at New Year, or where you're doing it." Did he think Toreth would be fishing for information on Sara's behalf? "What happens outside work is up to you."

At the slight stress on "outside," Morehen's expression hardened. "Para, there are plenty of other investigators and admins at I&I in relationships."

"You aren't breaking any rules, no. But I run an investigative team, not a bloody dating system. If this ends messily, or it screws up the smooth functioning of the team in any other way, then one of you will be heading for the pool. And, just to be crystal clear, it will be you."

Morehen didn't look in the least surprised by the prioritization. "Yes, Para. I understand. Neither of us is going to let it affect our jobs."

"Good."

Toreth finished his sandwich, crumpled up the cup and bag, and tossed them into a corner of the I&I car, then settled in to wait for their suspect to make a move. While Morehen continued, without any visible optimism, to monitor the surveillance results, Toreth took out his hand screen and rechecked the final information on the bed order.

He had never imagined it would cost so much to get something made out of dead trees. The cabinet had been expensive, but that was antique. Antiques ought to be expensive. Things like Warrick's ridiculous coffee brewer were antiques. A few years ago, during an investigation, Toreth had seen one in a shop in an upmarket shopping complex. It was the kind of shop that didn't show prices on anything so, as it was the end of the day and he had no other appointments, he'd wandered in to ask. He'd taken his time looking around the place, enjoying the forced pleasantness of the staff, who hadn't dared be openly rude to a para-investigator in uniform.

At the time he'd been in need of an apology present for Sara, for some long-forgotten reason, who'd previously gone on at great length about Warrick's fabulous kitchen and its contents. After he'd found out the price and left the shop empty-handed, Toreth had needed a stiff drink. Sara got her usual bunch of flowers.

And here on his screen he had the final bill for the bed, needing to be paid before the delivery date could be settled. Now that it had come down to actual money, the idea of making the payment was unexpectedly painful. He didn't particularly want the money for anything else, but these days he had a more acute awareness of how much he earned, and how much that differed from Warrick.

Secretly, Toreth had rather enjoyed the financial troubles at SimTech. Not that, God forbid, he wanted the corporation to go bust or be forced to sell out. Warrick would be utterly impossible to live with if that ever happened. But he had derived a certain satisfaction from Warrick having to think about money more often.

He'd delayed the payment as long as he could. Now, though, he'd finally decided on a date after New Year to have the bed sent to the flat, when it was easier to guarantee a day when he would be there but Warrick wouldn't. It had provided him with another potential headache in working out exactly how to arrange delivery to a building with a high corporate security grading. Fortunately, very few people who bought handmade natural wood furniture lived anywhere else, so he'd been pleasantly surprised to find the delivery staff already screened to a degree which satisfied the building security.

The numbers waited on the screen, and they wouldn't get any smaller for delaying further. A few seconds, and it was done. Toreth closed the screen and tucked it away. Now all he had to do was wait and hope that New Year wouldn't produce anything too traumatic or, with Tarin and his friends potentially involved, criminally political.

He snorted softly to himself, and Morehen looked up from his own screen. "Para?"

"Nothing."

"I thought you—oh, wait a minute."

Toreth sat up. "Something good?"

"Not really. But I think the meeting's breaking up. Yes, Richardson is definitely getting ready to leave."

"Thank fucking Christ for that." Another exciting day's investigation nearly over. It was moments like this which reminded Toreth of how much he enjoyed having a team to do his dirty, and boring, work for him.

Morehen began packing the scanner away. "Join I&I, see the world. Or at least Peterborough. In the rain."

Toreth laughed. "Maybe tomorrow he'll catch a flight to Monaco." He waited until Morehen's face brightened, and added, "Then you can call I&I Marseilles to take over surveillance, and get back to that training course."

"It'd be drier." Morehen shook his head. "The rental on the storage unit runs out on Friday, Para. Is anything likely to happen after that?"

"Probably not. But once the illegal tech is a dead end, Richardson's all we have, so we'd better keep a watch on him. Don't worry, I'll approve the overtime for the weekend."

Morehen sighed, although at least he had the sense to do it quietly. "Right, Para."

Chapter Seven

❖

U p for the gym this morning?" Toreth asked as he opened the fridge door.
Warrick was eating toast at the table, reading a hand screen. "What?" he
asked after a moment. "Sorry."

Toreth picked out some yogurt and the bowl of leftover fruit salad. A constant,
magical supply of fresh fruit in the house was one of the corporate luxuries he certainly wasn't planning to complain about.

"I said, 'Up for the gym this morning?' I was thinking we could play squash.
It's Saturday, in case you'd forgotten."

"I had planned to go in to SimTech," Warrick said. "We're still trying to complete the new scan data before the end of the year."

"What's the point in being a fucking corporate director if you can't order people to do things at the weekend for you?" Toreth poured yogurt into a cereal bowl
and wiped up a spill from the worktop with his finger. "I've got Morehen trailing
all over the country on a probably entirely pointless tail. He's fed up with it, Sara's
fed up with the lack of cock in her life—and do I look like I give a shit? It's his
job."

Warrick swallowed a mouthful of toast. "Well, there are technicians there, of
course, but we're still tightening things up, trying to keep costs down, and I like
to make sure it's done as efficiently as possible. We're renting that scanner by the
day."

"Of course." Control freak, as ever. "Never mind. Nice thing about housing
complex gyms, there are always plenty of people there Saturday and Sunday. Getting their exercise for the week. I'm sure I'll find a partner." Back still to Warrick,
Toreth spooned fruit into the yogurt. "I had a good game with someone last week,
actually. I hadn't noticed him there before, but he must keep himself fit somewhere—he had the most amazing overhead smash. Mind you, he could've just
been lucky. We only had time for a couple of games before I had to leave to get to
SimTech. Maybe he'll be up for a rematch. Martin, I think he was called."

Actually, Toreth had no memory of the man's name at all, but he liked the touch. He sat down at the table and smiled. "Is that tea hot?" he asked, pointing at the pot with the handle of his spoon.

"Yes. That's your mug next to it." After a moment of silence, Warrick added, "I'll call SimTech, let them know I'm not coming in until later."

At the gym, Toreth didn't mention the idea of squash; Warrick didn't say anything either. Warrick, so sure of himself in the sim, didn't have quite the same coordination outside it. Toreth could beat him easily, and Warrick hated to lose, which put him in a bad mood—amusing, but it spoiled the chances of really good sex afterwards. After going to all this trouble to get his Saturday fuck, Toreth didn't intend to throw it away for the momentary pleasure of seeing Warrick scrambling after another missed point.

("Why don't you let him win, then?" Sara had once asked, when he'd explained it at coffee time. Toreth shook his head at the memory.)

Toreth worked efficiently through his own repetitions on the equipment. After the second time around the circuit, he finished stretching and went to watch Warrick for a minute or two. Never a bad way to pass time, but to Toreth's annoyance he found himself thinking about work. According to Morehen's increasingly tetchy surveillance reports in the Investigation in Progress, Richardson spent plenty of time at the gym—irregularly regular time, as it were, always visiting a gym somewhere, sometime during the day, no matter where he was staying. Could that be significant? Gyms, with their temporary memberships and networks of secure corporate-grade facilities, were perfect places to set up meetings and confuse the evidence analysis systems. Making a habit of irregularity wasn't on its own even enough to raise a potential corporate sab flag on someone's file.

A dark-haired, leanly muscled woman Toreth didn't recognize stopped next to him and gestured to the leg press he was leaning against. "Sorry—do you want this?"

"No," Toreth said. "Go ahead and use it."

"Thanks." She hesitated, then said, "Excuse me?"

"What? Oh, I'm sorry." Toreth stepped away from the control screen, and the woman tried to register her ID. She had to do it three times before the machine reset the resistances.

"I told the gym supervisor last week that this machine's faulty," she said. "What do they spend all the housing complex fees on, do you suppose? I'll have to send a message to the management corporation."

"Maybe it just doesn't believe the numbers," Toreth said. "They're pretty impressive."

She laughed. "I like to keep fit."

The next obvious comment was *I can see that,* and in Toreth's judgment she wouldn't be unreceptive to it, either. But after all the effort of dragging Warrick here, he should probably avoid any negative reinforcement.

"I'll get out of your way," he said. "Have fun."

Toreth walked away a few steps and returned his attention, or at least his gaze, to Warrick.

Richardson could be meeting anyone at a gym. Doing exactly what Toreth had just done, pausing for a breather or changing machines, and casually talking to someone. A perfect way to exchange a few words with a client or their broker, in a face-to-face meeting that would leave no records. With gym equipment to interact with, and performance to analyze, comms and hand screens wouldn't raise comment, either.

Should he demand surveillance records from the gyms? It might be worth having Sara pursue that, but a lot of corporate facilities were protective of their clients, even temporary ones. And if Richardson was indeed a sab, he was a smart enough one to know not to talk to an agent anywhere in view of a camera. Smart enough, in fact, that he'd never even fallen under official suspicion.

Warrick replaced the bar on the rests and lay there, breathing deeply. Toreth went over and leaned on the frame.

"Ever met a man called Kelvin Richardson?" Toreth asked.

"Mm...no, I don't think so." Warrick pushed his sweaty hair back from his forehead. "Or if I have, he didn't make enough of an impression that the name means anything right away. Why?"

"Someone connected to a case I'm working on. He's corporate, so I thought you might know him. No particular reason—just hoping, really."

"There are rather a lot of corporates in the Administration, or even just in New London." Warrick cocked his head. "What does he do?"

"Runs a very small corporation, mostly software systems work. He calls himself a security consultant."

Warrick grimaced. "Well, that can cover a multitude of things, some more sinful than others. I take it from the original question that it's a difficult case?"

"Very. If it's even a case at all, and not just a flock of wild geese. Right now, a lucky coincidence is probably my best bet for getting anywhere."

"What has he done, if he's done anything?"

Warrick had become surprisingly willing to discuss I&I business lately. Or maybe not so surprisingly, now that Toreth was reduced to asking prisoners nicely if they'd like to confess. "Maybe nothing. I can put a reasonable question mark against his name for owning restricted surveillance tech, but that's the best I have."

"Corporate sabotage?"

"Who the fuck knows? Maybe he wanted good equipment because he's worried about his girlfriend fucking her gym partner behind his back."

Warrick laughed. "And is she?"

"No idea. Maybe I should check." Toreth paused. "That's not a bad thought, actually. Even sabs are sometimes stupid enough to talk to their partners. If he has one, then it'll give Morehen something to do other than sit on his arse and drink coffee."

Enough worrying about work, Toreth decided, especially a case which seemed likely to end as the most annoying kind of failure to have on his record—one that had never mattered in the first place.

They were in a corner of the large room, out of the winter sunshine shining brightly through the mirrored security glass. No one was close by; everyone was facing away or focused on their own workouts. He took hold of Warrick's wrists, pinning them to the metal rack supporting the weights. Warrick's eyes widened.

"Toreth?"

"Mm?"

"What—" He licked his lips. "Let go."

Toreth tightened his grip a little, rubbing his thumb over the pulse point in Warrick's left wrist, then digging it in for a moment. "Strong benches, these. Sturdy. Nice that they don't waste all those charges on security. Are you thinking what I'm thinking?"

"No," Warrick said.

"Liar. We should come here late one night, test how much they can take. Probably no one would walk in, but it adds something, don't you think?"

"Yes." Warrick cleared his throat, but then Toreth tightened his grip again, and Warrick's voice wasn't quite steady as he said, "It adds a high likelihood of being banned from the facilities. I'm sure there are cameras."

"Oh, do you think so?"

Warrick laughed. "There must be."

"There often aren't, you know. I can always ask building security." Toreth knelt down, still holding Warrick's wrists. "Are you hard?" he whispered in his ear.

Warrick didn't say anything. Toreth lifted his head, just enough to see Warrick's face.

"Come on. Tell me."

"Yes." Warrick stared straight up at the ceiling.

"You're so easy." Toreth breathed on his ear, feeling Warrick's arms tense, then let him go. "So fucking easy. Hurry up and finish, then we can head back to the flat."

Warrick sat up, breathing rather quickly. "We could go now."

"No. No skimping. Come on—the faster you get moving, the sooner you're done."

55

Chapter Eight

❖

Toreth decided he could at least give Morehen credit for having a good effect on Sara's timekeeping—although possibly not on her productivity. When Toreth arrived a little late at I&I on Monday morning, Sara was at her desk, with Morehen seated comfortably on the edge of it. They were so engrossed in conversation that neither of them spotted him until he was halfway across the office. He saw the moment when Sara caught sight of him. She sat up straight and said something to Morehen that made him jump smartly to his feet.

"Morning, Para," he said as Toreth came up to them.

"Morning." Toreth didn't say anything else, just waited until Morehen finally cleared his throat.

"I, uh. I had a message waiting for me this morning from Senior Para Zaleski in Corporate Fraud, Para. They've been looking at Richardson for a while, and someone noticed the new link on his file to our IIP."

"Why are we only hearing about that now?" Toreth asked. When Morehen shrugged, he said, "Sara?"

"I don't know, either. They never flagged his file."

"But they have a definite evidential link from Richardson to corporate sabotage," Morehen said. "Smuggling wasn't what they were looking for, apparently, and there's no specific tie to our case, either, but if they're connected it could be enough for both of us to start asking him questions."

Which sounded good, so long as "both of us" didn't mean General Criminal's case being relegated to a few cursory questions at the end of the session.

"Will they let us run the interrogations?" Toreth asked.

"They're asking us to, Para. There are no CF interrogators available, and the pool is totally dry."

"Great." Now someone else's questions would be pushed to the bottom of the priority list. "Tell Nagra I'll need her back for some real casework. Or at least for some more interrogation."

Morehen grinned; they both knew how disgruntled all the junior paras were about the heavy interrogation load which had been pushed onto them since the revolt. "Yes, Para."

"But before you do that, let me take a look at Corporate Fraud's IIP. And Morehen—no need to wait here while I do."

Morehen's gaze flicked reflexively towards Sara before he looked back at Toreth. "No, Para."

Corporate Fraud's "definite evidential link" proved to be less solid than Zaleski had suggested. Richardson's name was a statistical freak, showing up in relation to a dozen minor corporations which had failed over the past few months. Hardly conclusive proof of sabotage, and the corporations involved were so small Toreth wondered why anyone cared about them. Some of them were single-operator. After he'd read the IIP summary through, twice, Toreth decided he needed a more knowledgeable opinion.

"Hey, Liz," he said, when Senior Investigator Carey's distinctive red hair brought a glow to his screen.

"Toreth!" She looked back up from where she'd been putting something away in a drawer. "You're a nice sight after a morning justifying my budgetary existence. How are you?"

"Never better. You?"

"Hanging in there. But I'm sure you didn't call to ask about my health. What do you want this time?"

Toreth laughed. "Know anything about a corporate security consultant called Kelvin Richardson?"

"Oh!" Carey grinned at him. "You're the poor sucker who put the smile on Zaleski's face this morning. I thought he was just looking forward to New Year."

"Stinker of a case?"

"Like the estuary at low tide," Carey said. "And about as sticky to escape. The best thing you can say about it is it won't actually make your hair fall out, although Zaleski might've pulled out a clump or two. All they have is a clutch of coincidences that don't seem inclined to hatch into anything."

Sounded even less promising than Toreth's wild geese. "So why not ditch the whole mess? I don't know what it's like over there, but Tillotson's been kicking cases into touch if they don't get a result before coffee time."

"Chean has itchy bollocks about it, so until he loses interest, Zaleski's stuck with the dud. I hear that Vaughn thinks it's all rubbish, mind you. But she's up to her ears in end-of-year budget and...well, now that there are so few paras compared to specialists here, Vaughn doesn't always get the final say. So she's letting Chean have his way over this to keep him happy."

Corporate Fraud had what amounted to joint section heads, or at least posts with almost equal power—Vaughn the named section head, leading the para-investigator teams, and Chean in charge of the finance specialists. Toreth had always thought that was one more head of section than anyone needed.

Still, if the para in charge didn't want the case, that explained the thin IIP and careless lack of a flag on Richardson's file. "So what's Chean finding so gripping about failed minor corporations?" Toreth asked.

"Nothing, except that all of them were involved in some way in finance sector systems security."

Light dawned. "That's why they all have full corporate status, even the single-operators."

"Right. No serious financial corporations will deal with anyone who's not a hundred percent signed up to the corporate accords. But they're still tiny, nobody corporations and individually any of them going under wouldn't raise eyebrows, especially with things the way they are. Lots of corporations are cutting back, tightening budgets, and it's hitting the small independents hardest. But Chean's convinced himself someone's found a new trick, and this is all laying the groundwork for something bigger."

"And you think that's crap?"

"I think it's what my great-aunt Sharon calls 'a bucket from Australia'—farfetched. Although..."

"Although?" Toreth prompted when she didn't continue.

"Well, Phil thinks there might be something in it." She sounded reluctant to offer the information. "Zaleski borrowed him for a couple of days to try to improve the case modeling—or prove there was nothing there—and Phil went over all the files."

"He found something they hadn't?"

"Oh, no. And he says the evidence is thinner than this year's bonuses, which is why Zaleski can't get any decent target predictions out of the system. But Phil also says he's sure they're on to *something*. Apparently he has a feeling about it." Carey snorted. "I told him he can get all the feeling he needs from me. But at the same time, Toreth, he's not just a pretty face, and he's right a hell of a lot more often than he's wrong. I don't want to get your hopes up, but there it is."

Instinct. Toreth loathed instincts, especially when they belonged to talented investigators like Phil Verstraeten, because that made it a bad idea to ignore them. He just wouldn't be surprised if he ended up wasting his own precious resources chasing the shadows of CF management paranoia. Section heads had no business poking around in casework.

"I'll bear it in mind," Toreth said. "Want me to send the interrogation transcripts your way?"

"It's not my case, you know," Carey said. "Thank God. And I'd hate to step on any colleagues' toes. But I daresay Phil might like to take a look through 'em, if his ID happened to be added to the IIP by mistake."

"It could happen. Sara's being very careless these days. Too many distractions in the office."

"Wildfowl on the brain? I heard something like that." Carey chuckled, sending a pleasant little shiver down Toreth's spine. "You need to keep an eye on them, Toreth. Messing around inside the team's a terrible idea."

Nagra showed up in his office an hour after Richardson had been brought into I&I and processed into the cells. Judging by the light sheen of sweat on her dark skin, she'd run up the stairs all the way from Interrogation to the fifth floor.

"Lifts out of order again?" Toreth asked.

"Why the hell did you send me down there?" she demanded.

"Shortage of juniors or not, you get one chance to rephrase that."

She took a deep breath and tugged her jacket straight. "Sorry, Para, but really. I don't need this, not after a solid month on the interrogation rota. Have you looked at his medical file?"

"Not yet, why?"

"Because nothing we can do will touch him. He's got drug resistance genetic modification, long-term blocker dosing—he must take so many pills in the morning I'm surprised he didn't rattle when CF picked him up."

"And it's all in his medical file?"

"Yes, Para. Each treatment by itself is legit, all approved corporate security treatments. Just a lot more than most corporates have—and most of them are recent. Since the revolt. He's obviously read the new P&P, or his doctors have. I sent a blood sample to the labs to get them to screen for illegal extras, but he'd have to be a lot more stupid than he clearly is for us to find anything."

"Bollocks."

"That's about what I thought, Para. I'll bump the waiver as high as I can, but it won't help."

Unfortunately, and understandable as Nagra's irritation was, Toreth knew there was only one viable course of action.

"Run the interrogation anyway," Toreth said. "Because if I walk into Tillotson's office and tell him there's no point doing one at all, we both know what he'll say. And if he doesn't, Chean over at Corporate Fraud will. Save me the arguments."

"Yes, Para." The disgust showed plain on her face. "I'll get right on to it."

"Who knows, maybe you'll be lucky and he's all fur coat and no knickers." With that much preparation, Richardson was unlikely to have skipped the interrogation resistance training necessary to go with it, but there was no point depressing the junior even further. "And Nagra—don't half-arse it just because we also both know you're wasting your time. Do it right, or you'll only have to do it again."

Nagra sighed. "Yes, Para."

After two hours, Toreth pulled up the interrogation on the screen and watched for a few minutes. Nagra had obviously taken his instructions to heart and was grimly pushing her way through the whole extent of the pharmacy available to her.

Despite the prisoner's extensive precautions, the drugs were having some effect, and Richardson looked distinctly sweaty and pale. But while the blockers' interactions with the drugs might be making him feel like shit, they were also clearly doing their job. He kept up a stony façade of flat refusals to engage with Nagra's questions. The way Nagra had him cuffed, he had to be cramping badly by now, but even that extra touch wasn't doing the trick.

That was impressive, even considering his medical file. At the least, it was virtually proof of extensive interrogation resistance training to back up the biological advantages. Even when Warrick was high on endorphins, he'd still register cramps. Whether or not they'd make him want to stop was a marker of progress through the careful stripping away of self until Warrick was completely and unresistingly his. Toreth smiled.

Nagra wasn't enjoying herself, though, frustration written on her face. It seemed like the prisoner could see it, too, because the latest reply came with a faint smirk. Nothing like Warrick there, who'd be glazed and lost in the game.

"No comment. Again."

Nagra picked up an injector. Offhand, Toreth couldn't think of anything she could give Richardson which would do more than push him closer to an overdose. Dead prisoners were the least informative of all.

Toreth linked through to her comm. "That's enough, Nagra. Call it a day."

"Finally, thank you," Nagra said, at least remembering to subvocalize, and threw the injector she'd picked up back on the table. "Take him back to his cell," she said to the guards before she left.

Richardson leaned back in the interrogation chair. The cocky smile he directed up and around, obviously aimed at whatever cameras might be there, made Toreth consider going down there himself and bending the Procedures and Protocols for Interrogation until they snapped. Instead, he went along to Tillotson's office.

"What do you mean, the interrogation is over?" Tillotson asked.

"We've done everything we can. A lot of the drug resistance tech is legal for corporate use, if the work is licensed and entered into central medical records. In the past we could always step up to a higher level waiver to beat it, but with the new P&P..."

"Seems like you managed to hamstring us very effectively," Tillotson said.

"You'd need to talk to Socioanalyst Carnac about that, sir," Toreth said blandly. "We only wrote the technical specifics. He made the policy decisions."

"Yes, well." Tillotson frowned at the screen. "There's really nothing you can do?"

"Nothing inside the P&P, no. I can drop back down to level two and keep going for a few days—that sometimes works. But these days we get lawyers all over us demanding a release as soon as they get a sniff of that. They're starting to work out pretty sharpish what resorting to verbal only means, and I'm sure Richardson will know, too."

Toreth didn't hold out much hope of Richardson cracking for level two, anyway. He was clever, and he'd clearly had extensive training. Toreth would put money on CF's suspicions being correct and the man having at least a corporate sab past. Not that it would help the case, even if they could prove it—the new P&P cut off at the same level for everyone, sab or otherwise.

Just because they couldn't do anything useful with Richardson didn't mean they had to let him go. Toreth told Sara to send a standard "we are processing your request" to any lawyers who started to take an interest, and then went over to Corporate Fraud to talk to Phil Verstraeten. He found the pale, slight specialist investigator on his way out of his office, heading for lunch. Toreth walked with him towards the canteen.

"It's not really my case," Verstraeten said as soon as Toreth broached the subject of Richardson. "Senior Para Zaleski is in charge of it."

"I know. But Carey said you'd had a look at the files, and I wanted your opinion. The theory is he's planning something, and his involvement in these company failures is somehow setting it up, right?"

"That's the head of specialists's theory, yes, Para. Senior Para Zaleski's not entirely convinced."

Toreth laughed. "He thinks it's bollocks, you mean?"

To his surprise, the usually diffident junior investigator smiled back. "Something like that."

"And what do you think?"

"Well..." Verstraeten rubbed his left eyebrow, the hairs so blond they were barely visible. "There could be *something* there. Richardson has definitely picked up work as a result of each of these company failures, albeit only minor contracts. He's been on quite a spree—in fact, Urban Fox Security has expanded its staff, which makes him notably successful as an independent this year. Short-term contractors, mostly, who all seem to have clean records."

"That doesn't sound like sabbing. What about these contracts?"

"His name's recorded in the Department of Financial and Corporate Affairs files regarding the administration of the corporate assets, which we have free access to—it's part of asset monitoring, to make sure nothing that ought to belong to the creditors, specifically the Administration, gets spirited away. He gained just one contract from each failed company, six in total, all security-related. Well—" He ducked his head apologetically. "To some extent we're guessing about that. Exactly what each contract contains is buried by corporate accord rules that we can't break through without enough evidence for a warrant, and none of the corporations involved seem to want to be helpful without one."

"And Zaleski didn't push very hard," Toreth guessed.

"Well...no, Para. I don't think he did." Verstraeten cleared his throat. "Anyway, the one thing we do know is Richardson cherry-picked the contracts. He bid on one or two each time. Except for two cases."

"Oh?"

"Yes, Para. The first was the only one of the corporations where there's a suspicion their failure was due to sabbing. More than a suspicion, actually. The sole owner was stabbed to death as he walked home one night by someone who knew his route and the relevant surveillance. No one's been arrested, though—someone made a pretty poor attempt to frame his girlfriend, which even Justice saw through, and then a lot of nothing. And the second, most recent, incident where Richardson bid on multiple contracts was a few weeks ago."

"That was after CF started taking an interest in him?"

"Yes, Para. There could be any number of reasons why he didn't use covering bids in the other cases. Perhaps he was worried he might actually succeed in too many of the other bids—that's a more common problem than you'd think, because they all have to be realistic or there's no point making them. Or he was simply confident that no one was watching him at the time." Verstraeten frowned. "The funny thing about that last bid is he was accepted on three contracts, but eventually he declined them all."

"Mm. And there's nothing shady about any of these other company failures?"

"Apart from the one sab hit, nothing we've been able to find so far. They've been spread out over months since the revolt. The final one was at the beginning of November."

"Maybe it's genuinely opportunistic contract collection, then, chasing some easy Euros. Could he have a contact in the Department of Financial and Corporate Affairs feeding him good leads?"

"It's certainly possible, Para," Verstraeten said reluctantly. "From what I've been able to establish, Urban Fox has a solid reputation for quality and reliability. It *could* all be perfectly aboveboard."

They'd reached the lifts. Verstraeten put his hand out, then stopped short of the screen and looked questioningly at Toreth.

"But if it's not legit, the question is, why those exact contracts?" Toreth asked.

Toreth would never have expected the junior investigator to push his own theory against opposition from a senior para, but he did look happy that Toreth was willing to keep asking questions. He dropped his hand and stepped away from the lift door. "That's what we can't find out, Para, not without a warrant. Although..."

"Yes?"

"Easy Euros," Verstraeten said. "Even if contact details are confidential, we still have some tools to trace payments between corporations. If we're lucky, that could give us more clues about the contracts he took."

"Why hasn't Zaleski done it?"

"I did mention it in my report. But it isn't my case, and—" Verstraeten shrugged diffidently. "To be completely honest, Para, I suspect he doesn't want to encourage Head of Specialists Chean. And, of course, there are so many holding companies and 'independent' contractors that it's rarely a useful technique, anyway—anyone up to anything shady knows to hide it."

"But if Richardson is picking up originally nonshady contracts for shady reasons...?"

"I'd say it was just about worth a try, Para. I'll run the analysis on the failed corporations and the corporations they dealt with, see what comes up. I definitely can't promise anything, though."

"Don't worry about it." Toreth grinned. "It isn't my case, either."

With little else do to in the afternoon, Toreth decided to pretend Verstraeten's investigations would be fruitful, and so tidied up the case's IIP and went home early. As soon as he opened the flat door, he smelled dinner in progress. Curry, he guessed as he took off his coat, sniffing the spices in the air.

In the kitchen, Warrick was rinsing a large colander under the tap, with an inorganic sounding rattle.

"Mussels?" Toreth said, and added, "Evening."

"Good evening to you, and yes."

French fries tumbling in the fryer added another enticing smell, and lunch seemed like a long time ago. "Mm. Soon, I hope."

Warrick smiled. "Very soon." He turned off the tap and left the colander to drain in the sink. "Ten more minutes to finish the sauce, another few for the mussels to cook. I started the chips when you came through the gates."

Toreth almost said, "Spying on me?" but when he was this hungry he could let it slide. "Thanks."

"By the way, we've scheduled the next few directors' dinners," Warrick said as Toreth watched him stirring the pot on the stove. "For next year. You remember I'm going away for a few days?"

"No."

"It's on the flat calendar. Starting the 16th of January?" Warrick's voice quirked interrogatively, so Toreth just shrugged. Warrick gave a very tiny shake of his head. "Asher and I are taking the next generation sim to a couple of entertainment industry conventions, and giving some private demonstrations, in the hope of drumming up more business to keep the production facility schedule full. Anyway, when I get back, I'm hosting for the dinner, and, ah..."

It wasn't like Warrick to be so hesitant. "What? You want me out of the way? No problem, I'm sure I can find someone else to do."

Warrick's face didn't flicker. "That isn't what I meant at all. I'm always happy for you to attend, if you want to. Or not—it's completely up to you."

"Not" was certainly Toreth usual preference. He evaluated SimTech events largely by how much free booze there'd be and how good his chances were of a fuck from Warrick or someone else there. Directors' dinners were disappointingly light on both, with the bonus of a lot of boring work conversation. Toreth always had somewhere more fun to be, even if in the past that had been at home with a bottle of beer and some good porn.

So his first response was to refuse. Warrick still had an odd tension in his body, though, that made Toreth curious. "So what's the big deal this time?"

"Well, primarily, I thought I ought to mention it, since it's happening in your home."

Toreth stepped up close and took hold of Warrick's left wrist. Warrick didn't resist, letting go of the spoon at once. Keeping unbroken eye contact, Toreth pulled him around to face him. When he gripped Warrick's right wrist equally firmly, Warrick swallowed. Toreth pinned Warrick's wrists behind him in the small of his back and then pulled him forwards until they were chest to chest. He paused for a few seconds, letting Warrick feel it, and then applied the tiny extra degree of pressure to the bones in his wrists that made Warrick part his lips, breath coming faster. Yes, this was definitely the best way to hold a conversation about tedious domestic crap.

"You are a such a bad liar," Toreth said. "Actually, no. You're a good liar. I just have a lot of practice at spotting it."

Warrick's gaze shifted, over Toreth's shoulder.

"If you don't want me there, I won't be there," Toreth said. "If you want me there, just ask. I'm feeling very accommodating right now."

"Toreth—"

"But either way, you tell me why. Right now."

He eased his grip on Warrick's wrists, shifting his hold fractionally, and he felt Warrick brace himself, ready for the extra twist of pain. He was already getting hard. Toreth let go and stepped back in one smooth movement. Warrick glared, even more so when Toreth laughed.

"Okay. Tell me why, and then maybe if you're lucky I'll make you tell me, just for fun."

"Very well. Asher and Lew will be there, of course." Warrick rubbed his wrists. "And Asher's husband Greg, as he often is, but this time Lotte's coming, too."

"Who?"

"Lew Marcus's wife. Usually she doesn't have much interest in SimTech, but Lew said she wanted to come. I've no idea why."

"Ah." Toreth grinned. "I bet I do. Not allowed out on his own, in case he can't find his way home without taking a detour?"

Warrick's expression turned cool. "I wouldn't want to speculate. The fact is she'll be here, and, of course, she's very welcome and I want her to have a pleasant evening."

Two and two made an easy four. "So you want *me* to promise to be nice to Lew bloody Marcus?"

"No, I'd like you to be nice to Lotte. And by 'nice,' I mean please don't allude any of the topics you do sometimes bring up to make Lew uncomfortable."

"He should've thought harder about his future comfort when he was fucking underage prostitutes," Toreth said.

Warrick winced. "He's done nothing of the kind for years. I think your charming manner might've been the important incentive there."

"Which is why his wife suddenly won't let him out of her sight, I'm sure. Warrick, someone who's stupid enough to risk his whole fucking corporate existence to get his dick inside some prime blackmail material doesn't stop just like that. He's doing it, I guarantee. He's better at hiding it, that's all—from you, anyway."

"Lew's marriage isn't any of my business, *or* yours," Warrick said with frosty emphasis.

Toreth considered. An evening made even more boring than usual by removing the mild entertainment of needling Marcus didn't appeal. On the other hand, maybe he should think about moving this from problem to opportunity.

"Okay. I'll let everyone keep ignoring the teenager-fucking elephant in the middle of the room, but..."

"Yes?" Warrick said warily.

"We spice it up with a bet. I want to try a new scenario."

"What?"

"I don't know. Yet." Actually, the day had given him a couple of ideas. With some time to develop them, he could definitely come up with something special.

"The important part is, we finish it. You stop it, you lose. Marcus will have to take his chances."

Warrick looked at him measuringly. Finally he said, "Nothing illegal. Nothing in public. Nothing deliberately unenjoyable. Nothing—"

Toreth cut him off before the list became too boring. "Just you and me, in the flat. Having plenty of fun. And no blood, no tissue damage." He smiled promisingly. "I don't need that, anyway." After a moment, he shrugged. "Or we can forget it, and I'll find somewhere else to be while Marcus's wife is dragging him around on a short leash. Up to you."

Still Warrick hesitated. Toreth waited, relaxed and confident. He knew his cat, and unlike Bastard, curiosity would definitely kill this one for him without any further persuasion.

Warrick smiled, slowly. "A bet? All right, then."

He held out his hand. Toreth shook it, then gave Warrick what he really wanted, pulling him back against Toreth's body, wrists squeezed tight once more. Toreth mouthed over the side of Warrick's neck, then whispered, "It's on."

Chapter Nine

❖

When Toreth arrived at his office the next morning, Phil Verstraeten was waiting there for him, talking to Sara. The junior investigator looked positively sunny, smiling and making copious eye contact—which for Verstraeten was any eye contact at all.

"Got something?" Toreth guessed.

"I—yes—I—" The investigator ducked his head and cleared his throat. "Yes, Para."

Behind him, Sara was fighting a smile.

"Go into my office, then. Sara will make us a couple of coffees."

Sara rolled her eyes, then instantly assumed a neutral admin façade as Verstraeten turned. "Thanks," he said, "but I don't think I'll be here long enough to drink it."

"Run up against a brick wall, then?" Toreth said as he sat at his desk.

Verstraeten closed the office door and sat down. "Not exactly, Para. The good news is the trace went a lot more smoothly than I expected. Let me just—" Verstraeten opened his hand screen and linked with the screen on Toreth's desk. A table filled with plenty of data appeared. "Here it is—contract dates, payment schedules, everything you could want."

Toreth leaned closer, scanning the screen. "All the contracts Richardson picked up are for work with the Central Bank?"

"That's right, Para. Which is why it was so easy to find them—the Central Bank has an unusually strict set of rules governing how it pays external contractors. Payments have to go directly to the incorporated body providing the services. No agencies, no invisible subcontracts. The rules came into force after a fraud in which—" Verstraeten cleared his throat again. "Not relevant. The point is, however indirect the link in terms of contracted suppliers, all payments go from the bank to Urban Fox Security. And all the contracts are to do with Central Bank security systems and processes."

"Well." Even if it didn't actually make it any more likely that Richardson was a criminal, it certainly raised the stakes if he was. "So I take it there's bad news?"

"In a way, Para. It means Richardson won't be handling any other parts of the plan himself—assuming there is a plan, of course. He'll know the Central Bank contract rules as well as us, and that his name is tied to it. In fact, it's probably why he was so blasé about bidding for the contracts in the first place."

"But it also means if there is anything more behind it, he can't be the only one involved?"

"Exactly so, Para. Unfortunately, this also suggests he's not the main player. He was probably brought in on the strength of sab experience and training, to insulate whoever's paying him if anyone got suspicious. He's a firebreak."

Conspiracy. That always played well to section heads. "And what are the contracts? Any clue about what he's up to?"

"Ah. Well, that's some more bad news, Para. The contracts cover a wide range of fields. In fact, there's something from almost every part of bank security that a contractor could plausibly work on. Almost certainly only a minority of them are important, but—" Verstraeten shrugged. "I ran everything I had through the evidence analysis system, and it did pick out a couple of areas as particularly security-sensitive. The best I could get was a weakly positive risk assessment meriting further investigation. I'm sorry about the confidence levels, though, Para." Verstraeten did sound genuinely apologetic.

"What do you think about the case?" Toreth asked. Then, forestalling the cautious expression on Verstraeten's face, he said, "What's your general feeling about it? Investigator Carey says she trusts your instincts, and I'm willing to do the same."

Verstraeten ducked his head. "Very kind of you, Para. My *feeling*, then, is if there is anything to it, then this is where you'll find it. Richardson, or someone, has put a lot of effort into getting these security contracts, and by their nature taking Central Bank contracts as part of a sabbing operation is an exposure to risk. Either Richardson is completely honest—at least, as honest as a probable ex-sab ever can be—or he's very dodgy indeed."

"Okay. Well, thanks. Tell Carey I appreciate her letting me take up your time."

"No trouble at all, Para." Taking his cue, the junior specialist stood up. "If you need anything more, anything at all, give me a call."

"Don't want to miss out on credit for the case?" Toreth asked.

To his surprise, Verstraeten smiled and bobbed his head again. "Some credit would be nice, Para, if I can actually produce data worth it. Like I told Investigator Carey, if there's anything at all to it, then it's going to be big. That's my guess, anyway."

After Verstraeten left, Toreth considered what to do next. Central Bank could cut the contracts, but the damage might already have been done—some subtle weakening of security, or extraction of information which would allow the hypothetical plan to succeed. Being able to point fingers after some catastrophic disaster had befallen the Administration's finances wouldn't produce much in the way of commendations. Especially if he'd only be able to point his finger at an experienced sab who was probably being paid more than enough to compensate him for a few unpleasant days in I&I custody.

A knock on the door was immediately followed by Sara opening it. "Coffee for one?"

"Thanks."

She set it down on the desk. "Do you need me to do anything for the case?"

"No...not yet. Wait—have we heard anything from any corporate lawyers about Richardson?"

"Nothing. Although he put in his own preemptive application for release via his Justice rep." Sara snorted. "Timed down to the second from his booking in, too."

"Smart-arse." The man must be very confident of being able to resist interrogation. "All right. Get a new surveillance rota worked up for if we have to release him."

Sara hesitated, then said, "Can I leave Andy off it next weekend?"

"If you can find someone else who wants the overtime. If there's no one here, try Corporate Fraud. Zaleski might as well put something into the case, even if it's only an investigator or two."

"Thanks," Sara said, and slipped out quickly as though she were expecting him to change his mind.

Truthfully, it didn't much matter who carried out the surveillance—Justice could probably do it well enough. Once Richardson had been arrested, the chances of him slipping up were even smaller than before, but like the wasted interrogation, it wouldn't do to get sloppy with the IIP. And what else did they have to try? These days, precious little, as everyone at I&I seemed to enjoy reminding him.

Leaving the coffee to cool, Toreth pushed his chair back, irritated by the neatly tabulated but still largely useless results on the screen, and tried a therapeutic pace across the office by the window. Two issues of what had been the *Journal of the Association of Para-Investigators* made the beginnings of a pile there. Now called *Innovations in Investigation,* it was finally back in print after the revolt. They didn't like the reformed P&P, either.

Having more information, even sketchy information, ought not to feel so unsatisfying. In the old days he'd be consulting Sara, trying to work out the maximum level of waiver they could push for with the new facts. Now, though, there was nowhere higher to go.

Or at least nowhere higher within the I&I system.

If Toreth had to waste his time waiting to see a senior official, the Bureau of Administrative Departments was at least a pleasant place to waste it. The pickiest corporate would've struggled to find fault with the comfort of the chairs. Toreth had drunk an excellent coffee, and turned down a second, before the smartly suited admin at the reception desk finally looked over to him.

"I apologize for the wait, Para-investigator," she said. "Principal Secretary Turnbull has a short window to see you now. Come with me, please."

Toreth stood up to follow the woman—the same one who had been there on his previous visits to the Bureau—along the plushly carpeted corridor.

"You're lucky you caught me here," Catherine Turnbull said as Toreth closed the door to her office behind him. "I'm going back to Strasbourg tomorrow."

"I'm very grateful you'd spare me this time at such short notice, Secretary."

"Not at all." Turnbull stood to shake hands, although she was so short it didn't make much difference. "You've done a great deal for the Bureau in the past. And for relations with America, too. I had a real paper New Year card from Luke Elliot's grateful father via their embassy only last week—well, a 'Seasonal Wishes' card, which I suppose is a generic concession to cultural differences." She sat down and smiled genially. "Now, how can I help?"

"I have a problem with an investigation, and I didn't know who to approach with it." Toreth sat down on the chair she indicated. "Even if it's not something that falls under Bureau purview, maybe you'll be able to point me in the right direction."

"Sounds intriguing," Turnbull said, although Toreth detected a hint of the get-on-with-it tone he'd be using if it was one of his team trying to build up some piece of evidence.

Toreth ran quickly over the details of the case, watching Turnbull carefully for the first signs of her dismissing it as worthless. He didn't see the reaction he'd more than half expected, although he remembered from their previous interactions that she was difficult to read. No one who made it this high up in the Administration's hierarchy would be anything else.

Finally he got to the meat of Verstraeten's analysis, if anything so fragile could be called "meat." More like one of Warrick's fancy lace-thin tuilles, and as likely to melt away to nothing if you actually tried to get your teeth into it.

"The one thing which stands out, Secretary, and which is all Corporate Fraud has, really, is this collection of security contracts from the Central Bank. Richardson has gone to a lot of effort to acquire them, and it's all been since the trouble with the resisters earlier in the year. Exactly what advantage he's hoping to get from them we can't say, but it seemed significant enough that I thought it was worth bringing to you. Someone should look into it."

"Forgive me for speaking outside my area of expertise, but that doesn't seem like very much of a basis for a case."

"You're right, Secretary. That's why the someone will have to be outside I&I. I don't see what more we can do."

Turnbull nodded. "I see. But you don't actually know for certain if he has any plans regarding the Bank at all?"

"No, Secretary, we don't. We doubt he's behind any plan personally, though. He's more likely to be contracting for someone else. Could even be someone outside the Administration—we do know he has contacts in India."

"Know?"

"Have some suggestive evidence, then. He's possibly connected to illegal security equipment imports."

"But not, I assume, sufficiently connected that you could convict him of it?"

"I'm afraid not. But at the very least, I'd recommend passing the files to someone at Ext-Sec."

Turnbull regarded him steadily, as though she were trying to see through him to some ulterior motive. "Couldn't you have done that without involving the Bureau?"

"I could. But I'd have no way of making sure they take it seriously. And the Central Bank could be warned directly, too, and they can decide whether they need to terminate any contracts, but there's no way of knowing what information he already has, or what he could do with it. We know—we *suspect*," Toreth corrected himself, "that he has a history in corporate sabotage."

"Contacts in India, you say? Officially, the Administration has an excellent relationship with their government."

"Does it? I'm afraid that's outside *my* area of expertise, Secretary."

"Of course..." Turnbull compressed her lips, silent for a moment in thought. "It sounds as though he's potentially political enough to strip his corporate status."

Toreth found himself impressed once again by her knowledge of I&I procedure. "It wouldn't matter, Secretary. Even after that, we still don't have enough left in the Procedures and Protocols to touch him."

"Because of these treatments he's had?"

"He's right up to date with them. Not long after everything settled down after the P&P rewrite, Central Medical Services has a whole new set of fixes recorded. He was plugging the holes from his previous treatments. Up against the old P&P, the work he's had done would've been a marginal benefit. Now, they've made him practically cast iron."

"At least, if he's tough enough to hold out against questioning."

"He is, Secretary. Taking his corporate status away won't get enough extra leverage to change that. You can be sure any employer already knows we arrested him."

She sat in silent thought again for a moment, then shook her head. "I'm sorry, but I'm afraid I'm not convinced this situation merits special authorization from the Council for anything outside normal I&I procedures."

Despite the refusal, the way she said it had a certain promise. It sounded as though someone had at least thought about how a better waiver could be granted these days.

"Fair enough." Toreth shrugged. "I just thought it was worth bringing to someone's attention. Thanks for sparing me some of your time, Secretary."

"Oh? I expected you to press harder."

"You think I'm here trying to get higher level waivers back?" Toreth shook his head. "I do my job, Secretary, just like I did it before. If I can't get the results with the tools I'm given, it's not my problem. My gradings won't suffer—everyone on the interrogation levels is working to the same P&P, and I'm as good an interrogator as anyone there."

"So why the personal visit?"

"Because I thought someone ought to hear about it. Do you have any idea how long it would take me to persuade my boss to send a report here?"

She looked at him measuringly, obviously not convinced. Toreth kept his face impassive, trying to project how very much he didn't care whether he had a chance to interrogate his prisoner properly or not.

"Very well," she said. "But I'll need to know more before I take this further. Excuse me while I make a call." She picked up her earpiece.

"Should I leave?"

"If you wouldn't mind. You can wait outside—I'll let you know if I'll be longer than a few minutes."

Toreth was happy to find the corridor deserted. The Bureau didn't skimp on furniture and fittings, and the door to Turnbull's office was thick enough to thwart an ear pressed against it. However, when he set his I&I camera to the crack and linked it to his earpiece, he could hear Turnbull's faint voice.

"—right away, if at all possible." She paused. "Urgent enough that I'm calling from my office. But if Dupré isn't available...ah, good. No, I can hold."

Dupré—not a name Toreth knew. Whoever Turnbull was contacting, they didn't feel the need to take an urgent call from the Bureau immediately. Eventually, though, Turnbull said, "It's Catherine. Yes, I'm sorry to interrupt, but I think you need to hear this."

Toreth listened, too, standing with his back to the door and the camera held behind him, glancing casually up and down the corridor while Turnbull outlined the case. He missed occasional phrases, probably as she turned away from the door, but he got the gist of it easily enough. Turnbull didn't need to repeat herself often, if at all, Toreth noticed after a while. Was Dupré someone connected to the Treasury, or involved in monitoring compliance with the corporate accords at the Department of Financial and Corporate Affairs? Finance wasn't his specialty; maybe Carey would know the name. Turnbull had announced herself by her first name, and she was treating Dupré with the friendly respect merited by a peer, so the person must be someone important.

"I agree—the foreign connection is probably spurious. Fabric has to come from somewhere. But consider the serious effect an attack on the Central Bank could have on our key stability matrices at this time, if—*if* there's a genuine threat of such, yes. I understand." Her voice grew fainter; she must be moving around the room. Toreth shifted the camera, trying to catch it again. "...can, yes, of course. I do know what I'm asking. Yes. But under the circumstances, do you want to risk the consequences of refusing to consider all avenues? Overall policy consensus cannot blindly dictate every practical detail. Flexibility, exactly. Yes, quite—and also balancing those priorities, you might say."

After that, the conversation seemed to consist primarily of Dupré talking, with Turnbull agreeing and, occasionally, disagreeing. Then a long silence gave Toreth the hint he needed to move away and station himself in front of one of the old-style paintings hung on the walls.

Turnbull opened her office door. "Come back in."

Inside, Turnbull remained standing.

"I imagine releasing Richardson would be the next natural step?" she said to Toreth. He nodded. "Then do so, while I have this information investigated further. I'm afraid that so close to New Year it could take several days—what you're asking may even require a new legal instrument. Keep a watch on Richardson, and I'll let you know as soon as I can whether there'll be any further action for you to take."

Toreth offered his hand. "Thank you, Secretary."

Chapter Ten

❖

U ncle Keir! Uncle Val!"
Still unloading bags from the car, Toreth looked over his shoulder to see Valeria leaning out of an open ground floor window. Warrick waved to her.

"Hello, Val!"

She waved again, then vanished from the window, which closed behind her.

"Well, at least someone's pleased to see us," Warrick said.

"She looks more like Dillian every time I see her," Toreth said. "Don't you think?"

"Yes, she does," Warrick said. "And like Kate, too."

"Growing up fast. How old is she now?" Toreth cast his mind back to his last precautionary skim over the family security files. "Nine, isn't it?"

"Ten," Warrick said, his voice much frostier than the damp December weather.

"Give her a few more years, she'll be beating the boys off with a stick."

"Toreth..."

Toreth hoisted the nearest bag over his shoulder. "Mm?"

"Don't forget the presents."

Toreth turned back to the car, grinning to himself. Five more years to wind Warrick up before Valeria hit the age of consent and Toreth had to worry whether it would be possible to get anywhere with her without Warrick—or any other member of the family—actually taking out a sab contract on him.

By the time they made it to the door, the rest of the household had been alerted to their arrival, and Jen, Dillian, and Valeria were all waiting for them. Toreth got a determinedly affable hello from Dillian, a genuinely warmer one from Jen, and managed to sidestep Valeria's greeting. Too grown up to pick up, now, she hugged Warrick enthusiastically. She had news, too.

"Dad's coming." Valeria beamed at them.

"That's great," Warrick said. He looked up at Dillian, who nodded.

"We finally got the word from the rehabilitation unit. Philly's staying over there tonight, and she's bringing him here first thing in the morning. He might even be allowed to stay for a couple of nights, depending on how it goes. They'll be monitoring his condition remotely."

Toreth wondered idly how long the miraculous effect of Tarin's near death would last. Neither Warrick nor Dillian had particularly seemed to like their half brother before Int-Sec had almost killed him. Well, for Toreth's purposes, it only needed to last another day or two.

Toreth offered to take their bags upstairs. Valeria volunteered herself to help him; agreeing seemed like the path of least resistance. She picked up the smallest bag, and Toreth took the rest. She showed him to the same room he'd shared with Warrick last time he'd been here.

"Can I help unpack?" she asked.

Warrick would be thrilled if Toreth let Valeria catch a glimpse of some of the things in his bag. "No. And don't you have anything else to do?"

"I'm helping Aunt Jen with dinner, but I hate peeling potatoes."

"Looked more like you were watching out of the window."

"I have a camera on the windowsill in my room, and the house system calls me if a car parks outside."

Warrick would be proud of her. "Clever."

"I'm building a list of registrations, to let me know who it is. Most people use taxis, though, so I have to wait for the facial recognition when they get out."

Valeria sat on the edge of the bed and watched him unpack. Just to psych Warrick out, Toreth folded Warrick's clothes very carefully and neatly in the chest of drawers, then shoved his own clothes in the drawer below.

"Uncle Val, did you ever finish investigating what happened to my dad?"

He looked up in surprise. "What?"

"I haven't seen you since Auntie Cele helped us make the picture, and she said she didn't know."

If Warrick's family were cats, the whole lot would be dead by now. "Yes, I finished. It was an accident. The Department of Transport report said something went wrong with the transporter controls. Outdated software. They fined the corporation, and they updated the control systems in their other transports."

"Oh. So that man Auntie Cele drew, he didn't have anything to do with it?"

"No. It was just a coincidence. Which is one of the things you have to be careful about in investigations—not making too much out of coincidences. Otherwise it's easy to get it wrong."

"Oh," she said again. "So, Dad'll be safe tomorrow, then, in the car when he comes here? Him and Mum."

"Yeah, I should think so. You'd need to be stupidly unlucky to have that happen twice."

And Tarin had never seemed especially unlucky—stupid, sure, but lucky enough. If Sable decided Tarin was still too much trouble to keep alive, he'd have the sense to vary his methods a little. And, really, if Sable couldn't manage to kill unobtrusively a man who'd been expected to die any number of times over the past months, it didn't say much for Citizen Surveillance.

Leaving the more incriminating items in the case, Toreth zipped it closed. "Right, I'm done here."

To Toreth's relief, when they reached the bottom of the stairs Valeria was summoned away by Jen, presumably back to her potatoes. He didn't get long to enjoy the respite; Warrick was waiting for him, and he steered Toreth into the living room.

"Problems already?" Toreth asked.

"I don't know. I hope not. Jen had another letter from Kate." Warrick held out a couple of sheets of paper. "Handwritten this time, like the one on Val's birthday."

Toreth didn't take the letter. "To say happy New Year?"

"Yes. It arrived here, addressed to Jen."

"Was there a return address?"

"Of course not. How could there be?"

Toreth shrugged. "Never mind. I'm sure she knows why she didn't get a card from you."

To his surprise, Warrick went to the door, checked the hall outside both ways, then came back, closing the door behind him.

"Warrick? Did something go wrong? Have you heard from . . . ?" Toreth left the sentence hanging, knowing Warrick would understand.

"Is she dead?" Warrick asked.

Toreth eyed him assessingly. Would a truthful answer send Warrick off on another lethally dangerous crusade for revenge? "I don't know," Toreth said at length.

"Toreth . . ."

"I don't. Honestly. If I had to guess then I'd say yeah, there's a reasonable chance she is. But only because Cit Surveillance wouldn't want an ex-agent running around loose outside the Administration." Especially not right after the revolt, when IntSec had been full of panicking covert divisions convinced the resisters were coming for them next. "They have a very strict policy of tidying up after themselves."

"I thought the same thing. But then I took Val's letter to a corporate forensic service to have it analyzed. The report said it was genuine, to the best of their ability to tell." Warrick turned the new letter over in his hands. "Which ultimately proves very little. The writing, the genetic material on the paper...yes, I know that can all be faked. But they sound so much like her."

"Cit could be dry freeze-storing letters she wrote before she left," Toreth said. It was a risky suggestion, but better than having Warrick think he wasn't seriously applying himself to the problem. "I don't know if you've heard of it? It's a fucking annoying technique that sabs and fraudsters *love*. Done well it can be almost impossible to detect, and of course it completely screws up document dating in cases."

"No, it can't be that." Warrick smiled, tight and precise. "Not unless she had psychic powers she never mentioned. There are references to contemporary events."

"Then I was wrong, and she's alive," Toreth said.

"Or someone is taking a lot of trouble to make sure we think she is."

And they both knew who it must be. "Warrick." This needed to be done delicately. "You know even having the letters analyzed was a risk. People will be watching. If he—they—think you have doubts, and that you might try to do something about them..."

To his surprise, Warrick smiled. "Oh, don't worry. If she is dead, then in a very real sense there's no escaping that she brought it entirely on herself."

"So why ask me about her?"

"I thought you might know the answer, that's all. Knowing definitively, one way or another, would be one less thing to worry about. If only there were some way to—" Warrick sighed. "Sometimes it feels like this will go on forever, overshadowing the rest of the family."

"But no one else even knows about it. Do they?"

"That's not the point."

And the way Warrick sidestepped that question really hadn't improved Toreth's day. "No, the *point* is that you're such a fucking control freak you can't leave this alone."

Warrick stared at him.

"What? Don't give me that bloody 'you're overreacting' expression."

"But you are. I have no intention of—"

"Warrick, you've been in the cells at I&I once already this year. Wasn't that enough of a hint? There are places in Int-Sec I couldn't even fucking *find* you, never mind get you out."

"I'm not going to look any further. Or turn over any dangerous rocks."

"Thank Christ for that."

Warrick nodded. "I won't deny you're right that I don't like leaving it unfinished. But I fully appreciate the danger, I promise."

His tone was far too casual for Toreth's comfort. Maybe it meant Warrick had put further investigation out of his mind. Maybe it meant he thought he was too clever for it to matter who was involved.

He put both hands on Warrick's shoulders and looked dead into his eyes. "I'm sure I've said this before, but this time, listen. You don't know what these people are like."

"Of course I—"

"No, you don't. You know corporate sabs. And they're bastards, I admit. But they play percentages, and even these days they have to worry about people like me coming after them. The Int-Sec covert divisions aren't like that. Indigs, paras, corporates—it's all the same to them. They care about *security,* and keeping secrets. Theirs first, and the Administration's a very close second. We could both be stabbed to death in the street in front of fifty witnesses, but when the investigations hit a Cit flag on our files they'd be closed down so fast the IIPs would barely register."

A rare small crease of doubt appeared between Warrick's eyebrows.

"Sable might've been willing to go out of his way to help you once," Toreth said, "but I wouldn't bet my life on him doing it again. And I definitely don't want *you* betting my fucking life on it."

Toreth tightened his grip to emphasize the point. Warrick licked his lips and glanced down at Toreth's hand on his shoulder.

"Oh, for fuck's sake." Toreth pulled his hands back. "Tarin wasn't the only one who got a second chance, Warrick. We all did. Don't—just don't screw it up by being stupid again." He hated begging when he had no choice but to mean it. "Please."

"I won't," Warrick said.

"Won't what?"

Warrick smiled very slightly. "I won't investigate Kate's whereabouts, or her state of health. I'll try to forget John Sable is alive. I'll read the letters, and I'll tell Dilly and Jen that I think they're from Kate, and nothing more. I give you my word."

Toreth breathed out. "Thank you."

Toreth had been expecting more visitors; the last time he'd been at Kate's home for New Year's Eve, the house had been crowded with guests. But as the time for dinner grew closer, no one extra had arrived except for Cele and Asher Linton. Dinner was still set out as a buffet, but the atmosphere seemed a little awkward and uncertain, as though people were determined to carry on with the family traditions, even though the backbone of them had been splintered by Kate's departure.

Of course, Warrick would hardly have been so sanguine when Toreth invited himself along if he'd been expecting an influx of acquaintances whose friends had been arrested, or who had possibly even passed through Toreth's hands in person. Or had the guest list been dramatically cut back once Toreth had announced his intention to be there?

As they ate, the conversation began to flow more easily, lubricated by the usual generous supply of wine. Despite the alcohol, some topics seemed to be tacitly off-limits: Kate, the revolt, Tarin's accident and the aftermath. The only one who mentioned Tarin was Valeria, who kept making suggestions for things they could do the next day, when he was there.

"And we should go and feed the ducks," Valeria said. "Granny would want us to. It's a seasonal tradition. The ducks are a bit dirty but I'll make sure he doesn't go too close."

"You're going to wear poor Tar out!" Dillian said, laughing, and Valeria smiled. "I just want him to come home."

"Well, we'll have to see what your mum says," Jen said. "She's going to call in the morning, first thing, as soon as she talks to the medics."

Valeria's face fell.

"Speaking of medics," Cele said brightly, "how was it yesterday, Ash?"

"A bit scary." Asher picked up her glass of water, and for the first time Toreth noticed she hadn't touched the wine all evening. "But he or she passed the scan and the DNA screen. Nothing wrong, no need to retest." She patted her stomach. "Project Linton is moving forward."

"Fabulous!" Cele picked up her glass. "I'll drink to that. So, Dilly, what do you think?" Cele winked. "Us next?"

Toreth expected Dillian to protest, but she smiled very slightly and said, "Do you really want to talk about it here?"

Was she joking? Toreth couldn't tell.

Cele clearly couldn't, either, because she stared at Dillian for a few speechless seconds, then said, "So. Asher, I thought Greg might honor us with his presence this year, in view of the momentous news."

"Well." Asher looked down for a moment. "You know how it is. Work."

Work, or a healthy respect for avoiding the friends of convicted resisters.

"Quiet, this year," Toreth said during a pause, as everyone else tucked into their desserts and he picked at a plate of cheeses.

For a moment, no one replied; then Jen said, "We told people we needed to have a private dinner. We hoped Tarin might be here by now, and we had very strict instructions from his doctors about avoiding sources of infection. And—"

Warrick cleared his throat. "More wine, Dilly?"

"I imagine some people were relieved to have an excuse, anyway," Jen continued with a rather determined air. "With so many of Tarin's friends being arrested."

"I'm sure that's not true," Cele said, with a glance at Val, who was following the conversation with interest.

"Of course it is," Jen said. "It does no one any good to pretend otherwise. It means a lot to me that you still came, and Asher, too."

Asher glanced at Warrick. "Jen, that's silly. You know we'd be here no matter what."

"Whoever turned them in just then did them a favor," Toreth said, and then left the silence to develop.

"A favor?" Cele said eventually.

"Considering the stupid crap they'd done, there's never been a better time to be arrested. Most of them were recommended for light re-education."

Toreth picked up a cracker and reached out for the butter. Warrick passed it to him automatically, any emotions locked away behind a polite corporate mask. The other adults also stayed silent. Valeria had put down her spoon and was frowning at him.

"They'd have got a hell of a lot worse before the revolt, and they'd probably get worse, now, too," Toreth added. "We're being told to tighten up on sedition, and the Justice systems are handing out heavier sentences again."

"It's exactly what I said would happen," Dillian said bleakly.

Toreth nodded. "Didn't take a genius to work that out. People like to feel safe. And the Administration likes stability."

"And we've had how many different Administration councils this year?" Cele said. "That's certainly not stable."

"You can't think it would be better to go back to—" Dillian started, then stopped and looked at Toreth. She stood up abruptly, her chair almost tipping over before Warrick grabbed it. "Would anyone else like a glass of dessert wine? I forgot to get it earlier. I'll find a bottle now."

Warrick followed Dillian into the small pantry. Dillian stood in front of the wine rack, her hands on her hips. Warrick waited for a minute, but she didn't seem inclined either to say anything or actually choose any wine. And, yes, he'd meant what he said to De Nijs about talking to Dillian over New Year, but he hadn't expected to have his hand forced so soon.

Finally, he touched her gently on the shoulder. "Dilly, what was that about?"

She didn't look at him. "Don't you remember? When we were in the car coming back from the spaceport? I said it wouldn't take long before things were back the way they were."

Carnac had said much the same thing, although Warrick was glad that name hadn't come up in the already fraught conversation. "That's not what I meant. You jumped up like someone goosed you."

"It didn't seem like a very healthy topic of conversation, that's all. Considering Val was there—and considering the company, too."

"Dillian, after all this time you *can't* think Toreth would report anything anyone said here? You just can't. He does his job, which is investigating cases he's assigned." And, of course, interrogating suspects. "Yes, he does it very well, but his dedication doesn't extend to looking for more work over dinner."

"No, I suppose not. And he might like to have me arrested, but not when my brother is his registered partner."

"It's not because of that. He doesn't care about politics. It honestly wouldn't even occur to him to make a report." No matter whether reports of that nature were still being investigated. "Please, I know it's difficult, but I'd be grateful if you could...try to give him the benefit of the doubt."

"I think we'd all be better off if he and I aren't in the same places."

"Is that why you haven't been coming to the flat so much since he moved in?"

She didn't deny it. "He doesn't like me any more than I like him. Why spoil the atmosphere for everyone else?"

"I'm sure he doesn't *dis*like you." Mostly true, because Toreth put so little emotional investment into anyone.

"Really?" Dillian finally turned to face him, her eyes shadowed by the pantry lighting. "That's funny, because I tried to talk to him, to start again as friends, at the flatwarming, and I got it thrown back in my face as thanks."

"What did you say to him?"

"Why? Do you think it was my fault?"

"Dillian..."

"I didn't say anything! I just—" She frowned, and he thought she was genuinely trying to remember. "I told him I could see he was making a commitment to you by moving in, and I had to accept he was a permanent part of your life now. All right, I admit I could've phrased it more graciously, but the way he flew off the handle, he's just not *right*. He really..." Her voice trailed off. "What? Keir, what?"

He wondered if he looked as horrified as he felt. The reason for Toreth's sudden change of mind at the flatwarming party was now painfully clear. He couldn't blame Dilly, of course, for an honest attempt to come to a rapprochement with Toreth, but the way she'd gone about it couldn't have been calculated to backfire more vigorously if she'd employed a squadron of psychologists to help her.

"So what did I say wrong?" she asked. "Just spit it out."

"Well, to begin with, commitment is never one of Toreth's favorite subjects. I don't think bringing it up at that exact time and place would've improved his mood."

She frowned. "But—but it's true. How can he move in with you without it meaning *something*?"

"And that's precisely why it was an unfortunate choice of materials from which to build a bridge. I promise, I'm grateful you tried," he added diplomatically. "But you did probably make him rather uncomfortable."

"Well, we wouldn't want him to feel *uncomfortable*," she said. "It's not as though anyone else's feelings matter, is it?"

"Dilly." The venom in her voice shocked him. She'd never made any secret of her dislike, but her feelings had rarely blown up into open antagonism. "Please, don't make this into a choice between you and him."

"Choice? I'm not asking you to *choose*. I just hate the way you tiptoe around him sometimes. It's like having a spoiled child in the family, except he's much too big for anyone to send him to his room."

Warrick had to admit, however reluctantly, that there was some justice in the assessment. "Well, you didn't tell him that, at least."

Dillian shook her head. "Do you think he loves you?"

"Dilly, you can't ask that."

"I can. I just did. See?"

"Reasonably ask it, then."

She sniffed. "I can't ask if you think the person you're apparently intending to spend the rest of your life with loves you? Is it such a ridiculous question?"

"Well, then I have to say it depends on how you define—"

"Oh, no," she said. "If you have to redefine 'love' to make it fit, then he really doesn't."

"I don't want to redefine anything," he said sharply. "To make it fit or otherwise. You're the one asking the question, and apparently expecting me to be able to read someone's mind. I mean to say—does Cele love you?"

"Of course she does!"

"And does she love you any differently to how she loved you when you were just friends?"

"She—well, I don't—" Dillian hesitated. "It's not the same."

"Is it not?"

"No. You're Cele's friend, too. I don't want to go making statements about her feelings to you."

"And yet, you want me to do that for Toreth to someone who admits she doesn't even like him." It had started off as a purely logical argument, but Warrick could hear the edge growing in his voice. "And who's said she'd rather see me leave him, however miserable it might make me."

"What?" she exclaimed. "I never did that!"

"Not directly, but you suggested I should walk away while I had the chance and be grateful that I could. And you didn't ask—"

"Did it really make you so miserable?" she asked anxiously.

"They certainly weren't the most enjoyable few weeks of my life." And having come so close to losing both Toreth and Tarin, Warrick suddenly found he couldn't bear the risk, however remote, of anyone else disappearing from his life. Warrick rubbed his hand over his face, and it seemed to wipe some of the annoyance away. "Dilly. I'm sorry."

82

"No, I'm sorry." Now she looked worried; that had been her default expression for years whenever the subject of Toreth came up, but Warrick decided to assume this time it was about his feelings rather than his physical safety. "I keep telling myself I can't run your life, and then somehow I seem to have to try again."

"I don't want to fight with you," Warrick said. "Especially not about what someone else may or may not feel."

"Then we won't." She hugged him. "There, okay. I won't ever mention it again."

"Thank you."

"I'll try to stay away from him while we're here, and—"

"Dilly—"

"*And then,* in the New Year, I'll make a fresh start. Again," she added, rather pointedly, but this time Warrick kept quiet. "I'll come to the flat, and I'll be nice to him if it kills me. I just—I don't want to spoil the holiday for Valeria and Tar, now, if I try and it all goes wrong. But I promise I'll do my best to think charitable thoughts about him. Just for you."

Warrick had to smile, because while she was no doubt sincere, it was hard to imagine. "Like?"

"Like..." Dillian smiled, too. "Well, I suppose he's here, right? That's something. After last time, I didn't think he'd ever be back."

"No." Warrick frowned, because that was a very good point he hadn't perhaps given as much consideration as he ought. "Nor did I."

Warrick found Jen clearing up the remains of the buffet. Or, rather, looking at the table with a rather forlorn air, while she ate whipped cream out of a bowl with a spoon.

"Jen?" Warrick said

She jumped a little, then glanced over her shoulder. "Oh. I didn't hear you come in."

"No. You looked like you were a long way away." When she didn't say anything more, Warrick went over to the buffet table and picked up a profiterole. He bit into it, and there was no need to fake a hum of appreciation. "I have no idea how you do it, but these get better every year."

"Practice," she said. "Thank you for sending that chocolate, by the way. It makes such a difference, but it's so expensive."

"Any time. It's hardly pure altruism when I get to eat the result, too."

"Mm." She contemplated the buffet. "Do you think I should've made cassoulet?"

Fortunately, he'd just taken another mouthful of choux pastry. "No," he said when he'd swallowed. "There was more than enough. I don't think anyone missed it."

83

"That's not what I—but you're right, I made far too much food. I'll be eating it for weeks." She smiled. "You'll have to take some things back with you when you go."

"Of course I will. Thank you."

Jen contemplated the table for a moment longer, then shook her head. "It didn't seem right, my making it instead of Kate."

"I know what you mean. The first New Year without her is bound to be strange. You never know, there's still a chance that one day she'll be back to make it in person."

"Maybe. But—" Jen looked at him hard. "I don't think so. Do you?"

Lying under her direct gaze was always difficult. Finally he said, "If she were coming back, I think it would've happened by now. But we can't be sure."

"Is she dead?"

"I wondered exactly the same thing. In fact, I went to the trouble of having one of her letters authenticated by the best forensic document analyst I could find." This was a big one. "She's writing them, there's no question about it."

"Oh," she said, as though she'd really expected another answer. "Well, then. That's a load off my mind. I still can't imagine what she did that meant she had to go, but so long as wherever she is, she's all right...I can live with that."

After all that, he almost didn't want to bring up the reason why he'd gone look-ing for her. But better now than tomorrow, with Philly and Tarin in the house.

"Jen..."

"Mm?"

"I know she's mature for her age, but I'm not sure it's a good idea to be talking about some things around Val. Like the arrests. She doesn't need to know about that."

"No?" Jen shook her head. "I have been thinking about it, a lot. After Kate was arrested, Tarin told me you knew about your father. What happened to him, how he really died."

"He was arrested and interrogated," Warrick said, wondering if a question about Toreth was about to follow.

"Yes. Kate was always so insistent you and Dilly should never find that out. And so we always told Tarin he couldn't talk about it, either. Looking back...I'm sure she only wanted to protect you all, but I think she was wrong. Poor Tar was so angry about Leo. It changed him completely. Maybe if we'd been more open about it, acknowledged what he felt, Tar wouldn't have been pushed to—to asso-ciate with those kinds of people."

Sadly, she might well be right. No doubt the Citizen Surveillance psychologists had carefully worked out the optimum strategy for Kate to mold her oldest son into the tool they wanted. And it had given them a tool they'd used for over two decades.

"So you don't think Val needs protecting?" Warrick asked.

"Of course! But she needs to know she can ask questions, too—where it's safe for her to ask them. And that some things are dangerous and have consequences. Better to learn that with us than to find out a much harder way later."

"I suppose so."

"I'm not saying we have to make her face any brutal realities right now. Just that she needs to be prepared. She's ten, after all."

Warrick wanted to protest that ten was still too young, but while the age of criminal responsibility might be fifteen, danger wouldn't considerately delay itself until then. "Yes, of course. You're quite right."

"Good, I'm glad you agree. Philly did, too. Now, come on." She smiled. "Help your old aunt tidy up in here."

Warrick smiled back. "You'll never be old. I won't allow it."

Jen put down the bowl. "You're too late, I'm afraid."

85

Chapter Eleven

❖

The next morning, after eating his breakfast, Toreth left the kitchen full of activity and preparations for the rest of the day. Cooking bored him at the best of times; people talking about all the previous New Year meals they'd cooked was definitely not one of the best times. He found himself a comfy armchair in the living room, where he could get out his screen and check his IIPs. Morehen and Sara were, presumably, fucking happily somewhere away from New London; faced with the prospect of pissing off his team with pointless assignments or wrestling investigators from the overworked pool, Toreth had taken the third, easier route of deciding sabs would probably take the New Year off, too, and left a bare minimum of surveillance in place.

As a result, he half expected a sudden, significant break in the case, for which Sara would probably never forgive him. However, all was quiet. Whether or not he was enjoying his New Year's Day overtime, B-C was faithfully filing reports on his watch of Richardson, and his routine suggested nothing sinister. Meanwhile, the storage unit remained unapproached.

Nagra had submitted a disgruntled update listing the cases from all over the department in which she'd been assigned interrogations. He almost sent back a note telling her not to bother informing him in future, but on reflection he sent back a "well done" and a promise of an overtime bonus. It would do her good to blow off steam, and he didn't want her being poached in his absence by some senior para offering a lure of more exciting casework.

Then he opened the list of unassigned new cases at I&I, just in case he was missing something exceptionally prestigious. He could always send Nagra to take it on his behalf, and then he'd have a happier junior, plus a ready-made excuse to leave if he needed one. After a minute, though, he realized he wasn't alone in the living room. Valeria had crept in, and she was waiting a couple of meters away, in silence, watching him work.

Finally, when it became clear that ignoring her would have no effect at all, he looked up. "What?"

That seemed to be an invitation, because she came over and knelt by the chair. "Are you investigating again?"

"No, not really. No one's being bad out there. They're all on holiday for New Year. Or at least I hope so."

"Oh." There was a thoughtful pause, then she added, "Can I ask you something?"

Knowing the rest of her family? "I'm sure you can."

She didn't say anything, just stared up at him with the same frown she'd worn at the dinner table last night.

"Well?" Toreth said. "What is it?"

The frown vanished and she sat back on her heels. "Do you think my mum and dad might get back together?"

Toreth closed the hand screen and stared at her. "How the f—hell would I know that?"

"Um." She shrugged. "Auntie Dilly was talking to Aunt Jen, about you and Uncle Keir. Not today—on my birthday. I just sort of heard them."

"Were you listening behind a door?"

"And," she continued unblushingly, "she said you broke up with Uncle Keir. But then you got back together, didn't you?"

Toreth clenched one fist against his thigh, very tightly, and imagined it was around Dillian's throat. He smiled and said, "That's right."

"So. I thought you might have an idea about that. If Mum and Dad will, too."

Tempting as telling Valeria to fuck off and leave him alone might be, it was too early to be thrown out of the house. "I have no idea at all."

"I asked Auntie Dilly and Aunt Jen, and they said they didn't know, either. But Mum goes to visit him a lot, you see. Not just to take me there. And she talks about him more. And she's never said anything really mean about him," Valeria added, sounding hopeful. "Not like some people's parents talk about each other."

Clearly, she wasn't going away without an answer. "Well, then. Maybe they will, yeah. Depends on why they broke up in the first place, I suppose."

"I don't know. I don't remember. I was only little."

Somehow, it was hard to imagine either Philly or Tarin running around having passionate affairs. In fact, if Toreth had to guess anything, he'd point his finger at Kate, who certainly wouldn't have liked Philly's attack of good sense about avoiding involvement with resisters. In which case, Valeria might well be right about them getting along better, now that Kate was out of the way. In fact, assuming that Philly had acted purely in self-preservation when she left her husband, she might be perfectly happy to jump back in bed with Tarin now. At least once there was no danger of his skin coming off in her hands.

And if he kept away from resisters in future. That made Toreth's covert mission for the holiday positively altruistic. He'd have to remember the angle if Warrick caught him.

❖ ❖ ❖

The object of all the curiosity and anticipation arrived around eleven, in a car with Philly. Toreth had been expecting a wheelchair, but Tarin walked into the house by himself, with the aid of two sticks. It took him long enough to make the short journey from car to door that Valeria had summoned everyone to the door. Dillian and Warrick both embraced their half brother with gentle enthusiasm.

Obviously someone had let Tarin know that Toreth would be there, because he greeted him without surprise, and with a curt nod.

"Toreth," he said.

Toreth nodded back. "Marriot." Then, so Warrick could have no possible complaint (or reason to watch him too closely around Tarin), he said, "You're looking well. Better than I expected."

"Thanks," Tarin said with artificial politeness. "It's good to be out of that place, even for a day."

Toreth had checked Tarin's security file surreptitiously on occasion, to make sure no one else was taking an interest, so the changes in his appearance weren't unexpected. Toreth kept studying him as the party went into the house and through to the living room, though, curious to see in the flesh what he'd only seen on a screen.

His new skin, unwrinkled and undamaged by sun and weather, made Tarin look younger than when Toreth had first met him. Damage to cartilage and, in places, bone, had been repaired as well as modern medicine could manage, but even that had its reconstructive limits. The change to Tarin's appearance had been large enough that it had required updates and a special note on his file. Altogether, it made him look oddly more like a close relative of Tarin than Tarin himself.

Philly was settling Tarin into a chair encased in an antiseptic white shrink-on cover provided by the rehab facility. "Could you get a drink, Val?" she said, and it took Toreth a moment to realize she was talking to Valeria.

"I put a carafe of water in the fridge," Jen said.

"Okay," Valeria said.

"How are you feeling?" Philly asked Tarin as soon as her daughter had gone. "Do you need to rest?"

"No," Tarin said. He sounded irritable, like it was a question he'd heard far too often.

"If you do need to, I'll make sure Val doesn't worry," she said.

"I'm absolutely fine. I've done nothing today except sit in the car."

There was an awkward pause, everyone exchanging glances while Tarin shifted in the chair, clearly trying to get comfortable. Toreth retreated to the window and left the others to it. A whole day of fussing and stilted conversations seemed even less enticing than the chilly winter's day outside. Toreth would probably have more fun joining Nagra on level D.

Soon Valeria came back in, carrying the water and a glass. "Are we opening the presents before lunch, Dad?" she asked when she'd set it down.

Philly looked at Dillian, but Tarin said, "Of course. Just like always."

As before, Valeria passed out the presents. Luckily, the slightly uncomfortable sense of déjà vu was overshadowed by the anticipation of Warrick opening his gift from Toreth.

The package was rather larger than anything Toreth had given him before. That meant there was no chance of opening it discreetly, and the well-hidden but unmistakable apprehension on Warrick's face as he took the parcel from Valeria produced the first payoff.

Toreth hadn't planned to bother with a stopgap present—Warrick would have no trouble believing Toreth had simply forgotten—but Sara had suggested the gift. She'd thought the whole idea was hilarious, and now Toreth had to admit she was right. Paper finally, reluctantly, unsealed and folded back, Warrick stared at the contents, clearly utterly speechless. Toreth sat and enjoyed the novel sight.

Finally Warrick said, "Sheets?"

"And pillowcases," Toreth said blandly, although he had to swallow down a laugh at Warrick's expression. "Matching."

Warrick ran his fingers over the natural-grown, and stupidly expensive, cotton fabric, and Toreth wondered if he were checking for embarrassing surprises hidden inside. "Well. Thank you."

"I'm glad you like them. I remembered you said the old ones were wearing thin. Probably my fault, so replacing them was the least I could do."

Dillian cleared her throat. "Who's next, Val?"

As they finished the presents, Warrick kept looking between the sheets and Toreth, as though trying to work out the hidden catch. Toreth resolved there'd be no explanations, not when a lack of them had an excellent chance of keeping Warrick entertainingly off-balance.

Getting time alone with Tarin proved more difficult than Toreth had hoped. He began to suspect Warrick was deliberately keeping them apart. He couldn't ask outright if it was the case without tipping Warrick off, but it seemed likely. Toreth kept himself in the background, quiet and unobtrusive, volunteering to help with this and that until finally the gaggle of other people in the house claimed Warrick's attention. Then Toreth went looking for the only reason he'd come to Jen's house for New Year at all.

He found Tarin outside, walking slowly around the small garden at the back of the house. Toreth had never lived anywhere with a private garden; this one seemed like a miniaturized park, squeezing in as many beds and trellises as possible. Most of the beds were bare, with a few growing boring plants with plain green leaves. Some of them looked rather like cabbages, not an aesthetic plus in Toreth's book. The only color came from patches of red or yellow stems. The whole place was fussy, and a lot of work for not much of a result. At least not in midwinter.

Right now, though, the trellises were useful, as Toreth hung back considering how to approach Tarin. Partly it depended on what he knew. Hopefully, nothing. No one should know Toreth's name was connected to the case, unless they'd spoken directly to one of the interrogated prisoners. Philly had always seemed like a sensible woman, and Toreth hoped she had the intelligence to stay away from people convicted of political crimes. Of course, long experience told him that intelligence in other areas wasn't always enough to keep people away from political stupidity.

Toreth checked over his shoulder to make sure no one else had come in search of the invalid. Then he waited until Tarin was out of sight of the house, so someone could plausibly run into him without expecting it, and walked around the side of a little shelter entirely covered by leafless stems incongruously thick with small yellow flowers.

"Oh, Marriot."

Tarin was looking up at an evergreen tree, where a couple of small brown birds were hopping from branch to branch. He glanced at Toreth, but didn't say anything.

"I wasn't expecting to see you out here," Toreth said.

Tarin looked away. "I'm supposed to exercise. Gently, anyway. I'm still getting used to walking. New ankles."

"After all this time?"

"The first grafts didn't take. They delayed the second attempt."

"Sounds like fun. Isn't a garden an infection risk, though?" Toreth still harbored a faint hope some late-breaking medical emergency could solve this problem forever.

"Not particularly. Do you know what the biggest single source of infection is?"

"Other people?" Toreth guessed.

Tarin nodded. "The medics didn't really want me to come here. But I couldn't miss New Year."

Toreth had a sudden urge to laugh. Tarin's forced politeness was as unconvincing as Toreth's own attempt to sound interested in the man's medical mishaps. Better to get this conversation over with, since someone could come looking for Tarin at any moment. This was as good a place as any; this corner of the garden was hidden by trees, fences, and the small shelter, not directly overlooked by any of the neighboring houses.

"I wanted to talk to you, alone," Tarin said.

The words were so exactly what Toreth had meant to say himself that they confused him for a moment. "Me?"

"Yes. There's something I need to know. About what happened after my accident."

"You mean the Department of Transport investigation? That was nothing to do with us."

"But the arrests later—my friends. That was I&I, wasn't it?" Tarin turned painfully, facing him. "Please. I need you to be honest."

What fucking idiot—"Who told you there'd been arrests?"

"I worked it out myself. I've had a lot of time to think. There were people I expected to see, visitors who didn't come. Once I could use a comm again, there were a lot of missing contact details which someone had seen fit to erase, and blocked names. It wasn't hard to guess what must've happened. I badgered Philly until she told me people we knew had been taken in."

"So if you know all that, what do you need me to tell you?"

"Why I wasn't one of them. Why I still haven't been arrested. Philly let slip by accident that you might have had something to do with my name not coming out."

Toreth cursed under his breath. Had she guessed, or had Warrick, for some stupid reason, told her?

"But she won't tell me anything more," Tarin continued. "Why the arrests happened, whether my accident was connected. Which is . . . I appreciate she wants to protect me, but it isn't any less stressful not knowing. I realize it doesn't mean anything to you, but I worry about Val and Philly. If they're safe."

"They are," Toreth said, and watched Tarin's new face light up with instant relief.

"So, will you tell me what happened? I don't remember anything, from the morning of the accident until I eventually woke up in hospital."

"No, I won't. Except—okay, I will say this." Tarin had given him the perfect opening to deliver his message. Toreth leaned closer and lowered his voice. "The main reason you're here right now is luck."

"I know." Tarin rubbed the skin below his ear, like it itched but he was trying not to scratch. "The medics explained how close I came to dying."

"I'm not talking about the crash. I don't know anything about that. You're *lucky* that when Int-Sec was clearing up after the revolt, I had enough favors to pull in to get your name taken off the arrest list—because they knew your name, don't have any doubt about that. Most people who dig themselves a hole as deep as you did don't get a second chance. And if there's a next time, if you make yourself into a target again, I won't be able to do anything. Actually, I won't even try to, because if you can't take this as a warning, then you're too fucking stupid to help."

In fact, Toreth would happily help arrange the next accident himself, and make sure it went exactly according to plan.

91

Tarin's eyes narrowed, putting wrinkles in his baby skin, then he nodded slowly. "I did say I wanted you to be honest. And thank you for protecting us. I am grateful." The words had a surprising amount of sincerity.

Toreth took a step back. "I don't give a fuck. Anything I've done, I did for Warrick," he added, which was partially true. "No one needs to be related to a convicted resister."

"Or to be living with the brother of one?"

Toreth shrugged. "I won't deny I had an interest in it, too. Just not as much of an interest as you—or Philly and Valeria."

"I understand," Tarin said.

"Good. I really hope you do." Toreth shivered suddenly and looked around the garden. The sunshine gave some warmth, but in the shade the damp winter wind made itself felt. "Enjoy your exercise."

On the way back into the house, Toreth met Valeria.

"I'm looking for Dad," she said.

"Outside," Toreth said, and went past her and into the house before she could say anything else.

He hesitated in the hallway. With his mission to warn Tarin against any future stupidity accomplished, the house now felt abruptly claustrophobic. He'd always planned to leave early, but any more time spent here making polite conversation sounded like a re-education sentence. Even with Sara away fucking, home turf felt like a far more attractive option.

Toreth found Warrick in the kitchen, breaking up a head of garlic. A large joint of meat sat in a roasting tray, already covered in herbs. The air smelled sharply of fresh citrus, with the bitter oily undertone of grated peel.

"I had a call from work," Toreth said. "Sorry—crime didn't stop for the holidays after all."

"Your corporate sabotage case?" Warrick asked, to Toreth's surprise.

"That's right. Looks like there might be an arrest, so Tillotson won't take 'sorry, Warrick's cooking something special' as an excuse."

Warrick frowned, as though he guessed there was something more to it, but he nodded and started slicing again. "Well, thank you for the time you could spare. You'll be calling an I&I car or a taxi, since it's a case?"

Did Warrick guess he was lying? Well, as long as he was willing to let it slide, why care? "Yeah, I will."

Chapter Twelve

❖

Warrick couldn't deny, even to himself, that the atmosphere at the house relaxed after Toreth's departure. As he'd carved the roast lamb the evening before, he'd heard the difference in the voices chatting around the table. Asher had gone home, but Cele had stayed with Dillian, and she'd been in good form, telling outrageous stories barely on the edge of respectable enough for Valeria's young ears. Even Philly had unwound.

He felt almost guilty, waking up the next morning with an undeniable relief that Toreth wouldn't be there. No peacekeeping required. No worries about what might be said by whom. Three more days of hopefully relaxing holiday time before he had to go back to the stresses of SimTech.

Although it was early, Valeria appeared in the kitchen as soon as he started making noise in there, still wearing her pyjamas. Pancakes for breakfast without Toreth there seemed wrong, so he suggested churros and chocolate as a surprise for everyone. Hot oil for cooking meant that supervision was needed, but she assisted with enthusiasm.

"Aunt Jen never makes these," she said, as she broke pieces of chocolate into a bowl. Warrick had brought plenty of extra with him, beyond what Jen had requested for the profiteroles.

"No?" Warrick poured the boiling water into the flour and picked up a wooden spoon. Years of use had worn one edge of its bowl flat. Probably one of the spoons he'd used with Jen at the same age Valeria was now. "Actually, I don't remember her making churros with Dilly and me, either. Maybe she doesn't know how."

Valeria shook her head. "Aunt Jen knows how to make everything."

He smiled. "True. Maybe she doesn't trust either of us with the oil, then. We'd better be careful."

Warrick found Jen's baking dispenser, filled it with dough, and selected the star-shaped nozzle. Valeria stood ready with a pair of scissors and snipped off the lengths of churros. They cooked batches of three, Warrick scooping them out so

93

that Valeria could roll them in cinnamon sugar before putting them in the oven to keep warm.

They'd moved on to making the hot chocolate when Valeria said, "Uncle Keir, have you ever done something bad by accident, when you didn't know it was a bad thing to do?"

"I'm sure I have," Warrick said. "Everyone makes mistakes like that. It's okay, as long as you say sorry and don't do whatever it was again."

She nodded. "What if you can't say sorry because the person isn't around anymore?"

"Then you just have to learn from the mistake and do better next time. What are you thinking about?" Something to do with Kate?

She didn't answer right away. Warrick waited patiently until she said, "When Dad was in the accident, and then Uncle Val investigated it and Auntie Dilly was angry with him..."

Probably not Kate, then, thank God. "Yes?"

"Uncle Val took me to school. Do you remember?"

"Yes, I do."

"In the car on the way I told him something that Mr. McVade said in our Citizenship lessons, and Uncle Val said it was wrong and he was teaching us to ask questions we shouldn't."

Warrick's stomach tightened. His first instinct was to try to shut the topic down. But after the conversation with Jen, perhaps he should try to explain. "Well, some things can be dangerous to ask questions about. Especially if you learned about them in Citizenship."

"Uncle Val went to talk to Mr. McVade. Everyone in the class saw him. And then not the next week but the week after that, on Monday, Mr. McVade wasn't there. We had a new Citizenship teacher. And none of the other teachers said anything about it, but then Tina told me that her dad said he'd been arrested. Tina's dad asked her all kinds of stuff about Mr. McVade, what he'd said to her and if he'd ever done anything to her that he shouldn't."

"I see." Monday. Even after all these months, he remembered the day. When I&I had picked up Tarin's resister contacts, and Jen had called him in a panic, and Warrick had told her to sit tight, do nothing. Warn no one. Let the Administration arrest Tar's friends to protect him and his family.

Valeria looked up at him. "Was it my fault? Did it happen because of what I said to Uncle Val?"

"No," Warrick said firmly. "It had nothing to do with you."

"But Uncle Val was talking at dinner about Dad's friends being arrested. I didn't mean to get anyone in trouble."

"You didn't." Warrick put the dispenser on the counter. "The Administration is always watching for people who...it thinks might be dangerous. Who might want to cause trouble. Some of your dad's friends were people like that."

"People who misbehave?" she queried.

"Yes." She said the phrase as though it meant something significant, and he wondered if that had come from the Citizenship lessons. "Or at least the Administration thought so."

"Okay." She didn't sound convinced. "Was it Uncle Val who arrested Mr. McVade?"

What the hell had Toreth been saying to her? "I don't think so." After all, it was statistically unlikely that Toreth had carried out that particular arrest, and the half-lie seemed like the easiest escape. "But *if* he did, it was because he was told to do it. Listen, Val, if Toreth wanted to arrest your teacher because of something you said, he would've done it that day in the school. He wouldn't have waited for a week." Was that reassuring? Probably not. What he didn't know about explaining potentially lethal political crimes in an age-appropriate fashion felt as though it would fill a library.

"And what about Dad?" she asked anxiously. "Now that he's getting better, are they going to take him away, too?"

"Absolutely not. I promise." At least not as long as Tarin gave up his political views and accepted the Administration, which for Tar was cutting out a fundamental part of his personality. "Did you ever talk to your mother about this?"

"No." Valeria shook her head. "No. She was already really stressed about Dad. Granny always said you shouldn't tell people things if it would upset them."

Yes, she probably had. "If you're still worried, then you should talk to her. I'm sure she'd rather you did."

"But I don't want her to be angry with Uncle Val."

That ship, if it were leaving the harbor at all, had sailed a long time ago. Philly was good at hiding her emotions, though. "Don't worry about Uncle Val. He'll cope."

She nodded pensively. "I suppose lots of people get angry at him, when he has to arrest someone. That's not very nice, is it? Having people hate you just because of your job?"

"No, it isn't." Although if Toreth cared at all, it would only be because it might limit his pool of available sexual partners. "So does that mean you definitely don't want to be a para-investigator anymore?"

"No! I told you before, I'm going to be a research medic."

"Of course, I forgot. Sorry." He crouched down and hugged her. She squeezed back enthusiastically. "Okay?"

He felt her nod. "Yes."

"And you'll talk to your mother if you're still worried about anything?"

"I will, I promise."

"Good girl." He stood up, and she smiled up at him, apparently far more reassured by the conversation than she might one day realize she should have been.

Valeria picked up the next slab of chocolate and started to unwrap it. She looked so much like Dilly at the same age—surprising, really, when they shared only Kate in common in their family tree. It was like stepping into a sim recreation of their innocent—ignorant—childhood in this house. Maybe the resemblance was why he suddenly felt so protective of Valeria, and so angry at the idea of her being upset by Toreth's careless pronouncements of Administration leniency. But tempting as it might be to relieve some of the tension, it would be pointless to call Toreth and demand to know why the hell he'd talked about the arrests in front of Valeria. Whatever the reason, he'd no more care about distressing Valeria than about arresting Tarin's friends in the first place.

Maybe Toreth had done it out of boredom, or to annoy Dillian, or simply because the comment had occurred to him. Maybe, with his own special brand of subtlety, Toreth had been dropping a hint to those around the table accustomed to talking openly in Kate's house. With Kate's disappearance, they'd lost the dubious protection of being useful to Citizen Surveillance. Warrick remembered an evening on the rooftop garden of his old building, when he'd expressed far milder anti-Administration sentiment than he'd heard in other places, and Toreth's reaction to it. Defensive anger and fear. Toreth understood the potential consequences to a degree that probably no one else of Warrick's acquaintance could. Other people heard stories about the horrors of I&I; Toreth saw them—inflicted them—every day.

In a way, perhaps, he should be grateful rather than angry. It was a warning to be careful. And a reminder, again, of the fragility of the safety Toreth had bought through his bargain with Citizen Surveillance.

"Uncle Keir?" Valeria said, and he realized how long he'd been standing there, absorbed in thought. Valeria had snapped the last squares and was looking at him with expectation and a touch of worry.

He smiled. "Sorry. Miles away. Yes, let's finish the hot chocolate. Everyone else will be down soon."

Tarin was supposedly asleep, and everyone else had gone out for the afternoon—Valeria's trip to feed the ducks, although Philly had put her foot down over Tarin joining them. The suddenly quiet house offered Warrick the chance to look through some of the ongoing scan analysis from SimTech. He'd taken a break to make tea when he noticed that the door to Kate's office stood ajar. He walked down the hallway as quietly as he could, and looked inside through the gap.

Tarin was in there, searching through one of the drawers in the tall storage unit. Whatever he was looking for must be small, because he searched each drawer thoroughly before moving on to the next.

Everything in Kate's office had been bought for it, Warrick realized. He'd never noticed before. Around the house were various pieces of furniture that might've fitted in here—a set of drawers in the dining room that had belonged to one of Kate's grandmothers, a desk used by his father that had passed from Warrick to Dilly and was now in the corner of Valeria's room—but Kate had obviously preferred things without attached memories. Thirty-odd years out of date, now, but still a practical, unfussy matching set.

Warrick watched for another minute or so, then went to make the tea.

When he returned with two mugs, Tarin was sitting at the desk, leafing through the contents of a paper file.

"Tea?" Warrick said, and Tarin jumped and looked around.

"Warn a bloke, can't you?" He closed the file and laid it on the desk. "The facility will be calling, wanting to know what happened to my heart."

"Sorry. I thought you were resting?" Warrick asked.

"Obviously not. I thought you'd gone with the others."

"Obviously not." Warrick grinned. "To tell the truth, Philly asked me if I'd stay behind and pretend I needed to work, or prepare something for dinner, or some other unconvincing excuse."

"In case I had a sudden medical crisis that the monitors weren't capable of detecting?" Tarin shook his head.

"They're annoying because they care. Like corporate security, except you don't have to pay their wages."

Tarin laughed. "True, true. I suppose it must get tiresome having everywhere you go assessed for suitability." He held out his hand, and Warrick passed over the tea.

"It isn't so bad. I'm not actually a very high risk. Most entertainment complexes have an independent rating, there are corporate grade taxis—after a while, it's all second nature." Warrick sipped his tea, still too hot for a real mouthful. "And I did actually need to do some work, by the way, so I didn't mind staying."

It was the first time they'd been alone together since…waiting for Dilly at the café in the park, probably. The weight of imagined conversations weighed down Warrick's mind. If he asked the obvious question, it could open a door leading to God only knew where. But he was curious.

"What are you looking for?" Warrick asked.

"I was just wondering if there was anything around, any kind of clue about what happened to Mother. Stupid, really. I'm sure you've already looked. You've had plenty of time."

"No, I haven't been in here. Not since I checked her system that day."

"Oh, right." Tarin blew across his tea to cool it. Then he put the mug down with a decisive bump. "I talked to your—to Toreth yesterday. Out in the garden."

"What about?" Warrick asked in alarm.

"I thought he might be able to answer some questions I had about my accident. He said he couldn't. He did tell me not to do anything stupid in the future. I had the feeling that's why he was out there—looking for me. To warn me to stay out of trouble. And you know, he actually sounded worried. Can't blame him, I suppose. It must be a new experience for him, being associated even distantly with people who've done things that could get them arrested."

Not as new as all that. Then something else occurred. Surely Toreth wouldn't... "Did you ask him about Kate?"

"No. I assumed if he knew anything, if he hadn't told you then he'd have no reason to tell me." Tarin frowned. "Does he know where she is?"

"I don't think so," Warrick said.

"And I assume there's nothing in your letters. Philly said you'd had a couple, like Val." Tarin shook his head. "I've had a lot of time to think about what happened to her, and...well. I haven't come up with anything I liked."

Warrick looked around the office. So innocuous, just somewhere for a self-employed financial consultant to work, but without the full security sweep he didn't want to risk, how could they know for sure?

"Why don't we go somewhere else?" Warrick said.

He thought Tarin might ask him why, but after a moment he nodded. "All right. I was thinking about another stroll around the garden, anyway."

"Are you sure? Philly said—"

"My memory might not be a hundred percent yet, but I can remember what the doctors said would be safe."

As they stepped outside, Warrick wondered if Toreth had had the same idea about the house being unsecure, and that was why he'd spoken to Tarin outside. More likely he'd wanted to keep it away from Warrick himself. Would Kate have installed official surveillance beyond ordinary house security? Too risky for her cover, hopefully.

Compared to summer the garden looked bare, although Jen's carefully tended winter vegetables—cabbages in shades of green, cheerful kale, faded tops of root vegetables—kept it looking alive and welcoming. Tarin stopped in front of the gazebo covered with winter jasmine that almost glowed. Planted by Warrick's parents to mark their wedding, it had been one of the stories that Warrick had grown up hearing. A cutting brought back by Leo from their brief honeymoon, smuggled out of some public garden. Had that been true? Had there even been a real honeymoon, or just an opportunity for two agents to debrief and plan how the next stage of the operation should proceed?

In his memory, the flowers were beautifully scented and a vivid red-orange, but somewhere over the years the plant had lost the engineered-in traits. Warrick leaned closer to sniff a yellow bloom, but caught nothing.

Tarin sat down on the bench inside the gazebo. Warrick sat beside him.

"You can't imagine how much I hate to say it, but Toreth's right," Tarin said. "I should stay the hell away from anything dangerous. He said Int-Sec had my name on their arrest list, so I'd put everyone else at risk by being involved in any way. But—" He shook his head. "It still feels like surrendering to everything I've hated all this time."

"I understand," Warrick said. "But yes, he is right."

"Oh, don't worry. Philly's already being a one-woman security force, making sure I don't take any chances, with anything. And she's put herself at risk, I know that, sticking by me since the accident and . . . everything. I hope she realizes how much I appreciate it. We fought about the danger so much after Val was born. That's why we separated. Back then, Philly insisted that we had an information leak." Tarin paused and looked directly at him. "Keir, if you don't want to hear any of this, stop me."

"Don't worry about it," Warrick said. "I've heard less savory things in SimTech security briefings."

"Ah, but the Administration lets the corporations get away with it. The rest of us aren't so lucky." Tarin smiled. "Sorry, probably not a good tangent to head off after."

"Jen wouldn't be the only unhappy one if they came back now to find you'd punched me, true. I don't think your doctors would like it, either."

Tarin laughed. "No, I don't think they would. I'd probably miss, anyway. The hand grafts were some of the hardest to get used to."

They'd stepped back from the conversation. Maybe Tarin was having second thoughts about trusting him. "Go on," Warrick said. "Philly thought information was leaking?"

Tarin hesitated for a few seconds, but then he said, "Yes. And I did a full security screen—a differentiated information distribution program, targeting different parts of the network."

He paused, and Warrick said, "You gave out test information to specific parts of the network, and saw if any of it leaked. A binary chop?"

"Right," Tarin said. "I suppose you would know about it."

"Sadly, we've had to do it at SimTech, to pin down someone who was selling information. Did you find anything?"

"No. If anything had come back, I would've drilled down, but it didn't. I thought we were leakproof. Or maybe I just wanted to think I did, as it were, because I never could quite shake the worry. Something would happen, and I'd wonder if maybe Philly was right after all. I tested again, over the years, too; it was part of our standard process. The funny thing was, until recently I never thought that there was someone I didn't check. Never even crossed my mind that I should."

He looked sideways at Warrick.

"Really? Who?"

Tarin smiled slightly, making tiny, precise creases in his skin. "You're good, you know? You should take this up. You know something about it, don't you? Or you suspect. Why else suggest that Mother's office wouldn't be a safe place to talk?"

"Well, if she was arrested—"

"Ah, but that's it, isn't it?" Tarin interrupted eagerly. "Why *was* she arrested? In the only few weeks in this messed-up period of history when people could actually get away with doing what we did, why was *she,* out of all of us, picked up? We never even found out by whom—I didn't believe it was the Service, not from the moment they took her."

Of all the outcomes of the conversation, this one had never occurred to him—that Tarin might get there first, on his own, and take all the control out of Warrick's hands. "You think Mother was the informer?" Warrick said.

"I do. It's the only thing that makes sense, and believe me, I've tried harder than you can imagine to think of ways that it doesn't. Someone found out she'd betrayed us, and either they took her—" He grimaced. "—in which case I can't not think that she's probably dead, or the people she was reporting to found out she was about to be exposed and they pretended to have her arrested to get her away."

He'd hit so frighteningly close to the truth that it took Warrick a moment to come up with a suitable neutral-sounding answer. "That's all very plausible, yes."

Tarin nodded. "And like I said, you aren't surprised."

"No. No, I'm not." Warrick took a deep breath. "I'm so sorry, Tar. I should've said something."

"Oh, I don't blame you. I'm sure you thought I would've blown my top, told you you were full of it, and run off to tell her. Maybe I would've, too, before I had so much time to think it all through and work it out for myself." Tarin shook his head. "I just want to ask her *why*? How could she do it, after what happened to my stepdad? Did they have some kind of hold over her? Did they threaten the rest of us? Did she make a deal?"

"I never talked to her about it," Warrick said, which was true enough. "I found some things on her system that made me suspect, that's all."

"Oh, right—when you looked at it after the revolt? So you didn't know for long either, then. What was on the system?"

Better for Tarin to think that Warrick had only found out last year than to know exactly how long Kate had betrayed him. (How long Warrick had kept her manipulation secret, his conscience whispered.) "I don't think it would be a good idea to say."

After a moment, Tarin sighed. "You're probably right. After all, I'm out of all that for good, now. I have to be. But, Keir, what the hell am I going to do if she

100

comes back? All right, I can step away from doing anything 'criminal,' but she knows so many people. Do I try to warn them, even if they think I'm compromised and they damn well ought to know better than to listen to a word I say? Do I tell *her* that I know? Do I stop her from seeing Val, somehow? I'd have to warn Philly, at least, give her the chance to take Val away. It makes me sick just thinking about it."

"I don't have any answers," Warrick said. And he didn't, because Tarin had put his finger right on the heart of the dilemma. How could any of them make plans to stay safe without knowing if Kate would return? "We'll just have to see what happens."

Tarin didn't seem to hear him. "I had been thinking about talking to Philly. Not about Mother, don't worry. About her and me. Whether our situation's going to change. Philly and I never finalized the separation, you know. I was always expecting to hear from her about it, but no. She said she wanted to keep her distance, in case the network was exposed, but she never did the one thing that really would draw a line between us. And I suppose that means something."

"I'm sure it'd make Valeria happy."

"Yes, it would." Tarin sighed. "But how can I even suggest living together again to poor old Philly now, with everything hanging over us? Especially when she doesn't know the full story."

"I'm sorry," he said, the words already out before he thought how they sounded.

Tarin looked at him in surprise. "Sorry, why? None of it's your fault."

More than you think. And Warrick would have to find some way to put it right. "I just meant...I'm sorry we're all stuck in this mess."

"Oh, yes, I see." Tarin nodded, and reached out to flick a couple of dead flowers from the jasmine. "In a funny way I feel like I've been protected from it all, in that hospital. Out here everything feels so vulnerable."

Chapter Thirteen

Toreth sat on the brand-new bed and examined the ropes he'd bought and cut to length: plain, bright white cotton, their ends wrapped with thread to stop them from fraying. Then he spent five minutes practicing the knots until he was certain he'd got them right. Something that would tighten when tugged on, but only to a point—not so far it would turn into a tourniquet.

Stage one completed, he sat against the beautiful headboard, getting the angle right. He touched his shoulders, then moved his hands away from his body until he reached a comfortable spread. He tucked his fingers behind the sinuous narrow posts and waited. After a couple of minutes, he adjusted the position again. Planning. That was the key. Plan everything out to start with, and things would be so much better. Important at work, too, but sex was easier. To start with, Warrick never turned up dosed to the eyeballs on resistance pharma.

When he'd found the angle, he tied one end of each rope securely to the chosen posts, and the other into a loop. Standing up, he surveyed the results. Perfect. And still time for a shower and a snack before Warrick could possibly get back from Jen's house.

❖ ❖ ❖

Clean and fed, Toreth still had time to kill, so he fished out his screen and continued reading a terrible crime novel he'd started months earlier: *Three Voices from Beyond* by some woman who claimed to be called Colette Clousteau. It made Toreth remember why he'd stopped reading mysteries before. The other problem was that he kept leaving it for so long he forgot what had happened and had to start again. It didn't help that the plot made no sense, although at least that meant he wouldn't guess who'd done it before he'd got his money's worth.

Not that he'd actually paid for it—it had been an unexpected birthday present from Sara. Probably regifting an unwanted present from her mother, who Sara

102

claimed had the world's largest collection of completely crap mysteries. Toreth flicked to chapter six, where the irritating detective was receiving yet another unhelpful message from the dead, channeled by her equally annoying blind male sidekick. Apparently the killer was someone who hated the victim. If that was the most help the dead could be, Toreth didn't think he was missing out on much by getting his own messages via O'Reilly and her lab.

Once he reached a part he didn't remember reading before he began to get a little more involved. It was almost a surprise when the door to the flat opened.

"Warrick?" Toreth called as he closed the screen and threw it over to land neatly on the pile of his clothes. Chapter eight, he told himself, knowing full well he would forget what had happened by the time he opened it again.

"Yes?" Warrick sounded surprised.

Toreth slipped his hands through the loops and settled his shoulders into position. One knee up, one leg straight on the bed. He could see his reflection in the long mirror opposite, the bondage porn-perfect tied hands against the polished wood, the spotless rope elaborately knotted and making a contrast with his skin. Positively mouthwatering, if he did say so himself. He shook his head back, to mess his hair.

He could see the smooth curves of the headboard behind him as well, of course. That looked okay, too, but while Toreth was pretty fucking confident Warrick would like the body in his bed, the new bed itself was less of a sure-fire sell.

"Up here," Toreth called.

Warrick's footsteps sounded on the stairs, then along the hall. "I thought you might be at work. I know it's Sunday, but if the case was—"

Silence. Warrick stood in the doorway, mouth actually hanging open, staring. Toreth wondered if he were even breathing.

He hadn't tightened the ropes yet. If Warrick was about to blow a fuse over the new bed, Toreth could still slip free and argue from a position of more dignity. Didn't look like that would be necessary, though.

"Happy New Year," Toreth said, breaking the silence.

"Oh, God. God, it's . . . " Warrick crossed the room slowly, moving around the bed to end up standing beside it. "You remembered."

And that was it. The bed was a hit. Toreth let the ropes take the weight of his arms and the knots tightened beautifully, like a magic trick. "I remember some things, sometimes. Especially confessions."

For once the oblique reference to I&I didn't draw any kind of reaction. Not annoyance or disgust—Warrick was simply staring at him, his eyes flickering as his gaze moved over Toreth's body. The appreciation, the heat and hunger in his expression, felt like sunshine.

"Come on," Toreth said. "It'll be tomorrow before long and then I really will have to go to work."

Warrick smiled, still looking a little glazed, then he started to loosen his tie. "It was months ago."

"So? I'd hardly start replacing beds if you hadn't mentioned the idea. Not when you're so fucking anal about furniture."

"I am nothing of the kind," Warrick said without the slightest hint of offense as he stripped rapidly.

"Bollocks. No feet on the table, no glasses on the table without coasters, no eating in bed..."

"Do you enjoy having crumbs stuck to your backside so much?"

"Not the point." Toreth wasn't really listening to himself. The familiar argument produced itself while he watched Warrick's body appearing. That was also familiar, of course, but somehow he never got bored of seeing it. "The point is, when a scratch a couple of millimeters long on the mantelpiece means a major bloody incident investigation—"

"Shut up." Now completely naked, Warrick leaned over the bed and placed his fingers over Toreth's mouth. "Shh."

"Make me," Toreth said past the fingers.

Warrick kissed him hard, and Toreth smiled against his mouth. He didn't mind doing this every once in a while, because Warrick was ever so amenable afterwards. This had to be worth at least one semipublic fuck.

When the kiss broke off, Toreth shifted his shoulders and said, "Do you remember what else you said, when you were talking about a new bed?"

Warrick blinked. "Ah—not as such."

"Are you sure?" He twisted his hands in the ropes, and Warrick's cock leaped. "No, I bet you're still using it for wank material."

As ever, Warrick didn't blush. He did smile wryly and say, "You know me too well. As far as I recall, I said that as an optimum position, I'd like to fuck your mouth and be able to look at your wrists at the same time."

It took a few seconds before Toreth's circulatory system managed to divert some blood back up from his groin to his brain. "Ready when you are."

Warrick shook his head. "Not yet."

Had he remembered it wrong? He didn't think so. "What—"

"Shh. Keep still. Relax."

Warrick knelt beside him, his hands on the headboard, and kissed him again, slow and deep, lots of tongue. Nice. The kind of nonurgent kissing that somehow worked best with someone you'd fucked at least a couple of times before, which made it something different. Something that only happened between the two of them.

It was so different from kissing...fuck. What had her name been? He'd only picked the woman up last night. God, memory like a sieve sometimes. And the circumstances weren't helping. Too good to concentrate on the fading memory of a stranger.

Warrick kept kissing him, not touching him anywhere else. Toreth's skin felt cool, acutely aware of every air current in the room. The hairs on his arms and legs prickled, on and off, nerves firing randomly at phantom touches. He'd forgotten about the ropes on his wrists until he tried to move his arms and couldn't. Toreth tightened his grip on the smooth wood.

Come on, you bastard. Touch me.

Soft lips, hard pressure of teeth behind them, tongue in his mouth, teasing him. Really fucking good kisses, but he wanted more, needed more.

Surprise made him hit the back of his head against the headboard as Warrick's hands landed lightly on his shoulders. He gasped, taking down the air from Warrick's simultaneous laugh.

Warrick stroked down his arms to the crooks of his bent elbows, then up to his wrists, his fingers coming to rest on the ropes. They stayed there, rubbing over and around, into the palms of Toreth's hands, over his knuckles, across the posts, always slipping back to the ropes and knots.

It wasn't unpleasant—the semitickle made the muscles in his neck and shoulders twitch, which in turn had some weird autonomic nervous system synergy going on with his cock—but it made him more aware of the ropes. A part of his brain he couldn't shut up kept telling him he really preferred tying to being tied.

Still, however he felt about it, the New Year present was going over well. Warrick was breathing faster now, kisses turning sloppy and careless. Toreth turned his head away, pushed forward to find Warrick's ear.

"Fuck me. Fuck my mouth."

Warrick whimpered, his hands stilling, then he breathed, "Again."

"I want you to fuck my mouth. Let me taste you."

He felt Warrick shake his head. "Not yet."

"Warrick—"

"Not yet."

Warrick dreamed about this far more than they did it: literal dreams, and the occasional daydream, and in deliberately constructed fantasies. It meant that when it actually happened, on the few, random occasions when Toreth decided to indulge him, it never felt real.

It never felt as good as the dreams, either. Over the years they'd tried it several times. It worked best, oddly, in the Shop, where it pandered to Toreth's exhibitionist streak, as well as providing Warrick with the satisfaction of showing Toreth off. In private the dynamics were off, out of kilter. Toreth wouldn't offer the gift if he objected—he was far too selfish and far too much of a hedonist, and Warrick knew it. However, Warrick also knew Toreth didn't really enjoy it, not for its own sake. The sex, yes, always, whenever and wherever. The restraint, no.

Warrick wished Toreth could understand it, just once. Not because Warrick wanted to do this often, but because it was so unbelievably good when Toreth did it to him that he wanted to share it.

This is how you make me feel. This is why you're an obsession for me. This is why I could never give you up, let you go.

Perhaps there would even be some reassurance in it for Toreth.

Not that Warrick wasn't enjoying what he had. The contrast of the ropes and smooth skin against his fingertips was almost enough to drive him insane. He could imagine how good it would feel to be tied like this. Tied and taken. Begging, being controlled. No doubt, before too long, their positions would be reversed. Like the cabinet, the new headboard would always be there, ready for the game.

At night, he thought, I'll be able to reach up and touch it.

Awareness of the endless future possibilities rippled through him, leaving him suddenly so close to coming he had to stop moving, to close his eyes, to hold still and breathe. Toreth's mouth was only a few centimeters from his, and after a moment Warrick had to pull back even further, away from temptation. Unbelievable—ridiculous—that furniture (he reached out with his fingertips to brush the wood again) could turn him on so much.

Except it had far less to do with the new bed than with the man on it.

He opened his eyes and found Toreth watching him, squinting a little because they were still close. After a moment, Toreth smiled slightly, smugly, and closed his eyes again.

He moved to straddle Toreth's thighs, and the tip of his cock brushed Toreth's skin below his ribs. His stomach muscles twitched at the touch. Warrick ran his hands along Toreth's arms again, down and back up to his hands, to the ropes. The muscles were tensed, not pulling against the knots but because Toreth's fingers were hooked behind the bars of the bed head, holding his arms up so he didn't feel the ropes, the confinement. This was why it was wrong.

He thought about the recent scan at SimTech, how other people had fallen asleep in minutes. Through almost three hours lying on the scanner bed Toreth had stayed alert, ready to move at a moment's notice.

Warrick leaned down and kissed him again, mouthing over his lips and up to the line of his cheekbone, into his hair and back again.

"Relax," he breathed into Toreth's mouth. "Relax."

Relax? What the hell did that mean?

He *was* relaxed, Toreth thought with a twinge of irritation, tightening his grip on the bed. Having a naked man rubbing himself all over Toreth's body was about the best relaxant available outside a pharmacy.

What the bloody hell did Warrick want from him? Toreth knew Warrick was waiting for something, but Toreth had no idea what and he didn't think asking would help. He was here, he was in the bed, he was tied to the fucking thing, and he didn't have much of a clue as to what more he could do. It was all up to Warrick now.

It annoyed him a little because he hated the uncertainty of not having the scenario laid out ahead of him. Outside the game he'd got used to fucking with no plan years ago. Or almost. At least he could easily ignore the perfectly ridiculous twinges of unease it generated, the bizarre sense of danger he still sometimes felt when they were just together and when, for a moment, it was like walking on too-thin ice over deep, cold water. As long as he didn't think about it afterwards, which he never did, it was fine. The feeling would come and go, a hard, fast cramp of fear, and then he would forget it as quickly.

The game usually felt safer than that. Today he'd set up what Warrick had wanted. What, in fact, he'd described in loving detail while Toreth had been fucking him into the old mattress the delivery company had taken away on Friday afternoon. It should be perfect, except now that they were here, Warrick had promptly changed the script. Too late in the fucking day now that the ropes were tied.

No, there really *was* nothing Toreth could do to—

Then, finally, he understood. Not whatever it was about the ropes that turned Warrick on—which was probably impossible—but that the ropes didn't *matter*, that at this moment they were absolutely not the point.

Relax, Warrick had said, but what he'd meant was surrender. Everything would be fine. In fact, everything would probably be wonderful, but even if it wasn't, that wasn't Toreth's problem. Because, really, fucking wasn't so complicated it needed two people in charge. So. Relax.

If there was one person in the world Toreth ought to be able to trust to do this, or anything else, properly, it was control-freak, perfectionist Warrick, who probably couldn't force himself to do less than his best with a gun on him.

With the resolution made, it was easier to carry out than he'd expected. A lot of muscles he hadn't even noticed were tensed loosened all together. His fingers ached from holding on to the bed, although he hadn't felt it until then, and taking the weight of his arms on the soft cotton rope around his wrists was actually a relief.

Warrick had had an idea once—more fantasy than serious intent—of making a Toreth-Yes in the sim. Creating not just a shell, but an evolved expert system designed to copy him. It had never gone beyond fantasy because he acknowledged the concept was, frankly, deeply unhealthy. The corporate psychologists would not approve. But the one thing he'd most wanted to see, the one thing he would have happily spent hours working in the sim to create, was this.

Real surrender. Unspoken, implicit trust that was almost as much of a turn-on as Toreth's closed eyes, the warm skin under Warrick's hands, the mouth open to his. He drank in the sight, touching Toreth gently, randomly, not quite believing the gift.

He was about to say, "Turn over," when he remembered this was the real world, not the sim. As he started to untie the ropes from the bed, he thought Toreth might ask what he was doing, but he stayed relaxed, eyes closed, light from above catching in his lashes.

"Turn over, onto your knees."

Warrick watched as Toreth obeyed, admiring the muscles sliding under his skin, so beautifully defined it was like looking at a computer-generated image. He counted the wooden posts at a glance, and retied the ropes in the exact center of the bed. The cotton ropes, soft against his fingers, were long enough to give plenty of play. He could have Toreth like this, or on his back. Wherever he chose.

It's not real, Warrick thought. The evening can't possibly be real. Maybe this is the sim.

Touching didn't actually prove anything about reality, but he ran his hands slowly down Toreth's back. This time he didn't flinch away, didn't move at all, not even when Warrick trailed his fingertips lightly back up Toreth's sides. He simply waited, head bowed, breathing a little quickly, letting Warrick do whatever he wanted. Utterly perfect.

Now that Toreth couldn't see him, Warrick allowed himself to smile, allowed himself to feel everything without reserve.

Now, they could begin.

Chapter Fourteen

❖

Usually Toreth had no problem sleeping through Warrick's alarm and right up to his own, and anything that robbed him of the last part of his night pissed him off. He was willing to make an exception, though, for the smell of grilling bacon.

When he opened his eyes, he found himself looking up at one of the ropes, still tied around the bedpost. Toreth flicked the end, thinking about last night. It would definitely go down as one of the more memorable fucks of his life. His shoulders ached in the way they might if he'd added a new exercise into his gym routine, and maybe that was why he also felt oddly unrested, as though he hadn't slept as well as he thought. Funny. He didn't remember waking up, but there it was.

Sleeping in a different bed didn't usually do that to him. Was it something about the brand-new mattress, not yet broken in, or the smell of the new wood? Or maybe he'd had bad dreams he didn't remember. Whatever it was, he hoped it would wear off soon. It would be annoying, after spending all that money, if he had to sleep in his own bed every night just to feel rested in the morning.

He stretched and gave an experimental tug on the edge of the head of the bed. Just like last night, it was as squeak-free as promised. Good, considering how much the thing had cost.

He'd showered last night, after they'd finished playing with the new bed, so all he had to do was roll out of bed, find his uniform, and go down to the kitchen. Warrick was plating up bacon, poached eggs, and fresh tomatoes. He sprinkled chopped fresh herbs over the tomatoes and carefully examined the effect.

"Special occasion?" Toreth asked as he sat down.

"Well, I thought so," Warrick said.

Toreth laughed and flexed his shoulders. They twinged again. "I don't know what I'm going to get you next year."

"I can't imagine. Although I wouldn't say no to a repeat performance of last night." Warrick paused, then set the teapot on the table and sat down. "I hope you enjoyed it, too."

Toreth nodded. "It was interesting. A great fuck," he added when Warrick raised his eyebrows. "Fantastic."

"Well, good. I know it isn't your usual thing, but I hoped you might—yes. Find it interesting. Thank you, anyway. It was definitely much appreciated."

"It wasn't exactly a hardship." Toreth shrugged. "We don't have to wait until next New Year to do it again, if you want to."

Warrick nodded. "Perhaps. But the rest of the time, we can stick to our own specialties." He poured the tea, carefully adjusting the cups so the handles lined up parallel with the edge of the table. "After all, we work rather well together like that, don't you think?"

Toreth took a forkful of bacon and broke the perfectly runny egg yolk. "Yeah, we do."

The leisurely breakfast delayed Toreth's departure, but Sara still wasn't at her desk when he arrived at I&I. He shook his head and was about to go into his office when he noticed her coat hung up on the wall. Not late, after all.

Toreth found her in the coffee room with Kel, another couple of admins, and Chevril, going over their New Year's breaks. They looked up when he came in, then went back to their conversations. No one would be pushing for an early start the first Monday of the new year. Toreth made himself a coffee and went to join them.

"And then," Sara was saying as he sat down, "just as all the fireworks finished, Andy took a ring out of his pocket."

Toreth looked at her still-bare hands. "Oh?"

"Yes. It was lovely, too—sapphires. Synthetic, but pretty. I gave it back, though."

"*You* did?" Chev said, and Sara frowned.

"Not sparkly enough?" Toreth asked.

Sara apparently decided to let Chev's typically offensive honesty go. "I told him, I don't mind giving him the code to my flat, and he can give me the code to his, if he likes, but I don't want anything...too big. It'll only jinx everything."

Kel laughed. "So, you're having a relationship by stealth, is that it?"

Sara folded her hands in her lap and laughed, too. "That's about it, yes. How was your New Year, Toreth?"

"All right. I escaped early from Warrick's bloody family and had the bed delivered. They had to assemble it in the room."

"Is it good, then?" Sara asked, her eyebrows lifting.

Chev grimaced, but didn't say anything.

Toreth grinned. "Very nice. Lovely finish on the wood. Very solidly built."

He took a sip of his coffee and was about to elaborate when over Sara's shoulder he saw Morehen appear in the coffee room doorway. The investigator scanned the room, then came over to them.

"Good holiday?" Kel asked him.

Morehen grinned. "Not bad, thanks."

"I hope you got the money back on the ring," Toreth said.

Sara glared at him, but Morehen didn't even blink. "Oh, yes, of course. I buy all my New Year presents on sale or return. I was looking for you, Para. Or rather, Tillotson is. He wants to talk to you about the Richardson case, as soon as you're free."

Chevril snorted. "Pity we can't get section heads on sale or return, too."

Toreth had hoped for a longer respite before Tillotson thought of something with which to annoy him. He finished his coffee slowly, chatted to a couple of the other seniors, and then finally decided he couldn't put it off any longer. He'd only made it halfway down the corridor from the General Criminal central office to Tillotson's lair before he heard Sara call his name.

"Toreth! Hang on."

Toreth stopped and waited for her to catch up. To his surprise, when she did she looked carefully up and down the corridor before she spoke in a low voice.

"I heard something funny just now."

"Mm?"

Another check around. "Tillotson was reviewing Chris Doyle's file. He asked Jenny to find out if you talked to anyone in HCT about him when he applied for the senior post here."

Apparently Tillotson didn't understand that admin clan loyalty trumped loyalty to him. "So, did I?"

"Sort of. They requested a regrading assessment from you, and I wrote him a... fairly glowing one."

He could imagine. Doyle had been one of her favorite pet juniors. "How glowing are we talking? Visible from space?"

"No! Nothing OTT, and it was all completely true. You always said he was good. And I sent it to you," she added. "You authorized it."

"Yeah, I'm sure I did." Although he'd probably given it a glance, at the most. Toreth rarely bothered to write assessments for his current staff, never mind previous ones. "But he's been over at PC for years. His last senior would've had far more weight than me."

"Well..." Sara paused for a thoughtful moment, then nodded. "As far as the HCT scoring was concerned, you probably were his last senior. At least, his senior

111

before the revolt was killed, and of course so was the Political Crimes section head. Then I know he was working for Brewer, and *he* resigned just before Chris applied for the senior post here—he had a windfall, won some money or something like that, so he handed in his notice one Friday and never came back."

Toreth didn't have a bad memory for people, when he needed it, but Sara's effortless recall still surprised him sometimes. "So? Why does Tillotson care about a regrading assessment?"

"I suppose he thought you might've asked Chris to apply for General Criminal specifically. You know—because he owed you. Although I don't know why he didn't just turn Chris down." Sara frowned, then answered her own question. "I suppose if his HCT scoring was high enough, it would've looked weird. He'd need to come up with a good excuse, at least, or everyone would know that he's worried." She paused and looked at him significantly. When he didn't say anything, she added, "That you're building a power base?"

As reasonable as the conclusion undoubtedly was, Toreth's first reaction was to tell Sara she was being ridiculous. "He thinks I'm after his *job*? Seriously?"

Sara shrugged. "Some people must want to be section heads."

Presumably so, although Toreth found it harder to understand than Chevril's unbending straightness. Endless rounds of budgets and meetings sounded like a level eight waiver hell. "Other people," he said. "Not me. You heard this direct from Jenny?"

"Oh, yes. Well, Jenny warned Diann, so she could tell Chris, and Diann mentioned it to Senior Para Belkin's new admin who told me, but direct enough."

Toreth sighed. This was not a good omen for the start of a new year.

Despite Sara's warning, Toreth was still hoping the reason for the summons was nothing more sinister than an order to stop wasting resources and drop the storage unit case. The optimism lasted long enough for him to sit down in front of the section head's desk.

Tillotson had not, he noticed, made coffee for them both this time.

"I had an interesting message today, from Catherine Turnbull—but of course you were probably expecting that, weren't you?"

Toreth declined the bait. "What did she want?"

"To tell me we're taking a case over from Corporate Fraud. I've already had a call from Vaughn about it." Tillotson's grimace suggested the conversation had not been an enjoyable one. "She says the head of the finance specialists claims we're poaching. First Citizen Surveillance, now the Bureau of Administrative Departments?" Tillotson added, rhetorically.

Okay, maybe Toreth had cooked up the interrogation of Tarin's resister friends behind Tillotson's back, but cooperation with Cit wasn't that unusual. Of all the aftereffects of the revolt, who would've guessed Tillotson's paranoia would be one of the longest lasting?

"I used a resource to help progress a case, that's all," Toreth said as evenly as he could. "I told you the interrogation was a dead end."

"Toreth, this must stop. We have procedures and proper channels of contact for a reason. But instead you go behind my back, you consistently undermine my authority... well?"

There was a distinction to be drawn between actively undermining Tillotson and simply not giving a shit about him, but Toreth didn't think the section head would be interested in the difference.

"If I'd asked you to call the Bureau, or the Central Bank, or Ext-Sec, would you have done it?" he asked.

"I would've made a decision based on the evidence."

"So that'll be a no, then?"

Tillotson's eyes narrowed. "Just because you had a temporary promotion, that doesn't mean I'm not still your boss."

Pretty rich, considering Toreth wasn't the one who'd conspired with Psychoprogramming to have one of his staff almost mindfucked and killed.

Still, life was complicated enough without having to spend his time with one eye over his shoulder, watching out for a ferret with a knife.

"Listen," Toreth said with all the sincerity he could dredge up. "It wasn't my idea to get an Assistant Director label slapped on me while we were sorting out the mess after the revolt. I didn't want it, but Carnac insisted. I'm just a senior para. I work cases to the best of my ability, with whatever tools I have. Nothing more. So, with respect, stop worrying about whether I want your job—which I don't—" and start fucking *doing* it instead. "And we can both get on with our work. Sir."

To his surprise, Tillotson didn't respond immediately. After a few seconds of silent contemplation, he said, "Junior Para Nagra has applied for a promotion to senior."

Toreth nodded. "I know. She's an extremely solid para-investigator." He was tempted to add "loyal," but that would be overenhancing the evidence. Tillotson might generally be clueless, but not about office politics. "I'm sure she'd do an excellent job running her own team."

Tillotson's nose twitched. "She's still young."

"Well, you know how it is." Toreth shrugged. "With the revolt and everything. I was surprised when Chris Doyle got his post." He couldn't resist adding, "Nice to have him back in the section, though, don't you think? I always knew he'd make a good senior."

"Doyle?" Tillotson looked at him sharply, but then obviously decided to let it

113

go. "Well, just remember what I've said. Now, I think you should take a look at what else arrived this morning. You must've made quite an impression on Secretary Turnbull."

"Toreth—" Sara said as he approached her desk, but he hurried past her and into his office.

When he switched on his screen, his own copy of the message was waiting for him. He sat down and opened it.

"Justice sent a waiver," Sara said from the doorway, sounding puzzled. "Or at least I think it's—well, take a look at it yourself. I didn't ask them for anything."

"I know." Toreth was already studying the document. "That's more or less what Tillotson wanted to see me about."

"But what is it?" Sara asked, closing Toreth's office door and coming over to his desk.

"That, Sara, is a special exemption waiver." He knew that because it said so at the top. Underneath, it said "by special order of the Security Subcommittee of the Council of the European Administration."

"I've never seen one before," Sara said.

"This might be the first one ever issued. It authorizes me to use measures 'up to but not exceeding' the old level seven."

"I wonder why they didn't make it an eight?"

"Probably trying to make it look less heavy-handed," Toreth said. "Still, seven should be good enough. That's almost all the validated techniques, and no one's developing any new high-risk experimental drugs these days, anyway. Richardson's going to regret wasting his money on all that interrogation resistance crap now."

"—while using only the minimum levels of coercion required to gain cooperation," Sara read over his shoulder.

Toreth grinned. "Sounds good, doesn't it? Arse-covering from the Bureau, I expect. It has Turnbull's fingerprints all over it."

Sara pointed at the screen. "It doesn't have a prisoner name on, though, just the IIP number."

A quick check showed she was right. "Then...I suppose it must be good for any prisoners in the case." Toreth scanned through the document again. "Yes, there it is. Point five: 'Shall apply only to interrogations forming a part of the above Investigation in Progress.' Saves the Bureau having to mess around with a new waiver every time we get a prisoner." And kept them hands off from the messy end of justice.

"Well, that should help." Sara shook her head. "Wow. But why did she decide to give it to you?"

"She must've found something we couldn't. She passed the investigation over to someone called Dupré. Carey didn't know who that was, and I checked the obvious places and I couldn't find anyone who fitted. There's no point looking up the surname in Central Records unfiltered—could be any one of thousands of people. I doubt the job in their security file will be 'makes discreet inquiries for Secretary Turnbull.' Could be Cit Surveillance, or someone else in Int-Sec. Or Ext-Sec, or the Central Bank. God knows. Could be covert sabbing contacts for all I know. The point is, we've got a decent waiver at last. Richardson's still being watched, isn't he?"

Sara nodded. "The last time I checked, which was about fifteen minutes ago, he was on the edge of the financial district, having breakfast with a client. Not someone he's been seen with before. B-C and one of the pool investigators are keeping an eye on him."

Toreth smiled, already anticipating Richardson's reaction to the waiver. "Tell them to bring him in. And book me a room in Interrogation. Soon as you can."

After a few seconds, Sara said, "There'll be one free when he gets here."

One positive thing about the lack of interrogators—an excess of interrogation facilities. "I want to know the minute he's processed. Did anything else arrive with the waiver? Any evidence?"

"Nothing like that, no. There's a message asking us to keep Secretary Turnbull informed of anything we find, and the name of a contact at the Central Bank who's to be kept in the loop, too. Security Director Rina Lehman."

Well, if Turnbull didn't want to share her sources, she must be confident he could find out enough on his own.

"Shall I give them both access to the IIP?" Sara asked.

Toreth considered. He didn't want the whole of the Administration looking over his shoulder and rummaging around in his investigation, but he couldn't risk entirely ignoring Turnbull after the favor she'd done for him. Maybe he could strike a balance, with a little extra work that could be done by someone other than him, anyway. "Give Turnbull access. The Central Bank can get a report if we have something to tell them. Oh—with luck we're going to need some finance specialists. Ask Tillotson to borrow Liz Carey."

Sara looked at him eloquently.

"I'd call her myself, but it'll keep Tillotson happy. Proper channels of contact, and all that crap."

"I'll talk to Jenny."

When Sara had gone, Toreth leaned down and opened the bottom drawer of his desk. There, its case only slightly dented, he'd stashed a neural induction probe set salvaged from the interrogation levels after the revolt. Sentimental reasons only, of course. When he opened it and checked the switch, the power was dead, but that didn't matter. He wasn't the only one who'd hung on to the old equipment, and someone down on the interrogation levels would have a charged power supply.

Whistling cheerfully, Toreth set off to prepare a suitable reception for his prisoner.

For the first time since the revolt, the interrogation room felt like it should. The harshness of the lights on the white walls had never changed, of course, but even those seemed brighter. Everything the pharmacy could supply stood arrayed for his use. Toreth had scrounged up a full range of injectors, too, from the subcutaneous to the deep organ and muscle injectors with suitably intimidating needles. Only some of the more specialized tissue-damage tools were missing, and Toreth had faith someone would be able to produce them if things went that far.

"Hello, Mr. Richardson," Toreth said. "My name is Senior Para-investigator Toreth. But you can call me whatever you like—I've heard it all before."

Although the guards had already strapped him into the interrogation chair, Richardson didn't look impressed, or especially intimidated. "Why am I being questioned again? This is starting to look like harassment. I'm a legitimate—"

"Save it. I'm not interested in level two fun and games today." Toreth presented his hand screen to Richardson at eye level. "I suggest you read it carefully, and let me know when you're done."

He watched the steady flicker of his prisoner's eyes as he read, the contempt on his face changing to a puzzled frown.

"That isn't legal," Richardson said. "What the hell are you trying to pull?"

"I'll take that to mean you've read it and understand it." Toreth closed the screen and exchanged it for the NI probe sitting fully charged on the bench. "So we'll get started."

He placed the tip of the probe against Richardson's belly, just below his rib cage. After all the intervening months, Toreth's hand still went straight to the precise spot he wanted.

"You're bluffing," Richardson said.

"Brave guess," Toreth said, and fired the probe. Richardson jerked spasmodically in the chair, the initial scream cut short as the overstimulation shut down his diaphragm. "But—wrong."

Richardson's anti-interrogation treatments might not have been proof against the new waiver, but they were irritatingly difficult to work around. Daedra had done her best, but the I&I pharmacy no longer stocked most of what Toreth would've chosen to use. She was promising fresh supplies synthesized before the end of the day, but that didn't help Toreth right then.

After a couple of hours, Toreth sent the guards in to clean Richardson up and went in search of Nagra. He found her having lunch in the level D canteen.

The soup Nagra was eating had a suspicious gray tinge, so Toreth bought himself a cheese and onion sandwich that looked as though it needed at least an old level four waiver, and sat down next to his junior.

"Hello, Para," she said, sounding surprised.

"Nagra, I want you to take the rest of the day off, then run an overnight interrogation for me. Your favorite prisoner is back."

"Richardson?" She curled her lip disgustedly. "Para—"

"Before you go off on one, Junior, take a look at this."

Nagra put down her spoon and read the waiver over, her smile growing broader with every line.

"You mean it? This is real?"

"Absolutely. Direct from Justice. Level seven, no holds barred."

"Oh, my God." Nagra waved the hand screen at him, to take it back. "Let me at the smug bastard right now, please."

"Tonight. And don't get too enthusiastic. There's no annex—I don't want him dead." Turnbull wouldn't like that as the result of her generosity. "If he talks, great. I'll leave a full list of the information I want. But there's no need to push too hard. I just want him nice and pliable for tomorrow. If you need to take a break, get the guards to bounce him between cells, maybe walk him up to the interrogation level and put him in the chair, then take him back down again. No sleep, no food and water. He's still a tough, smug bastard, even after we take his toys away."

"Yes, Para." Nagra was so happy she didn't even protest being told how to run her interrogation. "He's going to have a memorable night."

"Good. I'll pick him up about 10 a.m. Pull someone else in whenever you like—I don't think you'll have trouble finding volunteers."

"No, Para. I'm sure not."

"But—Nagra?" He waited until he was sure she was paying full attention. "Don't run around spreading this everywhere, okay? The Bureau wouldn't like it."

"Oh. Oh, right, Para. I understand."

Toreth left her, confident the news would percolate through the interrogation levels, with his own arse nicely covered. The interrogation so far had shown how genuinely resilient Richardson was, and Toreth didn't anticipate any answers from him for a while. Toreth was happy to mark the rest of the day down as preparation. With Nagra's help, he felt cautiously optimistic about a result in a day or two.

Toreth stepped away from the prisoner and tapped his comm. "I'm here."

"Sorry to interrupt," Sara said into his ear. "I just want to let you know I'm going home now. It's after six. Unless you need me to stay?"

She sounded very unenthusiastic, which Toreth took to mean she had plans with Andy Morehen, presumably involving his cock. Pushing away a slight, annoyingly irrational irritation, he said, "Go ahead."

"Thanks. I'll see you tomorrow. Oh, I heard back from Corporate Fraud. Senior Specialist Carey is too busy with her own cases, but she'll lend us Phil Verstraeten."

By eight o'clock, with Richardson unconscious more often than he was conscious, Toreth decided to hand him over to the guards for a couple of hours before Nagra resumed business later. He went back upstairs and checked the IIP, which showed little development from the rest of the team. Searches of Richardson's office and home had turned up some edge-of-legal equipment, but nothing of great significance. Systems had started to go through the business files; initial reports showed nothing obviously criminal. Toreth's investigators had been talking to Richardson's staff and reported the majority of them as being bewildered and apparently convinced they worked for a legitimate security contractor; one or two of the longest-serving names had been marked for further questioning.

And that was that. Toreth sat back in his chair, tired but strangely reluctant to switch off the screen and leave. No, not leave—go back to the flat. He rubbed his wrist. The soft cotton hadn't left any marks, but he could feel a ghost of the pressure there.

Ridiculous. Still, even when he was standing in a chill drizzle on the edge of the Int-Sec complex waiting for a taxi, he found he didn't want to go straight home. Finally a taxi pulled up—Toreth wondered idly if, since the partial neutering of I&I, the taxis had dropped I&I calls lower down the priority list—and he climbed into the welcomingly warm interior.

About to give the address of the flat, he paused and said, "Gegi's Bar."

An hour's detour to Gegi's, and a pretty girl with implausible (and probably expensive) breasts and way too much perfume cleared his mind. Gegi's still held reminders of his meeting with John Sable, and although with luck that particular ghost from Warrick's past would never be an issue again, it lent a lingering spice of danger to encounters there. By the time Toreth climbed the stairs up to the flat, his mood had improved enough for him to catch himself humming under his breath.

As soon as he closed the door, he heard Warrick in the kitchen, clattering pans.

"It's me," Toreth called. "I'm going for a shower."

"No hurry," Warrick replied. "The food won't be ready for a while."

Upstairs, Toreth glanced into the main bedroom as he passed. The covers on the new bed were rumpled, he noticed, as they absolutely never were on Warrick's bed—unless someone had jumped off it in a hurry. Toreth smiled and went on to the bathroom.

Even after he'd taken full advantage of the corporate building's endless supply of beautifully hot water, by the time Toreth came back downstairs Warrick was still at the preparation stage, grating something from a gray block into a bowl. Onions sizzled in a frying pan, while water simmered in another pan at the back of the cooker.

Toreth licked his finger and dipped it into the bowl. The stuff had a grainy texture almost like sand, fishy and intensely salty. "Gah. What the hell is that?"

"Botargo. Dried, salted fish roe. Not natural, sadly—all the relevant species are protected, so the wild supplies are very limited and *very* expensive."

"And that's edible?"

"Extremely. Once it's on the pasta, I promise it will be a lot less salty. It was in a New Year gift basket from an appreciative supplier—oddly enough, I was the only one who wanted to take it home."

"I wonder why."

Warrick finished grating and went to wash his hands at the sink. Toreth leaned against the counter and watched him. Yes, there were definite advantages to coming home to Warrick and a meal, even if sometimes the food wasn't what he would've chosen himself. But if Warrick said the stuff was good, he was willing to give it a try.

When Warrick came back across, he touched Toreth's damp hair. "Busy day?"

"Hm?"

"I wondered if you'd been running around, if you needed a shower."

"No." Definitely not a day Warrick would want to hear about. "I stank of perfume, that's all. At least I assume I did—I couldn't smell it anymore by the time I got back here, thank fuck, but I didn't think you'd want to smell that flowery crap all evening."

Warrick paused, then nodded. "Well, thank you for the consideration."

"Any time. Although if I'd known the place was going to reek of fish, I wouldn't have bothered. And speaking of food, if we're playing investigators, you've been home a long time not to have finished dinner."

"Yes, well." Warrick turned back to the pans. "I haven't been home so long. I had a late meeting. And it's a very quick dish that needs to be prepared fresh."

"Liar," Toreth said evenly. "Remember, I'm better at this than you. I do it for a living." He put his hands on Warrick's waist, standing not quite close enough for their bodies to touch. "You were upstairs on the new bed."

"Yes," Warrick said.

"Thinking about last night?" The idea sparked off the same vague unease that he'd felt in the morning, but Toreth quashed it.

"No. Well . . . a little. Mostly other things, though."

"I thought you enjoyed it?" Toreth said.

"Yes, a great deal. But there seemed to be so many other possibilities, I didn't want to limit myself." Warrick turned and looked up at him. "It's one particular fantasy, and I'm extremely pleased you went to the trouble of making it real, but . . . it's not a fantasy I'd want to indulge every day. I'd rather keep it fresh."

"Good," Toreth said. "Because I have a few ideas for things myself."

"Really?" Warrick licked his lips. "This *is* a very quick recipe. We could postpone dinner until—"

"Hmm . . ." Toreth tightened his grip on Warrick's waist, then let him go and took a step back, smiling at the flicker of dismay that escaped Warrick's control. A little anticipation was good for him, especially now that they saw each other all the time. "No. Let's eat first. I'm starving."

Chapter Fifteen

❖

Richardson had a cut on his left eyebrow; according to the logs, he'd acquired it while breaking free of the guards and trying to run. Christ knows where he'd thought he was going, three floors underground, but prisoners weren't usually thinking very clearly at 4 a.m.

"Good night?" Toreth asked brightly. "Sleep well?"

"Piss off," Richardson said, but his heart definitely wasn't in it compared to the invective he'd managed yesterday. Nagra must have had a productive night.

Toreth strolled over to the racks of drug vials and inspected the new arrivals. Daedra had outdone even her usual pharmacological magic. He picked up a vial and read the name.

"Oh, this is a nice one. I haven't seen this for months." He showed the label to Richardson. "Enhances pain receptor activity and raises the threshold at which prisoners pass out. One of us is not going to have a lot of fun today."

Richardson turned his face away. He was breathing shallowly, and Toreth could taste the fear in the room. He set the vial down with a click and stood in front of the interrogation chair.

"Well, that can wait for a little while. Before we get down to business, I'm making an offer. I think we've established that I'm not bluffing. So I suggest you start to cooperate, and then all the unpleasantness stops."

He let the offer dangle, leaving Richardson time to think it over. Fifty-fifty, Toreth decided, between cooperation and defiance. Maybe with another nudge...

"You're a professional, too," Toreth said. "You know I can rotate interrogators in and out of here for as long as you make me do it. I hear there's quite a queue forming, everyone nostalgic for the good old days. Do us both a favor. Take a short-cut to where this ends, anyway."

Finally, Richardson looked up at him.

"If I talk to you, they'll probably kill me," he whispered.

"And if you don't talk, I'll definitely kill you. Eventually." Toreth lifted the prisoner's chin. "Your choice. Though you might want to think about where you are, and who's here with you."

After a moment, he felt Richardson try to nod.

"If you fuck me around, if the neural scanner so much as twitches—if I even *think* you're holding anything back—then I don't ask any more questions for twenty-four hours. Not unless you want to count 'How much does that fucking hurt?' as a question. So far we haven't even touched an old level seven. Barely a six. Just remember that."

Richardson shivered. "I'll cooperate. No holding back."

Toreth reached out to pick up another injector, and Richardson croaked, "No! I'll cooperate, I promise, I'll—"

The sentence choked on a sob as the tip touched the red circle of a previous injector mark on Richardson's neck. Toreth made sure he felt the sting of the drug delivery before he said, "Don't worry, this is the good stuff."

The stimulant should brighten Richardson up for a while. Of course, it would make him feel like shit in a couple of hours, but then he wouldn't feel too clever without it, either.

After a minute Richardson said, "Can I have some water? Please?"

"Right now you can be grateful you don't have an NI probe down your throat. Anything more than that requires payment up front." Toreth glanced at the calibration levels on the neural scanner. "You can start by telling me about your so-called security business."

"Okay. Yes, I . . . I used to be a sab." Richardson tried to wet his lips. "I won't deny it. Even back then it was nothing violent, though. Not really violent. I mean, we never killed anyone. Might've scared a few people, I suppose. But that crew broke up years ago, after Kat and I got together. When we had the conception license granted, I decided I'd rather watch my kid grow up than spend my time in re-education because some corporates didn't want to get their own hands dirty. So I set up Urban Fox and bought the incorporation franchise. I never touched anything heavy after that. Just some semilegit security system infiltration, comms pattern analysis, information collection for persuasive negotiation, that kind of thing."

"Persuasive negotiation." Toreth snorted. "Blackmail."

Richardson shook his head. "I supplied the information. What people did with it wasn't my business. Most of our work was completely legit. Even after things went south with Kat, when I thought about the old days the risk and reward seemed way out of whack."

The prisoner had been dosed with neural scan enhancers before Toreth arrived, and the readings on the screen looked truthful enough on this relatively medium-stress topic. It was one area, though, where they couldn't completely neutralize the treatments he'd had. Not without using drugs Toreth didn't feel like risking on a valuable prisoner so early in the process.

"So why all the medical work?"

"Policy. In the old crew. Mostly to defend against other sabs—it's a competitive business, which is another reason I switched to the purely technical stuff."

"And after the revolt?"

Richardson was silent for a few seconds, long enough that Toreth thought he might need to organize another twenty-four hours of interrogation rota. Then he said, "That was for the Central Bank work."

Now that they'd established a baseline for the scan, they could move on to more interesting topics.

"Tell me about that, then," Toreth said. "So far I'm not hearing anything that pays for water."

"I'm getting there." Richardson half closed his eyes. "Someone approached me out of the blue. Few months ago. The risk didn't sound too bad, especially when everyone said they'd pulled I&I's teeth, and the reward was—" He whistled blowily through his cracked and swollen lips. "Generous."

Toreth went to the dispenser on the wall and filled a paper cup. He held it so Richardson could drink. Two mouthfuls—a little positive reinforcement never hurt, but not too much.

"Thanks," Richardson said.

Toreth set the cup down on the table, in Richardson's eyeline. "So, tell me about this offer that was too good."

"My contact said the people who sent him had noticed some . . . irregularities. Financial ones. I don't know what kind," he said before Toreth could ask. "They never told me. He said they were trying to pin them down and find out who was behind it."

"And tell the bank, I suppose?"

Richardson shrugged, awkward in the restraints. "That's what he implied. I know, it sounds ridiculous, but the regulators offer huge rewards for that kind of information. And . . . the contact seemed pretty straight up. Honest."

So much so, he'd been able to find a sab like Richardson. "Trustworthy enough for you to hand over confidential information about Central Bank security systems to him, at least."

"I know." Richardson hung his head. "I know. I'm fucked. I get it." He looked up. "But I didn't even give him info. He gave *me* a piece of data. And no, I don't know what it was. I tried to test it—it didn't seem malicious in any way I could work out. Just a normal piece of comms traffic. My job was to send it into the system when I'd got access."

"And?"

"I don't know. He said they'd be able to tell when we found the right target. I hunted out bust corporations with suitable contracts, I picked them up, I sent his data, and I got paid really, really well. That's all."

"Were you given the targets all at once, or over time?"

"Both. Three to start with, then the rest over time." Richardson looked up. "I know what you're thinking—were they feeling their way deeper into the system? That was how it looked to me at first, but then I changed my mind. It was too... random. It was like they knew they were looking for *something,* but they didn't know where it was."

"One specific weakness."

"Yeah. That's how it seemed to me."

"Now, this is an important question." Toreth crouched down to get better eye contact, the neural induction probe held loosely in his hand. "Do you think they found it?"

"No. And I'll tell you why," Richardson added hurriedly. "I started to get the feeling someone was watching me. That was you, right?"

Toreth didn't answer.

"Okay. Well, it was enough to spook me. When I met the client's rep I told them I was done, no more contracts. But he offered me more money—double. He said it would probably be the last one. So... fuck. I was stupid. I thought, with the treatments, even if I was picked up..." He swallowed painfully. "So I said yes. I put my bid in for the target they wanted, covered it with a few others, and I got the contract. I sent the okay, expecting the time for the code send and... nothing. Then I got a message for an urgent face-to-face."

"You didn't use anonymous messages?"

"They were crazy paranoid about that. I mean *paranoid.* We met in a different public place every time. They always sent the same guy, though, I think."

"You *think*?"

"We didn't actually meet. We'd go to the same area, then subvocalize on secure short-range comms."

Paranoid, indeed. "So how did you make contact?"

"I had a dating profile—I had to post a specific sentence up there."

Sometimes the simplest codes could be the most secure. "And that's how they contacted you?"

"Yes. There was another profile I checked every day. So I saw the meetup request, I went to the place I'd been told at the last meet, a public park, but they never showed."

"Why was that, if they really wanted the last target?"

"I assumed... something bad. I tidied up as best as I could, pulled out of the last contracts, and then I planned to lay low." He swallowed again with difficulty. "Please, can I have more water?"

Toreth let him drink.

"I want all the data available," Toreth said. "Every scrap. We're taking everything from your home and office. Where else do we need to look?"

124

"Everything was on one data store. I destroyed it. Deleted it, purged the store, and put it into the recycling." Richardson gave a painful smile. "I didn't think it would do me any good to have it around."

The neural scanner gave that a weak but positive truthfulness score, as it had for most of the interrogation. Toreth didn't like to rely too much on the opinion of analysis systems.

"Well, that's a shame. For you, especially." Toreth tapped the NI probe in his palm. "So instead, we can move on to names."

"No." Richardson shook his head. "They never used any names."

"Mm-hm." Toreth set the tip of the probe against the prisoner's throat. "I told you what would happen if I thought you were holding back."

"I'm not! I just don't *know.* He never—please. Oh, God."

Toreth slid the probe down, pausing for a second over his solar plexus, then moving steadily down to nestle against his balls. Richardson went white.

"I'm sorry." Toreth shifted his grip on the probe a fraction and smiled. "I'm sure you appreciate—I need to be sure."

"Please," Richardson whimpered, and Toreth could see the hopeless knowledge in his eyes. The only words that would do him any good were words he didn't have to offer. "I don't know. *Please.*"

"All right." Toreth straightened up, the probe still unfired in his hand, and the prisoner stared at him incredulously. "We'll hold that for now. Just remember where we'll be starting from, if you make it necessary."

Richardson leaned his head back and closed his eyes, panting.

"We already have enough for the Justice system to hand out a heavy re-education sentence. Or, who knows, it might decide that attempting to sabotage the Central Bank for unknown third parties qualifies as treason. You're a sab, you should understand the routine. You're working for us now. The more you cooperate, the more lenient a recommendation we send to Justice."

"Anything you want," Richardson said hoarsely.

"Good. First we'll go over everything that happened with your contact. Every message, every meeting. As long you continue cooperating today, we might not even need to come back here next time we talk. If I ever don't like what I'm hearing, we can restart exactly where we left off. Clear?"

Richardson opened his eyes. "Clear. I'll cooperate, I promise."

"If I like the results, then you can have a shower, some food, and maybe a couple of hours' sleep. How much depends on how happy you make me. After *that,* you talk to a facial recognition expert and give us a picture of your contact."

The sleep wasn't really a reward. There was no point expecting someone sleep-deprived and still with interrogation drugs filling his system to provide a good description.

Toreth tapped his comm. "Sara?" he subvocalized.

125

"Yes?"

"Are B-C and Mistry still interviewing?"

"Mistry is," she said immediately. "With Jameson. B-C is down with Systems, going over everything recovered yesterday. Andy is running background on Richardson, with the pool investigators."

"We have a better source now. Get Morehen and Verstraeten watching the interrogation feed. I want facts verified as fast as possible." Toreth looked down at his prisoner. "And I want to know immediately if anything doesn't check out."

He'd promised Toreth, that was the problem. And just as Warrick rarely pushed his luck by making requests of Toreth, so Toreth asked for very little in return—largely because he didn't want much beyond regular sex and beer in the fridge, but that was beside the point. Toreth had been worried enough about the consequences to ask him, emphatically, to stay away from Citizen Surveillance.

That left Warrick with very few options if he were to have any chance of finding the way out Tarin had talked about. Their conversation had turned wondering about Kate's fate from a question that nagged only when circumstances forced him to think of her into an irritating, intrusive worry. He'd worried at it all the way back from Jen's house, and walking into the flat to find Toreth's spectacular New Year present had distracted him only temporarily. Warrick hated impossible problems, especially when they came in a flock. Was Kate alive? Would she return? If she did, could he somehow protect Tar from anything more Cit Surveillance might want from him?

Contacting John Sable (Leo Warrick—his brain still flipped between the two names, as though they were entirely different people) both broke his promise in spades, and made him feel queasy. He couldn't trust the man, and besides, Sable had tried to kill Tarin once. Giving him a reason to try again was out of the question. His safest option, contacting Carnac again, was also—from a personal point of view—possibly the least appealing. Certainly it would be the worst in terms of Toreth's likely reaction. And Carnac had no reason to help him, either.

A direct attack on Citizen Surveillance's systems to find out the information for himself carried far too much danger. He'd tried once, and been detected and arrested. Toreth might not be able to rescue him a second time—and might not take the risk to do it. But there could be another way. A long-standing corporate principle was that when it became too dangerous to proceed yourself, you called in the professionals. Either to provide technical expertise, or to take the fall.

Warrick knew that Emma Queen generally kept her schedule clear of meetings on Tuesday afternoons; the SimTech head of security liked to use the time to review current threats and long-term security assessments. That gave him a chance to talk to her without needing to put his own name on her calendar. Paranoid, yes, but only the tip of the iceberg of caution he'd need if he pursued this to the end.

The opaquable glass of her door had a single stripe clear, allowing anyone who made it past the security guard at the end of the corridor a glimpse of the office. Enough to see that Queen was alone at her desk.

Warrick knocked on the door, and she waved him in without looking up. Probably she'd already been alerted to his visit.

"I need to hire a sab," he said bluntly.

Queen's eyebrows rose. "If it's for SimTech business, then shouldn't that be my call?"

"This is personal. Ideally, I wouldn't involve you at all, but unfortunately I have no suitable contacts myself. It requires a *very* high level of expertise in information retrieval." Since she knew at least a little about Warrick's personal skill at ferreting out reluctant data, she'd understand the level of hazard suggested.

"Information retrieval?" She sounded surprised. "Something y—something no one here can get to, then?"

"Definitely. And I couldn't take the risk, anyway. The target is . . . noncorporate, and not a private individual." Leaving, more or less, Administration files.

"I see." Queen's expression grew even more concerned.

"Can you help?" Warrick asked.

She didn't answer right away. He wondered if she was weighing up her perfectly natural (commendable, even) instinct to tell him to forget it against the possibility of him going elsewhere if she refused. Finally she said, "Is there nothing that I can do to help, before you go outside?"

"I very much doubt it." Still, her expertise was greater than his. How could he phrase it most accurately while giving the least information away? "I'm trying to determine if someone is still alive. They've been completely out of sight since just after the trouble last year. The major roadblock is that I don't want to risk making inquiries that show I'm looking for this specific person."

She nodded. "Then, as a start, I'd suggest trying to access financial records belonging to somewhere this person might appear."

"There's also a very strong likelihood that they're outside the borders of the Administration, so the usual secondhand methods are no use."

She didn't look surprised; she'd probably guessed that he'd already considered and rejected the approach, if he were looking at sabs. "Tough one. And there's no one you know who might be in contact with this person?"

"Possibly, yes. Whether or not I should be in contact with them is another question." Either of them.

Queen grimaced. "If you're willing to spend the money on this level of sabbing expertise to avoid them, I suggest the answer to that is a very solid no."

"You're probably right."

127

"Then I can give you an introduction to an agent," she said with obvious reluctance. "They'll take my recommendation; they won't even know your name. That costs more, unfortunately, but I'd say it was well worth the extra security."

"And they know the right caliber of sabs?"

"They'll let you know, but I expect so. I've used them in the past."

"At SimTech?" That could prove an awkward connection.

"No, a previous employer." She smiled. "I've never found a problem here that needed quite the intensity they can bring to a solution. But Warrick—" Now she looked deathly serious again. "Before I give you the contact, I need to ask you to come to me for final approval before you go ahead with a plan. I respect your judgment, but my contract is with SimTech. I have to protect the corporation's interests, even over the directors'."

"I promise," Warrick said. "And thank you."

This time, with SimTech's immediate interests at stake, he couldn't break his word.

Chapter Sixteen

❖

Sometimes prisoners who'd come to their senses would have an attack of stupidity soon after, and decide they wanted another round or two. It was a hazard of not breaking them thoroughly enough in the first place, and in Toreth's experience sabs with extensive interrogation training were among those prone to sudden bravery. Maybe they wanted to get their money's worth.

So he'd half expected Richardson to clam up, which Nagra would no doubt enjoy. To Toreth's pleasant surprise, over the next two days Richardson was as eager to please as a top-class corporate-screened escort, although not always as satisfying. He certainly didn't satisfy the facial recognition expert.

"The reconstruction's no good, Para," she said. "Simply not enough detail—even skin tone's a broad range. It's pulling up every medium-height, medium-build, brown-haired man in the Administration."

Toreth found it hard to believe an experienced sab, even one allegedly mostly out of the game for years, wouldn't have contrived a good look at his contact's face. "Do you think he could give you any more?"

"Well, that's your field, Para. He *seemed* fully cooperative. I can say the end result we have is consistent with the type of meetings he described. Glimpses of a face at a distance, often concealed with a hat, glasses, and scarf. It is difficult."

Verstraeten at least managed to get a little more from his encounters.

"He identified all the relevant contracts, and told us where his client wanted their code sent. We're liaising with the Data Division to try to confirm the details, but even though Richardson's cooperating now, back then he was trying to conceal the traffic. So that's a work in progress."

"And what about the code itself? Do you know what it was supposed to do yet?"

"Unfortunately, he claims the client never gave him any hint about that, so he's as much in the dark as we are. The contracts give him access to an interesting selection of systems—the Central Trading Exchange auditing and communications, the Central Bank section of the Data Division, the bank's internal secure comm network. I'm afraid we haven't cracked the pattern yet."

"Richardson said the final contract was the one his client was getting excited about."

"Ah, well, that's been an issue. Since he ultimately turned down the contract, it went to the second tender, and of course that put the fine detail under their corporate confidentiality privileges. We had to mess around with a warrant."

"And?"

"It confirms Richardson's account, insofar as it would have given him access to what he said the client wanted. In a slightly different area than the previous ones—Central Bank staff security files. They're kept separate by the Data Division, with very limited access, like some of the Int-Sec division staff files."

Toreth wondered if the Central Bank and Data Division were more worried about resisters or corporations breaking into their files. "So what could this piece of data do?"

"As Richardson destroyed it, I'm afraid we can still only guess," Verstraeten said apologetically. "It's possible it altered files, changed clearances, or even just triggered a send-out of the files. I'm sure there's potential profit for anyone with free access to the names and life histories of highly placed Central Bank officials."

And that, at least, was something he could send to Turnbull to justify the faith she'd placed in him. They might not—yet—have the detail to pin it down, but Verstraeten's feeling there was *something* wrong seemed vindicated.

It was also enough, Toreth felt, to persuade the Central Bank that they needed to take the threat seriously and hopefully win their full cooperation. He'd told Sara to set up a case conference on Thursday morning to include the Central Bank contact Turnbull had given him. Maybe their cooperation could push the case forward.

Sara had arranged a conference room where a semicircular table stood against a screen wall. Toreth had wondered if Turnbull would show an open interest in progress, but neither she nor one of her staff appeared. Security Director Rina Lehman of the Central Bank in Frankfurt was already waiting when Toreth arrived, with two of her senior security specialists flanking her—both men, one blond and one dark.

The rest of Toreth's team had been waiting outside the room, tactfully not pointing out his slightly delayed appearance. As they took their seats, Toreth studied the room visible behind the Central Bank staff. The Central Bank certainly didn't stint on offices for its senior staff; while it wasn't top-end corporate luxury, a visiting senior corporate certainly wouldn't feel out of place. The Central Bank obviously didn't enforce a uniform, and Lehman and her specialists were dressed to match her office—immaculate, professional, quietly impressive. Lehman herself was plump, middle-aged, with a tan that suggested outdoor hobbies—a hint of pale skin showed at the neckline. She wore her long hair neatly rolled up, a few dark wisps escaping to make the only slightly untidy thing about her.

To begin with, Lehman required an explanation of the investigation so minutely detailed that Toreth almost wished he'd agreed to open up the IIP to her. He caught movement from the corner of his eye several times as members of the team shifted in their seats. Only Phil Verstraeten seemed utterly absorbed, and Toreth wondered if he'd ever considered a transfer to the Central Bank.

When they reached the I&I systems specialists' limited and understandably vague list of possibilities for the target of Richardson's code, the Central Bank vault doors slammed closed.

"There can be no viable targets here," Lehman said. "Nothing exists in any Central Bank system that isn't accounted for and thoroughly understood. It's impossible."

Laughing in the face of the head of Central Bank security would probably get him a memo from Tillotson, at the very least. "Forgive me, but 'impossible' is a big claim."

"Our code control-test cycling is the most robust in the Administration—we *defined* the highest standards in the industry. Do you have this payload?"

"Not yet. The sab involved destroyed—"

"Well, if you manage to find it, send it to us and we'll take a look. But I'm sure—if it exists at all—it's a fantasy. A scam. It's happened before, so-called backdoor keys sold to gullible would-be criminals." Lehman shook her head, then glanced down. "You're at I&I London—General Criminal?"

"That's right," Toreth said.

"Ah. Normally I'd deal with Caro Vaughn. She has a very good understanding of the Administration's financial systems."

Caro, indeed. Toreth couldn't remember ever hearing anyone use the Corporate Fraud section head's personal name, still less a nickname. He couldn't imagine many people taking the liberty and surviving, either—she had the face and body of a retired porn star, but the cold eyes and personality of a clever shark.

Lehman wasn't the only one who could throw names around, though. "Secretary Turnbull hoped we'd be able to cooperate," Toreth said.

Even though her expression didn't change, Toreth felt a chill fall over the link.

"And we will. We already are, in fact, with this meeting. I assure you, we take any concern from the Bureau seriously. Obviously we're grateful to them—and to you—for drawing this to our attention, and I'll assign a team to start investigating the areas you highlighted. I'm confident they'll find there's been zero breach of security."

Resentment at Bureau interference in another department, Toreth guessed. Coupled with her determination that the bank wouldn't be found at fault, he shared her confidence that the experts would find nothing.

Maybe she thought she'd overstepped the mark, because she leaned forward a little with what she probably imagined was a more sincere smile.

"Let me try to reassure you. The type of attack you're proposing's incompatible with our systems these days. In the old days trading involved much more automation, but it was regulated a long time ago, for security reasons."

Meaning security flaws that a clever person might be able to exploit in a new way? "What reasons?"

"Well, transactions were performed directly by trading systems, buying and selling at subsecond speeds. Trading was limited only by data-transfer rates. Corporations sited their offices to minimize physical distance to exchanges." She shook her head. "Craziness. The traders liked it, but unfortunately it was prone to fraud, sabbing, and critical instability events. Some events were caused by genuine software mistakes, some by corporate sabs. International espionage, too. There was a series of incidents, at corporate, national, and even global levels, until markets finally began to move away from microautomation. Actually, Europe was the first to propose a ban on subsecond trading."

"But now there's no automation at all?"

"Not of the trading. There're thousands of expert systems—who knows, maybe tens of thousands if you include smaller scale trading and highly specialized markets—working in market analysis, but all trades have to be placed and executed by humans. Of course, that brings in a whole new set of risks—corruption, collusion, and so on, but at a more manageable scale. And those are controlled by rigorous employee monitoring and screening."

To Toreth's surprise, her dark-haired sidekick spoke up. "Para-investigator, do you have any suggestion that someone here is colluding with this sab, this Richardson?"

"Not that he's admitted to us. And if his clients already had an insider, they wouldn't have needed to approach Richardson to get inside your systems."

"Unless it was a system outside their access limits," he said. "Or they wanted to maximize the pool of suspects. Given the timing..."

Toreth expected Lehman to at least give the man a frosty stare, but instead she said, "The ethical integrity screening?"

He shrugged.

Toreth cleared his throat politely. "Is this something that might be relevant?"

"Possibly," she said. "Karaca," she added, and he nodded.

"Until the trouble earlier in the year," Karaca said, "all high-level bank staff and some other key market-access corporate staff with certain risk assessments were required to undergo an integrity and loyalty assessment at random intervals

132

of up to a few months. We used a neural scan-based system." He glanced at Lehman, then said, "It included imaging, and basic reinforcement of loyalty to the Administration and the Central Bank's standards of ethics."

"That's restricted technology," Toreth said in surprise.

"Yes, but the Administration grants licenses for some uses. I've been scanned myself, multiple times. It wasn't pleasant, but it was part of the job. Everyone who takes a designated post has the process explained to them up front." Karaca rubbed his forehead above his right eyebrow. "Anyway, we lost the provider after the trouble last year, and we're still finalizing our replacement screening programs."

"So if someone wanted to infiltrate the bank, now would be a good time," Toreth said.

"A slightly better time," Lehman said. "Or at least someone might think so. It doesn't directly impact on this situation. Our system monitoring is still far beyond the scope where one, or two, or even ten employees could manipulate it and remain undetected. Whatever your sab was sending, it could have no technical effect here. But I promise you, we will be looking."

"Maybe you should start with recruits since the unrest? If you'd like us to help with background security checks, I'm sure I can get all the manpower needed."

Karaca opened his mouth, but Lehman answered before he could speak.

"Thank you, but no. We can take care of that more efficiently, I'm sure. Can't we?"

Karaca nodded. "Absolutely, Director."

"There," Lehman said. "And if we uncover anything suspicious, however small, we'll pass the names over to I&I."

After a run through their future plans—which seemed to be that I&I continued to investigate, while the bank continued to deny they could possibly have a security hole—the meeting ended. Toreth wondered if Turnbull had received the same adamant insistence that Central Bank's systems were beyond bombproof. If she had, she'd distrusted the assurance enough to give him the special exemption waiver.

As they all stood up, Toreth heard B-C say in an undertone to Verstraeten, "Did you know that they scan their staff over there?"

"Not know, exactly, but I've heard stories about it before. Supposedly there was a plan to extend it to parts of Corporate Fraud, but senior management here wouldn't have it." Verstraeten closed his hand screen and shrugged. "That was all years ago, though, and really just a rumor."

"Isn't that kind of reinforcement scanning dangerous?" Jameson asked dubiously.

"It can't be, can it?" B-C sounded surprised by the idea. "It's Administration policy, after all. And Karaca is head of systems security at the bank. He wouldn't be getting scanned himself if he thought it was risky, surely?"

Personally, Toreth's already low opinion of the Administration's ability to screen its employees had dropped to record depths after the failure to notice one of its own socioanalysts masterminding an Administration-wide revolt. Scanning or not, if Carnac could fail to trip alarms at Socioanalysis, how bulletproof could the Central Bank's staff screening possibly be?

Whatever the truth, he would clearly need some more concrete evidence before he could convince Lehman that a serious threat existed.

Even subvocalizing in the privacy of his home office didn't feel secure enough with Toreth in the flat. At the same time, he couldn't risk compromising SimTech by calling sabs from there. That made a lunchtime return to the flat Warrick's best option, since even if Toreth chose today to check up on him, he couldn't ask why Warrick was at home without revealing his snooping. The safest choice, yes, but Warrick couldn't shake the feeling of dishonesty. All he could do was tell himself truthfully that it was better for Toreth not to know. If this imploded, genuine innocence would be the only safety, however fragile.

The nameless male voice that answered Warrick's secure comm request today matched the initial contact he'd made, but that didn't mean much. The agent certainly wasn't hearing Warrick's voice.

"I found a possible team, but not for your specific target request. They're willing to contract for acquiring a named single file, or defined piece of information, with provisos."

And therein lay a large proportion of the danger. Even with Cit Surveillance involved, simple corruption might be able to abstract a single piece of information with low risk of tracing back to the corruptee—with an inversely proportional risk of identifying Warrick if the attempt blew up.

"No. It has to be a large enough data loss to obscure the target."

"Then you'll need someone with less risk-averse contacts than I have. The team offered a counterproposal, though, which is a personnel file search result log. They're substantially lower security. A search is carried out, and you'd get a record of which files matched the criteria."

That would answer the most basic question of whether Kate was dead. "I assume Cit operative file IDs don't include the operative's name, though."

"No. But they can get the ID for a particular operative."

Thereby giving the sabs Kate's name, thereby linking the operation back to Warrick if things went wrong. Every option seemed to lead to the same stumbling block. "How would it be done?"

"Are you interested, then?"

"Maybe. But I have to clearly understand the level of risk."

"The relevant hardware would be scheduled for repair with the logs still in memory. It'll be taken out of the building through the facility's own procedures, diverted for analysis, and then returned. The memory should be wiped anyway, so there'll be nothing suspicious left behind."

A plan that tidied up after itself. The neatness appealed. And while physical interaction was always riskier than remote access, it was an interesting approach he hadn't considered. Warrick made a note to discuss with SimTech systems security whether the technique was something on their radar.

"And how do they link an operative ID to a name?"

"A straight—and, I should warn you, substantial—payment to a contact in exchange for the information."

"A contact inside Int-Sec?"

"I don't have that information. I'd assume so, though. If you're interested I can ask for more detail—not a name, but perhaps some indication of how long they've used the contact, or the number of successful transactions."

"I need to think about it," Warrick said.

"Sure, I understand." He didn't sound surprised. "You know how to reach me, if we need to talk again."

How many sab contracts reached this stage and went no further, Warrick wondered. The agent had already taken his or her initial fee, and while they'd get more again if the plan carried through, this was money for very little risk indeed. A good business to be in, unless everything went wrong and some corporate or sab sold them out. Perhaps because that corporate or sab had found themselves at I&I, or in an even worse situation.

Inter- and intracorporate sabbing was one thing. Aiming a sab team at an Administration facility meant stepping into a completely different arena—although obviously one that enough people ventured into that an enterprising sab team had developed a system for discreetly "borrowing" Int-Sec hardware. Was it an arena he dared enter? Or... perhaps there was a compromise available, taking the least dangerous part of the sabbing plan and looking elsewhere for the key to use it. Although if he decided to look there, why not—

His comm chimed. Coming so soon after ending the call to the sabs, it gave him an irrational jolt of fear. Then he checked the caller's identity, and smiled.

The more solid evidence Toreth had hoped for arrived on Thursday afternoon, when B-C came into Toreth's office wearing a look of quiet triumph. He was still limping, but he'd come back from New Year with only one stick, which gave him a free arm with which to flourish his hand screen.

"Would you like to hear the good news or bad news first, Para?" B-C asked.

Normally, Toreth would've told him not to piss about. But Warrick was still showing his appreciation for his present, and anticipation for the coming weekend was already mellowing Toreth's mood.

"Give me the good."

"We have a possible ID on Richardson's contact. Evan Rupert Lake, 27, a trades analysis systems programmer. And he has an interesting background, Para. He was sponsored at university by the EFA—European Fisec Authority—which regulates finance sector corporations. He then worked at the EFA for three years, until some corporation called—" B-C consulted his hand screen. "—Equibon Investments snapped him up and transferred his training debt. Typical-sounding career path, but it may be significant, I thought, in light of Richardson's story."

Toreth sat up. "How good is the ID? I thought the reconstruction was useless?"

"It was, Para. But we located some images from one of the meetup sites. It was a pure fluke. Part of the increase in security in areas bordering corporate districts. A corporate security coalition operating near the meet location bought one of the newly licensed autonomous mobile security systems, and applied to have coverage extended outside the designated high security zone."

A concession wrung out of the Administration by the Confederation of European Corporations in the wake of the revolt. "They won't last," Toreth said. "I remember the last time they tried fliers. The assassinations and countersabbing were out of control."

"More cases for us, I suppose," B-C said philosophically. "Anyway, it came online the day before the meeting—the cameras probably weren't even flying when that meetup was arranged. It still gave us a pool of males in the area, but Nagra showed their security file photos to Richardson and we got a hit. He wasn't verbally confident, but Nagra said the neural trace was positive."

Which, given the complication of Richardson's treatments, was less certain than it could've been. "You can confirm Lake for the other meetings?"

"Well...yes and no. He had an unusually light touch on the c&p—pays a lot of cash, or just doesn't get out much—but we established a negative imprint for him for the times Richardson gave us."

In other words, the suspect hadn't definitively been anywhere else. "Do we know where he is right now?"

"Oh, yes. Although that's the bad news. He's dead."

Now Toreth wished he'd started with the bad news. "Hell. When?"

"Beginning of December, possibly the very end of November. He has no family in New London, but someone at Equibon Investments..." He checked the screen again, then gave up. "One of his colleagues, anyway. She reported him missing on the third, which was a Tuesday. She last saw him alive on the previous Friday, the twenty-ninth of November. His body only surfaced last week, dismembered and dumped at a building site out in the sticks. Lucky for us it was dug up again before they built something on top of it. Under the circumstances, I'd say a sab hit."

Richardson had been right—something bad had happened to his contact, and right around the date Richardson had given for the missed meeting. "Good work, B-C."

"Thank you, Para," B-C said, then added, "Although Jameson was the one who actually spotted the new autonomous security."

Toreth frowned at him. "Feeling generous for the performance reviews? Don't worry, I'm sure Sara's keeping track."

B-C cleared his throat. "Sorry, Para. I just didn't want to—"

"Mind you, you'll be lucky if anyone other than Morehen gets a bonus this year. Now we can call Justice—no, you go over there in person, and let's hope they haven't completely fucked up our evidence."

Being part of an active investigation, Lake's body was still stored in the Justice morgue. After B-C limped away, Toreth sent a request to O'Reilly to take a look at it once it had been delivered to I&I, with a tactfully worded hint that it was important enough for some overtime.

The rest of the evidence, once retrieved, appeared pleasingly complete. Corporate sabotage was high-end work for Justice, and they'd put respectable resources into the murder. B-C reported them as disappointed and grudging when requested to hand the case over so soon.

"Tough shit," Toreth said. "Send anything that can store information down to Systems, and tell them it's a priority. I want to know what was in that code he gave to Richardson. And give everything else to Forensics."

"Already done, Para. Well—what Justice had, anyway. Equibon Investments claims his desk was cleared two weeks after he stopped coming to work; all personal items were destroyed, and they wouldn't give Justice access to his work system or records without warrants."

"Stubborn enough to be suspicious, or they just think dealing with Justice is beneath them?"

B-C smiled. "Probably the latter, Para. Anyway, if they still want warrants we can get them. Meanwhile, he did have a high-end private system, totally secure— physically secure, with no outside connections at all. The Justice report says they found nothing illegal or evidential on it, but I've given it to Systems, and they'll call if they find anything."

The location of Lake's flat interested Toreth. He had, at least recently, prized security over space. He'd moved at the worst time for that, too, three months after the revolt when the corporate horde was in full flight away from the discontented masses and towards high security-graded accommodation. Perhaps that was why he'd ended up with somewhere even smaller than Toreth's old flat.

"He moved not long after he first contacted Richardson," B-C said, as they looked through the file detailing Justice's search.

"He must've been expecting trouble."

"Well, he certainly got that. No sign of a struggle, though, Para. Or search disturbance."

"No." Hopefully strong building security would've prevented whoever killed Lake from removing any evidence in the flat. "So what do you think, B-C? His security file says women, and you're the girlfriend expert."

B-C scanned through the pictures of the bedroom, then the bathroom. "Nothing that indicates a partner to me. At least, not one serious enough to leave a mark."

"Or to register. Shame. Even if he hadn't confided in her, she might've noticed something." Toreth skipped through the search, then asked, "It there anything else interesting in the flat?"

"Not really, Para. Evidence analysis reads it as a normal corporate lifestyle. The secure system's the only item of note."

"Did Systems give you an ETA for their report on that? There must be *something* on it, or why have it?"

"A couple of days, perhaps. I emphasized how important it was. And I mentioned the Bureau—I hope that was okay?"

Toreth nodded. "This time their interest's official. You don't have any plans for the weekend, I assume?"

"No, Para," B-C said immediately.

And neither would anyone else on the team, including Toreth himself. Turnbull would be expecting results and a demonstration of effort, but that had little weight. The case was starting to develop and he'd need to be here to make sure leads were followed up and snags were dealt with promptly. Warrick and the new bed would be there another weekend.

Toreth opened the IIP and started assigning tasks.

Toreth didn't get back to the flat until late, hoping that Warrick would have left some food for him. He didn't have the enthusiasm even to reheat something frozen. Halfway to the kitchen, Toreth paused—could he hear voices in the living room?

When he opened the door, he found Dillian there, on the sofa beside Warrick, looking thoroughly settled in. Used plates sat on the coffee table in the living room, along with a block of Parmesan and the grater, a blue bottle of mineral water, two glasses, and forks and spoons.

He couldn't stop the little stab of irritation. Eating in the living room, and not just anything, either, but pasta. Warrick only grudgingly let *him* eat dinner in the living room, probably because even though it was allegedly *their* flat Warrick had furnished it with the same sort of stupid light-colored shit he'd had at the last place, or at least only a few shades darker.

He said hello, and was about to retreat to hunt for leftovers in the kitchen, when Dillian smiled welcomingly.

"Toreth! How are you?"

Reflexes took over. "I'm fine. Can't complain. You?"

"I'm very well." She stood up and hesitated, waiting, so he went over to her, wondering what the hell was going on. She kissed him on both cheeks and smiled again. Up close the smile had a determined edge to it, but she sounded friendly enough. "I'm afraid I was so hungry I talked Keir into feeding me."

"No problem. I'm sure he made enough. Were you..." He couldn't think how to finish that. "Accidentally mindfucked" probably wasn't the tactful choice.

"Actually, I just dropped by to tell Keir I've been offered a partnership as a deep-sea installation consultant. Faroe Consultancies, in New London. Not much site work, at least at first. Office-based design and technical troubleshooting, mostly."

"Congratulations," Toreth said. If she'd come here to gloat about future chances to piss him off, he couldn't fault her technique. "No more off-world bases, then?"

"No. I do enjoy it, but being on Mars when the trouble started made me re-think. Not because of the danger on the base, but it was a long, long way from home."

"So I suppose we'll be seeing more of you?" He matched her smile. "Great."

Dillian frowned slightly, obviously suspecting him of taking the piss. Warrick's expression was absolutely blank.

Toreth forced himself to think about suitable family-based crap, then added, "You'll be able to see Marriot more, too. And Valeria. She'll love it, I should think. Wouldn't you say, Warrick?"

"Ah—yes. I'm sure she will." Warrick stood up and started gathering plates. "Do you want something to eat right away? You were quite right, there's plenty left."

"Yeah, thanks. And a glass of wine, if there's something open. Dillian, do you want another one?"

He ate slowly; it meant he had to say less, although Dillian kept including him in the conversation. Refusing to be beaten, he matched her smile for smile. It took an hour before she left, but by then she had begun to look as disconcerted as he felt. Good. Toreth even went to the door with them to say a cheerful goodbye.

Back in the living room, he picked up his wine glass and drained it, then turned to find Warrick watching him from the doorway, smiling.

"Poor Dilly will be awake all night, wondering if you've been abducted by Psychoprogramming and re-educated."

"Psychoprogramming doesn't exist anymore, which is the only reason I'm not blaming them, too. What the fuck was that about? And don't say 'what was what about?'"

Warrick, who'd already opened his mouth, closed it again and smiled wryly. "Truthfully, then, we had a somewhat lively discussion at New Year, which resulted in Dilly agreeing to make a fresh start regarding, well. Us. I think that must have been it. Thank you for meeting her halfway."

Toreth shook his head. "I was just worried she was about to start foaming at the mouth and bite me."

"I still appreciate the reciprocation, however motivated."

"Oh, yeah?" Toreth smiled, banishing Dillian from his mind. "How much?"

Chapter Seventeen

❖

Despite everything, despite Carnac's conviction at their last meeting that Warrick would never have reason to speak to him again, he'd never erased Carnac's contact information. The socioanalyst's comm supported the latest, most secure systems approved by the Communications Systems Assessment Division. Secure against Citizen Surveillance? Common sense suggested that could be a risky assumption. A speculative journey to Strasbourg might have an even higher chance of attracting attention. So. Make the call.

The seconds ticked past on his watch. A birthday gift from Kate, many years ago. He hadn't really thought about its origins for years. It had no inscription, no visible tie to her. Perhaps he'd wear another one for a while, though. Or none. It was only ornamentation, after all. No practical value. Time made tangible, with the tiny hesitation before each tick poised on the uncertain future.

He'd started to wonder if Carnac would simply ignore the call—no answer, no chance to leave a message—when the blank screen suddenly changed to Carnac's face. Despite the fact that he must have known who was calling, he performed a very creditable rendition of absolute astonishment.

"Keir!"

"Hello," Warrick said.

"My goodness, what a *very* unexpected end to the week." Carnac turned his head, looking across the office. "Adam, leave us, please. I'll call when I'm done. Until then, you can talk to the twins about starting the research we discussed."

What Warrick could see of the large room behind him suggested that the straitened circumstances in which he'd found Carnac on his last meeting had been resolved. The new office was large enough to be divided by a display bookshelf, and the glimpse of a city view to one edge of the screen pointed to a prestigious location.

Carnac, likewise, seemed to have repaired the scuffs to his polished manner. "Staff of my very own," he said, as though Warrick had asked. "Not even related to me, and still an entertaining novelty. I do believe I may be being seduced by the attractions of corporate life." He paused for a moment. "Now, I'm sure you didn't call for the pleasure of hearing my voice, even if that's why I answered."

If Carnac had left an ambiguous opening for a dig at his vanity, no doubt it was on purpose. Warrick ignored the tempting gambit. "I'm afraid I need another piece of information."

Carnac's expression of polite interest didn't flicker. "I'm listening."

"Before I ask, I need to know if I can rely on your discretion this time."

"You mean, don't warn anyone that you're placing yourself in potentially fatal danger?" Carnac shrugged. "Very well. I shall leave you to look after your own interests, no matter how badly. What do you want to know?"

"I'd prefer to discuss it face to face."

His eyebrows lifted fractionally. "Are you in Strasbourg?"

He could almost imagine that Carnac sounded alarmed. "No. But...I'm not sure that coming to Strasbourg would be a good idea."

The corner of Carnac's mouth twitched, but he sounded perfectly unemotional when he said, "You don't want to provoke Toreth with another visit?"

"I try to consider his feelings, which isn't the same thing."

"Consider his feelings?" He stressed the last word, and this time the twitch became a definite smile. "At least that can't waste too much of your time."

"Please don't—"

Carnac had already held up his hand before Warrick even began his protest. "Petty and irrelevant, yes. You know my long-standing views on your relationship thoroughly enough by now to make a consultation unnecessary, so this obviously relates to another topic. I suppose that 'face to face' means you want me to come to New London? Immediately?"

"No, it's not urgent. Difficult, but not urgent. But the next time you're here, if you could spare an hour or so? It's about...a family matter."

"Ah, I see." There was a long, thoughtful silence, then Carnac said, "I promised someone that I would keep my distance from you—and from Toreth."

Warrick frowned. "Promised who?"

"Perhaps I should've said something, not someone. Socioanalysis. It was one of several preconditions for the end of our legal wranglings and the restoration of my license."

Could it really be true that Socioanalysis had such a strong interest in whether Carnac met him? It sounded bizarre, but neither could he imagine Carnac making up an excuse to justify avoiding him. "I see, but—"

"No, you don't. But that doesn't matter." Carnac brushed his hair back with his left hand. "What matters is that I gave my word on the matter—a currency I try to keep sound while surrounded by widespread devaluation—and gave it freely. And yet here I am, accepting your call."

He'd had some strange conversations with Carnac in the past, but this matched any of them. "New London to Strasbourg is still quite a distance."

"People who make a living from the splitting of the finest hairs are generally not interested in excuses along those lines." Carnac looked away from the camera, frowning a little. He reached out, and when his hand came back into view he was holding a small chess piece. A rook; Warrick remembered seeing the same set on Carnac's temporary desk at I&I during the revolt. "Keir, in the past months I've come to understand—well, a great number of things. The pertinent revelation here, though, is that for some time I placed...an undue weight on both our relationship—" Carnac pointed the rook at the screen. "Which did not exist in any meaningful sense. That is, in fact, rather the core of the problem. Where was I? Yes. An undue weight on both our relationship, and on the intensity of my dislike for Toreth. Not that I'd characterize my current feelings towards him as anything other than profound loathing. But he is only one insignificant, if repellent, cog, grinding away in service of the greater machine, and my psychological need for him to bear the weight of my feelings towards that machine is diminishing. Somewhat. And slowly. Do you understand?"

Warrick fleetingly wished that De Nijs could be there to interpret. "I'm not sure."

"Well, perhaps on reflection it may become clearer." Carnac sat up a little straighter. "The practical consequence, though, is that to protect myself on multiple levels I cannot afford to reengage at this moment. Professionally or personally. I am genuinely sorry," he added, with apparent sincerity, "but then again, it's possible that's just another symptom of the underlying cognitive malfunction."

Perversely, annoyingly, the pity Warrick had felt for him at their last meeting returned. "I apologize for disturbing you. I won't call again."

"Thank you. I greatly appreciate it." Carnac looked at him meditatively for a moment, then sighed and set the rook down on his desk. "Yet I cannot deny that, as was once pointed out to me with some emphasis, I was the proximate cause of some of your current 'family matters.' Very well, let us see what can be accomplished in the moment. Is the problem fraternal or maternal in nature? Or regarding a mysterious dark stranger?"

Dark stranger? Ah—Sable. "Largely maternal," Warrick said. How to phrase it? "We've had letters. Paper letters. Reassuring in terms of content, but..."

"Unconvincing? Or unconvincingly convincing? Paper does provide rather pointed opportunities for authentication which, since you're here, one assumes they have passed?"

"Yes. But that isn't necessarily conclusive. I just need to know, first of all, whether she's dead."

Carnac's expression didn't change. "And your preferred answer?"

Warrick opened his mouth to say that of course he wanted to hear that Kate was alive. Then he stopped himself, and gave the question as neutral an examination as he could make. "I suppose 'dead' would at least be final." Worries about Tarin pushed themselves forcefully to the front of his mind. "'Alive' would have its own complications. Especially if she comes home."

If Carnac was shocked—unlikely—it didn't show. "I see. Well, I'm afraid that I have no specific factual insight to offer there. I'm not current on the situation—I've been keeping clear of matters that no longer concern me."

"Last time, you gave me a piece of information from a file. If you could give me one more small—"

"Ah, there I must stop you," Carnac said gravely. "All information I possessed has been disposed of, by way of removing temptation. I have nothing to give."

Would he remember her identification code? Whether he did or not, Warrick didn't need to ask to know the answer he'd get. He nodded. "I see."

"When we spoke previously, I suggested that you let someone stay dead. Did you?"

"No."

The lift of his brows and brief tilt of his head eloquently conveyed an utter lack of surprise. "How did that work out?"

"I got what I wanted, if not in the way that I wanted it," Warrick said honestly. "I was promised that we'd be safe. I've no reason to doubt that assurance, per se."

"And you must realize that events could've unfolded in a far less healthy fashion. Do you have any reason to believe that the current state of uncertainty poses a material danger to your friends or family?"

"Not as such," Warrick admitted reluctantly. "Not if the status quo remains unchanged."

"Good. Now, I'm sure you broached the question of your dissatisfaction with our mutual acquaintance." A tiny smile appeared on Carnac's lips. "I'm equally sure his reaction is what drove you to the desperate measure of actually contacting me."

"I promised him I'd drop it," Warrick said. "And I meant it. But later I had to reevaluate."

"Ah, well, it's some comfort to know that our words have been equally cheapened." Carnac reached out and adjusted the position of something out of sight on his desk. "And he's unaware of this reappraisal?"

"Yes. Anyway, he probably can't access that kind of information. Certainly not much more safely than I." Warrick paused, but Carnac merely regarded him steadily, obviously waiting for the rest to be spoken aloud. "He wouldn't agree to do it if I asked, as I'm sure you know. He wouldn't even understand why I'm willing to take the risk."

Carnac shook his head. "I must admit that in some circumstances, his deplorable personal qualities can be advantageous. He's a predator, with a predator's instinct for sizing up larger, more dangerous animals. Keir, you have unwisely ven-

144

tured into a very dark and deep jungle. Please be guided by his splendidly functional sense of self-preservation, and leave whatever dwells therein alone. That is the path I *strongly* recommend you choose to take."

"I can't. I need to—"

"As I believe I pointed out before," Carnac interrupted sharply, "'can't' is self-deception. Whatever you might think, I do know you better than that."

The chiding tone grated. Why couldn't he just say "I won't help," when that was the end result of his pontificating? "So that's it, then?"

"Yes. No. Let me conclude with a small prediction. You have already considered a range of options. As a good, law-abiding, but most pertinently *intelligent* citizen, I'm sure you realize that the less legal ones carry with them an unacceptably high chance of catastrophe. Let us discount them all." He flicked his hand, shooing away the thought. "But perhaps you're still contemplating approaching your mysterious dark stranger again."

"Yes, I have thought about that. It seemed...unwise. That's why I called you."

"How novel to be the lesser evil for once. But you're right, yes, it's vastly unwise. Your family's recent mishaps have demonstrated his, shall we say, robust approach to crisis management." Carnac raised a warning finger. "Do not become a problem he needs to solve, or force him into making a choice between duty and family, or this *will* end badly. Still." He shrugged and folded his hands. "I can't deny that he would seem to represent the least danger-filled possibility of acquiring information about the person in question."

"When we talked before, he lied to me...repeatedly." Admitting that to Carnac felt strangely painful. "I have no reason to think he'd tell me the truth about this."

"Then you must consider whether the game is worth the candle, especially with such poor and unreliable illumination." Carnac leaned forward, his voice gentler. "Keir, no one understands better than I how terrifying it feels to lack knowledge and control. Those are water and oxygen to a socioanalyst. Please believe that I empathize acutely. And among your many delightful attributes is a generous amount of observation-derived opportunity maximization—or luck, if you prefer—but you can't rely on that forever. To repeat myself, you should stop this. For your own safety, *must* stop this. Now. Forgive yourself, and others if you are able, and close the book on the matter, however unsatisfying you find the final chapter."

He sounded so emphatic that Warrick wondered why Carnac had chosen to point out the possibility of approaching Sable. Just a socioanalyst's professionalism in giving a client his best analysis of the situation? A desire to find out Warrick's intentions? Having taken the step of contacting Carnac, ignoring his advice completely would be foolish.

"Yes," Warrick said. "I suppose you're right."

To his surprise, Carnac sat back in his chair with obvious relief. Affected, or genuine? "Of course I am. Although you'd be surprised how often people don't seem to care."

"I should let it go," Warrick said. A repeat of his promise to Toreth, already broken twice. "At least while I don't have any evidence of immediate danger. And, yes, try to accept that I can't control everything."

"I suggest you make a strenuous effort in that direction. You might even find it refreshing. I have." Carnac smiled, suddenly, his vivid blue eyes crinkling at the corners.

"What?" Warrick asked.

"It has been, as ever, a joy to talk to you." Still smiling, Carnac shook his head. "However, ten minutes' conversation, and the merest hint of acquiescence on your part, and already I find myself prodding awake the sad fantasy that one day you might forgive me the unforgivable. I think that's a sign I should say good-bye. So. Goodbye, Keir. And bon chance. Please give yourself no reason to need it."

The connection went blank before Warrick could reply.

Carnac stared up at the ceiling for a good five minutes after ending the call, trying to empty his mind. It was a technique he'd learned a very long time ago, during his first few years at the academy. A roomful of six-year-olds, all unnaturally still and silent, being molded into obedient little socioanalysts. Perhaps that was why he'd abandoned the practice for many years. Or perhaps it was that, much as he hated to admit it, he still found it almost impossible to achieve.

Keir had once asked him, "don't you ever stop?", and the answer he'd given, that he couldn't, was practically true. The lie—or at least vast simplification—had been in adding that he wished he could. In fact, there was so much for a mind to *do,* and so little time in the day to think everything he wanted to think, especially after subtracting time spent on basic survival and tedious professional necessities.

Despite recent changes in circumstances, Keir's well-being still mattered to him. The point at which it no longer did would also be the point at which he could be confident that he could become involved again. Paradoxical, but not helpful.

Did he believe Keir's promise? In the short term, perhaps. In the longer? Not for a moment. The itching lack of knowledge would not remain unscratched for-ever. But whether Keir yet acknowledged it to himself or not, the promise made would've been the same. Disappointing, but understandable. He must know that Carnac had other considerations beyond Keir's personal safety.

Which led Carnac to the tricky question of whether to report the conversation. He could dismiss it as a contact from a potential client whom he had ultimately turned down, but that would be one more instance of the self-deception he had deplored. The odds of whether or not Socioanalysis might come to hear of the conversation anyway was only a single factor, albeit one that affected the weighting of several others: his own professional goals, Keir's interests, Kailynna Avens's possible well-being (not worth a great deal of his consideration), potential effects on Citizen Surveillance and the wider Administration.

And, as whimsical as it might be, he found himself wondering what was the *right* thing to do. Apparently the sting of the lesson he'd learned from the revolt had already faded.

As far as he had been able to discover, Socioanalysis had played fair and maintained the bargain struck that past autumn. He had his access to resources, his license, and his Socioanalysis-trained staff. For that, he owed them some loyalty. On the other hand, he had hurt Keir, and but for happenstance and Toreth's infuriating, improbable persistence in Keir's life, the hurt would've been worse, both deliberately and via unanticipated consequence. While Carnac's motives had been... if not impeccable, then at least excellent diabolical paving material, that also had left a debt to Warrick.

Another consideration—Adam may have taken note of Keir's uncommon name. The exclamation had been careless. While his assistant had his own charms, as a failed socioanalyst candidate with the same years of childhood indoctrination as Carnac himself, he was still deeply enmeshed in the influence of Socioanalysis. Had he been warned to watch for Keir? Would he report what he'd heard?

Carnac looked around the office, which sometimes gave him the impression of being very pleasantly but unmistakably gilded, and sighed. Possibly he should've fired the boy, and the two data analysts also supplied by Socioanalysis, weeks ago. He hadn't, though, and the current hiccup aside, they'd been more than satisfactory.

On balance, then, qualified honesty seemed appropriate. Camille du Pre answered her comm after only a slight delay.

To his surprise, the connection was voice only. Someone too interesting in her office, perhaps?

"Jean-Baptiste?"

Better to keep the conversation light. "You'll never guess who I talked to just now," he said. "Or perhaps you will."

To his surprise, she hesitated for a fleeting moment. "Guess?" Then she laughed, but the edge seemed forced. "You've left me a rather large range of possibilities. If you tell me what you talked about, that might help narrow it down."

"It was a figure of speech," he said. "Actually, I had a call from Keir Warrick."

"Dr. Warrick, I see. And...?"

"I'm sorry—are you busy? This can wait."

147

"No, not too busy to talk." Another tiny hesitation. "Although if it's likely to be a long conversation, it might be better to schedule some time."

"Not very long, no. I merely wished to inform you of the breach of my terms of reengagement."

"What was the call about?"

"He wanted some professional advice regarding a family matter. Nothing whatsoever to do with the para-investigator."

"Ah." She audibly relaxed, a more obvious reaction than he'd heard from her for a while, and he wondered what she'd been anticipating. "What family matter?"

Should he elaborate? As regrettable as some of the potential outcomes might be for Keir, the root cause of his potential messy demise at the hands of Citizen Surveillance was hardly something to shake the fabric of Europe's social and political landscape. "Nothing of great import to anyone but him. I gave him a brief consultation and told him I was unable to help further. As I never actually informed him of the new boundaries of our relationship, vis-à-vis not having one, one can hardly blame him for calling. I admit I merely assumed that given the strained circumstances, he never would. Now he knows."

"Then I think you have everything covered." And she was fully back in control again. Intriguing. "Thank you for the prompt call. Is that all?"

"Yes. No. Yes." Carnac pressed his forefinger against his lips and considered all the reasons why it would be a terrible idea to ask du Pre—"No. I find myself with an unignorable need to beg a favor."

"Regarding Dr. Warrick's unimportant family matter." There was no hint of a question in her voice.

"Yes. I'm afraid that...he might be about to have a conversation that could attract unwelcome attention from another Administration department. Citizen Surveillance, to be exact."

"What do you want me to do about it?"

"Warn them away—indirectly. Flag his security file. Just a note that he's of continuing interest to Socioanalysis. It isn't entirely untrue. The sim has social and political ramifications significant enough to warrant the study I carried out."

"Other departments aren't bound to respect our requests. Courtesy usually holds, but..."

"I know. Still, it might at least give them pause if anyone decided his removal would be the expedient solution." Carnac briefly considered the rest of Keir's family and friends before deciding they would have to take their chances. He could place only so many demands on his still-unseasoned arrangement with the rest of Socioanalysis. "It would be better if my name isn't attached to the note. Citizen Surveillance can't hold a favorable view of me at the moment, especially regarding this matter."

The silence went on long enough that he was about to prompt to see if she was still there, when she said. "Very well. You know, I'm starting to feel as though I need to meet this Dr. Warrick. I don't think his security file can entirely represent him."

"I'm sure you'd enjoy it," Carnac said. "He's delightful in person, especially when you can talk intelligently about his work. I wouldn't rely on an introduction from me, however. Not if you want a warm reception."

"No." She laughed. "No, perhaps not. And now, Jean-Baptiste, I'm afraid I must go."

After brief goodbyes, Carnac was left contemplating a blank screen. A minute's assessment of the conversation as he recalled it, then he pulled up the recording of the call and replayed the opening segment.

The idea of du Pre rattled by a simple call from a colleague was so unlikely he'd already half convinced himself that he must've been mistaken. Not so. Her reactions sat at the perfect point to ring maximum alarm bells—too small and disorganized to be deliberate, too obvious to be trivial surprise or distraction. Something was most definitely afoot at Socioanalysis, if not actually awry. That would bear watching in the future.

And now, he really should get back to work, since he had to finance all idle speculation and curiosity himself these days. Unfortunately, none of the professional options available seemed likely to soothe his lingering disquiet. He hated to give work, however uninteresting, less attention than the payment merited. Instead, he closed the files and called Adam back into the office.

The boy opened the door with no more or less energy than usual. No guilt on his face. No sign of conflict over whether he should inform his other masters of Carnac's conversation. Perhaps he'd already done it.

"When I sell *my* soul, at least I offer good value," Carnac said, unable to resist testing.

Adam looked at him blankly. "Socioanalyst?"

Carnac shook his head. "Just thinking aloud. It's a terrible habit, actually. Obnoxious, even."

Adam smiled. "You? Never."

"You'll be astonished to hear it's been suggested." By Keir, for one. And why did all his conversations with the man stay so clear in his mind that he could recall a pointless, low-information remark from nigh on two decades ago?

"Was there something you wanted?" Adam asked.

Ah, well. If Carnac couldn't empty his mind one way, perhaps another would help. "Yes, Adam. I've decided to go out of the office for lunch today, if you'd like to accompany me."

"Okay. Where? Are we meeting a client?" He brushed his hand through his thick, dark hair—a mess as usual. "Do I need to prepare anything?"

149

"Actually, I thought I might go home and order something to eat there."

Failed candidate he might be, but Adam could certainly pick up a hint. He grinned. "Sounds like fun! Um." He glanced back at the door, possibly wondering if he'd left it open and Colette might have heard him. (Carnac supposed it was possible his sister hadn't yet noticed what was happening; he hadn't cared to ask her.) Then Adam looked back at Carnac and licked his bottom lip. "Early lunch?" he asked.

As Carnac was well aware without looking, it was barely eleven. He smiled, and stood up. "Why not?"

Toreth had expected Lake's autopsy file to show up in the IIP sometime on Friday morning. O'Reilly was efficient and her reports thorough enough that they usually stood alone. To his surprise, she called him.

"I'm sending it right now, but one or two points were missed in the original examination that make it more interesting than the usual dice and dump. I thought I'd run over it in person, if you have the time?"

"Go ahead." Experts loved to talk about their jobs. "Are you saying Justice screwed it up?"

O'Reilly shook her head. "I wouldn't go that far. It was their typical PM standard. Not bad, but could be better."

"Better how? Cause of death?"

"No, they got that right. Seven or eight heavy blows to the head from behind with something like a metal pipe. Simple but comprehensive. And he was cut up immediately after death, more extensively than you might expect for ease of transport—and in this case I'd have to say 'cut up' rather than disarticulated." She smiled, and so did Toreth. O'Reilly liked the language of death to be precise. "It's much easier to slice through the joints, but they left several joints intact and cut through bone instead. There are even some diagonal and longitudinal cuts. I ran it through the system already, but no matches to patterns in previous cases."

Amateurs at work, or something more significant? Toreth made a note. "Anything else unusual?"

"Well, we're missing a section of left thigh, one kidney, half a lung, and some intestines."

Toreth nodded. "They're probably in a marsh somewhere. Or under a wall."

"Well, possibly. It's common enough for sabbed corpses to show up in so many parts when there's moving water to disperse them, less so for burials. But more interestingly, there are some unusual postmortem right lower limb injuries that Justice attributed to burial damage. According to the notes, the corpse was dumped opportunistically in a construction trench, then rediscovered roughly five weeks later during further digging. I don't think..." O'Reilly frowned thoughtfully at something Toreth couldn't see, then shook her head. "Some of the damage, yes, I agree. But below that is another distinct set of injuries, still postmortem, that look more regular. Mechanical scraping and crushing to the bones, with the most severe being at the most distal locations. Several of the phalanges are missing entirely."

"Left behind in the trench?"

"Even Justice usually remembers to collect human remains. A basic reconstructive scan at the scene would've shown the feet were incomplete. I think it's far more likely there was another event, after death but before burial."

A basic scan for I&I, possibly not for Justice. Toreth flipped back through the case report. "The body was found on the site of a bionutrient processing plant. Some corporation called Fresh Green Fields—I bet they aren't—in the protein sector. So you're thinking they'd have the right kind of machinery to produce that damage?"

"I hate to say it, but that's exactly what I was thinking, yes." O'Reilly grimaced. "The mix of transferred organic materials on the remains and especially within the questionable injuries would support the theory. It includes things you wouldn't expect to find in a hole in the ground."

Toreth grinned. "So, what are you having for dinner tonight?"

To his surprise, O'Reilly laughed. "Don't look at me. I cut up enough muscle here—I'm vegetarian."

Toreth had a general idea of where most of the food he ate came from. As everyone who had sat through the mind-numbing tedium of citizenship classes knew, clonal cells were seeded onto preformed scaffolds, allowing corporations to produce hygienic, nutritious, and affordable fish, meat, and other foods for all Administration citizens. Warrick, oddly, had been the source of most of his more recent knowledge when, exasperated by Toreth's lack of interest, Warrick had cooked a tasting platter of pork ribs. A rack of ribs from a real pig were the most expensive—and, according to Warrick, the best tasting—followed by vat-grown "replica" cuts, anatomically accurate with natural proportions of bone, muscle, and fat. After that were the generic ribs familiar from cheap restaurants and more expensive takeaways: oblong slabs with evenly sized bones. Finally Warrick had disdainfully produced entirely boneless rib strips, made from reconstituted vat-brewed protein, by far the most resource-efficient—and in Toreth's view absolutely perfect for any late night when your taste buds had drowned in alcohol.

Warrick's demanding palate had given Toreth more of an appreciation of "real" meat, but left to his own devices he'd never pay the exorbitant premium for barbecued ribs that had lazed around in a shed somewhere for months instead of sitting in a nutrient bath for days. Not unless he was slipping the bill past I&I expenses, anyway.

What he'd never given much thought to was the stage before the bioreactor.

"As you can see, this is the new breakdown plant," Tushingham said. The site director was a neat, fussy little man, with a bald spot and a pinched expression. "Still under construction, or at least it was. They found the, ah, *body* about fifty meters over there. Justice had promised we could start work again soon," he added anxiously. "Do you think you'll need to keep it sealed off for longer?"

"Let's hope not," Toreth said. He supposed he should be grateful to Justice for not already releasing the scene and letting Tushingham build a bloody great piece of industry on top of it. "But this is an I&I case, now, so I can't make any promises."

"Oh."

Toreth watched for a minute as Jameson picked her way through the sticky winter mud towards where the screens erected by Justice still blocked off an inconvenient area of the site. She had the appropriate equipment from O'Reilly to check for the missing pieces of Lake.

"Now, talk me through the process you'll be carrying out in there," Toreth said.

Tushingham gave him an odd look, then shrugged. "All right. It's rather cold out here. If we go to my office I can show you the plans of the plant, and—"

"There's an older facility here that was working when the body was found, right?" Toreth said. "You can show me that, instead."

"Well..."

"Is there any reason you can't?"

"No! No, of course not. It's just that, well. This will be our state-of-the-art breakdown facility, and..." He trailed off, while Toreth looked at him steadily. "The old plant, yes, of course."

The enormous construction site where the body had been found occupied only a corner of the industrial complex. The morning had started off with a thick fog, and it still shrouded the vast, windowless oblong buildings. Most were painted a pale gray, the only splashes of color being the green and yellow Fresh Green Fields logo on their sides. On the wide roads between them, large refrigerated transports displaying the same logo moved product. The damp air held a peculiar smell, reminding Toreth of a jar of yeast extract overlaid with the smell of cut grass in the Int-Sec grounds, with other notes he couldn't begin to tease out.

The old plant certainly didn't look in need of replacement. At the entrance, which made Toreth think of a Mars base airlock, he and Tushingham changed into the same white clean room suits as were worn by the occasional technician they passed. Inside the plain exterior, the building was packed with gleaming, spotless machinery.

"We process two main sources of nutrient material," Tushingham said as they walked between rows of giant tanks. "The bulk algal base is grown in the hydrotube systems on the other side of the site. We also take in organic material via our contract disposal division. Waste from further down the food supply chain, plant material, some, ah, animal byproducts."

"Human waste?"

"Oh, no. No, no, no." Tushingham paused for a moment, then kept walking. "Of course, you understand that *technically* there's no reason why we couldn't. Our processes produce the most basic biochemical components, absolutely sterile and safe. They'd be identical whatever the source. The growth factors and so on that we use are all biosynthesized, not recovered. But that sort of starting material would be unacceptable to *our* end customers. Dear me, yes. Completely unacceptable."

His emphatic tone made Toreth smile. "So no human bodies, then?"

Tushingham gave him a nervous glance. "Of course not. Why—why would you ask that?"

"Well, this makes an unusual dump site. Most victims go into the marshes, and if someone was looking for a building site, there are plenty in the city. Taking the body here was a risk, unless they were hoping to get rid of it completely."

"Oh, I see." Tushingham cleared his throat. "Well, I wouldn't pretend to know how the minds of people like that work. As I was saying, the nutrients are recovered, separated, and reproportioned into different formulations depending on product needs. The mixes from here go over to the meat production facilities, and also to our dairy expression plant, which of course is on a separate site a kilometer or so away."

"Of course?"

"The owners of the corporation . . . that is to say, Fresh Green Fields supplies a large and, ah, varied market. Some of our clients have customers with, ah—" This time the sidelong glance went directly to the badge on Toreth's uniform. "There are some dietary and, ah, *cultural* preferences the corporation finds it profitable to consider."

Fun as it was to poke Tushingham and watch him squirm, Toreth had other corporates waiting for his attention. While they walked, a noise had been growing steadily louder, a vibration and deep grind of gears. Up ahead, Toreth spotted the piece of machinery he'd found when studying the processing plant plans back at I&I. He stopped and pointed.

"Is that where you found Lake?"

"No!" The denial came so fast, Tushingham had clearly been expecting, and dreading, the question. His pale cheeks flushed slightly. "The body was outside. Buried in a trench. We called Justice and—"

"Mr. Tushingham, I can shut down this plant—the whole site, if I have to—and bring in a full forensic team to sweep every building from end to end. We can empty every vat, every storage tank, and open every pack of meat. Forensics has very sensitive equipment, and if there's any of Lake's DNA in here, we'll find it, even if it takes days. Which I guarantee it will. And then, that sort of investigation can be very hard to keep under wraps. In fact, I'd say information would be certain to leak out."

Tushingham sighed. "All right. You obviously know something about it already. We found the, ah, *parts* of the body in here, yes. The safety sensors spotted them during an overnight run—shape recognition. You must understand, Para-investigator, we were in the middle of the New Year production ramp-up. The celebratory joint is one of our most profitable markets, and shutting down then would've been a commercial disaster. Not just lost sales, but the inevitable rumors."

"I see. Well—" Toreth paused as Jameson's voice came over his earpiece.

"There's nothing here, Para. No little piggies at this market."

"Right. Wait outside for me." Toreth turned to Tushingham. "According to our postmortem, you didn't get all of Lake out of the machinery."

"We tried our best, I promise. And we junked the whole processing run," he added earnestly. "There's zero chance any of the contamination got into a nutrient batch. *Zero*."

"So then you took the body parts and buried them outside." Which all made perfect sense, from a financial standpoint, but—"Why dig them up again later?"

"It—well, it preyed on my mind. I couldn't stop thinking about the poor man, and how worried his family must be about him." Tushingham clasped his hands together. "What a nightmare it would be for them, never knowing for certain where he was. And once the new building went up over him, well, it would be far too late. So we uncovered him and I called Justice to deal with it."

Funny how his conscience had only kicked in after the New Year. "Very public-spirited," Toreth said dryly.

His tone sailed past Tushingham unheeded. "Thank you. It seemed the right thing to do. And, well. I didn't think telling Justice the, ah, entire story really mattered." He waved his hand to indicate the building around them. "Our sterilization cleaning would've removed any evidence from here, I'm sure. It would've caused trouble for the corporation, and he was a complete stranger, after all. Nothing to do with *us*."

"Is this building's access controlled?"

"Oh, absolutely. We take product security very seriously."

"Is there any chance the body came in here as part of a waste shipment?"

"Well…" Tushingham pursed his lips thoughtfully. "In all honestly I'd have to say no, not really. Most of the material categorization is done during collection, off-site, but there's a final checking step in here. Yes, I'm sure one of the supervisors would've noticed sorting poor Mr. Lake into mechanical breakdown."

"In which case the body must've been brought in here by one of your staff, mustn't it? Or by someone else Fresh Green Fields has given access to the building. Which makes it very much something to do with you."

"Oh. Oh, yes. Yes, I do see what you mean." Tushingham looked up at him unhappily. "You'll have to close us down after all, then?"

"Not if you cooperate fully. I need a complete list of everyone who worked here or had access to the building around the time you found your unwanted visitor. Found him the *first* time, I mean."

Although he'd learned relatively little that he hadn't at least guessed beforehand, Toreth didn't consider the visit to Fresh Green Fields wasted. He'd got a good feeling for the dump site, and that feeling said whoever had put the body there knew what they were about...to a certain extent. Clearly Lake had been meant to vanish, leaving the usual uncertainty as to whether he'd disappeared voluntarily or involuntarily. The plan had failed—except for half a left thigh, some internal organs, and a few toes—because of the safety system. Had the body dumpers not known about that, or had they thought the unusual dismemberment pattern O'Reilly had noted would be enough to fool it?

All interesting points that an investigator could pursue. Jameson would stay behind to begin the fun of picking through security logs and whatever month-old surveillance footage survived, and trying to match that to a sab. Toreth himself went on to the next corporation on his list.

Equibon Investments made an interesting contrast to Fresh Green Fields, at least on the surface. The initial reception area Toreth encountered was overfurnished with what he guessed to be reproduction furniture. He'd passed through enough genuine old-money corporations to recognize a pretender trying a little too hard. Maybe their clients weren't rich enough to see through it.

Doubtless any offices clients might encounter would be up to the same standards. After only a minute's wait, Toreth was escorted by a security guard into a lift and up a couple of floors. The lift doors opened onto a corridor Toreth believed a lot more than the reception: no carpets, no artwork on the walls, just slightly scuffed plastic flooring and neutral walls, with a background hum of working voices—the office equivalent of the gray sheds at Fresh Green Fields.

B-C and Mistry were waiting for him in a small meeting room. Toreth pulled out a chair—made of very unpretentious plastic and with the fabric fraying at one corner of the seat—and sat down.

"Where are we?" he asked.

B-C reported that his corporate confidentiality warrants had arrived smoothly and without objections, which made Toreth wonder if Turnbull was still taking an active interest in the case. "Their lawyers are looking over them now, Para."

"I asked them to find me the colleague who reported Lake's disappearance," Mistry said. "Emma Rutland. And there was another name in the Justice file, someone he'd worked closely with lately—Davey Cavendish. They're finding him, too."

"All right." Toreth looked over to the door; slightly to his surprise, the security guard had gone. "While we're waiting for the lawyers, B-C, you have a poke around. Get a feel for the place. See if anyone seems especially nervous to see you, or if they try to keep you out of any particular areas."

"Right, Para."

When B-C had gone, Mistry said, "Which one do you want me to take, Para?"

"Hm. What did Justice think about them?"

"Not a lot, Para, with good reason. The interviews look well conducted, and their stories are consonant. She was the more upset by the news, apparently. Justice turned up nothing suspicious in their backgrounds, and nothing to suggest either of them had much contact with Lake outside work. I glanced at the c&p, and it all seems in order."

"Let's talk to them together, then. Maybe that'll spark something one of them's forgotten."

When Rutland and Cavendish arrived they made an interesting contrast: she tall and square-shouldered, but graceful, her long, brown hair in a French plait, he short and stocky, with spiked blond hair and bad skin. They were both dressed for work, but Toreth's experienced eye rated Cavendish as the better, or at least more expensively, clothed.

They sat down at the table, opposite Mistry. Toreth stood to place the camera and then took a seat to one side, where he could see both the witnesses without being in their direct eyelines. He watched while Mistry introduced herself and Toreth and explained that I&I was taking over the case. Cavendish cast Toreth a cautious glance, then kept his attention largely on Mistry. Rutland looked over more often. Guilty conscience, or just a general nervousness towards authority in uniform?

Mistry consulted her hand screen. "You worked with Lake for almost a year, Mr. Cavendish. But you told Justice you never socialized outside work?"

"Too right," the man said emphatically. "Or inside work, either. Around here anything less than a ten-hour day, six days a week will get you a warning. Do you think I want to waste the time I do get to myself out with people who wouldn't know fun if it gave them a...good time?"

156

"And he didn't?" Mistry asked.

"Lake *enjoyed* his job."

Toreth smiled at the sneer of disbelief. Cavendish reminded him of plenty of I&I colleagues.

Mistry also smiled, more sympathetically. "And you don't?"

"I enjoy the money. Trading analysis is what brings in the profits, and they pay us well for it. A lot better than people like her—" Cavendish gestured at Rutland with his thumb. "Traders are glorified admins. Comm monkeys. If their jobs weren't legally protected, we wouldn't need them."

Rutland rolled her eyes. The aspersion didn't seem to surprise her. "There's a *bit* more to it than that. Strategy formulation. Client contact. And the systems don't always get it right, either, you know."

"The systems make the predictions and set the margins." Cavendish straightened the sleeve of his expensive shirt. "You just place the trades."

"How about you?" Mistry said to Rutland, heading off the argument. "Did you know Lake well?"

"Equibon doesn't approve of the traders socializing with the back office," she said.

"Too easy for us to conspire to break the rules," Cavendish interjected.

Rutland gave him an irritated glance, but all she said was, "I met Lake years ago, at uni. I was Finance and Accounting, he was Finance and Computing. We knew each other the way that you do when you have live-speaker lectures together. Then we lost touch until he joined Equibon. We used the same underground route—the line opened not long before he started working here, and I got on a couple of stations before him. He recognized me the first week. We'd walk here from the station together most days, and then sometimes we'd see each other on the train at the end of the day. That's all."

Mistry nodded. "Yet you were worried enough to report him missing after only a couple of days? Didn't you think he might be on holiday?"

"He would've said something. I mean, he hardly ever took any time off."

Cavendish snorted softly. "That's definitely true."

"But you didn't think it was odd he didn't show up?" Mistry asked Cavendish.

"Wasn't here. Like I told Justice, I was taking leave before the end of the year. Use it or lose it, so I had a crappy rainy few days in Manchester with my mum and dad, and another few in Amsterdam, where it was still raining, but at least I didn't have to listen to my mum wondering why I haven't met a nice girl yet. When I came back the team leader said Lake was gone and she moved someone else over to work with me. Honestly, I didn't miss him."

Which was all confirmed by Justice's report. Toreth caught Mistry's eye and gave her a get-on-with-it tilt of the head.

Mistry nodded slightly. "Now, Mr. Cavendish, do you think it's possible that Lake might've become involved in something illegal?"

Cavendish laughed. "*Lake?* Never. About as likely as my grandma joining the Service. Or taking up stripping."

"Ms. Rutland?" Mistry said.

Toreth thought he saw a hesitation before she said, "That doesn't sound like the Lake I knew at uni. That was years ago, of course, but...no."

"It's ridiculous," Cavendish said. "Really. He had a massive har—a mania for legality. He was obsessed. He could quote every tight-twatted European Fisec Authority rule that had anything to do with code compliance. From memory. Probably all the other rules, too, but luckily I didn't have to listen to those. That's where his office nickname came from—Rupert Rules."

"So why did he leave Fisec?" Mistry asked.

Cavendish shrugged. "*He* said—and this is just what he said, mind—that they pushed him out. Conflict of attitudes, he called it. He thought they were—" He glanced at Toreth, then said, "Not that I'm saying they don't keep on top of problems in the sector. But they weren't far enough on top for Rules."

Toreth made a note on his screen for someone to follow up with Fisec.

"Honestly, I can't believe anyone would have a reason to kill him." Cavendish looked between Mistry and Toreth. "I mean, he never did anything out of line. Really. Never. If we had biscuits in a meeting, you could see him counting them when he sat down, so he didn't take more than his fair share. He was the most boringly uptight person I ever worked with. Right?"

The final appeal was addressed to Rutland, and she nodded. To Toreth's surprise, hints of tears glistened in her eyes. Probably she was thinking about the last meeting where they'd shared custard creams.

"He always seemed like a perfectly decent guy," Rutland said.

With that tepid epitaph, Toreth decided to end the interview.

"It was a bit of a washout, I'm afraid, Para," B-C said as Toreth and Mistry prepared to leave Equibon. "People are curious, but not any more nervous than people usually are when we show up. But the lawyers okayed the warrants, and they're happy for Systems to start work. Did we get anything useful from the interviews? Anything I can chase up here?"

"No. Apparently Lake was a squeaky-clean saint who loved nothing more than following Fisec rules."

"Oh." B-C didn't look particularly surprised; he was as familiar as Toreth with the way that dead people always seemed to have better than average morals. "Well, shall I stay and supervise the Systems team, anyway?"

Toreth nodded, but after Rutland's and Cavendish's descriptions of Lake's meticulous nature, he found it difficult to imagine the man keeping secret files at work for the corporation's systems security to find. Anything important, if it existed, would be away from Equibon.

And on that front, disappointing news awaited them back at I&I. Initial analysis indicated everything recovered from Lake's flat that was capable of storing data was clean of hidden files. A request to the Data Division to locate any remote data storage he'd accessed was pending.

Finding the key to the case lying around unprotected on Lake's system would've been such a good break that Toreth wouldn't have trusted it anyway. Still, it would've been nice to be able to solve the whole case in time to spend the weekend in bed with Warrick.

Chapter Eighteen

❖

W arrick had seen little of Toreth over the weekend. If this had been before they'd started cohabiting, Warrick suspected he would've been entirely absent. The few times they'd coincided at the flat, Toreth had been distracted but not irritable, which usually meant a case that was complicated and unclear, but with open avenues of inquiry. A sort of mental prowling around problems—Warrick imagined it as the investigative equivalent of a fox outside a hen house. Over the past few months, Warrick had started cataloging shades of distraction; it was a new and interesting side of Toreth to observe, and sufficiently far removed from the details of I&I.

Toreth's absence had also made it easier to think about where Carnac's inability to help had left his plans to find Kate. He'd promised Toreth he'd leave this alone. Carnac's jab about cheapened words came back to him every time he thought about sabs or Sable.

He felt guilty. It was so unexpected, at least with regards to Toreth, that the feeling kept surprising him. But this wasn't a tactful omission of volunteering for a sex protocol in the sim, or even not mentioning Carnac's stay at the old flat during the revolt. This was something that, if it went wrong, could damage Toreth as badly as it could Warrick. And that helped him make his decision.

On Monday morning, he found Queen's door opaqued. Warrick knocked and waited until she called him in. There was no one else there; presumably she'd been hoping for peace and quiet. If so, she didn't show any hint of irritation when she greeted him. He closed the door and sat down.

"Is there something we need to discuss?" she said.

"No. Thank you for the contact; I did consult them, but I decided against pursuing that avenue in the end. The risk to potential reward ratio wasn't attractive."

"I won't say I'm not relieved."

"I'm sure."

"So what will you do now?" she asked, watching him closely as she waited for the answer.

"I don't know." As he'd told Queen before, he'd very few options to begin with. "Probably nothing. And certainly nothing that puts SimTech at risk, I promise."

She didn't look particularly reassured. "Warrick, do Linton and Marcus know about this investigation into…whoever it is?"

"No, they don't, and I'd rather it stayed like that. It was an entirely private inquiry. But if you feel you have to take it to them, then obviously I wouldn't hold it against you. I appreciate your loyalty to SimTech, and I respect your judgment completely." She'd offered him the same compliment when she gave him the name.

She considered the choice for long enough that he'd started to wonder how he could explain this to Asher and Lew without giving everything away. Asher at least might guess. Maybe "I'm trying to find my mother" would be enough.

"No," she said finally. "If you've definitely dropped the sabbing?" She paused, and he nodded. "Then I'll leave it up to you whether they need to know."

"Thank you." He smiled. "I promise you won't regret it."

The Monday morning case meeting was filled with reports of investigations in progress—financial, forensic, and interviews. Just before lunchtime, though, Toreth received an invitation that definitely didn't form part of a typical case's progress.

The rather scruffy café was well away from the Int-Sec grounds; Toreth couldn't ever remember passing it before, never mind having been inside. He almost walked past it, despite his comm's prompting. Downstairs was a takeaway, but eventually he found the stairs tucked away to one side that took him up to the café on the first floor. Liz Carey was waiting for him, squeezed in at a tiny table right at the back, away from the windows that overlooked the street below. She'd already ordered fish and chips for both of them.

"Why the high security?" Toreth asked as he sat down.

"Because Chean is spitting feathers. He's still convinced this will turn into the case of the year. Vaughn is catching it in the neck from him *and* she's pissed off that you're using Phil after poaching a case. If you need CF resources, why isn't it a CF case, etc., etc. Coffee-room scuttlebutt is she's already taken her grievances up with someone at the Central Bank."

And Toreth had a good idea who. "Great."

"Zaleski's happy, at least," Carey added. "Although he won't be if you do find someone trying to bring down the bank."

"So you don't want to risk your career being seen with me?" Toreth said.

Carey laughed. "Oh, my record's good enough for that. But I did want to run a theory past you without Chean bending my ear about section loyalty. Did you see the data recovered from Lake's flat?"

"Not in detail. The report from Systems this morning made it sound like they hadn't found much. Lots of financial records, they said, but nothing suspicious. All public information."

"Yes. Phil says it looks like trade analysis, tracking actual stock prices against theoretical stock rating indices and price predictions. Heavyweight modeling, too. According to Equibon it wasn't related to his work."

Toreth lifted the batter and looked at the fish underneath. Since the meat plant discovery, he'd found himself inspecting his food with a more suspicious eye. But it looked as unblemished and smooth as any other piece of fish.

A moment later, he realized Carey was waiting for a response. He replayed her last words in his mind. "Maybe he was making private investments."

"He had his own portfolio, yes, but not connected to that data. At least not in any way that Phil can find. He's already checked Lake's family and everyone the comms and c&p marked out as a possible friend or associate, of which he doesn't have many. I had a look at your IIP yesterday—just caught a glimpse over Phil's shoulder, you understand—and it made me wonder if you'd been looking at this backwards. Suppose it wasn't a firebreak hierarchy, with Richardson, then Lake, then the people he was working for." Carey drew a ladder of ascending horizontal lines with her knife as she spoke. "What if it was Richardson and Lake over here—" She flourished her fork in her left hand, and then her knife in her right. "—and over here the people Lake was working *against*."

Toreth considered the idea. "It's possible, I suppose. But how many times have you known anyone to hire a sab and go to meetings in person?"

"Almost never—and Phil agrees with you, incidentally. The evidence analysis system doesn't like the idea. But the money that paid Richardson exactly matches withdrawals from Lake's personal accounts. According to your investigators there's no evidence he had clandestine meetings with anyone other than Richardson. His comms messages are clear. There actually isn't a scrap of data that points to him having partners at all."

"So it's a good firebreak. Maybe he gets the payout at the end. Richardson said Lake was just a rep."

"And Richardson's a sab. If I were Lake, I'd have told him the same thing, whether it was true or not. But you remember what else Richardson said, right? That Lake might be planning to report anything he found?" Carey pointed her fork at him, a chip stuck on the end. "That struck me as such an odd thing for a sab to say. He had to know you wouldn't believe it. But Lake's friends said the same— he was honest."

"So does everyone's friends." Toreth paused to add more salt to his chips. "And that goes double for corpses."

"True enough. But let's pretend they're right, and also that Richardson wasn't just trying to make handing out Central Bank secrets look better, too. If Lake really was trying to close some exploitable flaw in the bank's security, what would he have done first?"

For someone who was supposedly too busy to help on his case, Carey certainly seemed to have time to try to complicate it. "Called one of his old mates at the European Fisec Authority. Liz, we did check that. B-C asked if they'd had any contact from Lake, and they told him they have an open anonymized reporting system. No records to search."

"Ah! Well, they would say that. *In theory,* all tip-offs to Fisec should be anonymized, whether they come through the public system or not. To encourage people to come forward, allegedly. But anyone who's worked with Fisec—like Lake—knows that's crap. If I wanted to make an anonymous report, I certainly wouldn't trust their system. Not if I wanted to keep my job at whatever corporation I was shopping."

And that was the problem with taking a case in someone else's specialty. "So I need to go back and demand the names?"

Carey smiled; she'd obviously expected his response. "You can try. Fisec is empowered by the Confederation of European Corporations to enforce the relevant corporate accords. It isn't directly part of any Administration department. The Treasury wants acceptable tax revenue—for which they don't use Fisec, because they aren't stupid—and a clear appearance of propriety to encourage investment. Fisec hands over a few insider trading and fraud scapegoats every year to Corporate Fraud for processing, and everyone's happy. Regulation sabbing, we call it. But Fisec doesn't like outsiders poking around in their business uninvited, especially I&I. Our job at CF is to wade in when someone oversteps the line and starts breaking the grown-up laws, so, as you can imagine, we're bottom of their New Year card list. Anonymity is more designed to keep the bad smells in-house than to protect informants."

"You're saying—what? We'll need witness warrants for Fisec to drag out any reports Lake made?" Toreth asked with dismay. Would Turnbull extend the special exemption warrant to evidence recovery?

Carey leaned forward, lowering her voice, which made it even sexier than usual. "Ah, well, luckily, I have a few contacts at Fisec myself. I made some discreet inquiries, with a promise of *real* anonymity. And guess what? Lake did send a report not long before he contacted Richardson, about suspected insider share trading. Apparently it wasn't the first time, either. He must've missed the good old days. Some of the tips were sound, some were, well. Overeager."

"And—" Toreth said indistinctly, then paused to swallow. "And this one?"

"Filed as overeager. They couldn't find any real evidence. By definition, insider trading needs inside knowledge. There's about to be a takeover announced, or a valuable contract, or an unexpected loss, something that produces a predictable effect on share price, and someone knows in advance. Lake spotted some

163

sharp changes in prices, and it sounds like he knew people were making money, but Fisec found no trigger events, so nothing for an insider to know. The markets have been understandably twitchy over the last year, and some lucky people cleaned up on the back of it. My contact said when they told Lake there was no case, he kicked up a bit of a fuss. Insisted they were wrong."

Toreth nodded. "Then you think he went out and found Richardson, to run his own investigation on the side."

"And ended up in the foundations of a processing plant." Carey heaped her fork with fish. "That's why Fisec investigators have a decent pay scale," she said through the mouthful. "Although, to be fair, it's also because of the corporate bribery. The place is still lousy with it, mind."

Toreth ate for a while, considering Carey's theory. At the very least, it fit the facts of the case as well as any other.

"Pity Richardson didn't mention anything about insider trading," he said after a while.

"Yes." Carey shrugged. "It's entirely possible hiring Richardson has nothing at all to do with this particular Fisec report. Apparently making reports was a hobby for Lake. On the other hand, the timing's a coincidence. And, for what it's worth, my contact said Lake hadn't sent anything to Fisec since, which they seemed to think was unusual for him."

"Can you get the file from Fisec?"

Carey put down her fork and fished a data store out of her pocket. "You can put it in the IIP. I'll be an anonymous source, too, thanks. I already gave a copy to Phil, to check if it matches any of the records from Lake's flat."

"I owe you, Liz." He tucked the store away. "At least we can pick up the traders involved in the trades Lake was tracking, talk to them, and see if anyone looks guilty."

Carey laughed. "They're traders. None of them look guilty, and they all are. Mind you, it won't be easy unpicking the legitimate trading from anything shady happening in the background. Make sure you pull some of your magic strings and get Phil decent warrants. I will say that if Lake got suspicious because someone was making big profits on unusual market movements, odds are the someone worked at Equibon Investments. I'd start looking there. Trading account information is locked down tight, and I can't see Lake having the sabbing expertise to break into accounts at other corporations just on spec."

"Okay. It's somewhere to begin, at least."

"Of course," Carey added cheerfully, "he could've heard it from someone who heard it from a friend who overheard a man in a bar. It's amazing how often there's a man in a bar at the root of financial shenanigans. Traders gossip like I&I admins, whatever the rules say."

Toreth looked at her silently, and she laughed. "Welcome to my world. By the way, since we're talking about gossip, you know Nik Christofi, don't you? Wasn't he at your flatwarming?"

"That's right," Toreth admitted. "I worked with him at Political back in the day. We still do each other the odd favor."

"Great." Carey leaned her elbows on the table. "You know he's moved to CF, right? What's he like? Other than extremely good-looking, I mean."

When Toreth finally made it home that evening, the flat had a familiar quietness that led him to Warrick's office. Warrick was so absorbed in his work that Toreth stood in the doorway for almost a minute, watching Warrick's face in profile, until Warrick suddenly looked around and said, "Oh! I'm sorry—"

"—you didn't hear me come in." Toreth shook his head. "Good thing I'm not a sab."

"Well, that's why SimTech pays the security fees here." Warrick checked the time. "I had no idea it was so late. Are you hungry? I already ate, but there's plenty left in the kitchen."

"Plenty left" turned out to be the remains of a pizza delivered from one of the restaurants in the complex associated with the buildings. Even cold, it was a definite step up from Toreth and Sara's favored takeaways. Toreth ate one slice, opened a beer, and took it and another couple of pieces of pizza back to Warrick's office.

Warrick sat absorbed once more, although this time he glanced around and said, "You found it, then."

"Yeah. Working on anything fun?" Toreth asked as he ate.

"Actually, yes. And I mean real fun, not neural modeling." Warrick sat back in his chair. "A private sim project, to distract me from . . . well. I'm making another stab at the game."

On this one area of the sim, Toreth was as confident as Lehman had been about Central Bank security, and with much better reasons. "It won't work."

"Maybe not. But if I gave up because people told me something was impossible, Lew and I would never have built the first sim demo."

"Whether I pin you up against that wall right now and fuck you, or take you upstairs and put you in the cabinet, it'll always be better than it would be in the sim."

"Mm." Warrick's small smile told Toreth exactly how clearly he was imagining the options. "But the rest of the world can't always have you on hand, can they?" His voice cooled slightly, although he didn't lose the smile. "No matter how hard you try."

"If I put that much effort into everyone I fucked, I'd be too knackered to catch any criminals." Toreth paused to lick tomato sauce from his palm. "And I still bet you won't crack it."

"We already have one bet running, don't we? Anyway, there's a principle involved. It's a problem I don't have a solution for, not even theoretically."

"Sometimes, however good the tools or the operator, there just isn't one." A depressing thought, with his level seven damage waiver in hand. "But still. If you need any help with tests . . ."

Warrick smiled. "I'll ask, don't worry."

Toreth left him to it and went to the living room. On the threshold he paused, looking around the place—the blue and gray tones of the furnishings, Warrick's ornaments precisely arranged, the nude portrait Cele had painted of Toreth on the wall opposite—and suddenly thought of Carnac. For no good reason, the socioanalyst still came to mind every so often.

Placing yourself into a domestic situation with a dominant presence over whom you have no control. It must . . . resonate for you.

Socioanalysts might be the masters of organizational and population behavior, but even they could be wrong. Despite all Carnac's doomy (and blatantly self-serving) predictions, things were working out perfectly. Better than Toreth had ever imagined.

He sat down on the sofa and balanced the beer on the arm.

"Housekeeping—screen on." Maybe he'd check a few of the financial news feeds, and try to get more of a feel for his case's world. That, or find some nice relaxing porn. And after that, if Warrick was still too busy to fuck, he could go out and try a bar or two.

Toreth folded the next slice of pizza in half and took a bite. Carnac could shove "it must resonate" up his arse, because he was stuck in his miserable little office in Strasbourg, like the also-ran he was, and Toreth was here, with Warrick. He'd fucking *won*.

Chapter Nineteen

❖

Verstraeten had taken up residence in B-C's office. Although, Toreth thought as he opened the door, it looked more like the reverse. B-C had moved to a temporary desk in one corner, and his old desk now sported multiple large screens. Verstraeten sat in the middle, thoroughly at home. Toreth wondered if he'd still show up for work if I&I didn't pay him. Maybe, although Carey would probably put a stop to it in short order.

"What is it?" Toreth asked.

Verstraeten offered him a seat. When Toreth looked at him more closely, the investigator looked exhausted, and Toreth wondered if he'd spent the whole night in the office. Exhausted but enthusiastic. He briefly reminded Toreth of Warrick in the middle of a coding binge.

"Good news, Para. With the file from, um—" Verstraeten glanced at B-C, who was busy with his own screen and apparently deaf to the conversation.

"From Carey, yes," Toreth said.

"Right. Well, I could finally make sense of the data Lake collected. He must've had an incredible memory to keep all that straight without reference keys."

Toreth mentally crossed his fingers. "And?"

"Lake was definitely looking at something real." Verstraeten smiled; maybe he was just happy, or maybe Toreth looked as relieved as he felt. "There's a detectable pattern of unexplained price fluctuations that people are exploiting. I'm calling them Unpredictable Profit-extracted Events. Some of them attract a much larger number of trades than others, and while there's a limit to how soon after an event I can say it definitely happened, I have picked up two further UPEs since Lake stopped collecting data."

Not a bad return for a crappy surveillance case even Justice hadn't wanted. "So whatever Fisec said, there's insider trading happening on a large scale."

Verstraeten opened two new screenfuls of graphs that Toreth hoped he wouldn't be expected to interpret.

"Not *exactly*, Para, no. Fisec rejected his insider trading hypothesis because there's no mechanism. It's far from impossible that we and they could both fail to find information affecting a single corporation's share price, but I'd be amazed if we could do it so many times. Now this is where it gets sticky. I wanted to test the robustness of the model we created from Lake's data, so I expanded it to examine fluctuations in various stock, commodity, derivative, and other markets. To be honest, I wanted a negative result, but instead I found even more UPEs, in places Lake never even looked. And all these UPEs display an identical event structure."

"You're sure it isn't the model that's the problem?"

Verstraeten stiffened. "Absolutely not, Para," he said in tones that suggested Toreth had insulted his mother, and probably his grandmother, too. "I wouldn't be telling you unless I was sure. I ran it on control data from a couple of years ago and I found nothing. I even tried some recent data sets from markets outside the Administration, with the same result. The model is sound. *Something* is driving these events, in completely disparate European markets. I can't begin to explain it, Para."

"Someone's manipulating the prices directly?"

"I don't see how it could possibly be done, even in one market. A 'price' is an aggregate of trades, defined by an exchange's systems. That kind of manipulation would have to trigger safeguards, even if it was happening in only one market. By-passing the security on multiple systems at the same time is unimaginable." Verstraeten shrugged. "But essentially, yes, that's how it appears. Either that, or someone's generalized a method for making market movement predictions orders of magnitude more sophisticated than anyone else."

"Would that be legal?"

"It depends on how they're doing it, but potentially, yes."

"Let's hope it isn't that, then." Toreth frowned. Something Cavendish had said at Equibon Investments, about collusion—"Is it possible someone's attacking the corporations' analysis systems? Manipulating them, instead?"

Verstraeten sucked in a sharp breath, then blew it out. "Para, that would be... well, I suppose we can't say anything's *impossible* at this point. But we've never run into anything on that scale at Corporate Fraud. Corporations run highly proprietory systems and tight security. There's a lot of technical sabbing, but that's usually between single corporations or small sabbing consortia."

Once again Toreth felt the handicap of working in someone else's field. But the case was far too significant to surrender now. "Well, you're telling me it's happening somehow. So we need to find the people involved and ask them." With the special exemption waiver, at least the second part of that would be easy. "Can you get me names?"

"If the Central Bank will cooperate, then yes, I should be able to."

"Show them your data. I think they will, this time."

Warrick could always find a reason to eat lunch alone in his office, allowing him to squeeze a little more time out of the day. But, as De Nijs would undoubtedly tell him, that wouldn't upgrade his Fitcherson's dependency-interest model scores. With SimTech's financial footing still not as solid as before the trouble, he tried to be seen in the cafeteria more days than not.

Today he was chatting to a couple of new contract programmers, when he noticed Lew Marcus enter the cafeteria and scan the room. He spotted Warrick and came over, sweeping emphatically enough across the room that people paused in their lunches and turned to watch him.

Lew glanced at Warrick's plate—almost empty—and said, "Warrick? Do you have twenty minutes?"

Ever since Toreth's confident pronouncement that Lew had got himself entangled in trouble again, Warrick had suffered from annoying twinges of apprehension any time his fellow director approached. Blackmail by another young woman didn't seem likely to produce the suppressed smile, though.

"I suppose so." Warrick excused himself and rose. "Where are we going?"

Lew was already striding away.

The test room was one of the development suites, but to Warrick's surprise, the pair of sim couches looked like standard production models. Usually that meant experimental software, but Lew's specialty, and the focus of all the projects he oversaw, was hardware. Valerie Earles, one of the senior hardware developers, was already there, working on the sim interface. She glanced over her shoulder as they came in and greeted them.

"He found you, then," she said, looking no less enthusiastic than Lew. "Don't go in just yet, but I'm nearly done."

Lew took one of the couches, and Warrick the other. These days, at least with the production models, no one was needed to fasten straps. Warrick slipped his wrists and ankles through the comfortable reactive bands that wouldn't tighten unless needed.

Earles had long, light brown hair, rather curly, and today she was wearing it rolled up at the back of her neck. As was often the case, a thick strand had escaped the arrangement. Warrick always tried not to let it bother him—objectively, it was none of his business—but he hated the asymmetry.

After a minute or two, he cleared his throat and said, "I'm so sorry."

Earles looked up questioningly, then smiled. "And I thought I'd checked." She ran her fingers along the roll of hair and tucked the hair back in place. "My quality control's rubbish. You'd think by now I'd have a foolproof system in place."

"Or that you'd have resigned in annoyance. I wouldn't blame you."

She grinned and went back to work.

Warrick thought about asking Lew what he wanted to demonstrate, but he was obviously enjoying the secrecy. As was Earles. Where she was working he could only see the side of her face, but she had a look of anticipatory excitement. Finally she stepped back from the screen.

"Ready," she said.

Voice-activated visors were another addition to the production suites. Lew lowered his visor, and Warrick followed suit.

The room that appeared around him was the plain testing room, with a table and two chairs. On the table lay a selection of objects, many of them standard items—bowls of hot and cold water, warm and cool plates, a piece of ice, objects with different textured surfaces. A real old-fashioned sim trial that Warrick hadn't seen for a long time. They sat down at the table and Warrick reached out for a square of sandpaper, stopping when Lew held up his finger.

"Just wait a moment," Lew said. "Earles needs to make a few adjustments. Your right arm's about to go numb—don't worry."

A few seconds later, the predicted effect occurred. Warrick stared at his right hand, trying to move his fingers.

"It'll only be a minute or two at the most," Lew said. "She's just attaching some new sensory-input hardware."

"I didn't see anything coming up on the testing schedule."

"No. It came from one of the side streams. A postgraduate project, actually. Rishika Scott?"

Warrick shook his head.

"She had an idea about adapting some new micropower sensor design for her project, and she talked to Earles about it. Earles thought it had potential beyond the one project, so she asked me if she could look into it."

Warrick suddenly felt his fingers flex in response to his command.

Lew nodded, probably at something Earles said to him. "The new hardware is only inputting your right index finger. Have a run through a few of the test items—just a subjective test. Don't look at the hardware, or the software, just yet."

Warrick pulled over the sandpaper.

"Hm. If anything, I'd say it feels a little less defined than usual. I'm getting a blur at very light contact pressure." Reflexively, he started to pull up the numbers describing the neural interface, and then remembered what Lou had said. Warrick changed to the hot-cold water. He closed his eyes and moved his fingers between them. "Excellent reactive change, good dynamic contrast. The evaporative chill... actually, I'm not sure if it's as good or not. I think I'm preconditioned to think that must always be difficult."

He thought the water off his hand and pulled over the pin pad. It was made of a very old sim material, known generally as "stuff"—a material not modeled on anything in the real world, the primary property of which was being extremely responsive to thoughts. Even inexperienced users could think it into what they wanted and lock it. A long time ago Warrick had called up a chunk of stuff and created a flat rectangle with two sharp and extremely strong pins rising from the surface. Seeing it survive unchanged in the sensory testing suite always triggered a pleasant nostalgia for the early days.

As soon as he touched the pin pad, Lew's expression changed infinitesimally, but enough for someone who knew him well. Concern. Warrick touched the pads of his index fingers to the pins, increasing the pressure gradually and evenly until they pierced the skin, all his attention on the indentations and the sudden peak of pain. He examined the tiny holes in his skin, squeezing out a near-identical pair of tiny drops of blood, then sucked his fingertips.

"Close. The right seemed marginally less focused, less intense, but..." Warrick shook his head. "You really should've blinded the trial."

"I've done enough of those already. I wanted to know what you thought."

"It's good enough that I'm wondering if any differences I felt were psychosomatic. Certainly good enough resolution that back when stuff was a novelty I would've been beyond ecstatic."

That answer seemed to more than satisfy. "Let's go out, then."

As the visor lifted, Warrick looked down at his right arm and blinked in surprise. His right index finger was covered in a thick gray-black ribbed sheath, with a signal-blocking strip between it and the sim. A thin connector led from the top of the sheath down to a system on the floor.

Earles must have been watching the sim session, because she said, "Ecstatic was how I felt the first time I tried it."

Warrick looked up at her, and then over to Lew. "That was all through this?"

Lew nodded. "Everything. Sensors and neural stimulators combined into the same microunit. The units needed some adaptation, but the biggest problem Earles and I had was how to mount them in the control matrix."

"And turning the matrix into something you could wear," Earles added. "Luckily I didn't have any other plans over New Year."

A sim suit. Freedom from the necessity of a couch. When Warrick had first described his idea of the sim to Lew all those years ago, that had been a step beyond a dream, an impossible ideal. Careful not to pull the connector, Warrick lifted his hand and rubbed his thumb against the sheath. It felt halfway between rubber and fabric, and when he bent his finger it flexed easily. Warrick looked up at Lew.

"So what are the problems with it?"

Lew smiled wryly, and Warrick wondered if he'd been expecting the question. "At the moment, the main one is depth of penetration. The sensors work down to a centimeter, and the neural stimulation a little less than that, at least maintaining the necessary precision. But I think that's a refinement and power feed issue, not a fundamental design limitation."

"Who makes the sensors?" Warrick hadn't heard a whisper of anything like them in commercial production. "You said this postgraduate found them?"

"No one makes them yet," Earles said. "The unadapted originals were prototypes from a university group, over in the biomedicine building. Scott did an undergrad research project there." Earles looked over to Lew.

"They've been trying to develop the microunit design into a product," Lew said. "They said they had some tentative interest before the trouble, but the corporation they were talking to pulled out and they've had no luck finding anyone since. Risk isn't popular in the current circumstances. Apparently they're running up against the problem of current solutions being good enough and much cheaper."

Solutions to problems other than the sim. "Do you think we can interest them in a partnership?"

"Well, obviously I haven't suggested anything so concrete to them, but I think so."

"We need to take it to Asher," Warrick said. "She and I are going away on Friday, but we should start negotiations as soon as we can. Before someone else hears about it and decides risk is back in fashion."

Lew nodded. "And speculative as it is, I don't think Asher'll complain about this one."

Warrick laughed. "I don't think she will."

Sara, fortunately, had reminded Toreth to leave I&I early—or, at least, just about in time. He'd considered calling Warrick to cancel for the evening, and if it had been some tedious corporate event he might've sent the message. This was an exhibition opening, though, organized by some mutual acquaintance shared by Warrick and Cele, or maybe Warrick and Dillian—or even Cele and Dillian. Toreth hadn't paid much more attention than it had taken to say yes to Warrick's invitation. For one thing, it wouldn't last too long. Then they could go home and enjoy an uninterrupted evening of fucking, always a pleasure in the middle of a case.

Of course, he was still changing his clothes in his bedroom when his comm chimed.

"I'm sorry to interrupt your evening, Para," Verstraeten said. "But you asked me to call when we finished the trading analysis? We've come up with a list of names of people who likely transacted in the suspicious trades with prior knowledge."

"Many?" Toreth asked.

"Well, that's one of the reasons why I called. It depends to a certain degree on the confidence levels you set, and when—"

"Never mind the details right now." Toreth opened the wardrobe. Shirts sorted exactly by shade, which meant Warrick had been at it again. At least it made it easy to find what he wanted. "I'll take a rough estimate."

"Roughly, then—at least a hundred people. That's using extremely stringent parameters, so tight there must be some number of false negatives. If you relax them to a level where you might expect false positives, it could be as high as two hundred."

Toreth stood still, the shirt hanging from his hand. "Two hundred?"

"Yes, Para. And not everyone we've spotted is a trader making trades for their corporations, or even with their own money. There are multiple transactions of various sizes being placed by people who aren't directly involved in the finance industry, using different brokers."

"Are you sure? You're saying *two hundred* random people are exploiting a critical flaw in the Administration's finance systems?" He tried to imagine Lehman's reaction to that suggestion. "How's that possible, without someone finding out about it?"

"Well, technically, that's what we're doing right now. Finding out, I mean. But, no, Para, I think knowledge of any actual flaw is still restricted. With full access to the Unified European Exchange records we were able to cross-reference every trader ID. Unpredictable Profit-extracted Events are getting more frequent, with new clusters of participants springing up, but the larger ones are still only happening twice a month or so. The number of traders involved is increasing, and every so often a new cluster is seeded, but security files and c&p checks support a model of primarily word-of-mouth spread of knowledge about selected UPEs between people with prior established social or professional connections."

"So if these price changes are being artificially generated, then either it's being controlled by a handful of people, or two hundred other people are spontaneously exercising a lot of restraint." The latter didn't seem to match up with Carey's opinion of traders.

"Between one and two hundred, yes, Para. And I agree with you, it isn't likely. They're already looking at the tragedy of the commons, simply by sharing information with a few people at a time." Verstraeten sounded unusually grave. "My prediction is that in just a few months the largest UPEs will become so blatant in scale that they can't be missed."

"And I imagine that would be bad for financial confidence in the Administration?"

"It's really very difficult to overstate how bad, Para, especially if we still can't explain how it's happening. 'Catastrophic' is a word that comes to mind."

Toreth tried to focus, but it was hard not to be distracted by the thoughts of commendations, or how sick Corporate Fraud would be that they'd thrown the case away. "How close are you to the source?"

"Unfortunately, the earlier and smaller the UPE the harder it is to pin down. We couldn't take it back much further than Lake managed to trace, and by then there are already several pools of suspects. There is a high-confidence subgroup who are placing the trades both with their own money and directly for their employer. I'd say they're most likely to know how it's being worked."

Toreth tossed the shirt onto the bed and picked up his hand screen. "Wait. I need to find Nagra."

The junior was still at I&I, so Toreth linked her into his conversation with Verstraeten. He briefed her quickly on the investigator's findings.

"That's incredible, Para," she said when he was done. "I hope the Central Bank remembers to say thank you."

In Toreth's experience very few people were grateful for having their flaws exposed. "I want you to go through the suspects' security files, starting with the ones Verstraeten's most certain are involved. Prioritize them by how early they were involved, how quickly we can bring them to New London, and by—"

—how easily we can get a damage waiver, he'd been about to say. How strong the evidence was, how important the suspect. Turnbull had rendered all that moot. He had a level seven waiver already in his IIP for anyone he wanted to arrest. He ran his eye quickly down the list of names Verstraeten had supplied.

"Para?" Nagra said.

"I'm thinking." How far could he realistically push it? Corporates were still corporates, no matter what the waiver said. Throwing fifty or so of them into high-level interrogations might have the side benefit of making the interrogators buy him drinks, but it almost certainly wasn't what Turnbull had had in mind. Subtlety, that was the key. "We might never have another special exemption waiver, so we should take advantage of it. Check if any of the best suspects executed trades in the names of close family members. Or, even better, if any of them have kids who interned at their companies since their involvement started. Any age, as long as they're old enough for level six."

"Got it," Nagra said. "Hold on." After a long silence she said, "Sara's still here. She's checking the records now."

"Good. Assuming you find some candidates, we'll start there. We can arrest the main suspects and the second-levels, and make it clear what our options are. If they're reluctant we can always put one of the secondaries straight into interrogation. Section N it maybe, if we can still find a few trained guards, or something else showy but safe, and give the others a front-row seat. *Someone* will talk."

There was another silence over the comm.

"Well?" Toreth asked.

"Just—the waiver does say 'minimum coercion.'"

"This will be minimum. Odds are it won't even come to anything, and if it does it's one, maybe two section Ns instead of a dozen other interrogations. No one can argue with that, and if we pick the right ones the traders will be heading for re-education anyway. Right?"

"Right, Para."

Nagra still sounded reluctant. Toreth snorted. "It's my name on the IIP. I'll be running any interrogations, too. You just find me the suspects, Junior."

"Yes, Para," she said promptly. "Shall I pick them up straight away?"

"No. We'll do it in the morning, nice and early. All picked up separately, and try to choose locals unless there's no other option. I want to be running the interrogations before news spreads too far. Tell Sara if she can't find enough with their own kids, move out to nieces and nephews. Siblings and partners, too, if the psych check looks promising. But they all have to be viable suspects—workplace access, or trades made in their names. I don't want corporate lawyers nitpicking afterwards."

"Got it, Para. Sara thinks she has one or two already."

"Good. And tell her to be there early tomorrow, too."

"Do you need anything more from me, Para?" Verstraeten asked.

Toreth had forgotten the investigator was still on the comm. "Just make sure that Nagra has the most solid suspects you can provide."

Toreth closed the link and stood for a moment in thought. Had he missed anything? He was half tempted to go back to I&I, but there was nothing he could do right that moment that Nagra and the others couldn't accomplish for him. As he'd told Warrick, what was the point of a team if they couldn't take the shitty jobs? Maybe the past weekend had been a write-off, but there was no reason to change his plans tonight.

A creak behind him made him look around, half expecting Warrick, but the doorway stood empty. Hell—Warrick had been ready to leave before Verstraeten's call. Toreth hurriedly donned his shirt and picked up his jacket.

Warrick was waiting at the foot of the stairs. Probably about to come up to look for Toreth. Pity Toreth hadn't taken a minute or two longer—he might have been able to persuade Warrick to skip the gallery altogether.

"I'm ready," Toreth said. "If we have to go."

"*We* do not have to, no. *I*, however, am." Warrick sounded frostier than a few minutes' delay warranted. "The taxi's waiting."

"All right, all right. Jesus fucking Christ."

Still half wondering if Warrick might be persuadable, he made a grab, but Warrick was already heading for the door. Toreth sighed and followed him.

Warrick knew he'd been unusually quiet in the car, but Toreth hadn't seemed to notice. He'd spent most of the journey absorbed in something on his hand screen. So absorbed that when the car stopped outside the gallery, Warrick had had to clear his throat twice before Toreth looked up.

"Sorry," Toreth said. He started to fold the screen, then hesitated. "You go on in. I'll hold the taxi for a few minutes—there's something I need to deal with. Work." He took his comm earpiece out of his pocket and smiled. "I'll get it done now, then I can concentrate on you later."

Warrick had almost said something then, but the right words hadn't come. He still didn't know what he could possibly say as he drifted around the large cruciform room, trying to look at the works on display. The exhibition was focused around historical art techniques, but the display was modern. The walls, floor, and ceiling had been painted some neutral shade Warrick couldn't even pick out in the low lighting. Active tracking lights followed the guests and lit the artwork with carefully calculated brightness and direction whenever someone looked at it from the angles and distances specified by the artist.

Eventually, Warrick halted in a quiet corner and distracted himself by trying to catch out the eyeline tracking systems, blinking the illumination of an elaborately cast abstract bronze off and on. Someone had placed the sensors very neatly. He was still turning his head back and forth when a voice behind him said, "Don't tell Hugo I said so, but I think that one looks better in the dark."

"Cele!" Warrick said, and turned. "How—"

He stopped dead. Now Warrick realized he'd seen Cele from the back earlier in the evening and not even recognized her. On one side her hair had been cut into the shortest of crops, with the other side grading from longer at the front to short at the back. The formerly rich brown had become almost black, with a glint of reddish tones that brightened to a red streak at the front.

"Well?" Cele asked, and Warrick realized he was staring.

"It's . . . different."

Cele laughed loudly. "That bad?"

"No, not at all. Just not something I'd ever imagined on you."

"There's a long and tragic tale behind it, which begins with me deciding to try a new type of resin this afternoon, even though I didn't have time, followed by an attempt to hurry the curing process and a small pressure kiln venting accident, and ending in half my head being declared an unnatural disaster zone by the stylist. It was this or an all-over crop, which is what I'll be getting in the morning. She swore this would grow on me."

"Well, I'm sure it will," Warrick said. "Eventually. That's the good thing about hair."

"Ha ha. Were I fourteen, which is about how old the stylist looked, I'd no doubt think it was amazing. Sadly, old age brings with it more sense."

"What does Dilly think?" Warrick asked.

"She hasn't seen it, thank God. She's back from Darmstadt tomorrow morning, by which time it will be a fading nightmare remembered only by the many, many people tonight who've taken photos to remind me about it for the rest of my life. In a blatant attempt at distraction, do you want to see my piece?"

176

"Please."

Cele's work was a large landscape painting of a view over New London. The view from her flat, he decided, a meticulously detailed sweep of buildings stretching out into the hazy distance. The screen beside it read *Overpainted*.

"What do you think?" Cele asked.

"Wonderful. But not especially historical. We've been modeling some of the same area, and that building wasn't built until—" Warrick paused, leaning back in surprise. A cloud he'd looked at only a moment before suddenly seemed different.

"I can see a finger," Warrick said.

"Really?" Cele said with mock surprise.

"Yes."

As they watched, patches of the landscape painting disappeared and reappeared, brush stroke by brush stroke, uncovering glimpses of a head and shoulders portrait of a woman. She lay on her side, her cheek pillowed on her arm, gazing wistfully off to the right past the viewer.

Warrick peered closer, but the medium definitely looked like paint. "Is it a textured screen?"

"No. It's a very old technique—I couldn't find anyone who's actually used it, so I had to work it out from the documentation, with some trial and error. You paint onto a backing board with an embedded copper mesh, and the pigment is responsive to changes in the current. It's a swine to get right, because it has to be done in different pigment mixes in exactly the right layers. It's supposed to represent lost love." She laughed. "Although I hope the model doesn't agree."

As she said it, the painting uncovered part of the woman's mouth, and Warrick exclaimed, "It's Dilly!"

"Yes. It's a shame she couldn't be here—I told her you'd recognize her. You look at practically the same lips and cheekbones in the mirror every day, after all."

"And the picture does build up, anyway. The brain's an amazing thing. How fine is the control?"

"Awful. Most of it has to be done in the paint. I tried cheating with multiple interlocking meshes, but I was never happy with the effect where they joined. Sometimes I used to stand there in the studio, brush in hand, and marvel that anyone had bothered to invent the process in the first place."

Of course, exactly the same effect could be achieved in no time at all with a screen, but that wasn't the point. Cele had done work for the sim, but she preferred a physical medium to a digital one.

"It's very impressive. Is it random, or a fixed pattern?"

"Fixed. They aren't the real brush strokes, though. I tried it, but it looked too bitty and messy, and not how people think creating a painting ought to look. So I had to paint the landscape in sections made to look like brush strokes. It took me bloody months, on and off. I had to take a lot of breaks, or I would've smashed the thing over the easel. I was fooled into thinking I could do it in a few weeks by the much less fiddly prototype, called *Watching Paint Dry*."

Warrick grinned. "Well, it's fascinating. Although, yes, it sounds like a lot of hard work."

"It isn't fun if it isn't hard, as my nan used to say." Cele looked around, squinting across the dim room. "Speaking of which, where's my Seven Inches?"

"Out in the taxi," Warrick said. "He'll be in later."

"Oh?"

"Yes. Nothing dramatic—just work." He kept his voice even.

"Want me to go lure him in?" Cele said.

She obviously meant it as a joke, which made Warrick even more annoyed with himself for the overly emphatic "No!" that escaped. "That is, I'm sure he'll be along soon."

Cele tucked the red hair by her face back behind her ear. "Keir? Should I ask?"

"Probably not. And I probably shouldn't tell you, either."

"Hm." She looked around the gallery, then said, "Not here, anyway. Come on."

Tucking her arm through his, Cele led him towards a door in the corner. Warrick knew if he resisted in the slightest, she'd let go at once.

On the other side of the door, the ordinary overhead lights in the corridor seemed harsh. Cele closed the door carefully.

"So, what's happened?" she asked.

"Nothing, yet." Warrick sighed. "I overheard a conversation. Toreth talking to someone at I&I."

"Well, you know what Jen used to say about eavesdropping. What was it about?" She hesitated, then said, "Not Tarin? Or Kate?"

"God, no. No, nothing like that. They were planning an interrogation, that's all." All. But he could see why Cele's fears might have been roused. "A...an especially unpleasant one." Section N. Sexualized interrogation. Rape. Reading the Interrogation Procedure and Protocols had seemed like a necessary evil at the time, but parts of it were hard to forget.

Cele frowned. "I thought your friend Carnac got rid of all the 'especially unpleasant'?"

"Apparently not. Toreth mentioned some kind of special waiver. I'd never heard of it before." But then, he'd always made sure Toreth wouldn't tell him. "And, well, it wasn't something I wanted to hear in my own home. Especially after what had otherwise been a rather good day."

"Keir, it's the same job he's always had." Cele sounded honestly perplexed.

"Yes, of course. And I know some of the things he's done, but that was past

178

tense. Immutable. I've never known what he was planning to do." Except, of course, with Marian Tanit's "accidental death" at I&I, when expediency and SimTech's survival had turned him into a co-conspirator, instead of merely a spectator. He could tell himself Marian had been guilty of the deaths of at least two innocents, but the memory of the interrogation room still sickened him.

Cele said, "Looks like Dilly was right, then, as usual. She's always said the reforms wouldn't stick."

"This warrant sounded as though it's something exceptional," Warrick said.

"Oh." Cele's voice brightened a little. "Then I suppose whatever he's investigating must be important enough to justify it."

"I suppose so. I'm sorry, I shouldn't have told you."

"No, it's—"

"Forget it, Cele. There's nothing to be done about it, anyway."

In the time it took for Cele to hesitate and nod, scenarios flashed through his mind: accessing the I&I system, finding the names of the people Sara had marked down, warning them, even helping them flee. Insanity.

"All right," she said. "I won't mention it again. Come on, let's go back and hunt down a drink."

Tarin would do something, Warrick thought suddenly as Cele opened the door. Or at least he'd try, if he possibly could. He wouldn't put the risk to himself over the children Toreth would arrest tomorrow . . . and look how that had ended for him. Still, he'd never before thought of Tarin as braver than him.

Toreth appeared a few minutes after they'd returned to the gallery. He spotted them across the room, looking between them with a familiar suspicion until suddenly he recognized Cele and laughed.

"Bloody hell," he said as he came up to them. "What happened to you?"

And then everything was normal again, until they were back in a taxi, heading home, seated opposite one another as before, and Warrick *still* didn't know what to say. There was no reason not to say something. Toreth wouldn't even be angry to be asked about the interrogations, at least not unless Warrick kept pushing the point. He'd just tell Warrick it was none of his fucking business, and possibly that it was his own fault for listening.

Toreth stretched. "Well, *that* was fun."

"It was a little on the pretentious side," Warrick felt obliged to agree.

"Still, free drinks, and Cele's always good value. And apparently, pretentious wank makes me horny."

Warrick couldn't help smiling. "Unlike everything else in the world."

"Hah." Toreth looked at him, considering, and even with the memory of the overheard call Warrick felt an automatic shiver of anticipation. "So, what do you want to do when we get home? I'm feeling generous."

Warrick hesitated for long enough that Toreth started to frown. "Nothing like— not the game. Not tonight."

"Oh?"

"No. I need to be up early."

"Me too. Cases don't work themselves, sadly." Toreth smiled lazily. "Come here." He beckoned Warrick over. "Come on. The sooner we start, the sooner we can get to sleep, right?"

Warrick took a deep breath. "I'm sorry, again. I'm really not in the mood. Apparently, pretentious art doesn't do it for me."

To his surprise, Toreth just laughed. "Next time I see Cele, I'll have to tell her she owes me one." He peered out of the car window, shading his eyes, then nodded. "Car control, nonurgent stop, as soon as you can."

The car pulled into a handy space, and Toreth climbed out. He ducked down to say, "I'll find my own way home. See you later," and then closed the door.

As the car eased out into the flow of traffic, Warrick looked back over his shoulder. The street was lined with open bars and restaurants, as well as a few small late-night shops. An ordinary, noncorporate sort of place, busy with people. Good hunting grounds for Toreth, who was already assessing the street, sizing up options, Warrick doubtless already forgotten. A tomcat out for his nightly prowl.

Warrick turned around and sat back in his seat. To think that last summer he'd worried so much about Toreth adjusting to life together. Well, Toreth seemed to be coping with it perfectly.

Chapter Twenty

❖

"B ut I don't know anything," Number Three said. Tears ran down her puppy fat-plump cheeks, but while she might be terrified, she was disappointingly quiet about it. "I was only there for two weeks. They didn't let me do anything important."

Two weeks participating in a very active intern program, worth a small education-related tax break for the corporation, which had provided Toreth with his best grouping of targets.

Prisoner number one hadn't believed Toreth until they had him half undressed; the point where he'd started screaming and trying to fight off the guards was about thirty seconds before Toreth got the call from Nagra to say the boy's father had started talking. Number Two had gone into hysterics once Toreth had read halfway through the waiver, and he hadn't even finished it before her sister had also started to spill everything.

Unfortunately, what they both knew was that they'd bought the shares on instructions from their trading section's analysis system. While they were willing to admit suspicion that something about the trades seemed odd, they were adamant about lack of complicity. Toreth had considered pressing their resolve on that, but mindful of the "minimal coercion" clause, he put those two on hold and moved on.

The results so far might be annoying, but they gave Toreth some optimism for his current prisoner—or rather, her father, watching in slightly more comfort through the reinforced glass from the adjoining observation room.

Number Three shrank back in the chair as Toreth put down his hand screen. "I don't know anything at all."

"Mm." Toreth checked her name on the file. "Well, Sarri, that's what we're here to find out."

"I'd tell you. I'd tell you if I knew anything." Her voice started to rise. "Dad will tell you I don't!"

"These guards will prepare you. If you resist, we'll apply a temporary pharmaceutical restraint."

The prisoner put her bound hands up to her mouth, stifling her sobs.

"When you decide to tell us what you know, then we stop." A nudge for the audience, who according to Nagra had sat through the waiver without a flinch. "It's entirely up to you." Toreth waited a moment, then motioned the four guards forward.

Once they'd pulled her out of the chair without meaningful resistance, Toreth called up the feed from next door on his hand screen. His own prisoner wasn't important now; the guards knew what to do, although after the carnage of the revolt, finding four section N-trained guards had been an effort in itself.

The disposable interrogation suit tore with a satisfyingly emphatic noise, and as Toreth caught the flash of pale skin being revealed in the corner of his eye, he saw the man on the screen take a sudden sharp breath.

"Stop this," he said. "Please, she's telling the truth. She knows nothing about any trades."

Nagra, standing behind him, smiled. It didn't show up in her cold voice, though. "Then she'd better hope someone else does, Mr. Sant."

"Open your legs," one of the guards said. "Open your legs, you stupid little cow."

Sant had flushed bright red. "I'm a corporate, I have friends who—"

"Not in here, you don't," Nagra said. "In here you're just someone who answers questions. Or doesn't, if you think your skin's worth more than hers."

"Para," the senior guard said.

Toreth left the screen on the desk, but kept the comm link open. Everything he wanted was laid out on the side, fully stocked now by Daedra. Sarri struggled on the floor, more effectively pinned than she even realized; the guards didn't need Toreth's help, but they followed instructions precisely. Toreth stood over her, weighing an injector in one hand and the neural induction probe in the other, waiting. Creating the sense that this was a point of no return. The black interrogation coveralls, stark white floor, and naked girl in the center often made an effective tableau, as Toreth knew from experience, and suddenly he heard Sant's voice.

"Stop! Tell them to fucking stop! I have a program. I bought it. A code that fixed the prices."

"A code," Nagra said skeptically. Toreth crouched down and placed the injector against Sarri's neck. Before he could even press the trigger she went limp, no longer resisting the guards, staring up at him with the terrified realization there was no way out.

"Yes," Sant said, his voice higher. "A code. It's true. I can give it to you. One of the back room techs, John Patel, helped me with fixing the analysis system. Please, tell them to stop it."

"Para?" Nagra said.

Toreth stood up, subvocalizing his answer. "Yeah, I heard him. I've got another room booked next door—put him in there and make sure he doesn't forget what happens if he changes his mind." He closed the connection, then beckoned the senior guard over to the door. "Tavinor, put her in the chair and leave her there until I call you. I'll have the cameras on." So behave yourselves, he didn't need to add.

"New suit, Para?"

"No. As she is, for now. Sorry to cut it short again." Interrupted section Ns had always been notorious for creating grumblings among the security guards. "If we're lucky, that was the last one. Thanks."

"Any time, Para." Tavinor hesitated. "Does this mean section Ns are going back in the P&P?"

"Probably not, I'm afraid."

He sighed and adjusted his cock through his uniform. "Pity. Beats a day of cell status checks. That, and I could use the extra cash." He looked optimistically at Toreth.

The guards behind Tavinor hauled Sarri to her feet and marched her back over to the chair. "I'll make sure you all get the bonuses for today's, at least," Toreth said, "even though they didn't complete."

Tavinor brightened. "Really? Thanks, Para, I appreciate it."

The first decent charges of the IIP went in against Sant's name, an impressive list by the time B-C had finished collecting offenses related to market fraud and manipulating Administration financial systems. More of Sant's colleagues would follow soon.

To a background of motivational weeping from the huddled figure on the screen, Sant had talked desperately, if without much organization, scrambling for new facts whenever Toreth feigned restlessness.

Carey's fabled man in a bar had actually been a man at a hotel. Specifically, at a traders' convention. No names had been used, and Sant had been skeptical, until the stranger had offered a demonstration. One price fluctuation later, Sant had been hooked. He'd paid a small fortune for the right to exploit two events a month, and the profit-related bonuses had rolled in.

The description he offered—a beard, sunglasses, thick hair—screamed disguise, but had done its job. The best Sant could offer was that the man hadn't had a local accent. Something mainland, Sant thought, and not south, which narrowed the search to only a few hundred million.

That had left Toreth with Systems as his main hope, and there was no rushing Systems. Back in his office, Toreth checked over the IIP, and he was about to go for a late lunch when his comm chimed. For a moment he was tempted to leave it until Sara caught it; then he saw the caller ID. He sat back down at his desk and readied a smile for the screen.

"Good afternoon, Secretary," he said.

Turnbull wasn't smiling. "I see you've made some progress."

The interrogations had only gone into the IIP an hour or so ago. Impressive. "It's very early days. The information seems sound, but we'll have to verify it technically."

"I wanted to talk to you about the methods, not the result." Her gaze flicked away for a moment. "The section N."

Bloody interfering outsiders. "It's a very low-risk protocol," Toreth said evenly.

"Physically, perhaps. Psychologically?"

"I'm sorry, Secretary?"

There was a pause, then Turnbull said, "If a relative, or someone at the corporation, complains about what you did to—"

"Don't worry, they can't."

"What do you mean, can't?"

Toreth decided he could take some lessons—Turnbull's polite confusion sounded far more genuine than his. Or maybe it was. "There's no mechanism for making a complaint about the interrogation process if it's inside the waiver," he explained. "That's what having a waiver means. Even if they somehow got as far as Internal Investigations, Internal would throw it out without a second glance. No one died." And even Internal would respect the Bureau's involvement. "Everything I did was fully covered—under the old system you could apply for a basic section N on a level five."

"I see." Yes, Toreth decided, she was genuinely taken aback. Usually she had an excellent understanding of I&I systems, so he wondered why this surprised her.

"Look, if you want some techniques taken off the table, let me know which ones," Toreth said reasonably. "That's why we have the system, after all, so Justice can—" Poke their noses in where they didn't belong. "—make that kind of decision about what's appropriate to the case. Just amend the waiver."

"I'm sure the Council would prefer to leave that to your discretion," Turnbull said, with a slight stress on the last word.

"Not a problem." Pretty much as Toreth had expected—results, so long as the Council's hands were no grubbier than absolutely necessary. "I'll make a note that section Ns are something to be discreet about."

The call from Systems came so late that Toreth had been about to leave for the night. As was often the case, in Toreth's experience with Systems, they brought good and bad news.

"It's easy enough, on the surface," Senior Systems Specialist Dale said over the comm. "You input the target, whether you want its price to go up or down and when, then it generates a simple output that looks innocuous enough in itself, and that's pretty much it. Assuming Sant gave us the real thing."

"How do we find out if it works?"

"We could always generate a code and send it off," Dale said brightly. "Pick a corporation, see what happens to their share price."

Toreth looked at him. Dale raised his eyebrows fractionally. It was tempting, but finally Toreth shook his head. "The Central Bank would explode. Tell me about this innocuous output."

Dale smiled. "Shame. Well, the program acts as a comms wrapper, generating something indistinguishable from a normal corporate-grade network encrypted comms message and sending it off. It would pass all the standard Data Division traffic inspections. Hidden inside the message is the stock manipulation input plus a small amount of information we can't definitely interpret yet—it could be something as simple as identifying the origin. It uses high-end black market encryption—one of the last-generation sab algorithms—but nothing we couldn't deal with. We still haven't traced where the message goes."

"Is it possible Sant was bullshitting us?" Toreth would've sworn not. He wondered if the daughter had been processed out yet.

"Possible, Para. The only good news is we aren't able to test the output on the various Central Bank systems."

"And that's good news?"

"Well, any hidden payload will be system-specific. The Central Bank knows their own systems best; maybe they'll be able to come up with something."

"And if they don't? What the hell's the point of it?"

"Well." Dale screwed up his face. "Assuming it isn't a complete smokescreen, it might trigger another piece of code that actually affects the prices."

"Or it alerts a person to do it," Toreth said, and Dale nodded.

"I might even say that's the most likely option, Para. Sant had the program installed on his private home system, not at work, and it didn't have direct access to any of the finance networks."

"I see." Toreth always preferred chasing people to hunting electrons. "How likely is it we can trace this message to its destination?"

"We aren't—" Dale hesitated. "When I spoke to Karaca, the bank's head of systems security, he said they'd handle the coordination with the Data Division for analyzing traffic movements."

Which was all very well from the point of view of solving the case, but less good for Toreth's record if everything was wrapped up in Frankfurt. "Would more copies of the program help you? I can pull in more of Verstraeten's names, get some search warrants."

Now Dale's discomfort became even more obvious. "I think Karaca wanted to handle that aspect, too. He said he'd be sending his proposed plan to you, Para."

"Oh, for fuck's sake."

Dale winced. "I'm sorry, Para. I'm just repeating what he told me."

Swearing at Systems was never productive. Toreth thanked Dale and cut the connection. Sure enough, a message from Karaca was waiting for him. It must have arrived while he was talking to Dale. Toreth opened it, scanned it, and swore again loudly enough that he was surprised Sara didn't open the door.

Case-stealing *bastards*. After all Lehman's fucking certainty that the investigation was a waste of time, Toreth would be cut out and demoted to making arrests at the behest of the bank. Crumbs of case credit, at best, even assuming Lehman didn't decide to let those go to *Caro* bloody Vaughn.

Toreth left the IIP and went over to the window. Technically—and as the message would no doubt explain when he calmed down enough to read it properly—the Central Bank could carry out the search more thoroughly and more discreetly than I&I. The Central Bank and Data Division between them probably had powers to examine the trading and communications systems of any finance sector corporation at any time, although the delicate balance between the corporate and Administration worlds meant they used those powers lightly.

Toreth had no doubt Lehman would spin the result as hard as she could to claim the Central Bank had needed minimal outside help to fix its security holes. Still, Turnbull had come through on her promises of commendations in the past. Maybe it would be good enough to sit back and leave the heavy lifting to Karaca and his team.

Good enough, but still infuriating.

Something about the view outside looked wrong, and it took a minute or so for Toreth to realize what had caught his attention. The window looked into an internal courtyard, the walls dropping down sheer to a small paved area with a square white stone plinth in the center which might have been intended as seating, although Toreth had never seen anyone use it. When the sun was directly overhead, light filtered down to otherwise gloomy offices; late on a January afternoon, the space was artificially lit, making it possible to catch the occasional sparkle of broken glass from the revolt, lingering in corners.

Apart from the glass, the courtyard had been bare since the revolt. Now someone had installed four tubs holding small trees, a straight stem topped with a ball of leaves—real or artificial, Toreth couldn't tell from five floors up. Were they a part of a maintenance plan established before the revolt that had simply shown up on schedule, or had someone thought greenery was a better investment of departmental budget than new para-investigators? Of course, it was probably easier to recruit trees than to persuade people that I&I was a sensible career choice.

Warrick had delayed and delayed at SimTech, finding things that could usefully be done before he and Asher left tomorrow, until he was forced to admit to himself that he was avoiding going home. And for that he blamed himself far more than Toreth. For months he had been impressing on Toreth that whoever paid the complex, the flat was home to both of them. Warrick thought he'd believed himself; why else did he still feel so guilty about the idea of contacting Carnac from the flat? Now Toreth's world had, perfectly reasonably, intruded, and dealing with that should be Warrick's problem.

Then, when he arrived home, the flat was empty and with the pristine look suggesting Toreth hadn't passed through that evening. Warrick was filling ravioli—pleasantly close enough to baking to have the same soothing effect—when the flat door opened.

"I'm in here," Warrick called with determined normality.

A thud outside announced a bag being abandoned in the hallway, then Toreth appeared. He had damp, freshly washed hair and a slight pink flush to his skin. From his expression, though, the gym had failed to work out whatever tension he'd been trying to lose. Without a greeting, he opened the fridge.

"Fuck. I thought there was a bottle of wine in here?"

"Over there on the side." Warrick pointed, with a slight flourish of flour dust.

Toreth poured a glass, splashing some onto the worktop, and sat down at the table.

"So how's your case going?" Warrick asked.

"Down the fucking drain," Toreth said succinctly.

Warrick kept his gaze on the pasta. "Would you like to talk about it?"

"Not especially." There was a moment's silence, then Toreth said, "It's all fucking politics. I hate that crap."

"Is it still the same case as before New Year? That—" Warrick reached for the name. "Richards?"

"Richardson, yeah. Okay, if you really want to know . . ."

Warrick listened as Toreth outlined the case. No mention of any special exemption waiver, or of arresting the children of suspects, but despite himself Warrick found he was being pulled into the background of the case. Privately, he agreed with some of the opinions that Toreth relayed that a magic code missile somehow manipulating share prices seemed wildly unlikely, but on the other hand, someone had believed in it enough to kill. An unfortunate, unforeseen consequence of a scam?

"So you actually have this so-called code?" he asked when Toreth paused.

"Yes, but it won't help. This is where the politics come in. After telling us we were wasting our time, Lehman swoops in today and takes the whole thing out of our hands: code analysis, comms tracing. The bank will grab all the credit—and your bloody Data Division, probably."

Even though Toreth sounded barely less annoyed than when he'd started the story, Warrick smiled. "It's a long time since they were mine."

"I suppose so." Toreth sighed. "Anyway, now I have a choice, if you can call it that. I can let the bank take the credit and hope enough trickles back to us, or I could fight to get the case back. But I probably don't have the clout. Turnbull won't care who solves it, as long as it's solved."

Why did it feel important that Toreth knew he'd been overheard? Warrick had kept things from him before, in the interests of smoothing their relationship. Like his call to Carnac, or his contact with the sabs—which was less smoothing and more preventing a somewhat justified detonation. Did overhearing the interrogation conversation feel so uncomfortable because of that much larger concealment?

Warrick crimped the last edge of the last circle of pasta, then turned around. "I heard you talking about the case yesterday."

Toreth lowered the glass from his lips without drinking and frowned. "What?"

"I came upstairs to see if you were ready. You were on your comm, discussing interrogations."

He watched Toreth's expression change from confusion to recollection, and then harden. "And?"

"No 'and.'" Warrick raised his hands placatingly. "You have a perfect right to talk to your colleagues here. But...yes, it bothered me. I wanted to—to—"

To have Toreth make the lingering discomfort go away. He wondered for a moment what De Nijs would think of that.

"Find out what happened to them?" Toreth shrugged. "Don't worry. We barely got anyone stripped before they all folded. Resisters and sabs hold up to second-level suspect targeted section Ns; most minor corporates don't have the spine. All the more annoying that Justice hated handing out section N waivers for them. Perk of corporate privilege. And in case you were wondering, the special exemption waiver was just for this investigation."

"I see."

"We might not even use it again. Lehman's given us the cold shoulder, and I can't see a thaw setting in. And definitely not the section N—I got that nixed from above today. Spineless fuckers." He downed the rest of his glass of wine and re-filled it. "Still, I'm sure the Council knows what's best. Shit like this happens all the time. I'll just have to forget about it, and hope someone bothers to mention my name when they submit to Justice."

Warrick could nod and they'd leave the conversation, and then soon the case would be closed and the special exemption waiver with it...until the next critical case, any-way. He dropped the ravioli into the simmering water and set a frying pan to heat.

"What about this murdered analysis programmer, though?"

"Lake?" Toreth sounded surprised. "What about him? Compared to the market fraud, he doesn't even rate as small fry."

"Well, small fry is better than no fish at all, surely? I can't imagine the Central Bank would be very interested in closing that part of the investigation. And he must have been at risk of finding something important, if he hadn't already." Warrick glanced over his shoulder. "Else why would someone kill him?"

Chapter Twenty-one

❖

A nd so the Central Bank has taken over the systems portion of the investigation," Toreth announced to the team. "I talked to Tillotson this morning, and he said the decision is out of his hands." The smug, vindictive arsehole.

Murmurs of disappointment traveled around the case conference like ripples in a pool. Finally B-C said, "Does that mean we're off the case?"

"Should it?"

"Well, the systems portion is pretty much everything." B-C glanced at the other investigators. "Isn't it?"

Toreth turned to Verstraeten. "Do you know yet whether these events are still happening?"

Verstraeten rocked his hand from side to side. "Honestly, Para, I can't give you a definitive answer. We need a long enough event tail to make sure it fits the model. But we still haven't detected anything substantive this year."

"So it's possible the operators have already spooked for some reason. If that's true, then the bank might have trouble finding them. In the meantime we still have a body, and that's *our* specialty. Lake didn't cut himself up and throw himself into the reprocessing plant. Jameson?"

The junior investigator stopped fiddling with her parti-colored hair. "I'm still working on the Fresh Green Fields security, Para. The files are coming slowly. I can't tell if they're being deliberately obstructive, or if they just have a lot of internal red tape and a fear of someone stealing their proprietary formulae."

"So give them a fear of something else. Explain the concept of impeding an I&I investigation to someone senior enough to get them all moving. And if they still don't cooperate, arrest them and explain it again downstairs. For fuck's sake, you aren't at Justice now. Take the bloody kid gloves off."

One thing he was willing to admit was that Jameson took discipline well. She never flinched or argued. "Yes, Para."

Mistry cleared her throat. "I ran out of things to do while you were interrogating, Para, so I prodded the forensic follow-up for results."

"Anything interesting?"

"DNA checks on Lake's flat. The usual sort of DNA traces showed up, mostly social contact patterns, but there was one belonging to Rutland inside underwear waiting to be washed."

"Really? Difficult to see how that happened on the underground."

Mistry smiled. "I think the other passengers would've noticed."

"Good. Bring her in and talk to her again. If she doesn't want to come, tell her we'll get a witness warrant and make it all nice and official on her security file. Speaking of witnesses, Richardson isn't doing us any good down in the cells. Sara, see if Justice is amenable to putting him on close location monitoring."

She nodded. "I'll show them the provisional evidence submission. I don't think it'll be a problem. Residence restriction?"

"Yes—no. Give him some leeway to go out. An hour or two a day, something like that. Morehen, you're in charge of him again. I want a twenty-four-hour watch. Maybe whoever killed Lake will decide to do some more tidying up. Ideally, catch them before they do it; if not, don't let them get away. B-C, go over all Lake's data again, especially comms and anything that doesn't look relevant. Do you have a list of his contacts?"

"Yes, Para. Anyone he ever spoke to directly. And I did run a broad c&p to generate possible names for face-to-face meetings, just in case." B-C grimaced. "The results are in the IIP."

The usual mess of false leads and time-wasting, presumably. "Leave those for if everything else dead-ends. Start with his known contacts and make sure that he didn't ask any of them to hold data for him. And recheck the details of his meetings with Richardson. Run some local c&ps, try to find anyone else who was in the area at the time. Jameson and Mistry can work on the leads when they have time."

Tasks divided up, Toreth sent the team on their way. Warrick had been right— Lake was still a viable investigation and now they had a new lead in Rutland. If Lake had confided in her she might still let them beat the Central Bank to the punch.

Toreth decided to leave Rutland to Mistry, at least at first. The woman had lied to them, but she could've had any number of reasonably innocent reasons for that. It was worth giving Mistry a shot at untangling them. With the now *almost* level seven waiver still in hand, they could move on to other options whenever they wanted.

Toreth watched on his office screen. Mistry had found one of the small number of interview rooms with a window. Even through the reinforced glass, interviewees found a glimpse of sky and grass reassuring.

Mistry laid out the DNA results clearly and with an encouragingly gentle air of puzzlement. "I wanted to give you a chance to explain it yourself, before my boss came to talk to you again," Mistry finished.

Rutland held her façade of bewilderment for a few seconds, then Toreth saw it crumble. "Oh, hell. Yes, you're right. We were seeing one another. The only reason I didn't tell you before is that Equibon is very strict about fraternization. We never even went to one another's flats. As part of our contracts Equibon has optional oversight of our accommodation, comms, finances—you name it. I liked Rupert, but I liked keeping my job, too. And it felt safer, after—" Her voice faltered.

"After?" Mistry prompted.

"I don't know. Nothing."

Toreth shook his head. Fucking Turnbull and her "take a real waiver but be nice to everyone" crap. Mistry was good, but it still irked him to have to slow down the investigation by easing information out of witnesses.

"Was he involved in something illegal?" Mistry asked.

"No!" Rutland sounded shocked. "No, of course not. He was...okay. He started investigating something at Equibon."

"So you knew about that?"

"Yes." Rutland frowned. "How do you?"

"That doesn't matter. If he was murdered because of it, we need to hear everything you know. It could be crucial in catching whoever killed him."

"All right. We talked about it a lot—he was obsessed with it." Guilt shaded her voice. "I was the one who told him something fishy was happening in the first place. I heard whispers about some kind of stock manipulation, big and getting bigger. I knew Rupert had worked for Fisec, so I asked him what he thought about the rumors."

With one eye still on the interview Toreth opened the IIP, comparing Verstraeten's list of guilty companies against Lake's Fisec report.

"Did you contact Fisec yourself?" Mistry asked.

"*Fisec?*" Rutland laughed incredulously. "Hardly. What could I have told them, anyway? I didn't have any proof, just stories. All I wanted to know was if Rupert thought it was even possible. If the whole company was going to end up in the soup, I wanted out before it happened. I didn't think he'd try to investigate it himself. In fact, I begged him to stop."

Toreth tapped his comm with a question for Mistry to relay.

"He didn't include Equibon's name in his report, although we've found evidence the code was abused there," Misty said, with no hint in her voice that the question wasn't hers.

She frowned. "Didn't he? I suppose he was trying to protect us. Me."

Obviously the existence of a code wasn't a surprise to her.

"And he didn't tell Fisec about the code, either," Mistry said.

Rutland's expression cleared. "Well, he didn't have it then. That was later, when he started hunting for some real proof to get them to listen."

"So how did Lake get hold of the code?"

"I'm not sure. That is—" She hesitated.

"We can't charge him with anything now, Ms. Rutland."

"No, I suppose not. Still, it feels like—sticking to the rules was so important to him. But when Fisec wouldn't listen to him, he said he needed concrete evidence, something they couldn't ignore. He got me to ask around, to try to get myself cut into the scam, whatever it was. I couldn't, but I did give him the names of some people I was pretty sure must be in on it. I think he stole the code from one of them."

"Did Richardson help him do that?" Mistry asked.

"Richardson?" Rutland tilted her head questioningly, then before Mistry could answer said, "Is that the name of the man helping him?"

"You didn't know?"

"I knew he was working with someone, but Rupert wouldn't tell me his name. He said it could be dangerous. They met in a bar, that's all I know. They got into a conversation about systems security, and it ended up with Rupert hiring him. I thought he was crazy. I made Rupert tell me the locations of the meetings, and I followed him a few times without telling him, to make sure he was safe."

Quite the little amateur sab. Toreth wondered how she'd managed to stay alive any longer than Lake. Did that mean whoever had killed Lake hadn't been watching his meetings with Richardson?

Mistry, though, had picked up on something else. "Ms. Rutland, not long after Mr. Lake disappeared Justice had an anonymous call directing them towards a certain location...?"

Rutland nodded. "That was me, yes. Rupert was meeting this Richardson at a storage facility—he called me to say the man had set up an urgent meeting. I didn't want him to go, but Rupert said this could be a big break. I waited for him to get back in touch, and I was afraid of getting Rupert in trouble. But in the end I knew something must have happened to him. So I sent the message to Justice."

"But when you spoke to Justice, and to us, you didn't say anything about all this."

"I was scared. Not about losing my job—about ending up like Rupert. I kept hoping he was okay, even though I knew he couldn't be, really, when he didn't call me for so long. Then the Justice officers arrived at Equibon, and they told us he was dead and what had happened to him..." She glanced nervously around the room. "If there's one thing you learn in our business, it's how easily information leaks out."

"How did Mr. Lake seem in the days before he disappeared?"

"Oh, he'd been very excited. He said he'd broken the encryption and he'd been wrong about the whole thing. I think he meant wrong about the mechanism, not that it was happening."

"Was that everything? Did he give you any more details? Ask you to take files or anything else for safekeeping?"

"No. That was it. He said he didn't want me involved. Oh..."

She paused, and after a few seconds, Mistry prompted her. "Oh?"

"He did ask if I understood comms tracing. Well, of course I told him I don't. I'm a trader." A small smile flickered on her lips for a moment. "You can't expect monkeys to understand how their toys work, can you?"

"Thank you, Ms. Rutland. If you'll excuse me a moment."

Mistry went out into the corridor, and a moment later Toreth heard her voice over the comm.

"Para? Did you see all that?"

"Yeah, I did. Very interesting. What do you think?"

"A storage unit is an excellent choice if you want to kill someone," Mistry said. "Soundproof, easy to shroud for the forensics, and no one will notice a large crate being taken away. Justice's forensic report said it had been cleaned down."

"And according to Rutland, Richardson was the one who wanted the meeting there."

Toreth was about to check the IIP, but Mistry said, "Richardson claimed that he was supposed to meet Lake in a park later that day. Lake's choice of location, only Lake didn't show up. Richardson's c&p confirmed that he went there."

"Yes." Toreth opened the c&p. "In a taxi that he'd know could be traced, even though he had access to that chipped car."

Inside the interview room Rutland had gone over to the window. After a moment, she made a gesture that suggested she was reaching for the comm that she would've surrendered when she was processed in for a witness interview, and then sighed. Her body language looked as relaxed as anyone ever did at I&I.

"So who do we think is lying?" Toreth asked.

"Richardson," Mistry said immediately. "I don't think he ever knew about Rutland, so he had no idea anyone could contradict him. And Rutland knows the content of the Justice message, so she most likely did make the call."

"Maybe she killed him, too. She's tall enough, and probably strong enough."

"I don't think so, Para."

"No, neither do I." Unless she was also a sab with a very solid cover. With the waiver there ready it was a tempting idea to send her downstairs and find an interrogator to make absolutely sure Rutland was holding nothing back. Rutland could thank Turnbull for a lucky escape—for now. "Thanks, Mistry. Good work. Go through it again with her, just in case there's anything she missed. If you have any doubts at all, let me know. Then check her alibis and c&p, see if it matches up with her story. If it does, she can go."

Leaving Mistry to finish the interview, Toreth opened his office door. Sara looked around at once. "Yes?"

"Did Justice process that location monitoring yet?"

"I'm afraid not, sorry. I was about to give them a nudge."

"No, that's good. Cancel the request. Then book an interrogation room starting right away. Open-ended. And tell Nagra she's back in business. This time I want Richardson wrung dry. The only proviso is she doesn't kill him—call it a steady level six, or a very careful level seven. Old level seven, obviously. Where is Nagra, anyway?"

"Running an interrogation for Senior Para Chevril," Sara said promptly.

Toreth grinned. "When he complains, tell him the financial security of the Administration is at stake."

Toreth spent a while working up an interrogation rota for the next few days. With Daedra's replenished pharmacy and an unlimited waiver, there would be no second chance for Richardson to cooperate. Everything he gave them from now on would be gone over and over again until the interrogators and Toreth were satisfied he had nothing left.

By the time he was done, Richardson was back in a level C interrogation room. Toreth had left the camera feed open on his office screen, and movement caught his eye as Nagra came into the room.

"You lied to us," Nagra said flatly.

Nonspecific and open-ended. Good. Let Richardson figure out what he needed to say to make it stop. Not that it would, not this time. Toreth watched Nagra at work for ten minutes, then switched off the feed.

Warrick went home early, working in the office at the flat until Toreth came home—unusually late. Progress in the case, or a side trip on the way home? At least Toreth's call of "It's me!" suggested he was in a reasonably good mood. A pity that wouldn't last for long. Warrick switched off the screens, tidied the desk, and collected four empty mugs from various perches that gave him an excuse to detour to the kitchen before he finally had no reason not to follow Toreth into the living room.

Toreth was standing by a chair, hand screen open, as though he'd been about to sit down and been distracted.

"Good day?" Warrick asked.

"Not bad. Nothing you want to hear about, though."

A well-understood warning.

"There's something I need to talk to you about," Warrick said. "Before I leave tomorrow."

"Mm?" He put the hand screen away. "Don't worry, I doubt I can trash the place completely in a week."

Warrick made himself smile. "I was planning to tell the vac to put in some overtime. But it wasn't that. Let me get a drink first."

"Okay. I'll have a whisky."

Warrick, aware he was still delaying, poured himself a modest gin and tonic and Toreth a much larger measure. As he handed the drink over, he realized that he'd chosen one of the plainer glasses, with no sentimental value. A subconscious indication of how he expected the conversation to go?

"Go on, then," Toreth said. He held up the glass. "If it needs a drink this big, let's get it over with."

He was joking, but on another level clearly not. Complaints to De Nijs notwithstanding, lately things had been going relatively smoothly. Please, God, this wouldn't turn into a blazing argument and one of Toreth's prolonged disappearances.

"I want to tell you about something," Warrick said carefully, "because it seems... too dishonest not to. I should've told you at the time."

"Is this about eavesdropping?" Now Toreth sounded amused. "You know, I can just let you take a look at the IIP if you're suddenly so interested in my cases."

"No, not that. Something that's of more personal importance to me, and less directly to you." There was no way to soften the truth, so he said, "I called Carnac last week."

The sense of relief lasted less than a second, until Toreth's eyes narrowed.

"About Kate?"

"Yes. He couldn't help me—he didn't know anything this time. And I'm afraid he isn't all of it."

Toreth groaned. "You didn't mess with Cit's files again?"

"No! That would be far too dangerous, I agree. But I did contact a sab team. In an exploratory sense only, to see if they could access information about her."

"Jesus fucking Christ!" For a moment, Warrick was sure Toreth would throw the glass—on to the floor, if not actually at him. Then Toreth downed half the whisky and slammed the glass onto the mantelpiece instead. His knuckles caught the copper cat sculpture that sat there and knocked it over. "Was one arrest not enough? Please, for fuck's sake, tell me you aren't going through with it."

"I'm not. I couldn't be sure they'd get the information, and the risk was too high."

"Warrick, what you've done already is a huge fucking risk." Warrick could hear the effort Toreth was expending to keep his voice level. "What if Sable—no, fuck Sable. What if someone else at Citizen Surveillance hears about it? Someone who doesn't give a shit about keeping you alive and out of re-education."

"I went through an agent, of course, anonymously. There's no way they could find out."

"Oh, really? Are you sure? Corporations aren't always as untouchable as they fucking think they are. Sabs weigh up percentages too, you know. There are teams out there working on sufferance because sometimes places like Cit need an extra level of deniability."

Warrick couldn't believe Queen would give him the contact unless she had absolute confidence in the security of the agent, and the agent themselves had seemed cautious but confident that Warrick's requirements could be met safely. But maybe Citizen Surveillance fell far enough outside the typical corporate sabbing field of interest that Queen might have a less realistic assessment of the hazards than Toreth.

"Well, either way, it's done now," Warrick said. "And it goes no further, I promise," he added. "I told Carnac the same thing."

"And I'm supposed to believe you, because you promised Carnac?" Toreth said, his voice tight. "That's the gold standard now? What was fucking New Year, then, with the 'I give you my word' shit you fed me?"

Too late, he recognized the tactical error of mentioning Carnac again. "I'm sorry. I know it doesn't make it any better, but when I said it, I meant it. But... the situation changed."

"Really?" Toreth said with bitter skepticism. "How?"

And there he was stuck. How could he even try to explain to Toreth? Carnac had understood the impulse, even though he hadn't approved of it. Toreth would be able to see nothing beyond Warrick provoking Citizen Surveillance over—what? The wounds in the family that couldn't begin to heal while Kate's limbo existence remained unresolved? Tarin's bewilderment and pain? Warrick's own guilt? None of those reasons would interest Toreth, for whom family existed only as leverage to hold over a prisoner.

"I'm sorry," Warrick said again, even though Toreth would give the apology the dismissal that, in all honesty, it probably deserved. "But I do think you're overestimating the danger. Citizen Surveillance can't monitor every—"

"Shut up. Just fucking shut your face, before I..." Toreth pulled out his hand screen and expanded it with an angry motion. He worked for a few seconds, then turned it to face Warrick. "Okay, pick one."

Warrick looked at the selection of faces, men and women, all unfamiliar. "Who are they?"

"The traders I was talking about on the comm, who thought they'd found a perfect scam. They screwed with something very important to the Administration and now they're all sitting in the cells at I&I, waiting to find out how hard they'll be fucked by the Justice system. Meanwhile, I have a blanket level seven waiver for all of them—old level seven, so plenty of the good stuff—so you pick one, and you can stand in the observation room and watch while I fucking *show* you where this kind of stupidity ends. Because just explaining it obviously isn't getting through."

Warrick stared at him. His hard, angry expression certainly made him look serious, but would he really interrogate someone purely as a demonstration, when he'd already said that people above were monitoring the special waiver closely?

"Come on," Toreth said. "Which one?"

Toreth had done it to Carnac, though; Carnac had told Warrick about it in the sim. Forced Carnac to watch an interrogation in what Carnac had described as a test of machismo, which was a trivial reason compared to the current situation. "You've made your point," Warrick said. "I do understand the danger."

"No, I don't think you do. When I talked to Sable last year, he asked me if I thought you'd keep chasing whoever put Marriot in hospital. I said you weren't suicidal. Looks like I was wrong. You won't choose? Fine." Toreth pointed to the picture of a woman in her fifties. "She'll do. We picked up her daughter as well. Maybe she can watch with you and you can explain why you don't give a shit that her mother's choking on a neural induction probe. Make sure you wear some comfortable shoes because you'll be standing there all night."

"Don't be ridiculous," Warrick said firmly. "Of course I'm not going."

"Then I'll record it and bring it back and you can watch every fucking minute of it here."

And now, finally, Warrick knew he was serious. "Toreth, no."

"Sorry, but you don't have the power to decide what happens at I&I." He turned away. "Or any other fucking place at Int-Sec."

As usual, Toreth had thrown his jacket over the nearest convenient piece of furniture when he took it off. This time, Warrick was grateful because as Toreth paused to pick up the jacket from the arm of the sofa, Warrick had enough time to dodge around the other end and get to the doorway before him. He closed the door and put his back to it.

Toreth pulled on his jacket, as impassive as if he hadn't even noticed Warrick move, which gave Warrick plenty of time to consider what the hell he could actually do to stop Toreth. Cancel the access on the flat security? That had worked once to prevent Toreth from leaving the old place, but not here, where Warrick had carefully given him equal authority. If it came to a real physical confrontation, he'd have a few seconds at most to produce something from his corporate training that might surprise Toreth.

He'd have to try, though. He'd felt like a coward before; he couldn't let this happen now. Why hadn't he kept his mouth shut about Carnac?

Toreth stopped too close, his face impassive, his eyes cold. This was the Toreth prisoners must see every day, no crack of humanity in which to slide the edge of a plea. Like the game, but not like, and even as he readied himself to try to stop Toreth, a sick twist of arousal threaded through the apprehension.

"Don't start this if you don't want to finish it," Toreth said.

"I'm not 'starting' anything. Can't we just—"

"Then get out of the way. I'm not pissing about."

The strength of the urge to comply surprised him. Years of training in another context completely. "No. This has gone far enough already."

Toreth moved, only a tiny motion shifting his weight, but Warrick reacted instinctively. He almost got a hold, his fingertips touching the shoulder of Toreth's jacket, then he felt his feet swept out from beneath him and he landed hard on his side, the carpet barely cushioning his fall. Before he could move, Toreth knelt behind him and wrapped one arm around Warrick's shoulder and upper arm. He grabbed Warrick's hand, pressing his wrist forward and down, folding Warrick's arm over Toreth's forearm. The movement crushed Warrick's biceps into hard bone, and Warrick gasped in pain.

"That hurts," Warrick said, the words shocked out of him by how *much,* how suddenly, and Toreth laughed.

"I know. That's what compression locks are for. Well? Anything else you want to say before I go?"

"Please don't interrogate—" He couldn't recall the name he'd glimpsed below the image. And a name wouldn't make Toreth care, anyway. "Please don't interrogate her. She doesn't deserve—" He broke off again as Toreth pressed harder on Warrick's arm, forcing another choked exclamation from him.

"Yes?" Toreth said. "She doesn't *deserve...?*"

"She doesn't deserve that," Warrick managed to say, and gritted his teeth. "Especially not because you mistakenly think you need to prove something to me. Please." He remembered watching Toreth at work on Marian Tanit, and the idea of being the sole immediate cause for that kind of torture sickened him. He touched the back of Toreth's hand. "Please, Toreth."

"Fuck."

Toreth released him, and Warrick curled away from him. The abused muscle throbbed, and he rubbed it cautiously.

"So she's worth your bloody consideration?" Toreth was breathing heavily. "Some greedy bitch you've never even met, you'll beg for her, but you're happy to screw around with Carnac and sabs and God knows what else until the rest of us are all down in the shit with you. If Cit starts looking too hard and finds out Sable frigged their operation files, do you think they'll stop there? I worked my nuts off in the interrogations you don't fucking want to hear about to make your bloody brother look like an informer instead of the stupid fucking resister he is. That's conspiracy to commit treason. Maybe we'll all be lucky and they'll just kill me, instead of making sure they find out everything I know first." He prodded Warrick in the shoulder. "*She* doesn't deserve it, but I do?"

"Of course not," Warrick said. He didn't think even Carnac could fault Toreth's self-interest in this instance. "You've made your point, and I accept it." His biceps twinged sharply as he straightened his arm. "Completely."

"Like you accepted it before, you mean?"

Warrick could only nod.

Toreth stood up, and for a moment Warrick thought he was about to leave—at best, to head for Sara's or a bar, at worst for I&I. Instead he went over to the fireplace, picked up the whisky from the mantelpiece, and took a mouthful. By the time he came back, Warrick had managed to sit up. As well as the lingering pain in his biceps, his hip felt bruised. Thank God they hadn't been out in the tiled hallway.

Toreth offered the glass to Warrick, who took it with his unhurt arm. The smoky taste in his mouth turned into the sharp burn of neat spirits as he swallowed. He drained the glass, and then Toreth took it back and helped Warrick to his feet.

"If you had to be so fucking brainless, why didn't you contact Sable?" He still sounded angry. "He might actually know what's going on, and at least he's got *some* reason to want to keep you alive."

Possibly. But also a proven disinterest in Tarin's life. "I agree he might know—in fact, if the letters from Kate aren't real, he may well be involved in faking them." Continuing the strange fantasy world of Kate's letters to Sable? The idea made him faintly queasy. "But he lied to my face about Tarin, so how could I trust him now?"

"So instead you'd trust sabs? I hope you realize that anyone who'd touch Int-Sec files has to be a fucking maniac. Any corporate sabs good enough to do it should be good enough to know not to try. And what do you think it would do to SimTech if you got caught sabbing *Citizen fucking Surveillance*?"

Wildly inappropriate as it was, Warrick almost laughed aloud at the idea of Toreth developing a pressing concern for SimTech's future. Another lever, just like family.

"Why does it even make any difference where the hell Kate is?" Toreth said, and Warrick was surprised to hear a background note of pleading. "She's either alive or she's not, and that's it—nothing actually changes if you know. Do I need to put you in the cabinet whenever you aren't at SimTech, just to keep your mind off this crap? Because that's starting to sound like a tempting idea. At least when you're fucking chained up, you can't go running off to fucking Carnac every time something goes wrong."

Twice in a year was hardly "every time." Warrick lightened his tone, trying to defuse the tension. "I thought we agreed that my wrists couldn't take it?"

"You know what? Yes, it'd probably fuck up the nerves for the rest of your life, but at least you'd *have* a rest of your life. And so would I." Frustration sharpened his voice again. "Why, Warrick? What happened? Why does it suddenly fucking matter enough to risk getting us both killed?"

Warrick shook his head. None of the reasons he could offer would do anything to satisfy the question.

"Upstairs," Toreth said abruptly. "My room."

"Why?"

"Because I'm sick of going in fucking circles about this."

Did this mean he'd abandoned the interrogation demonstration? Much as Toreth loved makeup sex, he was nowhere near as easily distractible as he sometimes appeared, especially when I&I was concerned.

"Well?" Toreth demanded.

Warrick hesitated. Real change of heart or a distraction ploy? Finally he shrugged. "All right."

Toreth fucked him steadily, controlled, silent except for rough breaths in time with each thrust. Warrick had his arms tucked under his chest, folded hands pressed between his breastbone and the mattress. Toreth's hands gripped Warrick's shoulders, his elbows tight against Warrick's sides. Enclosed, almost smothering, with a shivering intensity that felt like the game. Except Warrick had all the awareness he lacked then, feeling every point of contact between them, skin covering skin. Intent and impersonal, both at once. What was Toreth thinking about?

His body wanted to move, but Toreth had him held as securely as if he'd cuffed Warrick to the bed. Warrick shifted, trying to get some leverage, some friction.

He felt the breath on the back of his neck as Toreth murmured, "No. That's not what you do."

Warrick stilled. That was the first thing Toreth had said since they reached the bedroom. He'd started stripping as soon as the door closed behind them; Warrick had followed his lead. He didn't know if they were inside or outside the game. Whatever rules Toreth was applying now, Warrick didn't understand them. The uncertainty, the enveloping sensation of restraint, mixed with the lingering adrenaline from the living room confrontation and crystallized into a single feeling.

Possession.

Warrick moaned, trying to hide the sound in the pillow. Toreth's fingers dug hard into his shoulders, and the rhythm broke as he came. He kept moving, still silent, until finally he stopped. Warrick flexed his fingers, turned on, frustrated. With only one deep breath as warning, Toreth pulled away.

Warrick turned over onto his back, already touching his cock before he could think what Toreth would want to do next. The relief of the contact made him shiver, head to foot, and he grabbed the duvet with his other hand. He expected a comment—you're fucking insatiable—a laugh. Something. But he might've been alone in the room. No more movement on the mattress, either. Had Toreth slipped out of the bedroom?

No. He'd moved to lean against the foot of the bed, in the exact center. He wiped his hands over his face, back through his hair, and blinked a couple of times. Warrick looked at him questioningly.

"You finish it," Toreth said.

"All right."

Warrick closed his eyes, trying to concentrate, to pull himself back inside the moment. Shallow breaths, quicker in than out. His body was turned on, but the strange, unbalanced atmosphere in the bedroom left his brain lagging behind. Almost like being in the sim, he mused, software and neural stimulation dictating physical responses that the mind tried to integrate into its reality. As an experiment, he let himself think about what had happened downstairs, Toreth's icy anger in the moment before confrontation exploded into violence, and it made his balls tighten and his heart speed up. The spark of arousal dampened back down only a moment later when the thought intruded that De Nijs—and the insurers—would not approve.

Damn. Warrick opened his eyes, just a crack, enough to see Toreth at the other end of the bed. He had his knees drawn up and his arms resting on them. He must've caught the movement of Warrick's eyelids, because he said, "I'm watching."

"Are you—" Still angry? Toreth didn't look it, but Warrick right now couldn't read his face at all. "What do you want me to do?"

Toreth shrugged. "I don't mind. I can join in, if you like."

"No. If that's what you want, stay there. Or..." Call it a night, and return to the unresolved, and possibly unresolvable, argument.

"Mm." For a few seconds more he didn't move, then he crawled over. To Warrick's surprise, though, Toreth just knelt beside him and leaned over him, pressing down the mattress beside Warrick's shoulders. No skin touched, but he thought he could feel the heat of Toreth's body. His serious expression made Warrick hesitate, his hand stilling.

"I was just thinking," Toreth began, then said, "—no, don't stop."

His tone had changed completely. Game voice, or something very close. Warrick did as he was told. "Thinking about what?" he prompted.

"About who. You. Specifically, keeping you out of trouble. Keeping you *under control*." The soft menace shivered down Warrick's spine, making his cock harder. "I thought about locking you in the flat, but you've just demonstrated how much shit you can get into with access to a comm. So...no comms. I wonder if Fran rents out the side rooms at the Shop? Some of those have good sturdy chains. I'll get a long-term lease. The Shop's always open; I could drop in and fuck you whenever I wanted."

Warrick swallowed, distractions fading as the room seemed to shrink around them. "I'd be very bored. Between visits, anyway."

"So? Bored is better than running about loose, causing fucking chaos." Toreth was watching his face intently, reading every reaction. "And why the fuck would I care, anyway? If you complain too much, I can always gag you. Whether you like it or not."

By force. They'd done that before, Toreth's strong, trained hands—not touching him now, even though Warrick so badly wanted them to—holding him, shoving the gag into his mouth, tightening the strap. Goosebumps rippled across Warrick's skin, and his breathing hitched.

Toreth smiled coldly. "Or maybe not the Shop. Too many people there. Too many questions. It'd be a waste of money, anyway. New London's full of empty cellars, places hardly anyone knows about. Not on any official city plans, that's for sure. Sabs love them for kidnappings, because they hide infrared and they have soundproof walls. SimTech security could search forever. No movement notification now, either, so you could be anywhere. I'll just say you sneaked off to Strasbourg to cozy up to fucking Carnac. Must've used a fake name to travel, trust a fucking corporate to make things difficult for people who want to help. Carnac can deal with Justice asking stupid questions. And meanwhile, you'll be safely stashed away. Waiting for me."

The inactivity that probably would drive Warrick mad in a day or two was something to be glossed over, a shadowy length of time only there as a background to let him imagine the door opening at last, a dim light filtering into the prison to hurt his dark-adapted eyes. (Had Toreth said it would be dark? No, that was his own addition.) Chains holding him to the wall, the ghost of fresh air taunting him, Toreth a silhouette against the doorway—Warrick tensed, stroking himself faster.

"What would you do to me?" Warrick asked breathlessly.

"I hadn't thought about it yet. Does it matter?" Toreth leaned closer, and then his hand closed gently around Warrick's throat. "Anything I wanted. Fuck, that sounds good right now. No need to worry about marking you. No Dillian. No suspicious medics. No Justice officers deciding I went too far. Just how long I want to keep you alive."

Anything. Anything he wanted. Slaps. Blows. A leather belt, the bruising sting of the buckle. Chains, cuffs, a knife, ice or blistering metal, real whip drawing real blood, rough concrete against his palms and knees, Toreth fucking him, Toreth's fist inside him—

"Anyway, I think you should be worrying more about what you could do. What you could offer." Toreth's cheek touched Warrick's, his voice a whisper now. "I bet you could get very creative, trying to make sure I want to come back again. Because no one else will be able to find you. You'll be *mine*."

203

"Please," Warrick said, the word echoing in his mind from cobwebbed walls. He closed his eyes, wanting the darkness of an imaginary blindfold. He groped out with his free hand, finding the back of Toreth's neck, holding on to him as Warrick's other hand tightened on his cock.

"Scream all you want," Toreth breathed right against his ear. "I'll make sure no one can hear you, no matter how loud you are."

Warrick's heels dug into the mattress, pushing him up against Toreth as he came, giddy with release and relief. Toreth increased the pressure on Warrick's throat, holding, then loosening his grip perfectly in time as Warrick relaxed back onto the bed.

He lay there, warm and tingling with pleasant little jolts of memory and aftershocks. Toreth stretched out beside him, pressed close now, and Warrick stroked the short hair at the back of his neck. The atmosphere had changed, the tension of confrontation cleared from the room.

"My ear's ringing," Toreth said.

"Sorry." Warrick hadn't even heard himself. "You did say 'scream all you want.'"

"Yeah, I did."

A minute or so passed, then the bed shifted as Toreth propped himself up on his elbow. Warrick disengaged his hand at once, but to his surprise Toreth didn't move further away. Warrick opened his eyes.

"You should take some holiday," Toreth said thoughtfully. "A week, maybe. Although you'd need to tell Dillian and SimTech that you'd be out of comm contact for it, or it'd be security nuclear strike time."

"I really would be bored out of my mind," Warrick said, and let his fingers drift casually along Toreth's shoulder blade. "Not a very sexually satisfying experience."

"In a few days?" Toreth smirked down at him, self-confidence personified. "You wouldn't have time. Anyway, I think there are still some of the dyschronos on the pharmacy list. You wouldn't know how long it had been. Or I could just drug you unconscious when I wanted a break."

The practical solution. Warrick smiled. "I'm not saying definitely yes, but... I'm not saying no, either." The concept intrigued him, anyway. "We'd need to talk about it."

"Okay. You know, maybe with enough training time and the right incentive you could finally learn to deep throat as well as you do in the sim. Hmm. Food's a good reward. I'll take some prisoner rations from work to start with. No one will notice—I don't think anyone's wanted to steal any of that shit since I&I opened. Then you can earn something better. What do you think you'd be willing to do for a real juicy pork chop, after a few days on reconstituted protein slices?"

"Are you hungry, by any chance?" Warrick asked.

There was a pause, then Toreth laughed. "Yeah, actually I am."

"Let's clean up, and I'll make something."

By the time Warrick came out of the bathroom, Toreth had gone. The slight apprehension—had he really *gone*?—lasted until Warrick found him in the kitchen, grazing through the contents of the fridge.

"I decided not to wait," Toreth said through a mouthful of ham.

"Omelet? It's quick, and there's plenty of fresh bread and salad."

"As long as you put something in it." Toreth abandoned the fridge, taking a slice of ham with him, and went to sit on the edge of the table.

Warrick picked out a mix that should hopefully make the offering interesting and substantial enough—Gruyère, spinach, mushrooms, chives, the surviving ham. Aware of Toreth watching him silently, Warrick cracked eggs into a bowl and ground in salt and pepper. Omelets were one of the few areas where he and Jen disagreed about food. She insisted on adding milk for a lighter final result. Warrick preferred the unadulterated richness. It was a question of personal taste, obviously, but that didn't stop his fingers from itching whenever he saw her splashing in the milk.

Do it my way. Do it *right*. Even when it came to making an omelet.

So, yes, Carnac and Toreth were spot on about his need for control, and the fact that they agreed on it was simply more evidence that he was being stupidly stubborn. Kate's disappearance was out of his hands—and even if it wasn't, not entirely, the price of regaining control might be too high. Events would work out in their own time, and all that he seemed likely to do was put people in more danger while he indulged his own irrationality.

"Do I need to start shopping for abandoned cellars?" Toreth said.

Warrick realized he'd been beating the eggs long past the point he'd usually stop. He put down the whisk and turned around. Toreth looked absolutely serious; this wasn't a conversation about fantasies anymore.

"No," Warrick said. "And I am sorry. I was wrong. I should've kept my word about Kate." Devalued now, as Carnac had said. "I didn't consider the possible dangers carefully enough. Maybe I didn't want to. I don't know if there's any way I can convince you that I mean this now, but I'm done with it. Not because I promised Carnac, but because I know you're both right."

Toreth's gaze was as searching as it had been upstairs. Finally he said, "And what if 'the situation changes' again?"

"I don't know," Warrick said honestly. "Something could happen, yes, that would alter the risk/reward balance. But . . . I promise that if it does, I'll discuss it before I do anything. With you, not Carnac."

"Good." Toreth linked his fingers and stretched his arms out in front of him, then relaxed and sighed. "I think I'm going to blame Sara and the fucking Department of Population."

Warrick spent a moment trying to work it out, then gave up. "Why?"

"Five, six—Christ, I don't know—years, anyway, and you manage to stay out of trouble. Then Sara badgers me into sending a registration form to the DoP, and as soon as they've got my name officially linked to yours, suddenly you want to whip out your cock and wave it in Cit's face."

"Toreth!" Warrick couldn't help the horrified laughter. "That's—no. Sable's my father."

"All the more reason not to get into a moronic dick-measuring contest with him. You know, I told Sable I could stop you from pulling anything stupid."

"When was that?"

"At Gegi's. I hope he doesn't decide to hold me to it." Toreth snorted. "Although since you'd just walked into a bar looking for a Cit agent you shouldn't even have known was alive, at least he has to realize it wouldn't be easy."

"You could...deregister at the DoP," Warrick said, leaving the rest of what that would entail unspoken.

Toreth looked away. "Too fucking late for that, don't you think? I doubt Cit would buy it for a minute."

"Is that what you were thinking about upstairs?"

Toreth's expression closed down completely. "It doesn't matter, does it? Fuck it. We don't need to talk about it anymore. It's all settled, right? Then just make the omelet."

Now he'd pushed Toreth too hard; he'd known as soon as he said it. Warrick nodded. "On its way."

Chapter Twenty-two

❖

Toreth woke up early, but even so Warrick had already left for SimTech. He would've felt better if he'd had the chance to ask Warrick a couple of pointed questions about whether he'd changed his mind again and was planning to do anything fucking stupid. Instead, Toreth went to I&I, hoping that Richardson's interrogation would distract him.

A quick review of the overnight record showed that Richardson was still desperately trying to sell his "I never met Lake that day" crap. About what Toreth had expected from him, after a few days' rest and with a murder charge waiting at the end of it. No point in rushing the interrogation—quick, safe, accurate, pick any two, as the saying went. He'd rather have the right information and Richardson still alive. Hopefully, none of the interrogators would get *too* enthusiastic. The rota for Richardson was already full until Wednesday. Interrogators had started dropping in to see Sara in person yesterday as news spread, trying their largely nonexistent charms on her to bag a session.

He'd arrived early enough that Sara wasn't there, so he checked his own messages. Nothing caught his eye. He opened Mistry's report on the rest of her interview with Rutland, but there was nothing new. And as he tried to concentrate on the case details, he found the previous night's argument with Warrick kept intruding.

Fuck it. Toreth closed the IIP and sat back in his chair.

How was it possible to have a conversation that started out with Carnac, then actually got worse?

Toreth had obviously worried about the wrong person at New Year. He didn't blame himself; Warrick was supposed to be the cautious and (mostly) sane one, Marriot the fucking idiot who thought hanging around with resisters led to anything other than a visit from Political Crimes. Stupidity seemed to be far more infectious than the bacteria that had inconveniently refused to kill Marriot.

It pissed him off that he had to worry at all. Warrick was reliable. He said things, he did them. In the middle of a murder investigation, when he'd known nothing about Toreth at all, he'd volunteered evidence that seemed to incriminate the sim because that was the "intellectually honest" thing to do. Something about family brought out a devious, corporate streak in Warrick that screwed with his judgment. He'd sounded sincere in the kitchen, but he'd sounded sincere at New Year, too.

Warrick should be *grateful* that his fucking mother had vanished. Toreth couldn't think of much better news. But instead he kept picking at the scab. Presumably there was some supposed reason behind it that Warrick thought justified setting sabs loose on Citizen Surveillance. Presumably he didn't think Toreth would understand it.

Carnac would probably have the answers, and *that* pissed him off more than anything. Of course he knew more than Toreth—he was a fucking socioanalyst, so that was a given—but he'd also get more than a shake of the head if he asked Warrick to explain. He'd *understand*. That was the core of Carnac's speech to Toreth last year. *You're not* that *good a fuck and, really, what else do you have?*

Not whatever Carnac had that kept Warrick running back to him for help, obviously.

And with that thought, he couldn't sit down any longer. Nothing in the room he could throw, not without regretting it later or creating enough noise to attract attention from the admins. Toreth paced the room twice, then braced himself against the wall, arms out straight, palms flat, his fingers spread. He pushed against the wall, trying to crush the rage down to manageable proportions with tensed muscles.

If Carnac alone knew the answers, then fuck it. The only way Toreth would ask him for information was to fly out to Strasbourg and strip it out of him with an NI probe and the best drugs the pharmacy could serve up. And, God, he liked that idea. The image of Carnac screaming, spasming against a solid set of portable restraints as Toreth rammed the probe up his arse and fired it over and over, finally cleared some of the burning anger. The smug cunt wouldn't look so fucking superior bleeding out into a pool of his own piss.

Tempting as it was to linger on the image, Carnac was an impossible solution. Pretend he didn't exist. (And never in Toreth's life had he wanted so much for wishes to come true.) Toreth leaned his back on the wall instead and took a deep breath. What else could he do to rescue the situation?

Walk away? He'd been surprised last night by how strong the impulse felt. Just put as much distance between them as he plausibly could and wait either for Warrick to solve his imaginary problem or for Citizen Surveillance to arrange another unfortunate accident. And yet he couldn't, for the reasons he'd given Warrick last night, and for the biggest one, the one he'd never say out loud.

He just *couldn't*. He'd tried once, and failed as spectacularly as he ever failed at anything. Looking back, he struggled to remember exactly how it had felt to send the note telling Warrick he was leaving, but he recalled the consequences with humiliating clarity. Days-long drunks, too much pharma, too much sex that had only made him feel worse—Christ, how was it possible for not seeing Warrick to ruin *fucking*?—and, yes, the pathetic, disgusting neediness that left him wanting to punch something if he thought about it for too long.

Would the same thing happen if Warrick died? The sudden thought disconcerted him. Last year he'd told himself he could never see Warrick again, but that hadn't been literally true. Warrick had been there in New London all along, which at the time had seemed to be half the problem, the ever-present awareness of the *possibility* of Warrick. Without that, would it be better? Or, fuck, somehow even worse? There was no way to tell.

Ask Sara? Would she know? Probably not. He sometimes still caught her getting teary-eyed over people who'd died in the revolt last year, people she'd barely known. Once people were dead, what was the point of remembering them? So her judgment was suspect, and there was no one else.

So that left him with exactly one option—fix the situation with Kate, finally and completely, so Warrick would never feel compelled to fuck with Cit again. Hopefully he could do it before he or Warrick found themselves staring down an "out-of-control" transport tanker. For that he needed information, and for *that*...

Yeah. For that, he'd have to do something stupid, too.

Was Sable still in New London? Toreth considered a range of approaches, from credit and purchase checks on someone else's code to trying to find a contact at Citizen Surveillance to make inquiries, but in the end, he decided that the safest way was probably the most direct.

He called Cit, and made an appointment.

7-4, plain black on brushed steel. The Citizen Surveillance building had numbers, not a name. If you had a reason to go there, you'd know what to look for. Toreth had rarely been inside. His usual interactions with Cit were to find one of their flags on the security file of a suspect, and then back the hell off. Sometimes it was worth a polite inquiry as to whether an arrest could be negotiated. Cit didn't always object to losing the occasional low-level informer who'd outlived their usefulness or decided to abuse their protection to break the law.

As Toreth approached, he saw Sable waiting to meet him outside the front door. Pity. Toreth had been curious to see the man's office, to get a clearer idea of how senior he was—and so how much protection he could ultimately offer.

Sable was holding two insulated disposable cups. He offered one to Toreth. "White, no sugar."

No point asking how a Citizen Surveillance agent knew how you drank your coffee. "Thanks."

Sable started walking, and Toreth fell into step beside him. He found himself glancing at Sable, trying again to see something of Warrick in his face. There was nothing in looks, really—Warrick was all Kate—but something about the way he moved, the way he held his hands, had an echo of Warrick that once again pulled Toreth's mind irresistibly towards imagining how he'd be in bed.

"Rather fresher air than the last time we talked," Sable said, once they'd made a couple of hundred meters from the Cit building.

"I like Gegi's." They had beds to hire, for one thing. "It's very discreet."

"I think it should be safe to chat out here," Sable said. "We have a plausible connection—the arrests last summer. But since you didn't mention a case, I assumed this isn't I&I business."

"Not really, no." The main Cit building at London Int-Sec was at the other end of the complex from I&I. That had given Toreth a bracing walk across the grounds in which to decide what to say. "At Gegi's you asked what I'd do if Warrick kept pushing, and I said I'd ask him nicely to stop."

Sable nodded.

"Well, now he's trying to find out what's happened to Kailynna Avens. I asked him nicely to stop." Extremely nicely, under the circumstances. "And I do think he's stopped for now, but I'm not confident it will stick."

He frowned. "Why now? It's been months."

"That's the thing—I don't know what's wrong, not exactly. He wouldn't say. I know he was having doubts about the paper letters. But something must've happened since New Year." Having gone this far, he should lay it out, so Sable would properly understand the urgency. "He talked to Carnac—the socioanalyst—and he's explored using sabs to get information. He says he isn't going forward with that, but—" Toreth shrugged.

"I see." Sable's expression of alarm left no doubt he was as unhappy as Toreth about that idea. "What do you want from me?"

"Some evidence—something to convince him that she's alive. Or dead. Honestly, I'm not even sure which would work best. But something conclusive."

"Hm." Sable thought for a few seconds, frowning, then said, "Releasing that kind of information could have repercussions. I haven't been entirely transparent with my colleagues about events. Do you think it'd help if I talked to Keir in person, tried to reassure him that the situation is stable?"

What was a tactful way to tell Sable that his son thought he was a liar? "He'll take some convincing. But I don't see how else you can find out what set him off, unless Tarin Marriot knows."

"Short of having Tarin arrested, which I don't think any of us wants, I have no way to get information from him." Sable brightened. "Ah. You mentioned sabs. Do you have a name? A contact? There's a chance information he gave them could be retrieved."

"I don't have anything, sorry."

"I'll check—carefully—in case we caught wind of anything that might be Keir's approach. If not...then I'll have to talk to him." He sounded unenthusiastic. Maybe he guessed Warrick's feelings after all.

"Just for fuck's sake don't tell him it's because of me." No way was Toreth carrying the can if Warrick went ballistic.

"I'm sure I can find a reason why the contact's necessary. And I appreciate you coming to me. Hopefully if I can uncover the source of his concern, I'll be able to reassure him, although there are limits on how much Cit business I can expose to outsiders."

"I don't care what you tell him," Toreth said bluntly. "Lie if you have to—just for Christ's sake make it convincing if you do. Like you said at Gegi's, if everything blows up then we all go down together." Highlighting how much Sable stood to lose too couldn't hurt.

Sable looked at him sharply, but he didn't respond to the reminder. All he said was, "Is that everything?"

"Yeah, I think so."

"Any information I could provide about a current case?" Sable drank from his coffee. "Just in case anyone gets curious about why you wanted this meeting."

Toreth contemplated the clusterfuck of obstructive Central Bank officials and Corporate Fraud interference. Dragging Cit into the middle of the financial side of the case might do more harm than good. "Evan Rupert Lake. He was murdered at the beginning of December, possibly by a sab called Kelvin Richardson. Lake's clean as far as we're concerned, but if any of their contacts are on Cit files, that would be good to know. They were messing with the Central Bank, but I can't pursue that angle at the moment without pissing off my boss. Departmental politics."

Sable nodded. "Send me their ID numbers; I'll see if I can dig anything up. And if I need anything more, or I have any news, I'll be in touch."

Great. "Okay. And thanks."

Toreth stayed where he was, watching as Sable headed back. He took a sip of the coffee—not bad. Much better than the general I&I crap, and at least as good as the coffee he'd taken from Tillotson's office after the revolt. Did that mean Sable had personal access to section head-grade coffee, or just that Cit preferred to keep their staff happy and well caffeinated?

"Where were you?" Sara asked when he returned to his office. "Your comm's off."

"Just something I needed to do," he said, in the tone of voice he knew she'd interpret as "someone."

"Ah, okay. Well, Tushingham sent a message from Fresh Green Fields. He'd like you to go over to see him 'at your earliest convenience' to discuss the inquiries you asked him to make."

She sounded amused.

"Why isn't he talking to Jameson?" Toreth asked.

"He said it had to be you." Sara scanned the message. "And he is polite about it, at least. It sounds to me like he's found something nasty lurking at the reprocessing plant."

Toreth weighed the options. Bad enough when real corporates with the power to back it up treated I&I like their personal security; Toreth objected on principle to being summoned across the city by a corporate nobody like Tushingham. On the other hand, Tillotson had scheduled an all-hands senior para meeting over lunch. Toreth had only skimmed the notification, but he'd spotted the grim trio of "budget overspends," "appraisal returns," and "case closure rates." Doubtless there'd be free food, but only Chevril was enough of a cheapskate to think that I&I canteen sandwiches made up for a Tillotson lecture on efficiency.

"Tell Tushingham I'll be there."

The site of the new processing plant still stood silent, waiting for word from I&I to release the scene. There was no forensic reason to keep it tied up; Toreth had hoped the delay would provide a financial incentive for the corporation to cooperate. On this visit there was no fog, and Toreth could appreciate the true scale of the place. The giant featureless sheds wrecked his sense of perspective, turning distant people into insects crawling past the gray walls. He wondered how much of New London's food the site supplied—and how many bodies might have passed through its gates unnoticed. Hopefully he was about to find out.

Tushingham's office was smaller than Toreth had expected. Scale models of food processing machinery lined up in perfectly aligned and dust-free rows along the shelves filling one wall. Opposite them, behind Tushingham's desk, the Fresh Green Fields logo was screened across the wall. Other than that the room was utilitarian, with a handful of upright chairs for visitors. No corporate luxury here; even the drink maker on a corner table looked simple.

"Your investigator is very persistent," Tushingham said as he offered Toreth a seat.

"That's what I&I pays her for."

"Ah—of course. Coffee? Tea?"

"Coffee, thanks." Might as well start the interview off on a reasonable footing.

As Tushingham made the drinks, Toreth set up his camera and tested the feed. When Tushingham came back he paused with his cup halfway to the desk.

"Is that necessary?"

"We usually like to record interviews in murder cases, yes."

Tushingham looked at him sharply, then put the coffees down without further comment and took his own seat.

"Fresh Green Fields has had a security team looking into the unfortunate incident at the plant, and they delivered their report yesterday. As I'd already spoken to you about the matter, the security committee decided I should be the one to pass on the information."

"Very kind of you," Toreth said. Never mind that the fuckers had been supposed to give full access to Jameson to make her own investigations.

"Sad to say, what happened last December wasn't the first incident of its kind at Fresh Green Fields. Earlier in the year, part of a—" Tushingham gestured at his chest, marking out an area between his breastbone and navel."—was found in the processing machinery at another of our plants, outside Wiesbaden. The machinery jammed for an unrelated reason and the technician carrying out the repair discovered the, ah, contamination."

Toreth checked on his hand screen; Wiesbaden was pleasingly close to Frankfurt. "They found just the one piece?"

Tushingham looked at his desk. "Yes. But I regret to say analysis of the slurry showed that it probably wasn't the only one." He glanced up quickly, then down again. "It might well have been a whole body."

"I hope you junked that run, as well."

Tushingham's head jerked up. "Of course! And immediately afterwards the improved scan system was ordered and fitted to our plants across Europe—discreetly, you understand."

So discreetly that whoever had disposed of Lake obviously hadn't heard about it. "What happened to the body piece that time?"

"Someone at the plant arranged for it to be, ah, found elsewhere and taken to a hospital." Tushingham looked Toreth in the face, obviously deciding simply to brazen this part out. "I think he told them he stumbled across it while out on a forest walk. Over there, sabs often use the forests to dispose of bodies...or so I'm told."

"I'm surprised they didn't burn it at the plant. Doesn't it have an incinerator?"

Tushingham's eyes widened. "That would've been disrespectful. He could've been—well, he could've been anyone, couldn't he?"

"And who was he?"

"I've no idea, I'm afraid. Nor the name of the hospital. But they must have reported everything to the correct authorities, surely?"

"All right. Who took the body part?"

Tushingham beamed. "Ah, now, we thought you might want to know that! So we had the plant management make inquiries and—" His face fell. "Unfortunately, no one could recall their *name*, as such. But it was very probably one of the security team who might have left since, or perhaps one of the temporary staff members. You understand, it happened soon after the trouble last year, and there was a lot of confusion. Normally our staff records are *meticulous*."

Right at that moment, Toreth wondered whether leaving the case to Lehman wouldn't be such a bad thing. "I'm going to need the best records you have for all the staff who worked at Fresh Green Fields last year, and for... let's say two years prior. Not just here or Wiesbaden—anywhere in the corporation."

"Already prepared, Para-investigator." Tushingham smiled happily again. "All the records, for *ten* years."

Jameson had obviously noticed the additional Fresh Green Fields files even before Toreth arrived back at I&I. She was waiting for him in his office.

"Nothing about a matching body part in that area shows up in Central Medical or Justice, Para. But that isn't necessarily a dead end. It's the timing—there was a lot of chaos and lost files. All the hospitals were swamped with live patients, so it's more than possible they lost track of part of a dead one. But I think it'll take time and a lot of calls to be sure."

"Well, you'd better start making them. I'm sure you can find people to talk to over the weekend. And if you do locate it, I want it brought back here for identification. Not sent to I&I Frankfurt." Much too close to the Central Bank.

Jameson hesitated for a moment, then said, "Can I make the calls from home?"

"If you have to."

"I'm looking after Riley on my own this weekend, that's all. But it's okay, she loves hearing about dead bodies. She's at that age." Toreth just stared at her until Jameson said, "Right. Don't worry, Para. If it's out there, or it was out there, I'll find it."

When Toreth arrived home, the flat was empty. A nagging feeling he'd forgotten something persisted until he looked at the flat calendar. Of course, it was the start of Warrick's SimTech trip. He wouldn't be back until next Friday, and then— fuck. There on the same day was marked the SimTech directors' dinner, with a link to the list of ingredients Warrick had already ordered from the complex's shops. That left Toreth not much time at all to plan his end of the bet he'd made with Warrick, and even less time to put it in practice.

He spent most of the evening toying with ideas, and then called Sara; her comm was taking messages only. A quick c&p check showed that Morehen had taken a taxi to her flat, but despite the moment's amusement at the idea of interrupting, Toreth decided against it. Sara would only fulfill his requirements by calling the Shop, anyway, and he could do that himself tomorrow. Fran was always amenable to a rush order, probably because Toreth rarely bargained very hard over prices for equipment for the game—especially true now that there was an account for "flat-related expenses" that Toreth had freedom to dip into at will.

He was thinking about heading up to bed, when his comm chimed. His first thought was that something had happened to Richardson, but to his surprise it was Warrick. He didn't usually call from a conference. Had Sable contacted him already? Surely if he had, Warrick would have more sense than talk about it over what was marked as an ordinarily secure connection.

He answered with vision, and Warrick appeared on his hand screen. He looked calm enough, but then that wasn't much of an indication with Warrick. Over Warrick's shoulder Toreth could see the corner of a bed, so he must be in his room rather than a public space.

"Everything going okay?" Toreth asked.

"Yes," Warrick said. "It's been a long day, but a productive one. The New Year seems to have brought a certain level of financial optimism with it, if the number of people here is any indication."

He sounded absolutely normal, too. Toreth relaxed, at least partly. "Maybe they just wanted some better weather on expenses."

Warrick smiled. "Let's hope not."

There was a pause. "Did you want something?" Toreth asked.

"Oh, no. Not particularly. Just . . . " Warrick shrugged. "If you're busy, I can go."

"Not really. But you don't usually call from conferences, so I wondered if you'd—" What was something domestic that Warrick couldn't tell the flat system to do for him? "—forgotten to put something in the freezer?"

"No, nothing like that." Warrick half smiled. "I suppose that generally I don't wish to interrupt if you're . . . otherwise occupied."

Meaning that he didn't want to know what Toreth was doing or who he was doing it to. "Even I can't be out on the pull every night."

Warrick's left eyebrow twitched but all he said was, "I'll take your word for it. Anyway, as I said, there's no special reason."

He sounded positive enough about it that Toreth finally ruled out some complication with Kate or Sable. Maybe Warrick wanted to check if Toreth had been sufficiently pissed off by the whole mess that he'd decided to move out after all.

"Perhaps I just missed you," Warrick added lightly.

Right, sure. But instead of laughing, Toreth said, "Well, yeah, of course you did."

The easy agreement seemed to catch Warrick by surprise. He paused, then said, "I'm sorry?"

"It's Friday, right? What Sara calls 'kinky sex night.'"

Warrick laughed. "Yes, that must be it."

"Well, if you don't want to miss getting chained up you should arrange your conferences better." Toreth lay down on the sofa and stretched out. "Want to see what we can do over the comm?"

The image tilted as Warrick stood up. "That sounds like an excellent idea."

Chapter Twenty-three

❖

Saturday and Sunday Toreth split between checking in on case progress at I&I and enjoying his weekend with the novelty of not having to think about Warrick. At least, of not having to wonder whether he'd need to come up with a tactful lie for Warrick about what he'd been doing all night. Toreth still found time to spare a thought for Warrick in Valencia and to wonder if a casual browse of the conference attendance list would be too pathetic. But with the highly respectable Asher Linton there to keep an eye on Warrick, he didn't have to waste too much bar or bed time on suspicion. Right now Warrick away from home was a good thing, if it kept him too busy to think about going back on his word again and contacting sabs.

On Sunday Toreth started the evening off in Gegi's Bar. As he bought his first drink he found himself leaning on the bar next to a guy who, at least from a quarter profile, might've been part of Warrick's annoying family. At first that dropped him down in Toreth's mental scoring system, since he could fuck all the Warrick he wanted at home, plus it had sour overtones of last year's desperate bar crawling. Then three places further along, the barman handed another customer a glass of sparkling wine with some kind of red fruit liquor pooled at the bottom of it. Toreth blinked at the glimpse he caught of her face, then leaned forward slightly to get a better view. From the immaculately painted fingernails that tapped on the glass as she took it to the cut of her hair, she was eerily like Sara.

Sara and Warrick. Together. That really was a fantasy come to life. He watched the woman walk away, relieved when she sat on a stool alone. No competition yet, then. Then the man next to him glanced around, and Toreth caught his eye. He was surprised to find himself holding his breath with anticipation, hoping for any sign of interest, relieved when he saw it.

It had been a while since he'd wanted someone enough to be willing to work for it. The guy was the more reluctant of the two—which at least doubled his appeal—but an hour or two of flirting and conversation wasn't too big a price to pay.

Not for the chance to half close his eyes and fuck faux-Sara while watching her sucking off the guy who looked even more like Warrick in the dim light. Toreth kissed her afterwards, oddly disappointed that she didn't taste like Warrick. At least she sounded a little like Sara when she came.

The pair of them seemed to be getting along well when he left them in one of the upstairs rooms at Gegi's. Toreth almost wished he'd got their comm numbers, or just made a note of their names, to give himself the option of a repeat experience. Because sadly neither Warrick or Sara would go for it in reality. It would take more than red wine or fuck drugs for Toreth to get away with that scenario with his skin intact. Not a bad evening's entertainment at all, though, and Warrick's absence meant he hadn't even needed to come up for an explanation for why he was still smiling when he got back to the flat.

And the woman had paid for the room. He could always make a credit and purchase check on her if he cared enough.

Monday morning's team meeting centered about Richardson, who was proving to be the same pain in the arse as he'd been throughout the case.

"He's a tough bastard," Nagra admitted. "Georgiou finally got a new story from him last night, though. This time he says Lake wasn't his real employer. Someone contacted him out of the blue and offered him the job. The deal was he manufactured a meeting with Lake and wangled himself involvement in Lake's investigation, then reported back on Lake's progress. So he wasn't lying about it being good money—he was paid by Lake and by this unknown contact."

"And his real employer?"

"Still swears he doesn't know any names, which does make sense if they actually understood how to do sabbing properly."

"A firewall." Toreth nodded. "Did he kill Lake?"

"He maintains not, Para, and he's convinced the neural scan, if not necessarily me. He says that after Lake switched focus to comms tracing, his contact asked him to supply a secure location where they could meet Lake and talk to him direct. He offered them the storage unit because the rent was expiring soon and he'd already picked up the specified equipment he'd stored there and cleaned the place down. It was only later he missed the bits and pieces Justice found and realized he'd left them inside a case. That's why he went back."

"Not to make sure they'd tidied up their crime scene?"

"He says not. He *claims* he got to the door, and then just changed his mind. If there was a body in there, and if someone was watching the unit, he couldn't explain away not reporting it. He decided he'd rather bet on having kept the equipment clean enough that we couldn't trace him—which he had, so he was right as far as that went." Nagra shrugged. "In my opinion he might have more to give us, although the basic story does seem sound."

She didn't need to add that he convinced them before. "Have you got something to show me?"

"Sure." Nagra skimmed through the interrogation recording, then put it up on the wall screen. "I dropped in for an hour or two this morning. This is fairly representative, and it matches with what Georgiou said he was getting last night, too."

Richardson looked as bad as could be expected for a man who'd spent the last few days with interrogators working out their frustrations with the neutered P&P. His right wrist was bruised and swollen—fractured during restraint, according to the log. Nagra was taking full advantage of the brain's difference in pain perception between neutral induction and a broken bone. She applied pressure every time he halted in his exhausted, stumbling delivery.

"They contacted me out of the blue. I never knew names. I never—I—*fuck*. I never knew names. They paid everything into my account—the number—I don't remember—I gave you the number."

Nagra paused the recording. "Then he talks about contacting Lake in a bar, after being given his description. I'll be double-checking the transcripts to make sure no one got careless and dropped any hints about what Rutland told us."

"All right. Are you going back down after the meeting?"

"Yes, Para."

"Good. Keep him going until he won't remember what he told us, which shouldn't take long, then freshen him up and start again." Toreth looked around the room. "Where's Jameson?"

"She left a message," B-C said. "She found the hospital that took the missing body part. They never ran a DNA ID or even entered it into the system, but a technician remembered it arriving and called her this morning. Apparently someone tossed it into one of the freezers in the morgue and it's been sitting there happily ever since. Jameson went over to fetch it in person."

"Did she mention anyone called Riley?" Toreth asked.

B-C looked at him blankly. "I'm afraid not, Para. Who—"

"Never mind." Hopefully she wouldn't try to put two flights through on expenses, at least not without a reasonable cover story. "Sara, you can tell her I want the forensic report as soon as it's ready."

One of the more notable and annoying consequences of Warrick's absence was how quickly the flat ran out of food. No evening meals meant no leftovers for lunch the next day; while Warrick was no doubt enjoying SimTech expenses in Valencia, Toreth had been forced back to the I&I canteen. The most impressive thing about the place, he decided as he unwrapped a packet of anemic ham and cheese sandwiches, was how it managed to get slightly but consistently worse every year.

The first bite made him wonder if he had time to leave the Int-Sec grounds and find something at least marginally edible. He was still trying to summon enthusiasm for a second bite when a vibrantly warm voice right behind him said, "Hello, there, Poacher."

"Hey, Liz," he said. "Poacher?"

"Of cases." She leaned with both hands on the back of the next chair at the table. "It's almost your nickname over at Corporate Fraud now, in a completely unaffectionate way."

"They need to talk to the Central Bank about poaching."

"Oh, Vaughn does." Before he could ask what she meant, Carey added, "Are you done with Phil on the financial side? If you are, I could definitely find a use for him." She smirked. "On casework, too."

"You're welcome to him, since I don't *have* a financial fucking side to my case anymore." Fake cheese and even faker mayonnaise squished between his fingers, and Toreth realized he'd almost squeezed a hole through the sandwich. He dropped it on the plate and licked his fingers. "But I assume you knew that."

"You assume right. Like I said, Vaughn has friends at the Central Bank."

Starting with Director Lehman. "Good for her."

"You won't catch me complaining if my section head has a long contact list." Carey lowered her voice to a distracting husky purr. "Toreth, I'm not going to say you should drop this, because a, there's no reason you should listen to me, and b, if I were in your place I sure as hell wouldn't. But you know how twitchy people are right now about section results. If you close this first, at least throw some credit our way."

She sounded deadly earnest, although Toreth couldn't imagine Carey really thinking there was a chance he'd "forget" to mention Verstraeten. He valued her CF influence far too much for that. "Liz, you know I will."

"I just thought it was worth a reminder. It isn't all for my benefit. I promise you, you don't want to be on Vaughn's shit list. And *I* don't want to be on there because we've shared some cases before and you've pissed her off." Carey straightened up, her voice returning to normal. "Thanks, Toreth. I'll tell Chean I'm expecting Phil back at CF today."

Once Carey had gone, Toreth picked up the sad-looking sandwich and took a bite, and smiled. Not at the flavor, though. Vaughn might be trying to fuck with his investigation, but with Verstraeten off the case his access to the Investigation in Progress files could be canceled without comeback. From now on Vaughn would have to poach blind.

When his office door opened Toreth half expected it to be Jameson, possibly clutching a body part in a bag. Instead it was Nagra, all but clutching a security officer. When he hesitated in the doorway, she shoved his shoulder, urging him into the room and over to Toreth's desk.

"Para, this is Senior Security Officer Hamed." Nagra turned to him. "Now, you can explain it to my senior. You tell him why I'll be spending my time running level twos for Senior Para Chevril's corporate-grade housing burglaries."

The guard held up his hand to her placatingly. "I'm afraid we had an accident with your prisoner, Para."

Toreth stood up, his chair bumping the back of his legs as it rocked, then stabilized. "What?"

The man took a small step backwards, but his voice didn't waver. "He had a bad dosing marked on his file. Luckily the guards were on the ball and realized what had happened as soon as he started reacting, so they got him up to the medical unit in time. According to his Central Medical file the drugs would've had a very good chance of killing him."

"Who the fuck marked his file?" Toreth demanded.

"Not me," Nagra said.

Hamed shot her an annoyed glance. "A detention-level security officer, I'm afraid, Para. Clayton?"

Toreth shook his head.

"Anyway, he claims it was a mistake—he's new since the trouble and he's never used that class of drugs before. He says he mixed up your prisoner's file with someone else's." Hamed didn't sound convinced "There was another prisoner due to be given that dosing. Clayton's been suspended, of course, while we investigate."

By his neck, if Toreth had anything to do with it. "Any signs someone paid him?"

Hamed sighed. "Unfortunately, yes, Para. According to some of the other guards, he's been having financial problems. It should've been reported, of course, but what can you do? One of the people he borrowed from is another guard, and she came forward as soon as she heard about the dosing error. She said he promised her that he'd pay back all her money by the end of the month."

"So he's an idiot, as well."

"It looks quite possible, Para. What do you want me to do?"

Security officers weren't in Toreth's team, or even section, so he wouldn't be carrying the can. "Tell Head of Security Bevan everything, if he doesn't already know." Given that a fly couldn't fart in I&I without Bevan hearing about it, Toreth doubted this had passed him by. "Then keep looking for a payment. If you find anything definite, give Clayton to me and I'll get the names. Bevan can decide what to do with him afterwards. You can tell him I said he should call Internal Investigations."

Hamed looked less than thrilled at the idea of delivering that message, but he nodded. "Right, Para."

"When will Richardson be fit to interrogate?"

"Not for a few days, at least," Hamed said. "I'm afraid the turlmazine did a number on his liver and kidneys before they flushed him. The medic in charge says the regen drugs might bring his liver back online, but he'll probably need new kidneys. Either way, he should recover completely."

The hopeful note in his voice didn't fool Toreth. Transplants were effective, but from the point of view of an investigation, far too time-consuming.

"Well, we'll just have to see. Go on, then. And don't forget I want to hear as soon as you know anything more about Clayton."

"Absolutely, Para. And I'm sorry about this."

Not as sorry as he would be if the poisoning turned out to be deliberate.

"All right," Toreth said to Nagra, when Hamed had made a rapid escape, "where are we with Richardson?"

"Where we were this morning. I didn't get anything fresh, and then he stopped making sense so I put him in the cells like you said. I'll review all the transcripts and see if I can wring any more details out of it."

"Ask Sara to help you."

Nagra paused in the doorway. "Shall I tell the medics to order the new kidneys?"

An expense that for some reason always reliably annoyed Tillotson. "Yes, go ahead. I'm sure Secretary Turnbull will appreciate it if we don't kill too many prisoners on the Council's waiver."

Further disappointment came in the afternoon. Toreth was drinking coffee and listening with a tenth of his attention to Chevril moaning about his burglary case—the usual bullshit story about some corporate flexing his influential muscles and getting a Justice-level case moved to I&I—when Jameson came into the coffee room.

"Para? I thought you'd want the ID as soon as I confirmed it."

Jameson came up to them and then glanced uncertainly at Chervil. She stood waiting until Toreth said, "Yes? Well?"

"Sorry, Para." Jameson cleared her throat. "The partial torso belongs to a Service officer, a Captain Paul Martin. He disappeared in Frankfurt last year during the revolt. Nothing suspicious except that he suddenly wasn't there. The Service and Justice both looked into it, and the official decision on his security file is presumed killed by resisters or looters, body not found."

"Not found until now. Any connection with the case?"

"Except for Frankfurt, no. No close friends or family members work at a finance corporation or the Central Bank. No suspicious money movements in any accounts, before or after he disappeared. I'm trying to contact his commanding officer to see if anything about his disappearance didn't make it into his file. But Martin had a good Service record, with early promotions. If he's connected, it's deep."

Toreth hated to see a promising lead shriveling before his eyes. "Was it definitely the right body part?"

"Yes, Para. Well, as far as we can tell given we have no original scene. I asked Forensics Specialist O'Reilly to take a look while they were checking the DNA, and she confirmed crushing marks that matched Lake's leg and comparable organic contamination."

"But it still might be a completely unrelated body dump, not even by the same people. Did every sab in the Administration know about Fresh Green Fields's bloody awful security?"

Jameson shrugged. "I'm still working on the personnel data, Para. A name might come up in common if I can find the right parameters."

"Well, good work finding the thing, anyway. Sara will make sure the expenses go through okay, so check with her before you send anything."

"Will do. Thank you, Para."

"What's all that about?" Chevril said when Jameson had gone. "Sara told me you were working on a finance case."

"I am. Same old shit as before New Year. Some finance sector sabs have been throwing their leftovers into food processing plants, that's all."

"Food processing—" Chevril looked at the untouched sausage roll waiting on a plate on the low coffee table in front of him. "Food for *people*?"

"For *and* from, yeah."

"Christ All-bloody-mighty." Now Chevril was distinctly pale. "People used to joke about what happened to annexed prisoners, but—hellfire. How long has this been going on?"

"Months, at least. Years, most likely. Did you buy something special for New Year? Apparently, Fresh Green Fields is a big seller in celebratory joints." He hoped Tushingham would appreciate the free promotion.

"We went to my sister's for New Year dinner. We had a bloody great piece of lamb, which she knows full well I don't like. Gives me indigestion." Chervil picked up the paper plate, folded it around the sausage roll, and went across the room to drop them both into the recycling—possibly to begin their journey back into the filling of another sausage roll.

Toreth laughed. "Chev, don't worry about it. Fresh Green Fields put in new security months ago, so the sabs will have to dump bodies in the marshes like everyone else."

223

"Now you tell me." Chevril briefly touched the door of the recycling unit, like he was half thinking about checking if the sausage roll had caught inside. "I paid for that, you bastard."

"I'll buy you another one." Toreth paused. "Of course, I'm not guaranteeing the new security. Sabs are like rats—if there's any way to get in, the filthy little fuckers will find it."

Chevril grimaced. "Forget it. I lost my appetite. I'll send Kel down later for a packet of crisps."

Almost making Chevril throw up in the coffee room was the best result of the day. Going home to an empty flat seemed depressing; going out to pick someone up sounded like too much effort. The way his luck had gone so far today, he thought, the whole of New London would have decided on celibacy. That left a night of boredom, unless...

"Plans tonight?" he asked Sara.

"Nothing special. Why?"

"I thought I'd treat you to dinner." Then they could get drunk, and he could find out what Andy Morehen was like in bed.

She smiled. "Busy weekend?"

"What?"

"I mean, you're all fucked out, with Warrick away?" She gave him a commiserating look of faux sympathy. "Slowing down in *your* old age, too? I suppose it's only to be—"

"Shut the fuck up, or it'll be takeaway curry, not The Golden Squid."

Her eyes widened. "That Cambodian-French place in the complex by your flat?"

"That's the one. What were you saying about my age?"

Sara sat up very straight, hands folded primly on the desk. "Nothing at all, Para."

Sara stretched out lazily, with her calves resting across Toreth's thighs.

"Mm. I love Warrick's sofas."

"Yeah." Toreth patted the softly padded sofa back, over which he'd fucked Warrick more than once. "Better than my crappy old thing."

"Of course these are your sofas too, now."

"Not really. He bought them. I just picked the color."

He hadn't meant it as a joke, but Sara giggled.

"What?" Toreth asked. "What?"

"Nothing. Really, no. Nothing." She put her hand over her mouth, and when she took it away she looked almost serious. Sometimes, he thought, she was very strange. "Here, top me up."

She offered her glass and Toreth tipped in the last of the wine. It filled the glass rather dangerously high, and Sara drank some before she settled back again. She balanced the glass where it had been before, on her breastbone, her fingers flat across the base, and looked up at Toreth past the stem.

"Toreth, I was thinking about Richardson."

"I wouldn't guess he was your type."

"Mmm." Sara smiled. "Dark, good-looking. Nice cheekbones. Knows how to break into other people's systems. I suppose he's more *your* type, isn't he?"

Toreth considered. "Yeah, I'd fuck him. Not while he's wired up on level C, mind."

Sara laughed. "*Anyway,* Gene Tams left me a message—that's HoS Bevan's new admin, used to work for someone up in Forensics, I think. Really tall? I'm not sure how long he'll last down in security. You know how loud the HoS is, and . . . what was I talking about?"

"Richardson?" Toreth prompted.

"Right! Yes. I asked Tams if he'd make sure we were copied on any messages about Clayton's investigation, and I started thinking about why someone would try to kill Richardson here." She waved her hand around. "Not here, here. Here, I&I, I mean. 'S a big risk, isn't it? Finding a guard, and paying him, and . . . all that stuff."

"I suppose they must think Richardson has some information about them."

"He doesn't know their names, though."

Toreth poked the sole of her foot. "And when did you qualify as an interrogator?"

Sara shrugged, wine slopping in her glass. "Whoops, hang on." She craned her neck forward and took a precautionary sip, then leaned back again. "I've probably seen more interrogation transcripts than *you*, you know. That's what everyone was pushing him for—names, contact numbers. *I* don't think he has it."

On balance Toreth tended to agree, disappointing though it was. "Whoever tried to top him might still think he does. Or think . . ."

Toreth trailed off, wishing they hadn't taken advantage of Warrick's excellent wine stock. He was still working through the possibilities when Sara nudged his thigh with her heel. "Yes? Or think what?"

"That Richardson could work out who they are and tell us. Okay. How did they find him?"

Sara struggled upright and sat sideways on the sofa with her legs crossed. "Well, he's a sab. The usual ways clients find sabs, I s'pose. Word of mouth. Agents." She snorted. "Corporate security departments."

The reminder of Warrick's stupid stunt gave Toreth an uneasy moment before he directed his mind back to Richardson.

"Messing with Central Bank systems is ballsy stuff, though, and he claims he's done nothing for years except fringe work. I think it's more likely to be someone who knew him before, knew he'd be up to the job. Maybe someone whose name he *does* know."

"But..." Sara's forehead wrinkled. "He hasn't realized who it is?"

Toreth held up his forefinger. "Not yet. But he might, and so that's why they want him dead."

"Sounds good." Sara nodded and gulped her wine. "So... who?"

"Ex-client? Although it'd need to be an ex-client who didn't use an agent then, and who's connectable to the case now—someone in finance, at a corporation, at the bank. Or an agent—that's more likely. I wonder if he's got any old files?" Sabs tended not to record too many names, though. "We could run him through visual IDs on known agents. Problem is, there's no way of knowing if any agent he recognizes is connected to this case. He could've met dozens."

"And so why would they need to take the risk of killing him at I&I?"

"Exactly. And why meet him before but be so paranoid now? Contacting sabs is what agents do." So who else knew sabs? Well, the obvious answer was—"Another sab, maybe? Subcontracting the risky part. Do you remember Richardson said his old crew broke up not long after he started his relationship with his ex-wife?"

"Yes! And you're thinking those two things might be related?"

"I've known it to happen before."

Sara giggled. "Yeah. Sleeping with your boss's wife can be risky. Careerwise."

"Oh, fuck off," Toreth said without heat. "Seriously, though, I like this. Where's my screen?"

Toreth finally found the hand screen in the pocket of the jacket he'd abandoned in the kitchen. He brought it back to the living room, along with another bottle of wine. Sara crowded up beside him on the sofa, looking over his shoulder.

"Richardson... there we are. Wife's full name was Katja Winkelmann, now living near her parents in Düsseldorf. Sounds promising. And she—fuck. No registered partner immediately before Richardson."

Sara waved her glass dismissively. "Doesn't mean anything. I never registered with some of mine, not even all of the ones I was a bit engaged to."

"We can ask Richardson. If he doesn't know they hired him he won't have any reason to lie about it."

"Now?" Sara asked, sounded surprisingly eager.

"No, in the morning. I'm not turning up pissed at midnight and interrogating anyone." Toreth opened the new bottle. "Let's celebrate in advance, anyway."

Warrick's impulse to extend an invitation to Marley Thomas had paid even greater dividends than he'd hoped. Whether her clearly extensive number of contacts had come to visit the SimTech display out of interest in the sim, or in hope of gossip about her departure from UnLTD Ent, she'd fed them neatly into the hands of the more knowledgeable sim sales techs. They'd run all the evening demonstration sessions far later than planned.

Now the sim displays were being packed away by technicians, some to go home, some to travel through the night to the next scheduled demonstration. Asher had excused herself, claiming the convention combined with Project Linton had worn her out, so Warrick ate a very late dinner with Thomas.

Their hotel was part of the convention center, itself part of the much larger Turia Garden complex that curved through the heart of Valencia like a river. Outside the night was probably cool—Warrick hadn't left the complex since they'd arrived on Friday—but under the high, curving semidome of temperature-controlled thermal glass, they could've been sitting outside on a summer Mediterranean night.

Thomas's enthusiasm for the sim had only grown over the past few days. Warrick had wanted someone who had ideas for Yes markets, and he couldn't complain about the outcome. They'd finished a Creme Catalonia each and moved on to coffee and discussion of various of the Yes concepts.

"Maybe it's because I've always been sensitive to it," Thomas said. "My parents named me Marlene, but nobody, not even them, called me that. Eventually I changed my name legally, because I hated putting my given name on forms. And that's what I was saying—names are absolutely critical for customers. Otherwise identical virtual performers with different names will give you totally different fan responses." Thomas leaned forward. "Now, I bet you're thinking, 'we need to know the most popular names.'"

Warrick smiled. Actually, he'd been thinking about how much he loved watching someone else embracing the sim dream. "Something like that, yes."

"Right. But broadly appealing names are like the biometric-averaged virtual actors that were in fashion for a while. Everyone likes them, in a vague way, but no one remembers them. They can produce steady sales, but they don't build true brand loyalty—and please excuse the marketing, I can't help it anymore."

"It happens to all of us in the end," Warrick said. "Sadly, ideas and enthusiasm aren't enough. Someone needs to buy the product."

"People will," Thomas said with confidence. "Yeses and the sim are a whole new world. I mean, forget names. You can tailor shells to individual customers, down to smell, skin texture." Her arms were bare from the shoulders down, and she rubbed the toned curve of her left biceps. "Muscle feel. Adapting shells on the fly from direct customer responses. You'll be able to bring someone's dream to life for them—you could call it the Pygmalion System." She shook her head. "I can almost see where some of Dr. De Nijs's concerns come from. There has to be an addiction risk."

"As there is with a large number of other perfectly legal products," Warrick pointed out. "The sim had been assessed and rated, and future applications will be assessed, too."

"Obsessed customers were something I used to help deal with, though. Fantasy fixation, to the point where people let their real lives go. Rare, but—have you read the reports from your old psychologist about increased dissociative indicators?"

"Of course." De Nijs had obviously been as thorough as Warrick had asked him to be. "It's something we're monitoring closely in the Yes program."

"Yes, De Nijs showed me some of the work he's been doing." After a few seconds, she shrugged dismissively. "Tailoring shells through live feedback is an *incredibly* cool idea, though, isn't it? You could honestly say you were selling perfection—subjective perfection. And that's the only kind that matters when you're selling sex."

"Apart from technical perfection," Warrick said.

"True. Of course." Thomas paused to finish her coffee. "Speaking of subjective perfection, I was thinking about your sim issue. I have a few a questions, if you have time to—oh. Is it okay to talk about it here?"

Warrick looked around. The complex proudly listed its surveillance monitoring and countersystems, so the glass wall made long-range surveillance only a remote possibility. Tables nearby were occupied, though, and while his personal tastes were hardly proprietary information, some discussions he'd prefer to keep out of the public domain. "We could go to the demo suite."

The suite currently still resembled an emergency evacuation scene. The couches had been packed away into a line of shipping containers, and the techs had moved on to dismantling the fast scanners used to create the basic demonstration sim bodies. Warrick's reappearance caused a brief pause, everyone stopping midtask to see if the plan had changed, until he signaled for them to get back to work. He and Thomas found a couple of low, padded seats against one wall—part of the facilities provided by the center, and so not liable to be packed away from underneath them—and sat down.

"I shouldn't think I've managed to make any breakthroughs in a few weeks," Thomas said. "But I did have some obvious ideas that must have equally obvious reasons why they're no use as a solution."

"I don't mind answering obvious questions." Warrick paused, then added for the sake of honesty, "As long as it's for the first time, anyway."

She smiled. "So, the most obvious way to make the sim feel real would be for it to stop users from remembering they're inside the sim at all. Would that be considered illegal neural manipulation, or are there other reasons?"

"Yes." Reasons like interrogation. Since the reform of I&I, Warrick had half expected the Administration to renew its attempts to access sim technology for that purpose, but to his knowledge they hadn't. Had it been dropped, or was there right now a part of Int-Sec working on their own version of the sim? The Psychoprogramming Division had been most intensely interested, and everything he'd heard had suggested they'd suffered badly in the revolt.

Warrick realized Thomas was watching him, no doubt waiting for him to expand on his answer. As useful as she might be to SimTech, he certainly didn't know her well enough to reveal his (probably doomed, as Carnac had once told him) rearguard fight to prevent the Administration from perverting the sim.

"We never pursued the question of legality. Having had to jump through some interestingly shaped hoops for various regulators, we've always been conscious of the potential for the sim to be abused by sabs or in other criminal ways. Especially with the Yeses. Setting up an entire sim scenario to trick someone into revealing corporate secrets would be expensive and elaborate, but if the potential payoff were large enough...." He shrugged.

"I see." Thomas frowned. "What about drugs, though? I've never been rated a high-risk sab target, but everyone learns about amnesiac pharma in countersabotage training—self-awareness and signs to watch out for. Couldn't sabs just drug someone into forgetting they got into the sim? What would happen if a user was unconscious when they were put into the sim?"

Warrick nodded. "We can't guard against everything. But in that case the sim already establishes consciousness before initializing, and it also performs periodic memory integration checks. A failure triggers automatic ending of the session. Primarily it's an extra safety layer to ensure that experiences like sense-memory stacking are processing normally, but as a secondary benefit that does pick up pharma-induced amnesia."

"But couldn't that be disabled on a voluntary basis by experienced users? If someone consented—wanted to forget the sim wasn't real—why not?"

"In theory, I suppose we could make an argument for that. In practice, putting the code in place to allow that opens it up to abuse. In recent years, after an unfortunate incident of sabbing at SimTech—" Possibly the greatest understatement of his corporate career."—we even heavily restricted what can be done with test systems. We have to prioritize thwarting potential sab uses. If corporate security divisions classified the sim as unsafe, it could devastate sales."

As he'd guessed, Thomas was too experienced a corporate to pursue an "unfortunate incident" without an indication that inquiries would be welcome. "Right, I can see that. That's something else I don't know much about. The security implications of porn are pretty low." Thomas suddenly yawned, then looked at her watch. "Oh. Is it really so late? I need some sleep, and I'm sure you do, too." She stood up. "Good night, Warrick. I'll see you at breakfast—early."

She sounded a little dismayed at the idea, and Warrick laughed. "Too early, yes. Good night."

Warrick chatted with a few of the technicians still hard at work, and then set off towards his hotel room. As he walked through the quiet corridors, Warrick thought about Toreth, back in the flat, and wondered if—rather unlikely as it sounded—Toreth was missing him. Probably he was too wrapped up in his case to even notice Warrick wasn't there.

Chapter Twenty-four

❖

Someone moved in the bed, and Toreth murmured, "Warrick?" The movement stopped abruptly, and Toreth opened his eyes. For a brief moment he registered he felt like death not very effectively warmed up, and then he realized he was looking into Sara's dismayed face.

"Oh, *shit*," she said. "Shit, shit. Fuck, fuck, *fuck*."

"Jesus Christ. Not so loud." Toreth rubbed his aching forehead. "Ow. How much wine did we drink?"

"Far too much." Sara buried her face in the pillow, but he could still hear her muffled words. "I remember you opening that bottle of red after—we were talking about Richardson, weren't we? About who hired him? And then I don't remember a lot after that. I don't even remember if..." She looked up at him, makeup smeared everywhere, including the pillow. "Toreth?"

The response came automatically, a reflexive probing for information in her reaction. "It's all a blur."

"Oh, God." Dismay, shading into horror. And guilt? "Sometimes I'm so *stupid*."

Fuck. Why hadn't he just said no, they hadn't? The hangover must be slowing him down. "Sara—"

Before he could say anything more, Sara jumped out of bed, and Toreth noted she was still wearing her shirt, unbuttoned and very wrinkled, and her bra and knickers. She scooped up the rest of her clothes from the floor and dashed into the en suite bathroom. The door lock clicked.

Toreth himself was still wearing his trousers—unbuttoned—briefs, and one sock. That was another measure of how much he'd drunk, because normally that would've been too warm to sleep in. Maybe the house system had turned down the room temperature. Toreth rolled over very carefully onto his back, then laid his arm over his eyes and listened to the shower running as he organized his memories.

The wine gave everything a pleasant, jumbled fuzziness. Sara bouncing on the bed, laughing as she pulled on the bedposts and exclaimed, "No squeaks!"

He'd been sitting on his pillow, leaning against the headboard, and he remembered grabbing her, pulling her over towards him, and telling her to stop shaking him around before he ruined Warrick's New Year sheets. Her face, flushed from the wine and the bouncing, as they slid down together. Laughing in disbelief as he looked down and saw Sara's hands on the waistband of his briefs, and then her fingers on his cock. Leaning over Sara, not holding her down, just enjoying his strength against her slender body while he kissed her. The feeling of silk knickers against his fingers, heel of his palm rubbing against her, while Sara wriggled and panted and dug her nails into his shoulder.

He carefully felt the skin there, but if there'd been any marks they'd faded now. That helped the plausible deniability. A pity they'd been too drunk to do anything more—although then, it probably wouldn't have happened at all. Anyway, it didn't matter. They'd already acknowledged their long-ago one-night stand, and Sara hadn't carried through on her threat to resign. What difference did another semi-fuck make?

Logically that might make perfect sense, but he knew Sara. The shower was still running, and Toreth sighed. This felt like the start of a long day.

Warrick's drug supplies were in the bathroom cabinet, and so temporarily out of reach. By lying very still and taking occasional sips from the glass of water one of them had had the presence of mind to leave by the bed, Toreth kept his hangover under control until Sara appeared again, fully dressed.

She sat dejectedly on the edge of the bed. "You know, I must've told Andy half a dozen times that nothing ever happened between us."

"Well, that was crap to start with," Toreth said.

She must have been feeling bad, because she didn't even glare. "Okay, maybe it wasn't *technically* true. But, you know, I've always *meant* it to be true. And that was ten years ago! Getting older is supposed to make you more sensible. Why did I even come in here in the first place?"

"I don't know." Another memory stirred, both of them standing on the landing outside the bedroom door. "No, wait, I do. You asked to see the bed." He patted the headboard. "The one I bought for Warrick for—"

"I know whose bed it is!" Her voice cracked.

Whoops. "Calm down, nothing happened."

She paused, then looked at him closely. "Really? You're not just saying that?"

"Of course not. You were testing the mattress, and obviously it passed because we fell asleep. Look, we were still half dressed when we woke up. Would you have your knickers on if we'd fucked?" Hopefully she wouldn't be doing any DNA tests on them.

"No," she said slowly. "No, I suppose not."

"There you are, then. There's no reason to start carrying on. We've slept at each other's flats dozens of times. Fuck, you slept between me and Warrick at his old flat, right?"

He thought he'd cracked it, but after a moment, suspicion clouded her face. "Why didn't you tell me that as soon as we woke up?"

"Because I feel like someone smashed a case of wine inside my skull. Look, I'd better have a shower, too. You go make some coffee, I'll find some of Warrick's magic tablets. We won't even be all that late for work."

"Oh, God," she said again, and put her hands over her face. "Work."

"Trust me, the tablets are good." He tapped her hip with his foot from under the duvet. "And we have some sabs to catch."

In the end, Toreth was only a few minutes later than usual. Sara had needed to detour to her flat to pick up her I&I uniform, so Toreth checked his messages himself, to make sure Tillotson hadn't sneaked in an early meeting, then went down to the medical unit.

Richardson was sleeping. Apart from the faint yellowish tinge to his skin suggesting the regen drugs were still working on his liver, he looked a lot better than when Toreth had last seen him on the screen. Someone had even put a cast on his broken wrist—not protocol under an old level seven, without a request from the interrogator, but presumably no one had remembered to tell the medical unit about the special exemption waiver.

Well, bones could always be rebroken.

"Wake up." Toreth grabbed Richardson's chin. "Wake up, you sabbing piece of shit."

Richardson's eyes flew open and he stared at Toreth, obviously disoriented. Toreth waited until he saw recognition dawn, then released Richardson and leaned on the bars at the side of the bed.

"Good morning, Mr. Richardson," he said cheerfully. "How do you feel?"

"Like crap."

"The medics think you should make a full recovery. We'll have you back in an interrogation room in no time."

Richardson closed his eyes for a moment, then said, "Great, thanks. I'm looking forward to it."

Surprising how fast the bastards could get their composure back, sometimes. "Of course, that's assuming I tell them to continue treatment."

Now Richardson stared, face blank, then he said, "What?"

"If you'd rather not spend any more time with Nagra. Or if I decide I don't want to waste the budget. It might save me another memo from my boss. New organs are expensive. Bit of a waste if the Justice system decides to execute you, don't you think?" Toreth straightened up and stripped back the sheets. He tapped the artificial renal pack belted around Richardson's waist. "And if we don't pay for new kidneys, then there isn't much point in this, is there? Don't worry, you'll probably still have a week or two to think if there's anything you haven't told us."

"But—" Richardson looked helplessly around the room. "I already told you about watching Lake, about the bank. I told you . . ." He wet his lips. "Please. You can't."

"Really? Want me to read you the waiver again? Withholding treatment's inside a level seven. Technically we're not supposed to let it kill you, but Internal understands it's an imprecise technique. Tell me the names of your old sab crew."

Richardson's brow creased. "What? Why?"

"Why isn't any of your fucking business. I'm only going to ask once more: what were the names of your old crew?"

"Adrian Braune." He still looked confused. "Michel—he was Braune, too, Adrian's brother. And Uwe Balik."

"Just four of you?"

"That's right. We kept it small. If we needed expertise, we hired in. I—I don't know all those names. I can try, though. I can—"

"Later. Dates of birth? Come on, don't fuck around."

"Um. I can't remember." His voice rose. "I—I know their old addresses. Good addresses. We all had one legit residence, for movement notification."

Toreth recorded them carefully. "And which one was your ex-wife fucking?"

Richardson seemed to have gone past surprise. "Adrian was Kat's boyfriend. She left him for me."

"Then the crew broke up?"

"That's right. There was no way we could keep working together. Adrian hated me. But—"

"There." Toreth straightened up. "That was easy, wasn't it? I might be back later—don't go anywhere."

Richardson lifted the hand with the cast, as though to try to hold on to Toreth's arm, then winced and lowered it again. "What about the treatment?"

"I'll let you know." Toreth smiled down at him. "If they come in and take off the renal pack, that's your answer. Better start working on those other names, just in case you need something to keep my attention."

Toreth quickly spotted the head of security's thinning dark hair and long, lined face on the other side of the main Detention security room. But before he'd even gone into the room, he'd heard Bevan's raised voice as he instructed a group of security officers to "Fuck off and get on with it." When Toreth glanced up at the screen running the length of one wall, he found a large blank section. A cell monitoring failure would put Bevan in a worse mood than usual.

Bevan's perpetually sour expression soured even further when he saw Toreth approach.

"What do you want? Haven't you caused enough trouble down here for one week?"

"It's about Clayton," Toreth said. "I have some names for you to look into—people who might have a financial connection to him."

"Well, thanks for the contribution, but we won't be needing them. A night in the cells made the little prick see sense. He's been moonlighting."

"What?"

Bevan turned to a senior security officer nearby, whom Toreth recognized from the days immediately after the revolt. "Just get the fucking feeds fixed, Adams. I don't give two steaming shits about Maintenance's priority system. Tell them if I don't see our cameras working in the next hour, I'll personally make sure every lazy bastard up there regrets waking up this morning."

His tone didn't seem to faze Adams; the easily upset didn't last long working for Bevan. "Yes, HoS. I'll let you know what they say. Para," he said to Toreth, and nodded before he left.

"Maintenance." Bevan snorted. "Won't do anything before they get a coffee. Then I'll end up with paras whining to *me* because their prisoner had a bad reaction, or topped themselves, and no one noticed. We can't resuscitate what we can't see, can we? I'm not a fucking magician." He waved his hand in the air, then pointed dramatically at the blank part of the screen which, of course, stayed blank. "See?"

"What were you saying about Clayton moonlighting?" Toreth asked patiently. Bevan needed coddling, but Toreth considered the effort well invested because the head of security was such a critical part of the I&I infrastructure.

"Before he came to I&I, Clayton worked as private security. So when he needed money to pay the unlicensed gambling debts he lied about when he applied here, he went back to his old mates and got a part-time job, off-system, cash in hand. He's been working day shifts here and nights bouncing drunks." Bevan shook his head disgustedly. "That's why he was so knackered that he dosed your prisoner up wrong."

"Oh," Toreth said. Another lovely theory burned to ash.

"So now I have to give the thoughtless little twat the boot anyway for breaking regulations, when I'm so fucking short-staffed I had to escort a prisoner from Justice *myself* last week. So thanks for that." Bevan paused for a moment, then asked, "What were these names, then?"

"It doesn't matter," Toreth said. "Just an idea I had."

"Some of us can find our own arses without needing a para-investigator to show us where they are." Bevan didn't smile, but his frown relaxed slightly. "Not even one who knows as much about arse-location as you do. Was that everything?"

"Yes."

"Then piss off and annoy someone else. I've got cell monitoring rotas to keep an eye on."

As Toreth walked into the central General Criminal office, he spotted Sara at her desk, uniform immaculate and not a hair straying from its assigned place.

"Morning, Toreth," she said as he passed. "I made you a coffee."

"Come in, I've got something to tell you."

He sipped his coffee while he recounted the events of the morning, good and bad. Sara had taken a chair, rather then her usual perch on the end of the desk, and up close under the office lights he could see the dark rings around her eyes that her best makeup efforts hadn't entirely disguised.

"So it looks like we were wrong," Sara said when he finished.

"Not necessarily. So, okay, Clayton wasn't paid off. But someone picked out Richardson to watch Lake, knowing he'd need to mess with Central Bank systems. Richardson barely does anything that qualifies as sab work these days, so I still think there's a chance they knew him from years ago. We have the names of his crew, so if it wasn't one of them they might know who it was. Richardson might have more names, too. Last night wasn't a complete washout." He winked at her.

"We're not talking about last night," she said firmly.

"Sara—"

"No. Nothing happened, so there's nothing to talk about. And nothing is ever going to happen again, so there's no need to talk about that, either. There was no last night, or there'll be no me here tomorrow. Am I being clear enough?"

Toreth stared at her. "I should say so, yeah."

"Good." Sara stood up. "Now, I have a lot of messages to look through, so I'm going to do that."

She didn't slam the door; no one in the outer office would know anything was wrong. But it sounded firmer than usual. Toreth had another mouthful of coffee and shook his head. More or less what he'd expected, but he still didn't see the big deal. Last year, after the revolt, she'd *offered* to fuck him . . . okay, probably because she was worried he'd stagger out of her flat and under a transport, but the principle was the same, right? Sometimes she really *was* strange.

Leaving Sara to her messages, Toreth found Jameson and Morehen in their office. Briefly he wondered why Sara had needed to tell Morehen quite so many times that there was nothing between her and Toreth. Then he dismissed the irrelevancy.

"You two are still looking at the Fresh Green Fields employee data?"

"That's right, Para," Morehen said. "Any connections with known sabs or associates, links to finance corporations, the Central Bank, Fisec. The problem is Fresh Green Fields is a huge corporation and we don't have anything to improve stringency. Even limiting it to their facilities around New London and Frankfurt throws up too many results to investigate effectively."

"And that's a big assumption," Jameson added, "since we already have two body dumps hundreds of miles apart. Fresh Green Fields uses highly standardized plant designs. And the processing equipment is bought from a third party and used by corporations all over the place. The security flaw could even have been identified outside Europe."

Exactly as Toreth had expected. "I added three names to the IIP just now. Try those."

Toreth stood, arms folded, trying to contain his impatience as the two investigators found the files belonging to Richardson's ex-crew and ran the searches.

"Michel Braune," Jameson said after a minute. "He had a six-month contract for Fresh Green Fields, working in security assessment. Not at one of the plants where bodies turned up, but . . . yes. They had an organic waste processing facility. It was five years ago, though."

Thank fuck for Tushingham's comprehensive, if belated, cooperation. "That doesn't matter. For all we know he's been tossing corpses in there ever since without any problem until something got stuck."

"Credit and purchase checks, Para," Morehen said. "The two Braunes have significant matches, but—"

"They're brothers," Toreth said.

"Right, Para. They have regular contact. But I'm not finding anything linking them to Uwe Balik in the last few years." He switched between records, then nodded. "That fits with Richardson's timeline about the crew breakup. Balik moved to Vienna soon after and he's still living there." Morehen looked up. "Of course, that doesn't mean he's not still sabbing, too."

"If it's nothing to do with the bank, I don't care," Toreth said. "Put him on the back burner for now. Anything suggestive for the other two? How about around the time Lake was killed?"

It took only a few seconds before Morehen said, "Adrian was in New London for the weekend, Para. C&p pattern says holiday—visit to the Tower of London Park, that kind of thing. Nothing to put him near Richardson's storage unit or Fresh Green Fields."

"If he was stupid enough to leave a trail like that we'd have caught him already. Now find me something that links him to Captain Martin, and you can have the weekends off for the rest of the case."

If the Braunes were behind the whole thing, or knew who was, the case might not last many more weekends anyway. Still, Morehen grinned. "On it, Para."

This time he took longer, a frown slowly deepening on his face as he drummed his fingers on the side of the desk. At the other desk, Jameson was still making searches, although her attention seemed elsewhere. Her lips moved fractionally as she subvocalized on her comm—about something relevant, Toreth hoped.

"Nothing very evidential, Para," Morehen said eventually. "Both Braunes were in Frankfurt around the time Martin disappeared. Michel bought a drink in the same bar within two hours of Martin." He looked up hopefully.

"Don't make any weekend plans," Toreth said. "I need something better than that."

"Is the offer good for me, too, Para?" Jameson asked.

"Depends on what you have," Toreth said.

"I just called Major Bayer-Dabrowski—Martin's commanding officer, the one I talked to about his record—and sent him pictures of the Braunes. He didn't recognize Michel, but he met Adrian Braune in Frankfurt. When the Service went in to stop the riots and secure Administration property, Braune was helping to coordinate resister forces in the city. The major is sure Martin would have worked with him while they were restoring order."

"Worked with him doing what?"

"Bayer-Dabrowski wasn't sure. He said the Service tried to get the resisters out as fast as possible, and the less he had to deal with them the better. I asked about the Central Bank, and while the Service did protect the buildings for a while, Martin had nothing to do with that, officially, anyway. He was based in an Int-Sec complex there—or what was left of it, which doesn't sound like much."

"I though I&I Frankfurt came out of it okay?" Toreth remembered them as being one of the first places to implement the new Procedures and Protocols.

"Maybe, Para," Jameson said. "I don't have any data to hand. But Major Bayer-Dabrowski described it as 'a bloody mess,' and it sounded like he meant it literally. I asked him to open up the operational records for us to access, but he says he'll need to clear it."

Funny how everyone liked to keep what they'd done during the revolt under wraps. "Are the Braunes still in Frankfurt?" Toreth asked Morehen.

"I can't say for sure—" The annoying qualification that preceded any location query since the end of movement notification. "—but their most recent c&p suggests so. They've both been silent for the last few days, though."

"All right." Toreth had half hoped they might have run somewhere further away from the possibility of Central Bank interference. Or, less usefully for the case, they were dead. "You two keep digging, let me know if anything more comes up."

Time for Sara to arrange, as discreetly as possible, some arrests and flights.

"How's your leg?" Toreth asked when he opened the door to Barret-Connor's office.

"Para?" B-C's head jerked up from his screen. "My leg? It's fine, Para. Well—more or less. Do you need me to go somewhere?"

"No, but I might need some fancy footwork while I'm in Frankfurt." Toreth went over to his desk. "You remember Secretary Turnbull?"

"Of course, Para."

"And I bet she'll remember you." Along with probably everyone else she'd ever met. "Nagra's in charge of the investigation here while I'm gone, but I've told her you're to handle contact with the Bureau. We might need Turnbull's backup at some point."

B-C suddenly looked over Toreth's shoulder and said, "Good morning, sir."

Toreth turned, surprised, and found Tillotson standing in the doorway. Had the section head heard Toreth mention Turnbull? His frosty expression suggested yes.

"Toreth, about this jaunt to Frankfurt. Is it necessary?"

Toreth had sent the request for authorization to work outside I&I London's area directly to Jenny, and he'd hoped she'd be able to deal with it without involving the section head. Was he watching the IIP? "Either we go there, or we bring the prisoners here, which needs an escort."

He'd expected Tillotson to suggest using Frankfurt interrogators, but instead he said, "My understanding was that bank security is taking the lead. I don't want any interdepartmental conflict."

"These are hands-on sabs, sir, who might be responsible for the death of a Service officer as well as Lake. We have no evidence to suggest they have anything to do with the market manipulation," Toreth added, which was true enough, so far. "But we might be able to wrap up the deaths while the bank deals with the rest."

"Do you even have a location for these sabs?"

If Toreth said yes, Tillotson would only demand details. Toreth imagined trying "need to know," but who would authorize the trip if the section head had a stroke? "Not yet. We're looking."

"Wouldn't it make more sense to have I&I Frankfurt locate and arrest them?"

"Yes, if you want to lose the result to Corporate Fraud. Apparently, Head of Section Vaughn has a lot of friends in Frankfurt."

Tillotson shook his head. "I'm sorry, Toreth, but I'm not spending section budget on a speculative visit looking for two sabs whose last credit and purchase location is over a week old."

Yeah, *now* he could read an IIP. "Fine, sir. I'll let you know if that changes."

After he was sure Tillotson was out of earshot, Toreth said, "*Fuck.*"

"Is there anything I can do, Para?" B-C said.

"Not unless you can pull the location of two experienced sabs in hiding out of thin air."

"I'm afraid not. How about the third sab, though? Uwe Balik?" B-C consulted his screen. "His file doesn't say anything about him being involved with resisters during the trouble, but he might still be in touch with the Braunes."

"Nothing in the comm history says so." But mention of resisters suggested another possible approach. "I'll be in my office."

"Para-investigator Toreth?" Sable sounded understandably surprised.

"Sorry to bother you again so soon. It's nothing very urgent." By which Toreth hoped he'd understand "nothing to do with your idiot fucking son." "Did you have a chance to look into those names?"

"Not yet, I'm afraid."

Probably Sable had only intended to make the checks when he had something to report back about Warrick. "Well, don't worry about it anymore. We've had a break, and I'm trying to locate a couple of sabs—Michel and Adrian Braune. They were involved in the revolt, so I thought Cit might be keeping an eye on them still."

"Let me have their IDs and I'll see what I can do. Do you want me to call you back?"

"I'll hang on." Was Corporate Fraud already looking for the Braunes? The IIP was closed to them now, but that didn't stop Tillotson from handing the names over to Vaughn. If CF found them first, he could kiss any case credit goodbye. Sable finding something quickly might be his only shot.

But, fuck, he hated waiting. Toreth closed his eyes and imagined the scenario he had planned for when Warrick returned. Fran had promised the order would be ready by Friday. He just hoped Warrick would be back in time. Of course the order wouldn't be entirely wasted if he wasn't; they could use it another time. But they had the bet running, too, and if Toreth didn't follow through, that was a major loss in the game.

Sable's voice startled him into opening his eyes.

"I think I have something, Para-investigator. They're still in Frankfurt. It appears they've gone to ground in a currently unused Int-Sec site. Int-Sec Frankfurt South." Sable chuckled. "Unusual choice of hidey-hole. Although the information here says that it went up in flames during the trouble, and I suppose since your suspects were working with the resisters they knew it was still empty."

"Are you watching them, then?" Just what he needed—someone else who wanted his suspects for themselves.

"Not closely. They're on the list of citizens who received an official amnesty for their actions last year, so of course they're of more interest than entirely non-political sabs. But if we cared about what happens to them, we would've flagged their files. Actually, it was simple facial recognition. They were careless with a couple of cameras on the Int-Sec site perimeter, and we have access to surveillance data from the corporation managing it. Part of the new requirements for obtaining Administration contracts."

Good old Cit, finding ways around the movement notification changes. "Thank you. That's extremely helpful."

"Always happy to assist an Int-Sec colleague," Sable said. "If anything else comes up, I'll call you."

Already planning what to do next in the case, it took Toreth a moment to realize what he meant. Warrick. "Ah, okay. Thanks."

Call ended, Toreth sat back in his chair. Not home and dry, but at least heading in the right direction. Was he looking too smug? Probably. Toreth sucked in his cheeks, trying to erase the "fuck you for trying to screw up my career, you weasel-faced shitstain" he was doubtless projecting, then he called Tillotson.

"I've got a location for those sabs, sir," he said without preamble when Tillotson answered.

"Really?" Tillotson's nose twitched. "So fast? Where?"

"Frankfurt, like I said. I'd rather not put the precise location in the IIP for now. After all, we still don't know exactly what happened to Richardson. We might have a leak."

Tillotson looked understandably—and justifiably—skeptical. "I thought HoS Bevan said it was an accident?"

"Maybe," Toreth said. "Better not to risk it, though. I'll tell Sara to make the travel arrangements, shall I?" An idea struck him. "Or if it's the budget that's the problem, I could ask the Bureau for a contribution. After all, it's practically their case."

"There's no need to involve the Bureau further," Tillotson said after a pause. "But I want to see an arrest on the screen when you get there. Not a week later—today."

"You will. Thanks, sir. I'll—"

"And I talked to Vaughn, and she wanted you to take a CF para-investigator along with you if you went to Frankfurt, to make sure the financial aspect of the case is fully covered."

Or to make sure Corporate Fraud could steal his case back at the last minute. "I can ask Senior Investigator Carey—"

"Para-investigator, not investigator." The speed of the reply suggested he'd been expecting Carey's name.

Toreth debated for a good three seconds the usefulness of arguing, but Tillotson had obviously decided he was willing to lose a case closure to CF if it would stop Toreth from getting all the credit. "Okay, sure. And that's a good idea, sir. I have to admit the financial fraud angle is complicated, putting it mildly. Some knowledgeable backup would be useful."

His abrupt agreement seemed to take Tillotson by surprise. "Senior Para Zaleski had the case originally, I think."

"I remember," Toreth said. "Don't worry, I'll tell Sara to sort it all out. I promise I won't set foot on a plane without a CF para."

Chapter Twenty-five

Y ou'd better not be bullshitting me about this," Christofi said as they scanned their IDs and bypassed the main queue for boarding the first available flight to Frankfurt.

"I told you, Sara actually saw the cleared candidate list for the new teams, and you'll beat everyone on seniority alone, before they even look at your record. She has some friends in HCT, people she worked with after the revolt. They'll fix everything. You'll be at a desk in General Criminal before you know it."

"Good. Because Vaughn will do her nut when she finds out that I helped you, and I can see why corporates want to keep her at a distance because she scares the shit out of me."

"It's in the bag, I promise. You'll be weighted too high for anyone to do anything about it." And if Tillotson did decide to spend the political capital to block Christofi from moving to General Criminal, they wouldn't find out until well after the case was over. Then it would be Christofi's problem, not Toreth's. "You haven't even finished the CF training, so they can't argue you're essential to the section. Or are all those databases starting to get you off?"

"If I never see another per-transfer tax analysis again, I'll die a happy man."

They paused by the door to the boarding tube. Toreth stared impatiently down the broad corridor leading back into the airport, but Jameson and Morehen were still nowhere in sight. He should've told them not to bother going home and to pick up anything they needed on expenses in Frankfurt.

"By the way," Toreth said to Christofi, "don't mention anything about this to Nagra."

Christofi looked baffled for a moment, then smiled slowly. "Because her name's on the candidate list, right? I suppose that makes her the second bird, and me the stone." He laughed. "You really are a smooth bastard."

It was a relief when Toreth and the others finally went, leaving Sara with only Nagra, B-C, and Mistry, all busy in their offices and not bothering her. Of course, the relief only lasted until she reached a pause in her list of things to do and had time to think.

She should know better. She should know *him* better. She'd kept their friendship in balance all this time, and now she was the one who had disturbed the scales after the revolt by admitting that she remembered sleeping with him. And then, to make it worse, the offer of a pity fuck in her flat—stupid, stupid woman—which she'd tried to dismiss from her mind once he was back with Warrick. Why hadn't she thought through the possible consequences? Was is because she didn't want to? God, she'd rather just blame it all on him. But twenty-nine was far too old to pretend that the wine had made her do anything she didn't want to do. All it had done was allow her to forget why what she wanted was idiotic and selfish.

She'd almost messed everything up irretrievably by asking Toreth if anything had happened. Still, if there was one thing he could be relied on to do it was pick the easy route and lie his way out of trouble. Or maybe he really didn't remember, but she found that hard to believe when she could remember far too much, far too clearly.

Ten years ago there hadn't been any particular reason why she shouldn't sleep with Toreth, beyond the fact that he was a para, and the general disastrous consequences of screwing your boss. Now Toreth had Warrick, and she had Andy, and she'd been willing to risk wrecking everything...why? Because part of her was still secretly nineteen and deluded into being a little bit in love with him?

After all her "I don't sleep with friends' boyfriends" horseshit, too. She'd seriously think about taking up prayer if she thought it would stop Toreth from telling Warrick what had happened. Surely even *he* had to realize that would be a catastrophe? And she couldn't bear the idea of having to talk to Warrick, of seeing the hurt and betrayal in his eyes that would be of no consequence to Toreth. No doubt he'd think that Warrick shouldn't care, since it meant nothing more than any of his other one-night stands. Which, much as she hated to admit it, was no doubt the truth.

"You're a horrible person," she murmured. "Yes, you are. Don't try to deny it."

All the reasons why it would never work were still just as valid as they had been when she was nineteen. Even more so, in fact, now that she'd seen what Toreth in a relationship actually looked like from up close. How Warrick put up with his screwing around she'd never understand. The careless cruelty with which Toreth would say "Warrick doesn't mind" when it was obvious to anyone that he damn well did still shocked her sometimes. She should be grateful that knowing he'd never change for Warrick made it impossible to pretend that he'd change for anyone else, either.

So here she was, somehow feeling sad that she couldn't have something she'd had a decade to get over wanting. Maybe she *should* apply for a transfer, for everyone's sakes, and she thought about it for a whole minute before she acknowledged she was kidding herself. "Should" and "would" were definitely not getting together for coffee and biscuits over that idea.

"If I ever sleep with my boss, you'll know about it, because I'll resign the next day." How many times had she said that in the years she'd worked here and never thought about the consequences? If she'd been with anyone other than Andy, it wouldn't be such a disaster, but...

"This is why it's a stupid idea to date inside work," she said firmly to herself.

"Sara? Are you okay?"

It was Kel, looking over at her, with concern in his eyes and voice.

Sara blinked until the blurriness went away, and smiled at him. "I'm fine. Just something in my eye."

He gave her a look of affectionate skepticism as he came over to her desk, but all he said was, "Come on. Let's find you a nice cup of something."

Sara tidied up her desk with a few efficient sweeps, then stood up. "All right. But just so you know, I don't want to talk about it."

She'd overdone the emphasis, because Kel looked at her curiously as they headed for the coffee room. "No? Why the secrecy?" He nudged her with his elbow, letting her know he was joking. "Did you finally sleep with Toreth?"

Luckily, her first response was to laugh, because it was funny that that was apparently the only thing Kel could imagine she'd keep a secret. "Ha! No, I didn't lose my mind over New Year." Much. "But, okay, I—I was just worrying a bit, about Andy. Chasing sabs in Frankfurt. I know, I'm being silly. I'm sure they'll be fine."

"Andy's a sensible boy," Kel said. "He can look after himself."

"I know. And I'm sure they'll have security with them. I never even would've thought about it before... before. I think I only started now because I used one of Senior Para Hepburn's old codes. Still working, after so long. I don't think Systems bothers sweeping them at all anymore." She sniffed briskly. "Anyway, it made me think about, well, everything that happened."

"Ah, I see. That happens to all of us, my dear." He put his arm around her shoulders and gave her a comforting squeeze that made her feel momentarily guilty for getting sympathy when she'd messed up so badly. "Although," Kel added, "I have to say, I'd never have believed anyone would *ever* get teary-eyed over Tom Hepburn."

"Look over there."

Christofi pointed out of the car window. They were traveling on a high flyover from the airport toward Frankfurt; below them, in the center of an expanse of green near the river, lay an extraordinary building, gleaming silver in the sunlight. A great central building, round and shallowly domed, sprouted a ring of silver lines that linked it to other, smaller domes. It looked like an abstract flower, blooming from the landscaped grass and trees around it.

"What is it, Para?" Jameson asked.

"That's the Central Trading Exchange. The core holds the offices and main stock exchange, and each one of the outer buildings has a different specialized trading floor. It won awards for the design."

Toreth blinked at him; he probably would've felt less surprised if Sara's cat had started talking about architecture.

"I told you." Christofi grimaced. "Corporate Fraud. Training schedule as long as my cock."

"So you've finished it already, after all?" Toreth said, and he saw Jameson's grin before she turned away to look out of the window.

"Fucker," Christofi said. "Don't forget I'm doing you a big favor."

Toreth laughed. "As if you'll give me the chance to. And don't forget I'll be doing *you* one, too."

As everyone climbed out of the car, Toreth put his hands in his pockets to avoid the biting wind and examined their destination. The main I&I Frankfurt building was a giant slab of dirty concrete, surrounded by other buildings that seemed to have been plonked haphazardly into whatever open space had once surrounded the building. Small, square windows were sunk deep into the face of the building, and the rooms behind them must be gloomy. The only other break from the blank concrete was around the main entrance; Toreth imagined the plans coming back to the architect with a note asking him to add *some* kind of feature, resulting in a hasty sketch of two stubby triangular piers flanking the pair of wide double doors, linked by a giant pair of scales cast into the concrete above.

Black smudges here and there on the concrete, like day-old makeup, might be traces of old air pollution from the time of petroleum vehicles, but could be more recent. However, nothing about the I&I Frankfurt buildings suggested they'd been heavily damaged in the past year. Not that was visible on this side of the main entrance, at least—maybe the worse damage was elsewhere.

Someone must have been watching out for them, or following the car's journey. It had barely pulled up when the door opened and a man hurried out to meet them.

The badge on his uniform said he was a senior para. He had light brown skin, very dark hair that made the gray strands in it stand out even in the dull light, and dark eyes with laughter lines that grooved the corners. Combined with a perpetual slight smile, they made his expression hard to read.

His voice was friendly enough, anyway. "Senior Para-investigator West, General Criminal."

West offered his hand and Toreth shook it, then introduced himself and the rest of the team.

"I have a security team ready to go," West said. "Do you have a location? We can go inside to discuss it, if you like."

Behind him, Toreth heard Morehen tell the car to wait. Obviously, they were thinking the same thing. "My information is that the sabs are hiding somewhere in the Int-Sec Frankfurt South building."

"That's just over the river." West frowned. "It's a big site, though. I'll need more guards to secure all the exits."

"Can you get them to meet us there?"

If West thought there was anything strange about Toreth's mix of urgency and secrecy, he didn't comment. "If you like. I'll get my junior to organize them."

Five in the car made a snug fit. Jameson squeezed in between Christofi and Morehen, leaving the seat opposite for Toreth and the Frankfurt senior.

With the financial shenanigans starting right after the revolt, Toreth wasn't inclined to label the sabs' choice of hiding place as pure convenience. As the car pulled away, Toreth said, "Tell me about this empty site."

"A nasty mess." West cleared his throat. "A couple of years ago Psychoprogramming built a flashy new complex on the south bank. They've always run a medical sideline in Frankfurt, and when they found some juicy corporate sponsorship, they persuaded the Administration to match it. Neuropsychological Treatment Center at the front, Psychoprogramming at the back." West sniffed dismissively. "You know how it works—get the higher-ups excited about how Psychoprogramming will solve all Europe's social problems, then pick their pockets. Well, at least we could expand into Mindfuck's old buildings, but of course Int-Sec Frankfurt had run out of money for refurbishment, so we got half a coat of paint and told to make the best of it. The mindfuckers swanned around, lording it over the rest of us, but all it meant in the end was that the resisters knew exactly where to find them. Which we were happy about—it kept them busy, and stopped them from killing any more of us than they did. I'm sure we were next on the list, but then the Service showed up. First time I've ever been grateful to see those stuck-up swine."

"I know exactly what you mean," Toreth said. "Although we kicked them out as fast as we could."

West's smiled broadened. "That's right—you're *that* Senior Para Toreth, aren't you?"

Opposite Toreth, Christofi snorted.

"Probably," Toreth said.

"You wrote the new P&P," West continued. "Although I wouldn't go telling people that over in the Interrogation building."

"Procedural changes were all down to Socioanalyst Carnac," Toreth said, wondering how many people ever believed him. "The Socioanalysis Division bases its social strategies on the long-term best interests of the Administration as a whole—or so they say. I'm afraid I can't take any of the credit."

"That's *his* story, anyway," Christofi said.

Toreth added Christofi to his mental list of paras and interrogators he wished he'd let Carnac deal with. Ignoring Christofi, he asked West, "Can you get access to the security systems at this Mindfuck site?"

West nodded. "I'll do it now."

The resisters certainly hadn't held back when it came to revolutionary arson. The hospital section had burned along with Psychoprogramming, and scorched ground marked where burned-out vehicles had been removed. A reinforced double fence ringed the entire site, hung with regularly spaced warning screens. In response to West's orders, the access codes had been changed, and the site's cameras and alarms linked directly to the I&I officers' hand screens.

Everything on the surface looked abandoned—no sign of machinery or recent activity. Some areas of the buildings were marked on the site plan as in danger of collapse; others had already been demolished, before the reconstruction effort halted.

"Int-Sec was just starting to clear for rebuilding," West said as they waited for his junior and the extra security officers to move into position. "Then the Psychoprogramming leftovers were folded into the Department of Medicine—Health Care and Research, or whatever is it now—and the DoM decided they should get the site. They've been fighting it out and appealing Council decisions ever since. Just when it's sorted out, there's a new Council installed and off they go again."

Toreth rubbed his hands together. The wind cut down from the north, funneled into the space between two buildings where they waited. Tiny ice crystals, too fine to call snow, stung his skin. "Any sign of the suspects?"

"Nothing's moved since we started watching. A small transport vehicle from the site management corporation logged in through the gate just before we arrived, although they couldn't give us a sensible answer about why it was here."

"The Braunes trying to escape?" Rerouting a vehicle was well within sab capabilities.

"Maybe, but it won't work. The transport's still in there, and it won't get out

248

now." West studied the plan on his hand screen. "I think the Mindfuck detention section is the most likely location for them. It had the least damage—apparently it took the resisters a while to break in, and the fire system in there functioned until the main fire died down." He lifted his head. "Right. Everyone's ready. Say when you want to go."

They made an ironic entry through a fire escape door at the back of the building. The manual override cracked loudly as a security officer forced it, and Toreth half expected a reaction from inside the building. They waited, but the only sound was the distant city background.

They went through the building floor by floor, quiet except for the occasional low mutter of West coordinating with the other search parties. Following Int-Sec customs, the detention section was underground, and with no power they had to search by torchlight. One advantage of the fire damage was the layers of dust and soot thick on the floor. After only ten minutes, West said, "They've found tracks on the northeast emergency staircase, leading down to level three."

As they reached the foot of the closest stairs, the door crashed open and a man bolted through. He was looking back, over his shoulder, and that gave them the edge. Christofi reacted first, catching the man's arm in a professional and painful hold that made him cry out. Christofi slammed him face first against the wall and kept him still while Toreth cuffed him.

Toreth had just turned their catch around when two security officers ran up, one male, one female, the man panting harshly as though winded.

"Sorry, sir," he said to West. He put his hand to his stomach, breathing in deeply and carefully. "He caught us off-guard. Me off-guard," he amended, with a glance at his companion. "But we have the other one."

Two prisoners. Exactly what he'd come to Frankfurt for, and Tillotson could choke on it.

Under the dirt on his face and hair, and the blood dripping from a cut on his brow, Toreth wasn't sure of the prisoner's identity. "Michel Braune?" he guessed.

The man coughed and spat. "Adrian."

The female officer looked at Toreth. "We've got a prisoner transport waiting topside, Para. Shall we take them straight back to I&I?"

Back to interrogation facilities, and a medical unit that meant Toreth could use the entire box of tricks Daedra had packed up for him (which, along with the neural induction probe, had raised a few eyebrows at airport security). But if Lehman had high-powered friends at I&I London, she would certainly have more on her own doorstep.

"I'll talk to them here first," Toreth said. "I don't want to risk losing any physical evidence they've hidden. Find a couple of empty rooms upstairs with daylight and doors that lock, and put one in each. Then tell your officers to start searching the complex."

In a dusty office half full of broken furniture, Toreth and Christofi inspected their catch over the secure camera feeds. Cuffed and in leg restraints, the Braune brothers sat on the bare floors, each shifting occasionally to find a more comfortable position. Both had acquired a few scrapes and bruises during their arrest.

"Adrian was the one who worked at Fresh Green Fields," Toreth said, "and he was the one who went to New London, so he probably killed Lake. He has the biggest incentive to try to make a deal . . . I'll start with Michel."

"Sounds good," Christofi said. "If he starts talking, do you want me to try Adrian? See if we can get a little competitive cooperation going?"

"Yeah. But make sure you only ask him about the murders, not the fraud. And don't push too hard."

"Don't worry, I'm not planning to unwrap an injector without your say-so." Christofi sounded entirely serious. "If this comes off, I want plenty of plausible deniability to show Vaughn that poaching her financials case back wasn't my idea—which is why I'd rather not be watching your interrogation."

Toreth tapped his comm. "Sara," he said, and almost immediately heard her voice.

"Toreth? How's it going?"

"We found someone to talk to. How're things there?"

"Okay, so far. I saw Investigator Carey when I was queuing to buy lunch. She said Vaughn had had a call from the Central Bank, wanting to know if you were still looking at the financials. Carey told her you'd sent Phil back to CF, and you were tied up with the murders."

Good for Liz. "Tell her thanks, if you see her again. If Lehman wants a progress report, make sure you have something suitable written up."

"It's all ready to go. But I had a request from the bank—Karaca, the head of security—to open up the IIP for them."

No doubt they'd discovered Verstraeten's lack of access. "File it under I don't give a fuck. If they come back about it, tell them I'm chasing suspects and you couldn't get hold of me."

"Fine," she said, with exactly the same inflection as if he'd asked her to make a coffee. "What about the interrogation transcripts?"

Toreth debated for a moment, wishing he could've brought Sara along. "We might need to make a fast submission to Justice. I'll feed the interrogations straight into the IIP. Make sure they're locked down, though—my eyes only. If anyone argues, they're too politically sensitive. Tell them you don't have the authority to give access."

Sara snorted quietly. "Well, someone might believe me. I'll let you know if anything else happens." She paused, then added, unusually, "Good luck."

Why did she think he needed luck with this interrogation, out of all the ones he'd run over the years? Toreth switched off his comm, just in case Lehman wanted to get involved personally once she heard about the arrests, then went to see his prisoner.

Like Richardson, Michel Braune had long hair, blond rather than dark, that hung around his face as he knelt on the bare, dusty floor. If he'd worn it tied back, the guards had removed the band.

"I'm sure you have the same interrogation resistance as Kelvin Richardson," Toreth said. "The waiver I just read to you is here to make sure it doesn't matter a damn. It gives me the power to do just about anything I could do before your resister friends caused so much trouble."

Unlike Richardson, Michel Braune didn't express any disbelief. He looked down at the floor, head bowed, breathing slowly. Toreth had told the guards to leave his hands cuffed behind him and the leg restraints in place, because Toreth didn't want a guard in the room.

"Now, I know you didn't kill Lake. I could probably be persuaded you didn't kill Captain Martin, either." Braune was good, but Toreth caught the tiny twitch of his shoulders at the Service officer's name. "If you can give me complete details of the finance operation and the names of everyone involved, then I can guarantee you get out of this building alive. Maybe that doesn't sound like an especially attractive offer, but there are two of you, and I only need one to talk to me." Toreth paused. "Anything to say?"

Without looking up, Braune said, "I want a Justice rep."

"Sorry, they don't make home visits. You can ask again at I&I—if you get there." Toreth gave him a few seconds, then said, "Okay. You can wait here while I see if your brother is any smarter than you. You'd better hope you see me again, because if you don't, that means he's holding my attention better than you have so far. Then you'll get a guard who won't be interested in anything other than your unfortunately failed escape attempt."

Braune impressed him; Toreth actually had one foot in the corridor before he said, "Wait."

Toreth paused, his hand still on the open door. "Well?"

"How do I know it's a guarantee if I don't get a rep?"

"Because I said so. If you don't fancy that, maybe Adrian will."

Adrian, who had two murders to explain away, and so that much more reason to cooperate.

Finally Michel nodded. "All right. It's a deal." He stressed the last word.

"Good choice." Toreth closed the door and stood over him. "You get one chance, so talk quickly. If I don't like what I'm hearing, that's it."

"It all started here, with Psychoprogramming," Michel said.

Toreth smiled coldly. "Where the resisters were busy killing Int-Sec people."

Braune winced. "Yes. But I didn't make policy decision, I just helped implement them. They wanted to hit Psychoprogramming first, and I&I later. I heard that one of the local leaders had a sister go through a fast re-education and come out in bad shape. That's the sort of logic they had behind a lot of decisions."

Toreth tapped his foot impatiently. Every minute wasted was a minute Lehman—or Vaughn, and then Lehman—could find out what he was up to. "I'm not interested in resisters or their policies."

"I'm just saying, that's how I came to be here. The second day, one of the psychoprogrammers wanted to talk to me—a man called Ritter. The resisters were busy fighting over what to do with the few Psychoprogramming survivors they had, whether to kill them out of hand, or rig up some kind of trial and execute them publicly afterwards. I didn't care, I was just trying to keep everyone focused on doing the job I was being paid to do. Ritter obviously guessed Adrian and I weren't with the resisters because we believed in a better Europe. He claimed he knew a way we could make a lot of money—literally as much as we ever wanted. He said there were people walking around with these 'preconscious processing level adjustments' that could affect their judgment about corporate stocks. Send a simple voice message with the right tone pattern in the background and either they'd start to feel good about a stock, or they'd start looking for reasons why it was a risky investment, without questioning why. Temporarily—it would wear off after a few days. Ritter claimed there were enough key people conditioned to shift the market."

That sounded like the kind of implausible scam Lehman had talked about. Why hadn't he packed a neural scanner? With two prisoners, he could risk the drugs.

"And you just believed him?" Toreth asked.

"Not really." Michel smiled wryly. "But wouldn't you be curious? We thought it was at least worth taking him away from the resisters while we checked. The whole building was wrecked, chaos, so accessing the systems was no problem. Some of what Ritter said seemed to pan out. Psychoprogramming ran a commercial service, monitoring staff loyalty. Not just key traders in corporations and the Central Bank, but some military supply jobs, information security in the Data Division. We found the accounts—they were doing good business."

Did that mean that in the past I&I had had some of their requests bounced because Psychoprogramming was padding their budgets with corporate work? Bloody typical mindfuckers. "But what about the financial backdoor mindfuckery? Was that in the books?"

"No. And neither of us knows anything about conditioning, so even when we eventually found the protocols Ritter described, we didn't know what they meant.

So in the end, Adrian had the idea of making Ritter run a test. If it was real, the markets were already screwed up after the revolt. Who'd notice? And...it worked." Michel shook his head, then tossed his hair back out of his face. "God's truth, it still seemed too crazy to be true. But it wasn't—there were instructions buried in the finance sector conditioning. They'd been in there for years."

"So who put them there? Ritter?"

"No. He said it had always been part of the protocols, as far back as he could check—at least since the formation of Psychoprogramming. Probably before that, but he didn't have the clearance. But there was no official record. He only found it because he was working on upgrading the conditioning system after they moved to the new building." Michel's shoulders shifted, like he was trying to bring his hands around. "That's what he said. I don't know if it's true, and once we'd worked out it was real, we didn't care."

It sounded true; it fit the case evidence. Of course, the bad side of keeping the Braunes away from I&I and the risk of bank interference was the lack of neural scanners. "Tell me about Captain Martin," Toreth said.

Killing a Service officer was something anyone might prevaricate about, but Braune answered right away. "When the army showed up, we hoped they'd take over control from the resisters and we'd be able to get on with investigating the conditioning—this was before we ran the test. But Ritter must've decided he didn't like his chances with us. He got to Martin, somehow. Martin wanted to report it." Michel shook his head. "Can you believe it? I always thought Service loyalty was a myth."

"And then you killed him."

Now Michel hesitated, running his teeth over his bruised lower lip; then he said, "Adrian dealt with him. I was stuck with the resisters—we didn't want to create suspicion by dumping our contract with them. The next day, Martin was gone. Adrian said it was handled."

"Just 'handled'?"

Michel nodded. "We never share more details than that. We gave it a couple of weeks, just in case, and then we were done with the resisters and we could get on with the real work of getting rich."

Toreth loaded all the skepticism he could into his voice. "Just the two of you?"

"Yes. Okay, we aren't investment experts, but we didn't want to risk bringing someone in. I finally hit on selling the system as a service. One thing we do know about is handling greedy corporates who don't mind breaking the law."

"I'm going to need names."

Braune nodded wearily. "We destroyed the records. I can probably remember most of them. I made a lot of the approaches."

Luckily, they had Lake's data to provide a crosscheck. "And what about Rupert Lake? Where did he come in?"

"Lake." Michel sighed. "Lake was where it started to go wrong. Maybe we should've stopped then, while we were ahead, but things were just getting good. We had a contact at Fisec. He knew nothing about the conditioning—I told him we were interested in picking up potential blackmail leads for stock market frauds, and that we'd pay a bonus for passing on any tips sent to Fisec. As soon as I read Lake's report, I knew we'd been found out."

"So why not kill him?" Toreth asked.

"Doing it right after he'd made the report seemed too risky—even Fisec might start to think he was onto something. I wanted to cut and run, but Adrian came up with the idea of using Richardson to watch him, and dealing with him later if he got too close. If no one at Fisec believed him, what Lake thought didn't matter." He smiled lopsidedly. "I enjoyed that part. Richardson had no idea he was working for us. He made the perfect cutout. Then Richardson told us Lake switched tracks, trying to chase down where the messages were going instead of what they did. By then it was months after the report, so." He shrugged. "Adrian went to New London a few days later."

"And solved the problem with the help of Fresh Green Fields."

Michel nodded. "It's his favorite way. We hoped Lake would go on record as a disappearance, not a murder. It's easier to vanish these days."

"What did you do with the material from Mind—from Psychoprogramming?"

"We left it alone. I expect everything's still here. This whole site's sealed off and secured. I think they're busy arguing about what to do with it, now that most of the psychoprogrammers are dead."

"Including Ritter," Toreth said.

Michel nodded. "Once we were sure we had all the information we needed from him."

"I expect that was down to Adrian, too."

Michel lifted his head and smiled bitterly. "Sure. Why not?"

"And did anyone else help you with the escape transporter?"

"With—" Michel frowned. "Escape from where?"

"Here. There's a light transporter parked up above. How did it get in?"

"Nothing to do with us. With me, anyway. And...Adrian would've told me if he was planning to leave." He didn't sound entirely confident.

Well, the transport could be left to Frankfurt I&I. If the Braunes had a junior collaborator, that would give West a scrap of credit. "Right." Toreth crouched down and expanded his hand screen. "I have the building plans here. You can show me *exactly* where to look for these magic conditioning protocols."

Michel looked Toreth in the face. In the dull winter light filtering in through the room's high, narrow windows, his blue eyes were almost gray.

"My guarantee?" he asked.

Toreth smiled. "Is worth the paper it's written on, until I've checked out your story."

"Where are we going, Para?" Jameson asked as they hurried along an underground service corridor linking the hospital's catering section to the main treatment center.

"Did you see the interrogation?" Toreth asked, his eyes on their progress across the floor plan. Their target was in an area marked safe, but getting to it involved a circuitous route. Hopefully West's men wouldn't be there yet.

"No, Para," Jameson said. "Your feed was locked. Senior Para Christofi wasn't making much progress with his prisoner."

"Well, we're going to collect some evidence." Assuming it existed, and Braune's story wasn't a ridiculous play for time.

"Something belonging to the Braunes?" Jameson switched to a slow jog to keep up with her taller companions. "Senior Para West's junior got in touch while you were interrogating, Para. He said they'd found where the Braunes were living. It's back in the detention building."

"This belongs to someone else." Left at the next junction, and up a flight of stairs. The fire damage here was noticeably worse, forcing them to skirt sections of security-reinforced concrete in the stairway and in the next corridor. "And soon it'll belong to us. Then Vaughn and Lehman can say what they like about who's best placed to investigate, but we'll have all the cards."

"Are we sure about that roof, Para?" Morehen said, echoing Toreth's own thoughts. Toreth gave an apprehensive glance up at the ceiling ahead and hoped the Int-Sec surveyors who'd assessed the building had paid attention that day.

"Of course. Do you think I'd risk getting you killed? Sara would never shut up about it. Right, here we are."

The corridor opened into a long gallery, with a circular reception desk partly buried under a heap of damaged furniture and screens. Clear-up had obviously begun here before the Department of Health Care and Research stepped in—had evidence of the conditioning protocols already been destroyed? They picked their way along the length of the gallery, passing open and closed doors equally spaced, each one leading into an observation booth over a psychoprogramming suite below. The key figures in the Administration's finance sector had come into a place like this, year after year, and walked out with a back door implanted in their minds. At least, if Michel Braune was telling the truth. To Toreth it still sounded unbelievable.

"But that's what we're here to find out," he muttered to himself as he checked the plan again.

"Para?" Jameson said.

"Nothing." They reached the far end of the gallery. "It's right over there."

A murmur of voices from behind the door to the systems service room gave Toreth enough warning for the annoyed thought that West had somehow beaten them to it. Then Jameson opened the door, and Toreth realized he was wrong, and Braune's story, however implausible, might be true after all.

The five people busily occupied stripping and crating the contents of the room had no uniforms, no insignia. He had no trouble picking out their leader, though, a middle-aged woman with short dark hair and a creamy, smooth complexion, standing apart from the others and surveying their work. Of medium height and slim build, she held herself with the confidence of someone who rarely had her commands questioned. She definitely didn't look as though she worked for a building site security corporation. When the door opened, she turned to face it, with no sign of alarm or surprise.

Motion in the room stopped, everyone looking either at the door or the woman, until she said, "Get back to work. I'll deal with this."

Toreth wished that he'd trusted I&I Frankfurt enough to bring a few armed security officers along with them. Jameson took a step towards the doorway, and then stopped when Toreth put his hand on her shoulder. He moved her to one side and strode in.

A solid bluff was his only hope. "Who the hell are you?" Toreth demanded with all the authority he could project.

The woman inspected him carefully. Like the others, there was nothing about her that gave any clue to her affiliation.

"Senior Para-investigator Toreth, I assume?" Her cool, cultured voice matched her manner, and had a familiarity Toreth couldn't immediately place. "Principal Secretary Turnbull from the Bureau of Administrative Departments said we might see you here."

The brief relief—at least it wasn't the Central Bank—was tempered by the lack of any names. "What's your division? Something in Int-Sec?"

"As I said, at this moment I'm working with Secretary Turnbull. She alerted me as to the unexpected direction your investigation had taken. We've come to collect the evidence of irregularities at the Psychoprogramming Division."

Working with, not for. "That's my evidence, for my case. I can have twenty I&I security officers here in five minutes."

"No." Her voice was still quiet, but very emphatic. "Unfortunately, when you came to examine the Psychoprogramming systems, you found they'd all been destroyed. You'll have to make do with the confessions of the perpetrators who exploited the loyalty assessment system to defraud the Administration. I'm sure it will still reflect highly on your record."

Toreth looked at her; the woman held his gaze levelly. Finally Toreth said, "I'll need to call Turnbull."

"I was about to make that very suggestion." She turned her attention back to the rest of the room, and Toreth stepped out into the corridor.

He'd expected to have to wait, but if Turnbull had decided to screw him over, at least she had the courtesy to let his call go through directly.

"Secretary," Toreth subvocalized as calmly as he could, "I'm at the Psychoprogramming building in Frankfurt, and there's some...person here who says she has your authority to steal my fucking evidence."

Turnbull laughed, then immediately cleared her throat. "I do apologize. Yes, that's correct. I have direct orders from the Council to close this matter swiftly and finally."

"This is my case." Toreth clenched his fist with hopeless anger. Lehman he'd expected, not this. "You can't just bury it."

"Absolutely not. Not all of it." She paused for a moment, then said, "I appreciate that you've put a lot of work into this investigation. But it's vital to us that certain facts are kept completely confidential, for the good of the Administration. The existence of the corporate conditioning loophole is one of those."

Corporate conditioning loophole. The familiar way she said it made him realize—"This wasn't some rogue bunch of mindfuckers setting up a way to rig the Administration's trading markets, then. This was *policy*?"

One of the problems with subvocalization was that it could feel a lot like thinking to yourself. As soon as he heard Turnbull's intake of breath, Toreth felt cold. Why the fuck had he voiced that deduction aloud?

"Toreth—"

"Okay, I'm sorry." Fuck, fuck, fuck. "Not my business. Forget I said anything. Just tell me what the Bureau wants me to do."

"Toreth, please." A soft creak over the comm suggested she had taken a seat. "Now that we've gone this far, I feel you should understand the full ramifications of a leak. Consider that the Administration has various tools available for guiding its citizens. Think of compulsory citizenship classes, re-education, or reproduction control, for example."

"I thought repro control was because of the bombs?" Toreth said. "Mutations and so on? Or for making sure people could look after their kids properly?" Much good had it done with his fucking parents.

"Well, those are commonly presented reasons. People need to be given...a clear path to follow. Otherwise, as our colleagues at the Socioanalysis Division would tell you, they can become confused and pursue suboptimal strategies. Population control, as it was conceived, is primarily a tool for economic stability. With allowances for regulated amounts of migration, it optimizes the age structure and socioeconomic layering of the Administration. And corporations, if you like, are another type of citizen. Individually more significant, perhaps, but that makes guiding them all the more important. Like other citizens, a corporation can't be expected to act spontaneously against its own imperatives for the good of Europe.

So a group within the Administration created an indirect tool for... applying subtle pressures and distractions."

By fucking with market prices. "The Bureau?" Toreth asked.

"That's unimportant. What concerns the Bureau now is the risk that too close an examination by experts could uncover the whole corporate conditioning strategy. The consequences would be disastrous for us all. It could even trigger a civil war between the corporations and the Administration. European unity is fragile after recent events. Some corporates are already questioning our ability to protect their interests."

"I get it now." Turnbull had been dead right—he hadn't fully appreciated the ramifications, especially the ramifications that continuing to argue could have on his life expectancy. "The Psychoprogramming data's gone. Fine. What do you want me to do with the rest of the case?"

She didn't hesitate. "Where you have clear evidence of criminal conspiracies with these sabs, arrest the traders."

A little pushback against the corporations from the Administration. "There might be some big names involved."

"Yes." She sounded pleased at the idea. "I'm sure the corporations concerned will be relieved when the Administration is forced to classify the trials, for political security reasons. Details have a habit of escaping, eventually, of course. I suggest that the final case submitted to Justice concludes these sabs suborned one of the late Psychoprogramming employees before the revolt—whatever time frame seems appropriate with regards to whom you arrest. Stress the sabs' proven links to resisters. There must be no suggestion this enterprise was endorsed by the Administration. And there must be no risk of anyone contradicting that."

"Ritter—the psychoprogrammer—and Captain Martin won't be a problem, unless you're prone to indigestion. And no one else has seen Braune's confession." No one but, he suspected, Turnbull. Apparently I&I security classifications didn't worry the Bureau. "Adrian Braune can be killed resisting arrest. Michel will say whatever he's told to say. He knows he's looking at heavy re-education at the very best. Then... annex?"

As he'd expected, she knew the term. "I think so."

"The bank, or Corporate Fraud, might still try to take control of the prisoners."

"Let me deal with that."

Even Vaughn would back down in the face of the Bureau. "And what about Kelvin Richardson? Annex, too?"

"No," she said thoughtfully. "Perhaps not. As long as you're confident he didn't know about the conditioning?"

"I'm confident he would've told us if he did."

"Then... re-education for him. Too clean a sweep can draw unwanted attention. You're quite certain no one witnessed Braun's interview?"

Had Sara started the transcript? He'd told her to do it promptly. "Only me."

"And I'm sure you now appreciate the likely consequences, should this leak out?"

Toreth could almost believe he'd imagined the threat behind the friendly question. He knew that he hadn't. "You know, a few years ago I found something else stinking up the place at Psychoprogramming—another brilliant plan that would've had the corporations up in arms, at least. Of course, that time it was all their own stupid work, and the fuckers tried to have me killed, but other than that, I'd say there were a lot of similarities."

There was a pause, and Turnbull sounded genuinely surprised when she said, "I don't think I know the incident you refer to."

"No, you wouldn't. And that's because I know how to keep my mouth shut."

The next pause was longer, and Toreth wondered suddenly if the call included someone he couldn't hear. Then Turnbull said, "I think you may have misunderstood my intent; perhaps I was unclear. What I meant to convey was that I have the fullest confidence in your good sense and discretion, Para-investigator. You've proved both of them to the Bureau before."

"Thank you, Secretary."

"And thank you for your hard work. We'll speak again later—before the case is submitted to Justice, perhaps."

He closed the connection and turned to Jameson and Morehen. "Right, that's it. We're collecting the prisoners and heading back to I&I."

Chapter Twenty-six

❖

How many years had it been since Warrick had visited the Brighton virtual entertainment expo? It was held every January, and in the early years of SimTech the directors had always attended, since it was close enough to New London to allow them to avoid paying for accommodation. Since then he'd become a regular attendee at far larger and more important conferences and exhibitions, but being back had a comforting familiarity. The upcoming new sim model had meant a plea from the marketing group that at least one director attend.

These days, the price of a hotel room was cheap compared to his time. Staying here meant more networking, and the corporate-graded facilities gave him secure access to SimTech if he needed it. He'd planned to send Toreth a surprise invitation to join him—a night or two somewhere away from the flat appealed, and it was close enough for Toreth to get to I&I—but then he'd had a message from Sara to say that Toreth was in Frankfurt and wasn't expected back in New London for a couple of days. Clearly she'd correctly assumed Toreth wouldn't bother to let him know. The forced change of plan had been unexpectedly disappointing. Ridiculous that living with Toreth seemed to make Warrick miss him more when he wasn't there.

"Dr. Warrick?" the receptionist called after him as he crossed the open area. When Warrick stopped, she said, "There's a message for you."

She had to hunt around in a drawer—obviously physical messages were unusual there—until she found the note on folded plain paper.

The pier. 14:30. JS.

John Sable. Warrick didn't doubt it for a moment. The time gave him more pause. Warrick had an hour built into the schedule there, for arranging time with anyone they met during the course of the exhibition with whom an immediate meeting seemed urgent. So far, it was free. A coincidence? With an organization like Citizen Surveillance, it seemed unlikely. More probably a subtle reminder that corporate status was not an exemption from being watched.

Toreth had been confident that Cit kept tabs on sab teams. Had Sable heard about Warrick's inquiries? Trying to look on the bright side, a daylight, public meeting with Sable suggested he wasn't planning for Warrick to disappear into the untraceable clutches of Cit Surveillance.

Or maybe that was what Sable hoped he'd assume, to get him away from SimTech security and alone. Well, in that case it would work; he couldn't involve SimTech any more than he already had.

The extravagant golden arches and balustrades of the Central Pier grabbed hold of every ray of winter sun that broke through the clouds. The riot of intricate curlicues gave the pier an air of historical decadence, an unlikely jewel in the gray backdrop of the sea. A memory came suddenly of one particular family holiday here, of running onto the pier, holding Dillian's hand, Kate and Jen following behind with his grandparents. Everything had been bigger and brighter, the smooth deck hot beneath his bare feet as they dodged between the crowds of adults. He'd had money in his other hand, held tight, a holiday treat. What had he wanted to spend it on? He couldn't remember.

Today, on a cold Thursday in January, only the facilities running down the central spine were open. Most of the other people on the pier were hurrying to or from the shelter of one of the entertainment complexes. Warrick spotted Sable waiting at the entrance to one of the virtually deserted side piers, in the meager shelter offered by a security scanner arch.

There should be something more, he thought as he walked over. He felt that same strange intellectual disconnection as he had at the bar last year, unable to reconcile his long-idealized father with the reality of the much older man in front of him. He wondered how Sable would react if he greeted him with "Dad."

"Hello," Warrick said, and Sable nodded. The wind was strong enough to whip up choppy waves, and Warrick shivered. "Couldn't you have chosen somewhere warmer to meet?"

Sable smiled. "Come on."

The walked along, further from the main pier. They met just one or two other people, carefully scrutinized by Sable as they passed.

"I like it out here, even in the winter," Sable said. "Katy did, too. She said even when she was a child she thought it was better chilly and quiet than warm but so crowded you couldn't move." He waved his hand eastwards. "Her mother came from Saltdean—just along the coast."

"I know." Did Sable happen to recall that, or had he refreshed his memory from Cit's files? "She and Granddad moved back when they retired. I do remember them."

"Yes, of course."

Honestly, Warrick probably remembered the novelty of visiting the seaside more clearly than his grandparents themselves. From the guest bedroom at the top of their house, he'd been able to catch a glimpse of the sea, at least if he dragged over a chair to climb on. Had they known anything about Kate's other life?

"Katy used to call the pier in the winter 'bracing,' which I think meant 'freezing cold.'" Sable paused, but Warrick didn't comment. "Do you know anything about its history? It's been damaged many times, destroyed almost entirely twice. But structures can be rebuilt, as long as the ideas they embody endure. Over the centuries it's become part of the essence of Brighton. Part of the soul, to be equally anachronistic."

Poetic. Pointless. "Why do you want to see me?"

"How's the conference going?" Sable asked, as though he hadn't heard the question.

Not until they reached their destination, clearly. "Very well. Interest is picking up somewhat. The next-generation sim model is helping. A lot of the refinements are about making it cheaper and easier to install."

"I tried your sim, last year, at a new P-Leisure entertainment complex. I know some people who're surprised it was allowed to be developed."

Giving citizens somewhere to escape their surveillance probably wouldn't appeal. "We had to deal with a lot of compliance. What did you think about it?"

"Very impressive," Sable said, although without the enthusiasm Warrick expected these days. "Disconcerting, though."

"Funny, Dillian thinks the same."

"Really?" Sable smiled, with a sudden, unsettling warmth. "That's interesting—that we have something in common, I mean. I was thinking on the way down here that I'd like to meet her, too. Katy talked so much about her. Impossible, of course," he added, to Warrick's relief.

"I didn't tell her anything about you or Kate," Warrick said. "I don't plan to, either."

"No doubt it's for the best—for all of us. Ah, here we are."

"Here" was a small building, filling one of the semicircular platforms that dotted the length of the side pier. A blank screen ran across it, giving no clues about the building's function.

Sable expanded his hand screen, and a few seconds later, the door opened. He went inside, then turned to Warrick, who still hesitated outside. "It'll be safe to talk in here."

Well, if Citizen Surveillance wanted him dead, thwarting them here wouldn't change the ultimate outcome. And the pier was freezing cold.

The lights had come up when Sable opened the door. The place was deserted. No furniture, plain white walls, a gray floor slightly scuffed in places, a counter that ran partway across the room from one wall—perhaps a café or some small shop, waiting for new season occupants. On the side facing the sea, the curved wall was made of one unbroken transparent sheet, floor to ceiling, that had the familiar tint of high security protection. Oddly, he could still hear the wind and sea; as he watched, a gull swooped across the width of the window, and its cries tracked with it. The sounds must be fed inside, speakers recreating the outside world. It seemed somehow an even more artificial seaside experience than the sim.

"It's corporate security rated," Sable said. "Almost more useful out of season than in."

"So why do we need it?"

"A meeting seemed like the best option out of several bad ones. The cleanest, anyway. I didn't want to commit anything in writing, considering who was involved. When we met at SimTech, you warned me about a particular socioanalyst."

Warrick nodded. What had Carnac done now?

"A few days ago, a note from Socioanalysis appeared on your security file, saying that you were an of-interest asset to them. His name wasn't the one attached, but I know the position held by Camille du Pre, and it's nearly certain that she's in close contact with him."

"What does 'of-interest asset' mean?"

"It could be a lot of different things to them. But externally, it's a request for other departments not to interfere or do anything dramatic without consulting whoever placed the flag."

Something there'd no doubt been on Tarin's file, at least before Kate's disappearance.

"Anyway, I...thought you should know." Sable smiled wryly. "I'm sorry I don't have any more detail, but hopefully this will help to some degree. SimTech security is the best placed to protect you from here, but they can't do that if they're entirely blindsided by a threat."

"Could you find out more?" Warrick asked, with more curiosity than intent.

Sable hesitated. "Well, yes, I could, if I had to. Do you want me to?"

The timing of the note couldn't possibly be a coincidence. "No. I shouldn't worry too much about it. If anything, Carnac's probably trying to protect me from you."

Sable frowned. "What?"

"I went to him with some questions. I suspect he decided that despite what I told him, I'd eventually take them to you, and that I might not get a good reception."

"From me?" He sounded genuinely surprised.

"Maybe he was thinking about Tarin's accident."

He wondered if Sable would repeat the weak denial he'd made before, but instead he gave a rather exasperated sigh. "The climate's changed since then. The political situation is less volatile. A socioanalyst should know that."

Did he realize that he'd just implied Tarin's attempted murder had been ultimately unnecessary? "I suppose he thought if you could...if that could happen to Tarin, it could happen to anyone. After all, it's been a long time since any of us were your family."

In the silence, the crying gulls outside sounded like an alarm.

"I wouldn't want you to think that I have no regrets about the choices I've made," Sable said, his voice unemotional. He might've been talking about a poorly arranged office party.

Do you regret having me and Dillian as part of your cover story? Do you regret letting your colleagues destroy your stepson's life? Do you regret trying to kill him, or just failing? None of those seemed like sensible questions to ask a Citizen Surveillance agent. "Oh?"

"Even if they were right, even if they were the only thing I could do at the time. When I left you and Dillian behind..." Sable stopped, looking out over the sea. "No. I don't think I have any way to explain it that would make sense after all these years. It was a difficult time. The Administration was in a period of unrest."

The chill was entirely imaginary, but Warrick still had an urge to put his hands in his coat pockets. He kept them free, instead, and waited.

"After I was compromised, they could've closed the whole operation down," Sable said. "I know the possibility was discussed. But we'd committed ourselves. The operation was too important to abandon with no attempt to salvage. The recovery plan was to use Katy's position working with Marriot's associates to see if she could maintain a viable flow of information that way. If not, she would've had to choose between resigning from the section or moving on to a new assignment. If she'd needed to leave you and Dillian behind, Jen was in place to take care of you. We planned that together. And I'm sure Katy thought that she made the right choice, too, even though at the time we had no idea how productive it would become. How many lives she'd save."

Before the revolt he'd done everything he could not to think about her double life. He'd played his part in the family charade with such dedication the role had felt real. Now sometimes it seemed as though every memory had been tainted. She could've taken him and Dilly to the pier for the day, and then called Citizen Surveillance to discuss Tarin's resister activities. Did he want to try to understand why she'd done it? Right now, no.

"Over time, I thought about her less, I admit," Sable said. "I'd assumed she did the same. I looked at your security files from time to time—yours and Dillian's—and you both achieved so much. I really thought everything worked out as well as it could have. But when I read the letters she wrote to me, all those years." Sable shook his head. "So, yes, I do regret not sharing that life with you all."

How could he phrase it, for the maximum chance of an answer? "Are you with her now?"

He cleared his throat. "It isn't possible for me to release any information about the current location of agents or former agents. Aren't you getting letters from her?"

Former agents? Was that a hint? If so, he needed more. "Yes. And if those are genuine, then they're very welcome," Warrick said carefully. "If they aren't, then it would probably be better for everyone's peace of mind if they stopped and we had a definitive answer. Not knowing if she's coming back is...stressful. Especially for Valeria, Tar, and Philly. And Aunt Jen."

"Jen." He smiled briefly. "But, yes, I can see that. Well, I can say that the operation has been permanently closed down. No one from the files is of active interest to Citizen Surveillance—provided that they continue to behave as good citizens. Those convicted of anti-Administration activities will receive the standard periodic assessment of their readjustment to healthy social norms, nothing more."

"Tar wasn't convicted of anything."

"No. But we both know that wasn't for lack of evidence."

Warrick had to nod agreement. "He's still my brother. Kate's son."

The quick frown suggested that the reminder displeased him. "I understand your loyalty—"

"Do you?" Warrick said bitterly, and for a moment even the sound of the waves and gulls seemed to pause. Maybe Warrick's heart, too. It had been years since he'd lost control like that in the middle of a negotiation, and what the hell could he say to recover it? Or now that he'd taken the first step, why not keep going? Hadn't he carefully proved to himself that he had no other options? "Tar loved you. I was so young when you went away, I don't remember much of the details, but I remember that. When they told us what happened to you, it devastated him. Everything he did later traces back to the lie that you died."

"He's an adult," Sable said firmly. "He made his own choices."

"Oh, yes, of course." The anger kept him looking Sable in the eyes, fueling exhilaration and fear in equal parts. "Helped along by a section of psychologists and agents working on the operation, of course. You have no idea how Tar's life would've looked without Citizen Surveillance meddling with it, with you pulling his strings through Kate."

"You can't blame—I had nothing to do with any of that." He sounded almost defensive.

"So was it her idea to use Tarin?"

"I don't know. I was moved on to Warsaw, with a new identity. I heard nothing from Katy until you gave me her letters. By the time the strategy evolved to include Tarin, years had passed."

"The operation file must say something about who came up with it."

"I told you—the operation is closed," Sable said with a hint of impatience. "I only looked at the file once, after you contacted us last year. I don't remember the fine detail."

265

A little off-balance? "You can ask her," Warrick said bluntly.

"Not when she's—" Sable stopped.

The words alone said nothing. They left open so many possibilities. Out of contact, outside the Administration, in hiding, on the run—but only one answer explained the flash of panic, or the immediate recovery into assessment of damage done.

Carnac would be shaking his head. Toreth would be horrified. Warrick felt a giddy elation at the dual success of the gambit and an end to the quest.

"Are you sure?" Warrick said.

After a moment, Sable nodded.

"How can you be?"

"I." Sable brushed his palms together, then said, "I saw her body myself. Not an image or a recording. Katy."

Who, how, where, why—none of those were questions important enough to dig this hole any deeper. Not when he was standing on a thin skin of artificial ground over the deep, cold water of the Channel.

"The letters stop," Warrick said. "There's some kind of death notification."

"I'll see what I can do," Sable said. "It may take me a little time, but there'll be something."

"Thank you."

And that was it. Exactly what he'd wanted, directly from the (somewhat unwilling) hand of Citizen Surveillance. He could walk away now, not look back, and Sable would be gone from his life again. Goodbye. Somehow, though, he couldn't take the first step.

"Is that everything you wanted to know?" Sable asked.

So much he could ask. "Yes."

"Then it's probably best we part ways now. I have things to do in New London. And you should get back to your conference before you're missed."

"Yes." SimTech had already suffered from his arrest last year. He shouldn't risk more rumors or signs of instability.

They went outside; after the illusion of standing on the open pier, the chill slice of the wind shocked him. Warrick shivered. He paused, waiting while Sable relocked the door.

Sable turned, tucking his hand screen away. The wind through the metal supports, and the sea slapping against them, filled up the lengthening silence until Sable said, "I may be leaving New London in the near future. My assignment here was initially supposed to be only temporary, after the unrest." He half smiled. "If I hadn't been here, I never would've seen the message you sent about Katy. As much happenstance as the damn arrest that compromised my cover."

"Goodbye, then," Warrick said, and still he couldn't make himself be the one to walk away.

266

"Yes. I—oh! I almost forgot." He reached inside his coat, and Warrick tensed until Sable pulled out a flat paper bag. "I got here early. The shop was open. I thought Katy would've liked it if..."

He offered the bag, and Warrick took it. Inside he could feel something a centimeter or so thick, smooth on one side and covered in small bumps on the other. He didn't ask, or open it.

"Yes, anyway," Sable said. "Goodbye, Keir. Give my regards to Toreth."

Not in a million years. Warrick nodded.

Sable walked away, back towards the town, and Warrick watched him leave. Kate was dead. As Toreth had said at New Year, it had always been a possibility. After so long, even a likelihood. Now it was a certainty, but he had no idea what to do with the knowledge, not even how to make it feel real. Maybe he should try to leave it alone, unexamined, until the official news came. Let his reactions be as natural as possible.

Now—what the hell was in the paper bag? He opened it cautiously and pulled out a large, two-dimensional gingerbread house. A model of the pier's main pavilion, baked a dark golden, elaborately hand iced and decorated with gold foil and tiny sugar gems in vivid colors.

That was what he'd wanted to buy with Dillian, all those years ago. Of course. As clearly as a sim room, he could see the shop in his mind, the window filled with buildings, people, animals, boats, glittering in the sun. For a moment, he wondered if Sable was trying to tell him Kate was alive after all—that she'd asked him to buy the gingerbread because she knew they were meeting here today. But then he remembered Kate's letters. No doubt she'd written all about the holiday, about how wonderful it had been to be there with the three of them, Tarin safely back in New London, out of mind.

Infuriating and unfair that Sable thought he knew so much about their lives. He weighed the gingerbread in his hand, considering skimming it out into the sea for the gulls to fight over. He couldn't bring himself to do it, though. It would be too much of a waste. Whoever had placed the little windowpanes and cornices deserved that much respect for their craft.

Warrick paused in the reception area, trying to compose himself. He'd taken a taxi back to the conference complex, arriving in plenty of time for his next scheduled meeting, but the solitary journey had given him far too much time to think. He glanced around; Asher might be wondering where he was and he wasn't sure if he could face her and give nothing away.

Why the hell had Sable decided to meet here, in the middle of the day? Why couldn't he have chosen an anonymous bar in New London, in the evening, when

Warrick would've had a chance to compose himself properly afterwards? However much he pushed it aside, all he could think about was Kate. And everything, every family memory flooding his mind, was colored by her double life. Tainted, like the gingerbread, with the lie she'd lived. With her had died even the remote chance of explanations or understanding. No possibility of that now. Not one honest moment between them, where he could look her in the face and see that they both knew the truth.

He sniffed, trying to tell himself it was just the temperature change from the cold outside.

"Not the time or the place," he said firmly, under his breath.

His eyes stung. He turned away, pretending to look at one of the historical murals on the reception wall. Exaggerated caricatures of men and women wearing strange costumes, with the men in tight trousers and the women in voluminous skirts. He didn't recognize the period. Warrick ran his thumbs under his eyes. This was stupid. Yes, it might seem reasonable that he should be upset by the news, but he'd said himself to Toreth that her fate was self-inflicted. He might even say to some extent deserved. This reaction was just . . . whatever is was, it was bloody inconvenient. He breathed in and out slowly until the tension in his throat and across his forehead eased. There, he was done for now. He'd set all this mess aside until—

"Warrick?"

He didn't recognize the voice right away, but when he turned, Marley Thomas was crossing the reception area towards him. As she stopped in front of him, he saw her expression change. Obviously he hadn't hidden the signs as well as he hoped.

"Are you okay?" she asked.

"Yes, fine." Warrick wiped his eyes again. "I had some bad news, that's all. A death in the family."

"Oh, no. I'm sorry."

"Thank you," he said. Now she was looking at him expectantly. He should've come up with a concrete lie instead of a vague truth. Thank God she knew nothing about his family—no one at SimTech really did, except for Asher. "I won't bore you with a long-winded explanation, but she was part of my parent's generation."

"Were you close?"

"We were, yes." She was like a mother to us. He crushed down morbid laughter. "When I was a child, anyway. Then I grew up and things changed. I haven't seen her for a while, now. And, well. It's not entirely unexpected news."

She nodded. "Still, it's always a shock to hear it."

"True." He considered asking her not to tell anyone, but making more of a mystery out of it seemed as bad as the alternative. Hopefully, if it did get back to Asher and she later connected it to whatever notification Sable arranged, she'd be willing to believe that he'd had the news through an Administration contact before official word arrived. That was more or less the truth, anyway.

"I'll leave you alone, then," Thomas said.

"No, not at all." Warrick sniffed. "I'm absolutely fine. As you said, it was just the shock. Now, what did you want?" he asked as briskly as he could.

"There's someone who'd like to talk about the sim, that's all. Another refugee from UnLTD Ent, but he's in virtual talent merchandising. I didn't promise him anything, though—I can tell him you're too busy and arrange another time. He's spending a few days in New London after he's done here."

"Now will be fine." SimTech always made the best, most absorbing distraction from the rest of the world, at least when Toreth wasn't available. "How about over coffee? I got some gingerbread on the pier—we can share it."

Chapter Twenty-seven

❖

So they took everything?" Sara asked.

"That's right. Jameson suggested looking for backups when they'd gone, but then to be fair, she didn't talk to Turnbull. I didn't tell anyone what Turnbull said, of course."

They were eating lunch in Toreth's office, with the door locked and the windows opaqued. Arriving back at New London airport on Thursday afternoon, Toreth had detoured to pick up fish and chips at the same little café where Carey had given him Lake's file. While they ate, Toreth laid out the events of the days in Frankfurt—a very unofficial IIP, for Sara's ears only.

"The funny thing is, if I'd let Corporate Fraud have the arrest, they would've locked down the site earlier, and Turnbull's techs might not have made it in. Then they'd have all the Psychoprogramming evidence." Toreth considered that while he ate some more fish. "And if news got out, they'd be absolutely fucked."

"So you did Head of Section Vaughn a favor, really." Sara grinned. "Pity you'll never be able to collect. And what happens to the traders?"

Toreth wiped up a splash of vinegar with a chip. "They all win a free visit to the brand-new Neuropsychological Division loyalty program, opening very, very soon at a Department of Health Care and Research Center near you. They'll never know what happened."

"Wow. And you were right, you know, I did finish that transcript." Sara sounded remarkably sanguine. "But I ran the new system on it, under your name. Even if Turnbull looks it'll show the transcripter originating the file."

Lingering paranoia from the case made Toreth ask, "Why do that?"

Sara shrugged. "Just luck, really. You said you wanted me to tell people I didn't have access to the file, so I thought that might cover my arse if the Central Bank really threw their weight around and had the IIP unlocked. But in the end no one asked."

She tipped the rest of her chips on top of his, screwed up her wrapping paper, and dropped it in the recycling system. Toreth opened his desk drawer, and Sara took out a cleansing wipe and tidied up her hands and face before throwing that into the recycling, too.

"Oh, speaking of transcripts," she said, "Nagra's cracking through her trader interrogations, and they're all folding like Kel playing poker. So I was sorting out the files for Justice, and I found something dumped to your personal notes. There's no location or interviewee ID, and the quality's horrible, so I didn't know what to do with it. I thought maybe you'd recorded it by mistake somewhere."

Sara played the file, and the first few words told Toreth what she'd found.

"Bollocks. I made it at the Bureau. That's why it sounds so bad—I picked it up through a door. I was in such a hurry I must've forgotten to tell it not to record."

"You were snooping on Secretary Turnbull?" Sara sounded understandably shocked. "I'll delete it, then, shall I? Before someone else finds it."

"Yes—no, wait." Immediate deletion would be safer, but a possibility awoke his curiosity. "She was talking to someone about the case. I wonder if they had anything to do with whoever stole the Mindfuck evidence? Although I don't remember her saying anything useful."

"Let me listen to it again. I'm good with transcripts."

He relinquished his desk to Sara. She sat down and ran the file all the way through, elbows on the desk and her chin on her clasped hands, her eyes closed. "Once more," she said when it was done, without opening her eyes.

"Well?" Toreth asked when she finished listening.

Sara looked up at him. "Didn't you search the name?"

"Dupré? I already looked at the Central Bank and Fisec, but there aren't any Duprés important enough to be on first-name terms with the secretary of the Bureau. Beyond that, there are thousands of them. Without a first name—"

"There is a first name."

"What? Where?"

"Right here." She played the transcript again. "You lose the sound completely, and then when it comes back, she says 'Can, yes, of course. I do know what I'm asking.' Trust me. You have to listen to the inflection. She's saying a name. Can. That could be a nickname, of course. Male or female?"

"No idea," Toreth said.

"Well, if it's a nickname it could be from Candice Dupré. Or Candy? Cansu? Can you think of any?"

"Not really." Toreth frowned, hunting for inspiration. "Maybe it only caught the second half of the name. Lucan? Duncan? Hakan?"

"Could be, I suppose." Sara played the short section again. "Yes. Or, actually, that might even be an *m*. Cam's a name. Um. Cameron, Camilla, Camille. There used to be an admin in Political Crimes called Campbell. I always liked that. And then any variations with *k*, of course. The system can sort that out. Listen."

Toreth still couldn't hear any inflection in the muffled voice, or the elusive *m*. "Don't worry about it. The case is over—I'm not getting my evidence back, whoever they are."

"True."

Sara's finger hovered, but she didn't delete the file. They both sat—or stood—in silence, looking at it. Poking around in Bureau business was likely to bring them nothing but trouble, Toreth knew that. Chasing crap like this out of pure curiosity was exactly the kind of thing that got Warrick in so much trouble. And yet . . .

"What security—" Toreth started.

At the same moment, Sara said, "Maybe we should—"

They stopped together, too. Sara looked up at him and grinned. "You first."

"What security codes do you have at the moment?"

"Mm. Really high level? I have one from Senior Para Hepburn's last case."

"He was killed in the revolt," Toreth said.

"I know *that*. But the last time I checked the code was still active. Honestly, I think someone persuaded Systems to look the other way. There's at least one person in ADCF using it, and a couple in Corporate Fraud, and that's just people I know."

Which should make it slightly safer. "Go on, then. Look her up."

"All right," Sara said, but she entered the code slowly, as though she were half hoping he'd change his mind.

A quick combing of the first search yielded nothing obvious. "Maybe Dupré has a cover job," Toreth said. "Something completely innocuous."

"Maybe we're looking in the wrong place." Sara tapped her finger thoughtfully on her lips. "Let's add a phonetic search for surnames, too. There must be some odd spellings around."

Surprisingly many, as it turned out. Duprée, DuPree, Du Preez . . . Toreth left her to it and went back to his chips. Finally Sara said, "How about that one? Camille du Pre, aged sixty-four, resident in Strasbourg—that's where the Bureau central office is, right? Her employment's just listed as 'freelance.'" She cocked her head thoughtfully. "Nice home address. It's in an enhanced security zone."

The sort of place where an Administration higher-up might live. Toreth reached over to bring up the basic security photo, and then stared at the familiar face. "That's the woman I met in Frankfurt."

"Are you sure?" Sara said.

"Yes. I thought she was younger than that, but it's definitely her." He crumpled the wrapper around the remaining chips and put it on his desk. "She wouldn't have had long after we started looking for the Braunes, but Strasbourg to Frankfurt . . . that's doable."

"How did she know where to go?"

Cit Surveillance—that was where the names had come from. Then Toreth thought of an alternative. "Turnbull? She was all over the IIP."

"So do I pull her full file?" Sara asked.

Toreth debated for a moment, then said, "Go on."

Almost as soon as the security file appeared, Sara said, "Oh!"

A second behind her, Toreth realized what she'd seen. "Jesus fucking Christ."

Sara sat back in the chair, leaning away from the screen like it might bite. "She's a socioanalyst."

Toreth stared at the division name, his mouth suddenly dry. He didn't even know what the threat might be, but if Socioanalysis was involved, he couldn't foresee anything good coming from it. And not some minor spook, either. Du Pre's personnel file would be locked safely away at Socioanalysis, barring a special request he certainly wouldn't be making, but the brief outline on her security file indicated an impressive client list, corporate and Administration, and a note marking her as Socioanalysis's Independent Coordinator.

"Independent Coordinator of what?" Sara asked.

"I have no fucking clue." Du Pre's bland, expressionless security photo stared back at him from the screen. "Independent cockups? According to Turnbull, 'a group inside the Administration' came up with the idea of mindfucking traders and bank employees under their control so they could fix the market for everyone's benefit."

"Socioanalysis?"

"I should've guessed. It sounds like exactly their kind of game. Overly complicated and bloody stupid. I wonder how long Turnbull knew?" The more he thought about it, the worse it looked. "I can't see Socioanalysis pulling a stunt like this without Council or Bureau approval, but if they did... or if they fucked up and let someone go rogue, like Carnac."

Sara said, almost in a whisper, "What do we do next?"

"Nothing. What evidence do we have? Du Pre took all the conditioning protocol files from Mindfuck—and I'd bet a year's salary any other Mindfuck location that ran the same protocols has had a visit. They won't be seeing the light of day again, especially if there's anything in them that ties back to Socioanalysis. Every storage device that information ever touched has been ground to powder by now. And no one else is talking, unless Justice has started taking evidence submissions from fucking mediums."

"Well, you saw her there in Frankfurt." Sara scanned through the file. "She took an awful risk, going in person."

"Right. So if Socioanalysis finds out I know who she is, that makes *me* evidence. I have no intention of ending up as someone's celebratory fucking joint. Can you delete the record of those searches—completely delete it?"

"I could try, but I'd probably make a mess of it. I'm not Warrick."

"No. You're a lot quieter in bed, for one thing."

His response had been automatic, and probably the glare he got in return was, too. The pressing circumstances stopped her from flouncing out, though.

"The best we can do is mark the result as no-store," Sara said. "But if they were watching the files when we searched, well."

"There's nothing we can do, I know." Du Pre's name—on Hepburn's widely abused code, yes, but using the security code of a dead senior para to pull her file only made them look guiltier. "We'll just have to hope they won't want to risk drawing attention."

It was not, Toreth thought as he watched Sara flag the search, a very solid hope on which to hang anything important, like his career or his life. Only time would show them if it was strong enough to bear the weight.

"Do you want to go for a drink when we're done here?" he asked.

She looked up. "You mean with everyone in the team, for the end of the case? I'll see who's free."

"I was thinking about you and me." With their new discovery, the case felt a lot less closed than it had this morning. "I could do with some unwinding."

"Sorry, I can't." She looked back to the screen, frowning suddenly. Before Toreth could start to panic, she added, "Well, the search is gone. So now we just cross our fingers. Anyway, yes. I've got a thing to do tonight."

"Does Morehen know you call him that?"

"A *family* thing." She stood up and moved around the desk. "I thought Warrick was coming home today?"

"No, that's tomorrow." It wasn't like Sara to forget something while he remembered. Then another thought distracted him. Fuck—he hadn't checked the progress of his order at the Shop. If it wasn't ready tonight, when could he test it? "Don't worry about it, I can make my own fun for the evening."

Sara smiled. "I'm sure you can."

Chapter Twenty-eight

❖

W arrick was unpacking his bag in the bedroom when he heard Toreth come home. It was only four o'clock, so the case was either going very well or very badly.

The cheerful "Warrick?" suggested the former.

"Up here." Had Toreth been watching for access to the flat?

Toreth arrived a couple of minutes later, with two beers and a broad smile.

"I take it the case worked out well in the end?" Warrick asked as he accepted a beer.

"Touch and go for a while, but well enough, yeah." Toreth took a deep drink of the beer. "Tillotson can go fuck himself, because my record is so fucking shiny right now you could see it from Mars."

"I'll be sure to have Dilly ask one of her engineer friends to look out of the window and see if they can spot it." Warrick zipped the empty bag closed. "By the way, Sable came to see me in Brighton."

"What?" Toreth said.

"I didn't call him. He wanted to warn me that he'd found a flag on my security file, from Socioanalysis."

"Carnac," Toreth said with disgust.

"Yes, I'm afraid so. But I think it was more protective than anything else."

"I suppose the bastard thinks you'll need it, if you keep asking stupid questions."

"Which I won't."

Toreth shook his head. "So you didn't ask Sable about Kate, then?" He sounded more resigned than angry.

"I rather lost my cool, and the topic did come up." Warrick picked up a shirt that he hadn't worn and shook out the creases. "He said that she's dead."

"Well, thank fuck for that."

Sometimes, even though he'd known Toreth for so long, he still surprised. Warrick stared at him, honestly wondering if he'd misheard, and Toreth frowned.

"That's what you wanted to know, isn't it? Don't you believe him?"

Warrick took a moment to think back to the conversation on the pier. If Sable had spontaneously volunteered the information, there would always be a lingering doubt. But he hadn't. "Yes, I do."

"There you are, then. It's over." Toreth raised his beer. "Goodbye Kate, hello sanity." He paused. "Warrick?"

"Yes. There's nothing more to know now. Nothing that matters, anyway. Sable said that he'd make sure we got a death notification. I don't know what we'll do then. Organize some kind of memorial, I suppose. Jen would want that. Dilly, too. Tarin, I'm not sure now if he—" Warrick stopped dead, staring at a mark on the otherwise pristine fabric of the brand-new pillowcase. "Why is there makeup on my pillow?"

"What?"

Toreth actually came over and examined the pillow, as though it were genuinely a surprise to him.

"Well?" Warrick said, with what he felt was laudable restraint.

"It must be Sara's. She came over here Monday evening, and we ended up epically hammered. She wanted to see your new bed, and then we both fell asleep in here." Toreth scratched experimentally at the streak. "Good luck getting it out. That mascara she wears needs a special enzyme to take it off."

"Oh," Warrick said, and then had no idea what to say next. In a few seconds, a whole scene had unfolded in his mind, Toreth's admission of breaking his promise, of bringing one of his endless fucks back to the flat, probably with a few details of what they'd done in the new bed carelessly thrown in. Anger, escalated by Toreth's bafflement and annoyance at Warrick being unreasonable *again*, until Warrick walked out or suggested Toreth find someone else's bed for the night. And now . . . already assuming Warrick would accept his explanation, Toreth had lost interest in the pillowcase, put down his beer, and wandered into the bathroom.

Did Warrick believe him? On principle, very rarely. In this case, if he wanted to be sure then he could check the security footage. Sara wasn't a registered occupant; the cameras would automatically record everything she did in the flat. Of course, Toreth ought to know that, too. So. On balance his account was probably true.

Warrick stripped the pillowcase and the rest of the bed linen, anyway.

Warrick added the potatoes to the bubbling sauce around the lamb, squeezed the juice out of the lemon halves, and dropped them in, too. He fitted the lid tightly and put the casserole back into the oven. Something nice and warming for a cold winter's evening. And he had plenty of time before the other SimTech directors arrived to check—

Warrick stepped out of the kitchen and stopped dead. Where the entrance hallway widened by the foot of the stairs, a metal plate sat in the middle of the floor, almost a meter square. It had staples at the corners that looked more than strong enough for chains, and some kind of socket slightly offset from the center. Toreth stood to one side, his arms folded, watching Warrick with an anticipatory smile.

Warrick pushed the edge of the plate with his toe. It didn't move.

"Soluble bonding," Toreth said. "It's interesting stuff. Pour the solvent around the edge and you can lift it in about a minute. Don't worry, I did a patch test yesterday. It won't mark the tiles."

"Thank you."

"I don't want you going off on one about your fucking floor. So, any ideas?"

Several. Warrick shook his head. "It's intriguing."

"Hm."

Toreth opened a drawer in the hall table. From inside he pulled a set of chains—including collar and wrist and ankle cuffs—which Warrick didn't think he'd seen before, and a thick but not excessively long dildo, which fitted neatly into the socket on the plate.

"This," Toreth said, "is payment for getting all the way through dinner without me mentioning that case Mike Belkin was working at the end of last year."

"I thought you'd forgotten. Or that maybe it was the bed."

Toreth smiled. "Did I say it was?"

"No. And the bed didn't really fit, anyway."

"There you are, then. Your assumptions aren't my problem. The rules are very simple. If you come, you win. If you don't, you lose."

Warrick's stomach flipped. "They'll be here in an hour." One advantage of being known as something of a control freak—or at least, it had always been an advantage in the past—was that when he gave a time, people who knew him stuck to it. No one would arrive before eight, and no one would be later than quarter past, either. Toreth knew that, too.

"It's an interesting case," Toreth said conversationally. "Belkin's, I mean. There's a sab group running a great system, trapping corporates with underage girls and then blackmailing them. Of course, you'd have to be a real idiot to fall for something like that, but it's amazing how stupid some corporates are, don't you think?"

"Move it upstairs," Warrick said. "If you do that, I'll—"

Toreth could move from relaxation to violence so quickly it never seemed possible. He slammed Warrick back against the wall hard enough to knock the breath from his lungs, leaving him gasping, dizzy from the impact and Toreth's grip on his wrist and arm across his throat.

"Should I have fucking written it down and had you sign it?" Toreth said into his ear. "I know you remember what we agreed. We do this my way, no negotiations.

If you want to cancel the bet, then say so, and I'm fucking gone. I don't need to stay here and have my arse bored off with SimTech crap. Now, are you going to strip?"

Still unable to get breath to speak, Warrick nodded.

Toreth released him, watching silently as Warrick undressed. He was torn between not wanting to waste time—an hour, no more—and enjoying the anticipation. Toreth picked up the chains and locked the collar around Warrick's neck.

"Kneel," Toreth said.

Toreth positioned him, brusque and silent. Warrick tried not to whimper aloud as Toreth pushed his fingers wetly inside him. Then Toreth jerked on the collar, shifting Warrick back an inch or two, and then pushed down on his shoulders. Warrick bit his lip, struggling to keep silent at the bite and stretch of the dildo sliding into him.

"There," Toreth said. "Perfect. Don't move."

Toreth linked the chains up with equal efficiency, not touching Warrick more than necessary, leaving him craving more contact even before the last lock clicked. With his ankles locked tight to the points at the back of the plate, his wrists chained behind his back, and another chain leading back from the collar pressing against his throat, he knew without testing how restricted his movements would be.

Toreth checked the chains one last time, and then his footsteps faded, heading back into the flat.

He hadn't said to move. Warrick held still. Could he come like this? For once, he wasn't sure of something. In the sim it would be nothing, easy, just a thought. Here he had to deal with the limits of a real body that Toreth somehow knew better than he knew himself. But he could do it. He had to be able to. Toreth had given him a chance to back out, and he'd refused it. Warrick waited, muscles already quivering in his thighs, anticipation drying his mouth and hardening his cock.

Behind him he heard footsteps again, and then a clatter of something on the tiles. "You can move now."

Warrick gave one glance over his shoulder. Behind him, Toreth sat in a dining chair, ankle crossed over his knee, watching. He leaned on the arm of the chair, hand supporting his chin, and he was smiling. No mistaking the expression—he thought Warrick was going to lose.

Then Warrick turned away and flexed his shoulders, feeling the confinement of steel and the stretch of muscle.

What time was it? No point asking when Toreth wouldn't tell him. Ahead of him was the main door to the flat. If he took too long, if he couldn't do it at all, then the others would arrive and Toreth would let them in, and they'd see him like this. Toreth's new scenario. A new kind of danger. The idea—the foretaste of humiliation—turned his stomach to ice, and already he couldn't separate the fight-

or-flight adrenaline from the buzz of arousal. He wanted it, and he didn't want it. It would be over when the conflict had been driven away and there was only the need. That was something he couldn't do by force of will or logic. It was something that, normally, he couldn't do alone.

All of which, he thought as he straightened his back to ease his breathing, was very interesting and philosophical. But now, right now, he had a bet to win.

He twisted his hips and the plastic inside him shifted, stroking over his prostate and back again, and he clenched his teeth trying not to moan with relief. Then he settled down to explore the full range of limited movements, turning and jerking, tugging at the chains and feeling the bite on his wrists which was almost as good as the flares of sensation from within.

The twisting movement was the best he could manage, though, and the only one that felt as if it had a chance of getting him anywhere, and he quickly discovered it was as tiring as hell. He could keep up a steady rhythm, but it was too slow to do anything other than frustrate him to the verge of tears. Anything faster, anything which started to build the arousal to the point where he might, God, please, come, he couldn't keep going for long enough. The burning ache in his thighs forced him to stop, panting.

By the fourth time he shuddered to a halt, almost sobbing, he had to fight not to call Toreth's name, to surrender and admit he'd lost. No. Toreth wouldn't set him up to fail completely. Without an outside chance of Warrick succeeding, winning the bet wouldn't mean anything. Toreth would know what was possible, what Warrick could and couldn't do.

An image hit him suddenly of Toreth kneeling like that, eyes closed, twisting and turning, trying out the scenario, smiling as *he* imagined Warrick doing this. The recursive excitement hit him like a blow.

He twisted in the chains until he choked himself, whispering Toreth's name. Finally he went still. He ached everywhere, inside and out, thrumming with arousal and frustration, but he forced himself to relax every muscle he could.

Rest. Five minutes, and then start again, slowly this time. Slow and steady, and build up—

The loud smack of the strap over his shoulders was so unexpected that surprise delayed the sting of pain for a second. When it came, it merged into the other, more diffuse pains, surprising a gasp from him.

Toreth chuckled. "Did I tell you to stop?" he asked and despite the laughter his voice was harsh with arousal.

Jaw clenched, Warrick started to move again, breath catching in his throat.

Toreth dropped the strap on the floor and came to stand in front of Warrick. He watched for a few seconds, then said, "Open."

Was this part of the plan, or Toreth deciding he'd skip to the end? If Warrick stopped now, he didn't think he'd be able to—

"Open." Toreth had already unfastened his trousers. "You don't want me to have to tell you again."

Toreth gave him no help, making Warrick do all the work, mouth sliding up and down Toreth's cock. Thirty seconds, a minute, and his jaw already ached.

"Deeper," Toreth said. "Come on, you can do better than that."

The chains and the trembling stiffness in his muscles—lactic acid burn, his brain supplied helpfully—made what should've been easy difficult. He couldn't lift up, couldn't find the right angle to deep throat and breathe. And still Warrick tried to work his hips, moving at least a little, wanting it and thinking about the ticking clock.

Warrick choked, gagging, and struggled to catch his breath, to control himself. Toreth didn't let up, and a moment later Warrick gagged again. Immediately Toreth pulled back and slapped him hard across the face, and behind the ringing burst of pain, a tiny part of Warrick thought about marks and darkening bruises over dinner.

"Pay attention," Toreth said. "Why do I bother teaching you this shit if you can't fucking concentrate?"

"I'm sorry," Warrick gasped.

"Liar. But you will be, if you don't get it right." Toreth caught a handful of Warrick's hair and twisted hard. "Open up, and keep still."

As Toreth pushed his cock in deep, Warrick relaxed, opening up, breathing in sync. This time Toreth moved, holding Warrick in place, his cock a brutal pressure in Warrick's throat. Toreth pushed him backwards, now onto the plate, harder than Warrick had managed alone, and the dildo stretched him open. He moaned, and Toreth's fingers tightened.

"That's better. Fuck. That's much better."

His other hand gripped Warrick's jaw, keeping him just as Toreth wanted him. Warrick swallowed as Toreth came, the rest of the game forgotten, fixed only on the idea of doing what Toreth demanded, doing it right. Then Toreth released his hair, and Warrick's shoulders sagged forward until the collar brought him up short, hard across his throat.

The bet—the clock.

"Please," he panted. Was he allowed to talk? Toreth said nothing. "Please. Can I move?"

"Do whatever the fuck you want." Contempt thickened Toreth's voice. "You've lost."

Warrick began to move again, wanting so badly to come. If he'd been this close at the beginning, it would've taken a few minutes, but now his whole body ached, his back, shoulders, and, God, his thighs, burned, throbbed, *hurt*.

He didn't realized he'd closed his eyes until Toreth said, "Look at me."

Blinking away sweat, he obeyed. Toreth crouched in front of him, trousers fastened, clothes straightened, his gaze intent on Warrick's face.

"Nearly time," he said. Toreth touched his cock, a feather-light brush of fingertips. Tormenting. "Mm. So close. But you aren't going to get there, are you? I fucking win."

"No," Warrick managed to gasp. "I. *No.*"

Pain flared in his left shoulder, fierce, breathtaking and almost too vicious to arouse. It took him a moment to make sense of it, then his left arm tried to straighten, jerking the collar back and digging it into his throat.

"Shoulder cramp," he gasped.

"That's right. Few minutes later than I expected, though." Toreth brushed his cock again, and Warrick whimpered through clenched teeth. "You want to stop it now? Take a break? Waste more time? Just say the words."

"Plas—" The first treacherous syllable escaped before Warrick pressed his lips closed. The pain came in pulses, sickening. Not nerve induction, not a carefully measured slap, but real pain that reminded him of the time he'd broken his wrist. He remembered Toreth's words from then, too, or at least the words as he'd shaped them in his memory over the years.

I know what you really want. I know how it starts. I ignore the safe word, don't I?

"I can leave you there all night. No timers on those locks. That'll be something to talk to Lew about over dinner, right? Wonder what his wife will think about that."

You can tell me to stop, you can beg, it'll do you no fucking good. Whatever the hell I want to do to you, I can, you can't stop me. I only stop when I want to stop, and there's nothing you can do about it.

"They'll be here any minute," Toreth murmured, and Warrick shook his head blindly.

He rocked back and forth, pushing through a new wave of pain as his thigh cramped up. No rhythm now, just a desperate search for anything to carry him over the edge. Toreth's fingers brushed his cock again, and Warrick strained forward into the ghost touch, and the collar dug in. Tears ran down his cheeks, helplessness and pain.

"Please," he gasped.

"Sorry, what was that?"

"Please." Just meaningless syllables. "God, *please.*"

"I don't think so. Not now."

I'm stronger than you. I'm trained.

Scream if you want. No one can hear you.

The door chimed, and Toreth's fingers tightened a fraction, but the fraction that Warrick needed. He had a second to think of Lew and Asher, outside the door, able to hear him, and then he came, the scream muffled only by the collar choking him.

The wrist and collar chains unlocked from a single point. Warrick slumped forward into Toreth's expert hold. Something stung his shoulder, and the pain eased almost at once. Warrick looked up, startled, and saw the injector in Toreth's hand.

"Analgesic relaxant. Very popular down on level D at the moment, so I didn't have any problem picking some up. There's a fast-acting agonist, too. Maybe we'll play with that sometime."

Past Toreth, he could see the front door. A minute or two must have passed, but the comm hadn't chimed again. Or at least, he hadn't heard it. Not the same thing.

"You'll—" He licked his lips. "You'll have to let them in soon."

"There's no one there." Toreth smiled. "You keep telling me it's my flat, re-member? Well, that means it's my security system, too."

However deep he breathed, he didn't seem to be able to get enough oxygen. "What time is it?"

"About a quarter to. I'll get you upstairs. If they show up before you're ready I'll tell them you're in the shower. I can hand out the drinks and make small talk."

"Lew," Warrick croaked.

"Don't worry, I'll be on my best behavior." Toreth kissed him. "Enjoy it while you can—you won."

Warrick stood in front of the mirror, carefully smoothing the vasoconstrictor gel over the red handprint on his cheek. When it had faded to invisibility, he traced more gel around the line of the collar on his throat. He'd need something to take down the bruising, too. He hadn't noticed at the time how hard it had dug in.

I ignore the safe word, don't I?

A new approach to that dangerous fantasy, making the safe word part of the game, locking it away behind the threat of defeat. Warrick still could've said it at any time, of course...but he hadn't. As Warrick tried to take the sim a step closer, Toreth moved the game a step further away.

Washed, dressed, and with no visible reminders of the evening so far, Warrick went back downstairs. He paused in the hallway, rubbing the toe of his shoe over the squares where he thought the bonding agent had been. No change in the color, no residue. No clothes and no chair, either. The only clue was a faint scent of sol-vent in the air.

Now, the thought of the door opening and his fellow directors seeing him in chains held far more horror than arousal. Bare flesh in the sim was one thing—in the early days, they'd taken volunteers from anywhere they could, and Warrick recalled even Greg taking part in a few trials—but that was a long way from traumatizing innocent dinner guests. Was he blushing? Dillian always swore he never did, but...Warrick put the back of his hand to his cheek, but he couldn't tell. When he checked in the mirror, he looked perfectly normal. Cool and collected, his damp hair the only sign anything had happened. He watched himself smile, and then shake his head, before he went on into the living room, following the sound of voices.

They couldn't have been there long. Everyone was still standing, while Toreth poured wine. Asher already had a glass of apple juice in her hand, and she spotted him first. "Keir! There you are."

He thought for a moment that Lotte hadn't come after all, but then everyone turned, the group rearranging, and he saw she'd been hidden behind Asher's husband. If bearlike was the description he'd heard applied to Greg more than once, not just for height and breadth, but his thick hair and gruff voice, Lotte was more of a bird, dark-eyed and fine-boned. A little plumper than when he'd first met her, years ago, but still looking tiny beside Greg.

As he greeted everyone he suddenly realized the one thing they'd neglected— he had no idea what, if anything, Toreth had said to explain his absence. And he doubted that had been a mistake on Toreth's part as he left Warrick still feeling dazed in the bedroom.

Then Warrick was distracted by Lotte. She looked happy enough, but he wondered whether Toreth's assessment of the reason for her presence was right.

"Lotte." He leaned down to kiss her on the cheeks. "Lovely to see you."

"Thanks. And you." She stepped back. He thought she might elaborate on why she'd chosen this month to come along, but all she said was, "The flat's looking great."

Toreth handed him a glass, and with his back to the other guests, he smirked wickedly.

"I was just telling everyone why you were in the shower when they arrived," Toreth said.

Warrick raised one eyebrow very slightly, but of course Toreth didn't elaborate.

"Yes, sorry about that," Warrick said to the guests.

"I broke a bottle of olive oil once," Greg said, and Warrick saw a fleeting second of disappointment cross Toreth's face. "But that was on a carpet, not tile. It ended up almost destroying the vac. Clogged up all the filters."

"Did you have carpet in the kitchen?" Lotte asked.

Asher glanced at Greg and laughed. "Not exactly. *Anyway,* Warrick, tell us what we're having for dinner. It smells fantastic."

It might be said with truth that the Administration never slept. Sometimes, though, it dozed. Now was one of those times, at close to midnight, Central European Time, on a Friday in January. Catherine Turnbull looked out of her office window, the bombproof, bulletproof glass only slightly distorting the view of the buildings outside. The snow that had started on Tuesday had been falling steadily ever since, but underground heating kept pathways clear. Few lights burned in the windows, but the broad avenues between them were well lit. The rebuilding of bomb-damaged Strasbourg into the administrative core of the new Europe had been carried out on a defiantly lavish scale, the buildings solid, enduring, and in Turnbull's opinion surprisingly attractive for political architecture. Still, from her vantage point Turnbull could count three patrols. Sometimes the continual armed presence in the heart of the Administration made her feel as though she lived her life under siege.

She held a plain glass tumbler in both hands, warming the whisky. After the past few days it didn't seem like too much of an indulgence.

The door opened. Without turning around, Turnbull said, "They told me you were coming up. The tea should have brewed by now. Chamomile."

"Thank you."

There was nothing suspicious about a socioanalyst visiting the seat of Administration government, even at this late hour. Certainly it occasioned fewer raised eyebrows than the Secretary to the Bureau of Administrative Departments turning up at the Socioanalysis Division. So on the rare occasions when a face-to-face meeting was necessary, Camille du Pre came to the Bureau.

Liquid poured, the cup and saucer clinked, and Turnbull heard du Pre blow on the tea. She didn't come over to the window, though.

"The para-investigator I met in Frankfurt accessed my security file," du Pre said.

Turnbull smiled. "I thought he might. He has a track record of unhealthy curiosity."

"The emergency oversight group accepted your recommendation, but surely something has to be done now? It's no exaggeration to say that the survival of Socioanalysis depends on the continuing protection of the corporate guidance strategy from broader scrutiny. It's regrettable, of course, but—"

"Cam." Turnbull shook her head.

Du Pre paused, then said, "Are you serious?"

"Para-investigator Toreth won't cause trouble; you can rely on that."

"Are you really suggesting someone with the psychological profile of a para-investigator can be trusted to keep his mouth shut about *this*?"

"Yes—except that it isn't a mere suggestion. I'm quite sure." She turned around and the whisky swirled in her glass to leave trailing legs. "Perhaps it's only natural that our perceptions of him are divergent, given our angles of approach, but along with curiosity that would make a cat blanch he also has a record of exemplary discretion. He understands the gravity; that's why I gave him even a partial explanation. The unfortunate matter is currently closed, and there's every sign that our version of events has been accepted everywhere that matters. Would you want the death of the para-investigator in charge of the case to draw attention back to it?"

"No, of course not, and that's precisely why the oversight group agreed with you, but—"

"Well, then. The risk assessment is perfectly simple. Killing him has a higher disadvantageous outcomes score than letting him live."

Du Pre gave a small, precise, and skeptical smile. "Easy to say standing here, outside the division."

"Speaking of which, if I'd been informed earlier about the exposure risk, then the situation never would've escalated to the point it did."

"That wasn't my decision, and it has nothing to do with the current issue."

Now she sounded defensive. Good.

"There would've been no last-minute scramble," Turnbull continued, "and we could've destroyed all evidence long before I&I reached the scene. Para-investigator Toreth seems to have developed an unfortunate habit of being required to pay for the mistakes of Socioanalysis."

"Better him than us," du Pre said flatly. "There's nothing personal there, either. Any one socioanalyst is a far more valuable asset to the Administration than *any* para-investigator. Fairness is not a primary strategic consideration."

"Maybe it should be, at least occasionally." For no other reason than it might make the division an easier sell to the rest of the Administration; some of the departments were showing increasing wariness in the aftermath of the revolt. Turnbull tried a conciliatory smile. "And perhaps I've been a bureaucrat for too long, but I hate to waste a resource."

Irritation flickered openly on du Pre's face. "Cathy, there's a difference between shepherding valuable assets and hoarding hazardous, broken junk."

"Toreth certainly isn't that. Did you read Darcy Grimm's report from his investigation in America?"

"Yes. Yes, I did," du Pre said slowly. "Insofar as it applies to the current situation, it appears to agree with your assessment."

"There you are, then. A current opinion from someone inside Socioanalysis who had personal contact with him, and uncolored by your protégé's idiosyncratic opinions."

"Carnac never said Toreth was inefficient, simply unstable and dangerous."

Turnbull raised her eyebrows, challenging du Pre to reinforce that statement, but apparently she was not inclined to argue the pot's assessment of the kettle's mental hygiene issues.

"You know, Carnac's tacit readmittance to the division had far from universal support," Turnbull said.

Du Pre frowned. "What do you—"

"For whatever my opinion was worth, I backed the position that he was still an asset too valuable to discard. Some considered him an excessive liability, though. I imagine some still do."

Du Pre said nothing, but after a few seconds her gaze dropped to her tea. The surface rippled slightly, a tiny tremor of her hand, and Turnbull wondered if she was angry, or simply tired after a long week.

"So we're agreed where the weight of evidence lies? Toreth will be left alone?" Turnbull waited until du Pre nodded. "Good, I'm glad we can see eye to eye on this, Cam. Obviously, if his threat level rises in the future..." She shrugged, offering the concession. "But I think it's more than likely the Administration will want his services again. One might even go so far as to say need."

She lifted her glass and, reluctantly, du Pre clinked her cup against it.

"What are we drinking to?" du Pre asked.

"The future." Turnbull sipped the mellow malt. "Long may there continue to be one."